Cancelled Vows

A Mac Faraday Mystery

BY

Lauren Carr

CANCELLED VOWS

Published by Acorn Book Services

For information call: 304-995-1295
or Email: acornbookservices@gmail.com

Designed by Acorn Book Services

Publication Managed by Acorn Book Services
www.acornbookservices.com
acornbookservices@gmail.com
304-995-1295

Cover designed by Todd Aune
Spokane, Washington
www.projetoonline.com

ISBN-10: 0692578080
ISBN-13: 978-0692578087

Published in the United States of America

To the unappreciated,
who must do the unimaginable,
and see the unthinkable to protect the ungrateful.

Thank you
to all members of law enforcement
and their families.

Cancelled Vows

A Mac Faraday Mystery

Cast of Characters

(in order of appearance)

David O'Callaghan: Spencer police chief. Son of the late police chief, Patrick O'Callaghan. Mac Faraday's best friend and half-brother.

Dallas Walker: investigative Journalist. Daughter of famed investigative journalist, Audra Walker and Buddy Walker, Texan rancher. Hails from Texas.

Chelsea Adams: David O'Callaghan's fiancée. Suffering from epilepsy, she has Molly, a service dog trained to sense and warn of seizures.

Mac Faraday: Retired homicide detective. On the day his divorce became final, he inherited $270 million and an estate on Deep Creek Lake from his birth mother, Robin Spencer.

Gnarly: Mac Faraday's German shepherd. Another part of his inheritance from Robin Spencer. Gnarly used to belong to the United States Army, who refuses to talk about him.

Robin Spencer: Mac Faraday's late birth mother. As an unwed and pregnant teenager, she gave him up for adoption. After becoming America's queen of mystery, she found her son and made him her heir. Her ancestors founded Spencer, Maryland, located on the shore of Deep Creek Lake, a resort area in Western Maryland.

Police Chief Patrick O'Callaghan: David's late father. Spencer's legendary police chief. The love of Robin Spencer's life and Mac Faraday's birth father.

Archie Monday: Mac Faraday's wife. Former editor and research assistant to Robin Spencer.

Ali Hudson: Yvonne Harding's assistant. Hails from Texas.

Yvonne Harding: David's old flame. She and David O'Callaghan grew up together on Deep Creek Lake. Four years ago, she moved to New York City to host *Crime Watch* at ZNC. Her star has been rising ever since. Last journalist to interview Audra Walker.

Ryan Ritter: One of ZNC's most popular news show hosts.

Pam Wiehl: Lead host of *Crime Watch*. Married to childhood sweetheart Jim Wiehl, the show's executive producer. On the wrong side of forty, she is past her prime. Is she so desperate that she would kill the competition to hold on to the spotlight?

Audra Walker: Prize-winning free-lance investigative journalist. Disappeared under mysterious circumstances shortly after Yvonne Harding interviewed her about her latest book.

Sergeant Caleb Roberts: Retired homicide detective. He originally had the lead in the investigation into Audra Walker's disappearance.

Jim Wiehl: Executive producer of *Crime Watch*. Witnesses say he is devoted to his wife. Just how devoted is he?

Lieutenant Wayne Hopkins: Homicide detective. Worked under Sergeant Caleb Roberts on Audra Walker's disappearance. Quickly closed the case after Roberts' retirement. Frequent guest expert in law enforcement on ZNC news shows.

Ruth Rubenstein: Internet troll. Murdered after Yvonne Harding outs her as a troll on *Crime Watch.*

Melissa O'Meara: Young author driven to suicide by Ruth Rubenstein's troll attack.

Preston Blakeley: ZNC's CEO. Big supporter of Senator Patrick Brennan, heir of the Brennan political dynasty, which had been threatened by Audra Walker's book.

Carl Rubenstein: Ruth Rubenstein's husband. It's debatable about whether he is mourning the murder of his wife.

Edward Willingham: Mac Faraday's lawyer. One of the top lawyers in the country, Robin Spencer had had him on retainer to handle her business affairs. He had hunted Mac down and chased him for three city blocks to inform him of his inheritance.

Deputy Chief Arthur Bogart (Bogie): Spencer's Deputy Police Chief. David's godfather. Don't let his gray hair and weathered face fool you.

Officer Warren Tate: Murdered New York City police officer. His body is found in the same alley where Yvonne Harding's assistant is attacked.

Lieutenant Abigail Gibbons: Internal Affairs investigator with New York City police—on the trail of a group of crooked police officers called "the Dirty Six."

Polly Langley: Carl Rubenstein's girlfriend.

Lieutenant Andrew Van Patton: Middle-aged career detective. Head of the homicide squad. Lieutenant Wayne Hopkins' supervisor.

Dr. Dora Washington: Garrett County Medical Examiner. Bogie's girlfriend.

Clint Brown and Kimberly Castillo: Texas' Romeo and Juliet. Audra Walker had been working on a book telling their story for several years. She had returned to working on this project the night she disappeared.

Officer Milt Sauer and **Officer Stan**: New York City police officers.

Detective Winslow: Lieutenant Wayne Hopkins' partner.

Jeff Ingles: Manager of the Spencer Inn, the five-star resort owned by Mac Faraday. Mac likes to keep Ingles' life interesting.

Don't marry the person you think you can live with; marry only the individual you think you can't live without.

James Dobson, Noted Psychologist

Prologue

East River, New York City, New York

Police Officer Dan Sauer collapsed onto the pavement. Blood spilled from his gunshot wounds and pooled around him.

All David O'Callaghan could see was the silver police badge pinned to Officer Sauer's chest. *I shot a cop. One of my own. A brother. Two brothers.*

"This one's buzzard bait." Dallas Walker's announcement broke through his thoughts. "How 'bout that one?"

Stunned at what he had done, David could only stare down at the police badge shining off of the late morning sunlight. Later, he would not remember seeing Dallas come around the car, extract the ninja spikes from his hand, and kneel down next to Officer Sauer to check for a pulse.

"They're both dead." She took Officer Sauer's gun from his holster and handed it to David. "You're gonna be needin' this."

David's hands were so numb that he could barely feel the cold metal when he took the weapon. He tucked it into the waistband of his pants and covered it up with his sweater.

"Take his spare magazines, too." His own voice sounded like it was in a fog.

She was already handing him the magazines, which he slipped into his pockets. Seeing the bloody tear through the left sleeve of his sports coat, she gasped. "You've been shot."

Squinting at her, David shook his head. He didn't understand what she'd said until she started poking through the hole in his sleeve to examine the wound.

"Looks like Stan managed to clip you before you took him out," she said. "You might be needin' a couple of stitches. Right now, we need to get out of here."

She dropped back down next to the dead police officer to search his pockets. She extracted the backup weapon that he had taken from David earlier. While David placed his weapon back in his ankle holster, Dallas removed Officer Sauer's backup weapon and placed it, holster and all, around her own ankle.

"Do you know how to use a gun?" David asked.

With a grin, she unholstered the thirty-two semiautomatic, extracted the magazine to check the rounds, shoved the magazine back into the grip, and then checked the sights. "I wouldn't be a real Texan if I didn't know how to shoot a gun." She slipped the weapon into its holster and pulled down her pant leg. "Sugar, police are gonna to be here faster than a prairie fire with a tail wind," she said while urging him to his feet. "Since we don't know which ones are the bad guys, we need to go underground till we get it figured out." Clutching her shoulder bag close to her with one arm, she tugged his arm with the other.

David took one last look at Officer Sauer. "I'm sorry," he murmured.

Grabbing him by both arms, Dallas forced him to look at her. Her tone was gentle yet firm. "You had no choice, hon. They were gonna *kill* us."

Far in the distance, David heard police sirens growing nearer.

"It's time to blow this pop stand, partner," she said. "Now!"

Forcing one foot in front of the other, David allowed her to lead him down the river and through the alleyway back toward the city—away from the approaching police sirens.

Chapter One

County Clerk's Office, Oakland, Maryland: Two Days Earlier

David O'Callaghan could feel the excitement pulsing through every fiber of his fiancée's being while they stood in line. Trying not to look like a fool, he fought the smile that grew broader with every step they took toward the license window at the county clerk's office.

"Do you have your wallet?" Chelsea Adams tightened her grip on his arm and grinned up at him.

Even Molly, her service dog trained to detect the onset of epileptic seizures, seemed to sense the excitement. Panting, she rubbed against Chelsea.

David patted his police chief's jacket—the inside breast pocket contained his wallet. "And my checkbook." Lifting her chin up, he leaned in to kiss her softly on the lips. "Don't be so nervous."

"Not nervous," she said, "Excited. In six days, we're going to be married." In spite of her effort to remain calm, she let out a girlish squeal of delight. Her ivory complexion held a hint of pink on her cheeks. There were sparks in her pale-blue eyes. She was glowing.

David looked down into her face.

"I love you," she whispered to him.

"Me too."

The clearing of a throat sliced through the moment. "Next," the clerk snapped.

As if they had been shocked with a bolt of lightning, David and Chelsea hurried up to the window where an older woman wearing turquoise-framed reading glasses regarded them. Her face was devoid of humor. "Chief David O'Callaghan, what brings you here today?"

David slid the application across the counter to her. "We're here to get a marriage license." He felt Chelsea's fingers digging into his bicep.

Molly squeezed in between Chelsea and the counter to press her snout against David's thigh. While the clerk studied the application, David patted Molly on the head.

"Hm." The clerk's eyebrows rose up into her bangs. Died dark brown, they didn't match her pasty complexion.

"Is there a problem, Edna?" David asked her in a low tone that dared her to find one.

"No." The corners of Edna's lips curled. "According to your birth date on this application, you're thirty-five. Seems like only yesterday that I caught you peeing in my pumpkin patch."

"Because you yelled at me every time I rode my bike across your footbridge to meet my friends at the lake." David let out a laugh. "I was—what? Five years old? And my dad took my bike away for a full week because of that. Don't you think it's time we put all that behind us?"

Chelsea cleared her throat. "As interesting as this history lesson is, can you please just give us the license? I have a final fitting for my wedding gown in an hour."

Her eyes narrowed, Edna turned her attention from David to her computer monitor. "Still got that speed trap along Lake Shore Drive in Spencer?" she asked in a casual tone while typing the information into her computer.

The smile dropped from David's face. "That was never a speed trap. The sign clearly states the speed limit is twenty-five. Always has been. Always will be—which is what I told you when I gave you those speeding tickets how long ago?"

"Yeah, I remember." She pushed her reading glasses up on her nose to read the monitor. "I see Mac Faraday speeding along in his fancy red sports car all the time. How many speeding tickets have you given him?"

Chelsea tightened her grip on his arm, sending a silent message to say nothing.

"I used to think you and your officers never pulled him over just because he's Robin Spencer's illegitimate son and owns half of Spencer," Edna said while working at the computer terminal. "But then when it came out last year that your father was—"

"I have no problem with Mac Faraday," David bit out. "Not only is he my brother, but he's also my best friend. As a matter of fact, he's the best man at our wedding. If you have an issue with the circumstances of his birth, which took place back when Robin Spencer was a teenager, long before she became a world-famous novelist, and when my dad was just graduating from school, years before he even met my mother, then that's your personal problem, not mine."

"David," Chelsea whispered, "please."

Forcing civility into his tone, he asked the clerk, "Can you please process the application and give us the license, *please?*"

"Certainly, Chief O'Callaghan," Edna replied. "As soon as you show me proof of divorce."

David stared at the clerk.

Slowly, a smirk came to Edna's lips.

"Huh?"

"Proof of divorce … from your *wife*." Edna removed her reading glasses. "The law clearly states that you can only be married to one person at a time. Now, unless your other wife is dead, you need to provide proof of divorce. Otherwise, you'd be committing bigamy, *Police Chief O'Callaghan.*"

Chelsea released her grip from his arm. The glow evaporated from her face. The sparks in her eyes turned to fury.

Edna was the happiest David had ever seen her in the decades he had known her.

"This is a joke," David said through gritted teeth. "Who did I marry?"

Shaking her head, Edna turned the computer screen around so he could see it for himself. David and Chelsea stepped forward to read the name.

Upon reading the identity of David's current wife, Chelsea uttered a shriek. Spinning around on her heels, she gathered Molly's leash and ran sobbing from the clerk's office.

In Western Maryland, Deep Creek Lake turns into a ghost town in late fall—the month between when the trees dump the last of their colorful fall foliage to the ground and the first snowfall beckons winter-sports enthusiasts to the ski resorts surrounding the lake.

One corner of the lake is home to the small town of Spencer, the birthplace of the late Robin Spencer, a direct descendant of the town's founder and America's answer to Agatha Christie.

Four years earlier, the world-famous author's sudden death from a brain aneurism had revealed her secret that as a teenager, she had given birth to a baby who had been put up for adoption. Her baby boy had grown up to become a homicide detective named Mac Faraday, and he'd inherited her vast fortune, which included the Spencer Inn, the five-star vacation resort that rested on top of Spencer Mountain.

After the snow-bird residents fly south to warmer climates, quiet descends on Deep Creek Lake. The only sign of life was found in an out-of-the-way cove tucked in a far corner of the lake: it was David's police cruiser, and it was parked in front of his luxurious house, a contemporary cedar-and-stone roundhouse.

Mac Faraday parked his SUV next to the police cruiser and turned off the engine. In the passenger seat, Gnarly, his German shepherd, stomped his feet. His regal ears stood at attention. He uttered a growl mixed with a bark.

A hundred pounds of fur and teeth, Gnarly was another part of Mac's inheritance. The German shepherd dog was the only K-9 to be dishonorably discharged from the US Army, who got very defensive when asked about him.

Following the dog's line of sight, Mac spied four ducks frolicking in the water next to David's boat dock. "No! We're not going to have a repeat of last time. It took a week to get the wet-dog smell out of this SUV. No chasing the ducks."

His ears drooping, he hung his head and pouted.

Mac opened the driver's side door and climbed out. Seeing an opening, Gnarly hopped over the center console and jumped out to run across the deck and down to the dock, where he ran back and forth barking at the ducks.

"Remember what I told you!" Mac called after Gnarly before pounding on the front door. "David, I know you're in there! Open up!"

After a long silence, the door opened.

Their shared DNA could not be denied. Even though Mac was several years older than David and they had grown up with different families and backgrounds, the common traits they'd both inherited from Patrick O'Callaghan were apparent to everyone—and especially to those aware of the family secret that had only recently been made public. Their blue eyes were identical in hue and shape. They had the same tall, slender build. While David had inherited his mother's blond hair, Mac's was dark brown with a hint of gray at the temples.

"Rough day?" Mac asked with a note of sarcasm.

David's hair was disheveled, as were his clothes. Mac saw that he had untucked his white button-down police shirt and unbuttoned it, exposing his white undershirt.

With a jerk of his head, David invited him inside. Leaving the door open, he went back down into the sunken living room, plopped down onto the sofa, and took a swig of beer from the bottle. "I'm sure your wife told you."

"Only that for some reason you and Chelsea didn't get the license." Mac held the door open to allow Gnarly to run inside.

Without stopping, the dog galloped inside and jumped up over the back of a cushioned chair to land on the seat. He turned around several times before lying down.

"And then you two had a fight, and she called Archie to go pick her up because she refused to ride home with you." Mac went over to the kitchen and opened the fridge. "Why wouldn't they give you a license?" He reached inside to take out a bottle of beer.

"Because bigamy is against the law."

His hand on the cold beer bottle, Mac froze. Over his shoulder, he asked, "What?"

"I'm already married."

With a laugh, Mac turned around to peer across the kitchen counter at David, who was in the sunken living area. "Obviously, they made a mistake. The clerk was looking up the wrong David O'Callaghan. You know Edna. She's a nasty old biddy. You'd know if you were already married."

"That's what I thought," David said. "Until I read the name of who I'm married to." He took a long sip to finish his beer.

"And you had no idea?"

David shook his head.

Mac glanced at the beer bottle he was holding in his hand. "I need something stronger than this—and so do you." He reached up into the kitchen cupboard for the brandy. "Married?" he asked. He repeated the word over and over again while pouring the two drinks and carrying them into the living room, where he held a short glass of brandy out in front of David.

After David took it, Mac sat in the love seat across from him. "I never would have believed it," he muttered before taking a sip of his own drink. "Who would have thought—how did Chelsea take it?"

David turned his head to meet Mac's eyes. "How do you think?" He took in a deep, ragged breath. "I've worked all these years to gain her trust again after everything that happened, and now she finds out not only that I'm married but—" He drained the glass in one gulp. With a grimace, he set it down on the coffee table. "She wouldn't even get in the cruiser with me."

"If you don't mind my asking"—Mac shook his head—"how could you have gotten married without knowing it? Who did you marry?"

David groaned.

"It's a logical question," Mac asked. "Who is she?"

David responded in a low mutter.

Mac leaned over to hear him better. "Who?"

"Yvonne," David breathed. "Yvonne Harding."

Mac sat up straight. "Yvonne? You started dating her back when we first met."

"I know."

"That was—" Mac sat up. "How long have you two been married? You two haven't been together for years. She moved to New York—how long ago?"

"Four years ago," David replied. "Do you remember that little trip she and I took to Las Vegas to go to that conference?"

"The one where she was hired by Zenith News Channel," Mac said with a nod of his head. "That was the beginning of the end for you two."

"Well," David said, "we went out to Vegas a day early just to have some fun. And we were drinking quite a bit of champagne, and we were feeling really good, and we went through a drive-through—"

"Wedding chapel," Mac finished.

"I thought it was a joke!" David jumped to his feet. "We got the value pack for two. Two deluxe cheeseburgers, fries, milkshakes, and nuptials."

"Obviously, it wasn't a joke," Mac said with a laugh.

"How could you laugh?"

"How could a man get married and not know it?" Mac asked. "All these years—"

"Six weeks after that trip, Yvonne moved to New York. If I'd known we were really married—" David shook his finger at Mac. "I had no idea that that was a real wedding chapel. What kind of wedding chapel has a drive-through?"

"Only in Vegas."

"Well, they should have huge signs out in front that say in big, bold block letters, 'Hey, drunks! Sober up! This is for real!'"

Mac stood up and grasped David by the shoulders. "Calm down, and take a deep breath. The important thing now is to get you *unmarried* so that you can marry Chelsea on Saturday."

"How can I marry a woman who won't even speak to me?"

"Archie will talk sense into her," Mac said.

"Chelsea knew Yvonne, Mac," David said. "We all went to high school together. Yvonne and Katrina were friends. Katrina broke Chelsea and me up. When Chelsea read Yvonne's name on the monitor—and she didn't even know I *dated* Yvonne—she found out that I'd *married* her."

Mac cocked his head at him. "You never told Chelsea about your dating Yvonne Harding?"

David shook his head. "Yvonne and I were over long before Chelsea came back into the picture."

"That's a lie." Mac backed up a step. "You didn't want Chelsea to find out that you'd been involved with Yvonne, because you knew she'd react the way she did today, and you didn't want to deal with it. So instead, you kept the truth from her, which made it worse when she did find out in the worst possible way."

"Mac, what am I going to do?" David asked.

"First things first," Mac said. "We need to get your marriage dissolved. We need to track down Yvonne—"

"That'll be easy." David took his cell phone out of his pocket. "I'll call her—"

Mac snatched the phone from his hand. "You have her phone number?" He studied the contact information. "You have her address—and you've been texting her!" He held up the phone for David to see. "I thought you two broke it off four years ago when she moved to New York."

"It was a long breakup," David said.

"When was the last time you saw her?" Mac asked.

David swallowed. "Are you talking casually or in the biblical sense?"

Mac's blue eyes bore into David's.

"We have not been sleeping together," David said. "We haven't slept together in a year." He added under his breath, "At least."

"You've been seeing Chelsea for *two* years."

"It was a *very* long breakup."

With a growl, Mac thrust the phone back to David, jabbing him in the chest with it. Disgusted, he stormed across the room before turning back to David. "You have no right to be getting married!"

"I love Chelsea!" David rushed up to him. "I know all of this is fallout caused by the dumb things that I've done going back to when I was in school, and I let the best thing I had going slip out of my hands because I let Katrina seduce me. But if you just help me out, Mac, I swear I'll do right by Chelsea. You should have seen her running out of the clerk's office today." He hung his head. "Mac, you're my best man. You have to help me."

After uttering a growl, Mac said, "Okay, first thing we'll do is get my lawyer to draw up papers to dissolve the marriage." He regarded David. "Am I correct in assuming you have no property or children together?"

"Not that I know of."

"We'll have Willingham send the papers to his New York office." Mac turned David around by his shoulders and pushed him toward the circular staircase leading upstairs to the bedrooms. "Go pack. We're going to New York to get your marriage dissolved, and then we'll come back here and get you married again."

Chapter Two

"David had no idea he got married?" There was a doubtful tone in Archie Monday's voice, and Mac could hear it all the way in the bathroom, where he was packing up his toiletries. Carrying his shaving kit, he went into the master bedroom, where he found his wife standing in the middle of the room with her hands on her slender hips. Her emerald-green eyes were narrowed to slits.

Stretched out on his back with his head hanging upside down over the edge of the king-sized bed, Gnarly was chewing on something. Mac guessed it was a new toy that Archie had picked up on her way back from comforting Chelsea. Archie was always buying Gnarly playthings to keep him occupied. It helped to keep the kleptomaniac from stealing from the neighbors.

Mac's inheritance included Robin Spencer's stone-and-cedar home located at the end of Spencer Court, which ran the length of Spencer Point. The court ended at the stone pillars marking the entrance to Spencer Manor, a multimillion-dollar estate that included Robin's famous floral gardens, which were tended by Mac's wife.

Robin had stipulated in her will that her assistant, Archie Monday, a stunning young woman with ultrashort blond hair, be allowed to live in the guest cottage on the estate for as long as she wanted, a condition for which Mac was eternally grateful. Before long, Archie had moved into the main house. They had only recently celebrated their first wedding anniversary.

"They were drunk and in Vegas." Mac slowed down on his way across the room to peck her on the lips. Seeing the anger in her eyes up close, he added, "Don't be mad at me. I knew full well what I was doing when I married you."

Pausing to reflect on how much he loved this woman, he brushed his hand across her soft cheek, letting it slide down to her shoulder, which he then squeezed. The curl of her lips told him that she was fighting the smile his touch had caused.

Turning serious again, she said, "You know what David's big mistake was?"

"Getting married without knowing it?" After tossing his shaving kit onto the bed, he went to the closet to retrieve his suitcase.

"Never telling Chelsea that he'd been involved with Yvonne in the first place," Archie said. "He dated Yvonne for a long time. They were so hot and heavy that I couldn't believe it when they broke it off the way they did. I actually thought they'd end up married."

"Frankly, it was a long breakup." Mac regretted his statement as soon as the words came out of his mouth.

Those lovely emerald eyes were glaring at him again. She folded her arms across her chest. "What?"

"You know those reserve weekends David does in Quantico once a month?" Mac muttered. "Well, there are several commuter flights from New York to Washington, but as soon as David got serious with Chelsea ..." He set the suitcase onto the bed so he could pack.

"I knew it," she replied. "Why did Yvonne even take that job in New York if she was going to be running down to Quantico once a month for a booty call? If she wanted David, she should have stayed here."

"Maybe David didn't ask her to marry him." Realizing what he said, Mac laughed. "No, wait! He did! He was just too drunk to realize it at the time and then didn't remember it afterward."

"This is serious, Mac."

"I can see Yvonne trying to have her cake and eat it, too." Mac forced himself to become serious. "She always wanted to be a star. That job hosting *Crime Watch* was her golden opportunity." He chuckled. "David married to a television star? Who would have thought?"

"But are you sure David's *ready* to get married *to anyone*?" Archie asked. "Chelsea's asking that question herself. She's seriously thinking of cancelling the wedding."

"Why are you asking me?" Mac demanded. "I'm only his best man."

"The job of the best man"—she pointed to him—"and the job of the matron of honor"—she directed her index finger to herself—"is to stand up and witness the bride's and groom's vows. If we stand up there on Saturday and listen to David vow to love, honor, and cherish Chelsea for the rest of his life, knowing that he has this commitment problem, then we're both lying—not just to everyone in that church, but to God." She lowered her voice. "Never lie to God. He doesn't like it."

"You make David sound like a scoundrel," Mac said. "He's not. I've known a lot of scoundrels. They'll have sex with anything that moves. That's not David. He honestly has feelings for every woman I know he's slept with."

"What about the ones we don't know about?" Archie let out a sigh. "I love David. Truly, I do. He's like a brother to me.

But he honestly has this problem when it comes to women. Is he going to be able to keep his wedding vows?"

"Only David can answer that." Mac placed his hands on her shoulders and forced her to look up at him. "I think he's scared to death of making his—our—father's mistake. Imagine growing up in a home where you know that your father is in love with someone else—someone he can never have because he's married to your mother. Imagine watching your mother go mad with jealousy and resentment because she knows, deep down, that her husband loves someone else."

"Pat never cheated on David's mother," Archie said.

"But he was in love Robin," Mac said. "How would you feel if you realized that I was in love with someone else—even if I never slept with her—that my heart was with her?"

"I would want to die," she said.

"The fact is, David grew up in the middle of that. He once told me that if he'd been in his father's place, he would have divorced Violet and married Robin."

"Pat was too honorable to humiliate Violet by doing that," Archie said.

"Deep down, David's scared to death of marrying one woman only to discover afterward that he's made a mistake." Mac went to the closet to gather socks and underwear to pack.

"He's going to break Chelsea's heart—I can feel it," she muttered while sitting down on the bed next to where Gnarly was still chewing on his toy. "He should have Chelsea about dating Yvonne."

"Yvonne was friends with Katrina." Then, as he folded his clothes and placed them in the suitcase, he corrected himself. "Actually, Katrina and Yvonne were frenemies. The same Katrina who seduced David to break him and Chelsea up back in high school."

"Which was ages ago," she pointed out.

"First loves can be very powerful—and painful." He smiled at her. "By this time next week, David will have divorced Yvonne and will be married to Chelsea, and we'll all have a good laugh about this on their first wedding anniversary." He grasped her by her shoulders and kissed her.

"I hope so." She returned his hug.

Mac closed the suitcase and zipped it shut. With a swipe of his arm, he said, "Gnarly, get off the bed."

The German shepherd rolled over onto his stomach. The object he was chewing tumbled out of his mouth and bounced onto the floor. With disappointment, the dog peered over the edge of the bed.

Mac bent over to pick it up. His eyebrows furrowed when he saw that the object was a box and that its felt cover had been torn by Gnarly's sharp teeth. The slimy object was dented and mutilated.

"What?" Mac sucked in a deep breath. He swallowed.

"What is it?" Archie took the box from his hand. "It's a jewelry box. What was in it?"

"David's and Chelsea's wedding bands," Mac said with gritted teeth. "The box was on the dresser."

Meanwhile, Gnarly gazed up at Mac, who moved in closer to him. Seeing the growing fury in his master's eyes, the German shepherd's ear lay back flat on his head.

Archie opened the box. "Where are the rings?"

"Good question." Mac then asked Gnarly, "Where are the rings?"

As if to answer him, Gnarly jumped down off the bed and burrowed underneath it.

"They have to be here someplace," Archie said.

After two hours of searching, Mac and Archie took Gnarly to the vet, who confirmed their worst fear with an

X-ray. The German shepherd had swallowed both wedding bands.

"You're lucky he didn't swallow the box," the veterinarian said.

"I can get another box," Mac said. "I *need* the rings—those rings. They're custom made."

"But the box could have obstructed his intestines," the vet replied. "From what we can see in these X-rays, I believe the rings will pass through fine." With a grin, he said, "In other words, he'll give them back to you in good time."

Cringing at the thought of how Gnarly would give the two wedding bands back, Mac asked, "How long?"

"Could be anywhere from one to ten days."

"The wedding is in five days," Mac argued. "How about pumping his stomach?"

The vet looked at Gnarly, who was on the examination table. The great dog lifted his head from where he was resting it between his paws and uttered a low snarl. "I don't think so. That could be very dangerous."

"Then how about surgery?" Mac asked.

"No!" Archie ordered. "We're not putting Gnarly under the knife."

"I need those rings back," Mac said.

"Well," the vet said, "as my mother used to say, this too shall pass." Laughing, he looked at Mac, who regarded him without humor. Unnerved by the glare in Mac's eyes, the vet dropped his smile.

With a sigh, Mac turned his attention to Archie who was lovingly petting Gnarly while making cooing sounds. "I'd hate to be you for the next few days."

Archie stopped petting Gnarly in mid-stroke. "What's that supposed to mean?"

"You're going to have to monitor Gnarly's bathroom breaks until he gives up those rings."

"Me!"

Her mouth was still hanging open when Mac said, "I can't do it. I'm going to New York."

"Why are you going to New York?" the vet asked.

"To make sure the groom gets a divorce," Mac said.

"The same groom whose wedding band is in Gnarly's stomach? He's married?"

"It's complicated," Mac said. "You see, a few years ago, he went with his then-girlfriend to Las Vegas and they got drunk and went through a drive-through thinking it was a joke, but it turns out it wasn't and he didn't find out it was for real until—Why am I telling you this?"

Her arms folded across her chest, Archie said in a firm tone, "I am not monitoring Gnarly's discharges. You're the best man. It was your job to take care of the wedding bands. Not mine. Besides, I'm going to be running around all over the place with Chelsea getting these last minute wedding details taken care of. I don't have time to inspect his poo."

Hands on his hips, Mac returned her glare. "Well, there is no way in hell you're going to make me take Gnarly to Manhattan."

"You are aware that we're going to New York City," David said to Mac shortly after the chartered plane took off from McHenry's airport early the next morning.

Mac followed David's eyes to where he was staring at Gnarly, who was sound asleep in the seat that Mac had pushed back into a fully reclining position for the large dog. The motion-sickness pills Mac had given him had knocked Gnarly out, which he preferred over having to deal with his vomiting.

"Yes, I know," Mac said. "Archie's spending the day with Chelsea."

"So?" David asked. "Gnarly loves spending time with Molly."

"Yeah, but the bridal shop doesn't love Gnarly since he tackled the pizza delivery man and ruined one of their most expensive gowns with tomato sauce. Cost me two thousand dollars." Mac waved at the flight attendant. "Could you get us two coffees, please?"

The attendant rushed back to the kitchenette to retrieve the drinks for the plane's only two passengers.

"Imagine what he could do in Manhattan," David said. "I mean, I love Gnarly, but between the air sickness and hauling him around Manhattan, wouldn't—"

"Have you talked to Chelsea?"

"She won't talk to me," David said in a firm tone. "I left her a voice mail and sent her a text. Who in their right mind marries a woman who won't speak to him?"

"Look at it from her point of view." After thanking the flight attendant, Mac accepted the two coffees from her and handed one to David. "This is supposed to be the happiest week of her life, she's about to marry the man she loves, and then this comes up. Give her some time."

"How much time? We're getting married in four days. What if she doesn't get over it by then?"

Sipping his coffee, Mac shot a glare at the dog snoring in the seat across from them. Considering what he would have to do to get their wedding rings back, he said, "She'd better."

Chapter Three

News Corps Building, Avenue of the Americas, Midtown Manhattan

On the thirty-fifth floor of the skyscraper that served as home to some of the country's major news networks, Ali Hudson gazed with remorse into a box of chocolates. She'd already eaten every truffle. Upon studying the chart on the underside of the lid, she saw that there was nothing left to satisfy her craving for more—only chocolate-covered coconut pieces, caramels, and various fruit creams remained.

Makes me feel lower than a gopher hole.

Like a doctor proclaiming a patient dead, she placed the lid back on the box of candy. Picking up her oversized coffee mug filled with coffee and double helpings of cream and sugar, she returned to her desk in the outer office of Yvonne Harding, one of Zenith News Channel's most distinguished investigative reporters.

Four years earlier, when ZNC had signed Yvonne on to serve as one of four journalists for their new crime reporting show, she had been regarded as simply another pretty face with a flawless figure and a great pair of legs. They'd intended for her to cover the fluffier news stories, like the ones in the weekly "stupid crooks" segments.

It didn't take long for Yvonne to prove that she was as tenacious and capable as less attractive journalists when it came to pursuing serious stories. Between breaking huge crime stories miles ahead of the competing networks and looking sensational while doing it, Yvonne had "popped," as they say in show business. She'd even outshone the lead host, Pam Wiehl, whose name was intended to draw in *Crime Watch*'s initial audience. In her late forties, Pam Wiehl was ZNC's award-winning veteran investigative journalist and the wife of the show's executive producer.

Since garnishing the star slot was an impossibility, Yvonne Harding had been compensated for drawing in big ratings with a huge salary and a prestigious window office with a view of midtown Manhattan.

Yvonne's research assistant was not so lucky. Ali Hudson had been given the outer office, which didn't have a view. She didn't mind, as long as she was allowed to slip off her four-inch heels while seated behind her desk.

Seeing that it was after ten o'clock, Ali peered down at her full mug and told herself that she'd probably had enough. With a sigh of resignation, she lifted the coffee to her lips.

The office door opened, and an arm bearing a small bouquet of yellow roses wrapped around the door. It was followed by the arm's owner, ZNC's most notable news show host, Ryan Ritter.

The attractive, broad-shouldered journalist was a favorite with the network's female viewers—so much so that his show, which followed *Crime Watch* at nine o'clock, was one of ZNC's top-drawing programs.

Beaming, Ryan handed the roses to the research assistant.

Her face filling with confusion, Ali hesitated before taking the flowers. "What's the occasion, sir?"

"How many times do I have to tell you, Ali? Call me Ryan." Grinning at her sultry voice, which was heavily laced with a Texan drawl, Ryan hitched a leg over the corner of her desk. "I was passing the florist on my way in, and they were putting these out. Yellow roses. Instantly I thought of ZNC's most lovely yellow rose of Texas."

The phone on Ali's desk rang. The caller ID indicated that it was the reception desk on their floor.

While picking up the phone's receiver, Ali chastised him. "Shoot! You didn't have to buy 'em for me." She uttered a sigh. "People are gonna think we're fixin' to do somethin' inappropriate."

"Who says we're not?" Ryan asked with a toothy smile. "What are you doing for lunch today?"

"Researchin' a missin' person's case for Yvonne," she replied before saying into the receiver, "Office of Yvonne Harding. This is Ali speakin'. May I help you?"

After the receptionist informed her that she had two visitors to see Yvonne Harding, Ali told her to send them in. As soon as she hung up, the outside line rang. The caller ID read "Caleb Roberts."

"Looks like it's time for me to get back to work, sir." Then she said in a tone oozing with Southern charm, "Thank you for the yeller roses."

The toothy grin dropped from Ryan's face while he muttered something under his breath that she couldn't hear. She assumed it was a curse over her turning down yet another invitation. *Can't he see that I'm half his age? Dirty ol' man should be 'shamed of himself.*

She shooed him off her desk with a wave of one hand and picked up the phone with the other. "Good morning. Yvonne Harding's office. Ali Hudson speakin'."

She arched an eyebrow at Ryan Ritter, a wordless demand that he leave. Slowly, he made his way out the door.

"Hello, Ali," the elderly man on the other end of the line replied. "This is Caleb Roberts returning Yvonne Harding's call. Is she in?"

"I'm so sorry, sir. She's not in yet," Ali replied. "But I'm sure I can help you. I'm her research assistant," she continued to tell the caller. "I was the one who left you the voice mail askin' you to call our office."

She started when the office door opened and two men with a very large German shepherd on a leash entered the outer office. At a gallop, the dog made a beeline for the break table containing the box of chocolates in the corner, only to be pulled back by the dark-haired gentleman with a bit of gray at his temples. Judging by the two men's similar builds and facial features, including their square jaws and blue eyes, Ali concluded that they were related. *Probably brothers.*

Holding up her index finger, she nodded her head to acknowledge them while continuing her phone conversation.

Directly behind the two men and the dog, Pam Wiehl charged in. "Is—"

Waving her hand to indicate she was on the phone, Ali continued to speak into the receiver. "I'm workin' with Yvonne on the Walker case."

There was silence on the other end of the line.

Refraining from exhibiting her impatience by tapping her pen against her notepad, Ali raised her light-brown eyes from the slender hips of the blond-haired man who had come in with the German shepherd. While admiring his firm, athletic build, she noticed a bulge under his sports coat—on his hip.

How did he get that gun through security? Must have a permit.

She looked up and saw him peering down at her with the clearest blue eyes she'd ever seen. The charm of his grin made her heartbeat kick up a notch. In spite of her effort to remain cool, she felt a girlish gasp escape her lips.

"Hello? Ali?" the retired detective said, sounding annoyed. "Are you still there? I thought Yvonne Harding backed off on the Walker case."

"Yes, sir!" Turning her head to avoid her visitor's pretty blue eyes, Ali forced a casual tone into her voice. "It's been two years ..."

Pam Wiehl was also looking the visitors up and down and drumming her long, manicured nails on the desktop directly in front of Ali. She tapped the toe of one of her red high-heeled pumps while the man with the dog tried to move the beast behind him, as if doing so would keep her from noticing the hundred pounds of fur and claws.

"Told you we should have left Gnarly at the hotel," the blond-haired man whispered to his companion.

"You're Mac Faraday." A wide grin crossed Pam Wiehl's face.

Seeing that they were not about to be booted out, Mac smiled and offered her his hand. "That's right."

"And this must be Diablo," she corrected herself. "I mean—"

"Gnarly."

The news journalist bent over to pat the German shepherd on the head. Instead of being his usual friendly self, Gnarly directed his attention to the corner of the office where the chocolates were resting.

"Super, sir," Ali said into the phone while writing down a note on her memo pad. "I'll see you at eight o'clock tonight. Thank you, Sergeant Roberts." With a grin at David O'Callaghan, she hung up the phone. "Can I help you, sir?"

"Yes," Pam interjected before David could respond. "Tell me why Yvonne Harding is wasting her time digging up the Walker case again."

"Why wouldn't she, ma'am?" Ali waved her hands and shrugged her shoulders. "The two-year anniversary of Audra Walker's disappearance is comin' up. She was a Pulitzer award–winnin' investigative journalist. Yvonne Harding was the last person to interview her. Yvonne figures that if she can make some headway with findin' out what 'appened to her—"

"She's wasting her time," Pam said forcibly. "The police already investigated Audra Walker's disappearance. They said there's no evidence of wrongdoing."

"Why would a famous journalist voluntarily disappear?" Mac asked.

"In the middle of a book tour while her best-sellin' book was still top ten with the *New York Times?"* Ali asked.

"David?" Yvonne Harding's voice interrupted their conversation.

When David turned around to face her, the leggy blonde rushed from the open doorway of her office to jump into his arms. After a quick hug, she greeted him with a kiss on the mouth that turned into a full-fledged lip-lock.

"I guess they know each other," Pam murmured.

Ali stood up from her seat behind her desk. "Looks to me like she's gonna be tied up for a while, Ms. Wiehl. How 'bout if I have her call ya? And I'll pass on your thoughts 'bout her workin' on the Walker case." She shot Pam a wink.

"You do that," Pam replied. "Tell her to call me as soon as she's through with her latest boy toy."

While shaking Mac's hand, Pam said, "If you're going to be in town for a few days, Mr. Faraday, I would love to interview you about your cases on my show, *Crime Watch*."

"I've seen it," Mac replied. "Maybe another time. We only have a bit of business to conduct here in town today, and then we'll be leaving first thing in the morning."

"Well, maybe you could just squeeze in an hour—the interview doesn't have to be live," Pam argued. "Tell you what—I'll e-mail you my information, and you call me. Leave your e-mail address with Ali." She grinned at the research assistant. "You don't mind taking down Mr. Faraday's contact information for me, do you, Ali?"

"No problem t'all, Ms. Wiehl."

Seeing that she refused to take a definite "no" for an answer, Mac consented to calling her. With one last reminder to Ali to have Yvonne call her, Pam Wiehl hurried out.

Staring and whining in the direction of the break table and the chocolates, Gnarly tugged at the end of his leash.

"Mac, how good it is to see you again!" After releasing David from the lip-lock, Yvonne hurried over to hug Mac. "And you brought Gnarly!" She bent over to pet the German shepherd, only to have him try to drag Mac toward the table.

"Chocolate is not good for you." Mac jerked on the leash. "Stop it."

"Did you bring Archie?" Yvonne asked them.

"No, she couldn't make it." Mac answered. "She had several appointments."

"I thought maybe you brought her shopping," Yvonne said. "Are you in New York on business?"

"You could say that." Mac jerked his head in David's direction.

David uttered a deep sigh. "Yvonne, can we talk … in your office?" He took her by the arm.

"Gnarly and I will guard the chocolates." Mac leaned on the corner of Ali's desk while David escorted Yvonne into her office and closed the door.

After slipping her shoes on, Ali deposited the roses in a small vase resting on top of the file cabinet and crossed the office to pick up the box of chocolates. "Maybe if I put these over yonder, sir, it'll take Gnarly's mind off 'em. He looks like he'll eat anything that doesn't eat him first."

"That's Gnarly," Mac said with a smile.

As Ali strode across the office, Mac noticed that unlike Yvonne and Pam, who were dressed in women's suits with short, form-fitting skirts to accentuate their legs and figures, Ali was dressed in a mustard-brown double-breasted pant-suit with matching pumps. She was tall and slender and had the walk of a runway model. She wore her long, dark mane in an updo with tendrils along the sides of her face. Her dark hair against her creamy white complexion accentuated her light-brown eyes, giving her an exotic appearance.

Once the candy was put away, she knelt down in front of Gnarly and cupped his head in her hands. "You're not only big. I can see just by lookin' at you that you're brave, too. I bet you'd shoot craps with the devil 'imself, wouldn't ya?"

Ali's Southern drawl was not only unmistakable but also familiar to Mac. "I knew Audra Walker."

Standing up, she continued to stroke Gnarly on top of his head. "Really?"

Mac nodded his head. "She was investigating a murder case that I was lead detective on back when I was a homicide detective in Washington."

He shot a warning glance at Gnarly, who was still staring at the corner, even though the chocolates had been moved. The dog gazed back at Mac over his shoulder and uttered a whine.

"*Before* you became a multimillionaire, Mr. Faraday?" Ali asked.

"Before." Mac flashed her a good-natured smile. "Audra Walker had excellent instincts. That's not something you learn in journalism school. It's something you're born with."

"Then ya know she wasn't one to just light out somewhere without lettin' anyone know ..." Her voice trailing off, Ali peered down at the top of her desk.

"Audra Walker was totally devoted to her two children."

"The police detective in charge of the case says she went loco because of her husband's death," Ali said. "Yes, she was choked up when he had that massive heart attack and died, but he was twenty years older than she was. She knew she'd end up bein' a young widow—" Seeing Mac watching her, she cleared her throat. "Rather, that's what I've found durin' my research 'bout the case for Yvonne."

"The Audra Walker I knew was too strong to have a breakdown and walk away from her family," Mac said.

As soon as she closed the door, Yvonne wrapped her arms around David's shoulders and pressed her lips to his.

Enjoying the feel of her body in his arms, David welcomed the kiss—until he remembered why he was there. Peeling her arms from his shoulders, David clutched her hands in both of his. "I can't do this."

"That was one area where we never had any disagreement," she said breathily. She reached up to stroke his face. "I've missed you so much, David. Those weekend get-togethers at Quantico–"

Her alluring scent, which was not unlike that of the sea, was evaporating his resolve. Stepping away, he went to the window to take in the view and clear his head. "I'm getting married this weekend ... to Chelsea."

Folding her arms across her chest, she narrowed her eyes and glared at his back. "Then what are you doing here?"

"Taking care of some unfinished business."

"David, we haven't seen each other in a year."

"We're married." David waited for her response. Hearing nothing, he turned back to her and saw her staring at him with wide eyes.

Her mouth hung open. Finally, she said, "Cute, David. Really cute."

David removed the papers that Mac's lawyer, Ed Willingham, had sent to their hotel that morning from his jacket pocket. "It's true, Yvonne. I found out yesterday when Chelsea and I went to get our marriage license. They refused because I was already married to you."

She moved to take the papers from him. "Seriously? When did that happen? How did we not know?"

"Las Vegas, four years ago," David said. "Remember the drive-through? We got the value pack."

"The place with the lukewarm cheeseburgers and wimpy fries?"

"That's the place," David said. "Seems their meal deal included bonus nuptials."

A sensuous grin came to her lips. She placed her hand on his chest. "I vaguely remember the drive-through, but my memory of later … at the hotel … in the heart-shaped tub …" She slid her hand down his chest to his stomach.

Before she could reach his belt, David pulled back. "I need you to sign these papers, Yvonne." Taking them from her, he leafed through to the last page, where Willingham had marked the signature line with an *X*. David had already signed on the line across from it. "Mac's lawyer drew these up. All you have to do is sign them, and Mac and I will take these papers over to the courthouse, and our marriage will be dissolved." He thrust the papers toward her.

Instead of taking the papers, she gazed at him with wide eyes.

❖ ❖ ❖

"What's wrong with you?" Mac dropped the leash to allow the dog to run over to the corner, where he sat down and stared imploringly at the wall. Mac rose to his feet.

"No offense, sir," Ali said, "but looks to me like keeping him in line is 'bout as easy as puttin' socks on a rooster."

Searching his mind, Mac recalled the last time Gnarly had behaved in this manner—that is, the last time he'd refused to be deterred by something that only his hypersensitive senses could detect.

"If I recall the details correctly ..." Mac said. "Yvonne Harding interviewed Audra Walker for *Crime Watch* in this studio."

"The interview was for her new book that had just been released—the one 'bout the death of Jolene Fitzgerald. She was a sex symbol in the eighties who was rumored to be having an affair with Senator Brennan, who was fixin' to run for president. Audra Walker found proof that he'd had Jolene Fitzgerald killed because she was going to go public 'bout their affair. Of course, he still failed to make it to the White House and died of cancer about fifteen years ago. His son, who took over his father's senatorial slot, was all worked up 'bout Walker's book."

Mac moved the table out of the way and searched the floor underneath for any treats that may have captured Gnarly's attention. There was nothing on the floor, except an empty mousetrap.

As soon as the table was out of the way, Gnarly parked in front of the wall and whined mournfully. Kneeling next to Gnarly, who turned to gaze pleadingly at him, Mac asked, "After the interview with Yvonne, didn't Audra Walker go back to her hotel?"

"Four Seasons," Ali said. "She and her assistant. As soon as they got back to their suite, Audra Walker went to work on her next book. She was working away like a hound during flea season when her assistant went to bed."

"What book was she working on?"

"Oh," Ali shrugged. "It was just something that she'd been working on off and on for years, sir. During the night, Audra left the hotel and was never seen or heard from again."

"But they found the cabdriver whose taxi she got in after leaving the hotel." Standing up, Mac pressed his hands against the wall.

"He dropped her off—"

"Here in midtown," he said. "Didn't I see a couple of years ago that many of ZNC's shows were getting new sets and that ZNC got a new studio? These floors were being renovated."

"Less 'n two years ago, sir." Her voice, breathless with excitement, sounded even sultrier. She hurried out from behind her desk. "What're ya thinkin'?"

Mac was tapping the wall with his ear pressed against it. "The last time Gnarly behaved like this, we found a dead body."

"Whatta ya mean?"

Mac rapped his knuckles against the wall up and down. "There's something behind this drywall."

Agitated, Gnarly began clawing at the wall.

"Do you have something I could use to make a small hole in it?" Mac asked her.

"How 'bout a sledgehammer?"

Before Mac could answer, she yanked open the bottom drawer of the file cabinet behind her desk and hurried over to him with a small sledgehammer. "Why do you have a sledgehammer in your desk drawer?"

"Contrary to what experts may tell you," she said, "when it comes to makin' an impression, size does matter."

"I'm afraid to ask what you're talking about."

Sensing that things were about to happen, Gnarly stood up and barked at them.

"You'd better not be lying," Mac told Gnarly before swinging the hammer at the wall.

"David, I haven't seen you in a year," Yvonne said. "Now suddenly you show up here at my office, telling me that you and I have been married for the last four years, and you want a divorce."

"That about covers it." David held the papers out to her.

She refused to touch them. "Are you happy with Chelsea?"

"If I wasn't happy with her, I wouldn't be marrying her."

"If you were happy with her, you wouldn't have slept with Katrina," Yvonne shot back.

"Now that's a low blow, and you know it," David replied. "We were kids back then. I was a fool."

"You weren't a foolish kid when we were together a few years ago," Yvonne said. "When we got *married.*"

"No, then I was drunk."

She brushed his cheek with her hand. "Remember all the good times we had together?" She added in a whisper, "We were so happy."

"If we were so happy, why did you leave me as soon as you got the offer to come to New York?"

"Did it ever occur to you to ask me to stay?" she replied.

David stared back at her.

"I didn't think so," she said.

As soon as the sledgehammer hit the wall, sending drywall dust scattering, Gnarly plunged through the opening and clawed through the mess. Spying plastic, Mac reached inside to yank away hunks of drywall.

"What's going on here?" a booming voice demanded.

Whirling around, Mac saw a tall white-haired man wearing a black suit and a red tie charging across the office toward him like he meant business.

Ali stopped him by putting her hand on his chest. "There's somethin' behind this wall, Mr. Wiehl."

Pam Wiehl was directly behind him. "There's nothing behind that wall except electrical wires and—"

"Who is this guy?" Jim Wiehl asked. "What's that dog doing here?"

"He's Mac Faraday, dear," Pam explained. "The detective I was telling you about. He's famous."

"I don't care how famous he is. He has no right tearing up our walls?" Turning back to Mac, who was yanking out clump after clump of drywall, he said, "I'm Jim Wiehl, an executive producer with ZNC, and I'm ordering you to—"

"What's going on?" Yvonne threw open her office door to learn the cause of the yelling. Upon seeing the sledgehammer, she asked, "Mac, what are you doing?"

"Ali, call the police," Jim Wiehl said.

"You'd better do what he says," Mac told Ali.

"Gnarly was chewin' his bit like there was no tomorrow, I swear," Ali argued. "He smelled somethin' inside that wall."

"Maybe that's because the dog is nuts," Jim countered.

"Gnarly is a lot of things," David said while moving in closer to peer inside the hole Mac was creating. "But nuts isn't one of them." He whispered to Mac, "What did Yvonne's assistant just tell him?"

"Gnarly was upset because he smelled something behind this wall, and she'll swear to it." Mac squinted at him. "Weren't you paying attention?"

"What's this all about?" Yvonne asked everyone, hoping someone could answer.

David turned around from where he was examining the space on the other side of the drywall. "A dead body."

Mac stepped back from the hole he had created. He revealed the plastic he had torn away and exposed the skull with long, dark hair that was peering out at them from inside her drywall coffin. "I'm willing to bet whoever this is didn't crawl into this wall and die of natural causes."

Chapter Four

"Why can't you just read a magazine while waiting like a normal person?" David asked Mac while keeping curious onlookers and news journalists thirsting for exclusives out of the office. Taking in the sledgehammer and the drywall dust littering the outer office, he shook his head. "What possessed you to smash a hole in the wall in the first place? Where did you get the sledgehammer?"

"Ali gave it to me," Mac stopped examining the skeletal remains to jerk a thumb in the direction of the desk where Yvonne's research assistant was sitting with her head down between her knees. "Gnarly was doing that thing he does when he senses a dead body in the area. I knocked on the wall and could tell something was behind it."

David went over to Ali, who looked like she was going to be sick. "Are you okay?"

Slowly, Ali sat up. Gnarly laid his head in her lap. She stroked him on his head and down his back. "I just don't believe it. I've been workin' here for five months, and she's been no more 'an a foot away." Her hands trembled when she wiped the tears from her eyes.

"Here. Take this." David took a handkerchief from his jacket packet and held it out to her. When she took it, their fingers touched. The touch of his hand made her jerk back into her seat. Feeling his eyes on her face, she concentrated on the dog resting his head in her lap and on wiping away the tears in her eyes.

"You're going to need to develop a thicker skin if you want to make it as an investigative journalist on the crime beat, Ali," Yvonne said in a harsh tone that surprised David.

"Audra Walker was a human being worthy of tears," Mac replied.

"I'm simply saying that if you let these types of atrocities get to you, you're not going to last long in this business," Yvonne said. "You're going to end up at the bottom of a bottle, in a rubber room, or bitter and unemployed."

"Audra Walker was one of the most compassionate journalists I'd ever met," Mac said. "But she was none of those things. She channeled her outrage over the injustices people perpetrate against one another into passion for uncovering the truth."

David broke the glare between them and asked, "When was this wall built?"

"These two floors, the offices, and the studio downstairs were renovated two years ago."

"Back when Audra Walker disappeared," Mac noted.

"Yes, they were being renovated then," she said. "I remember because I interviewed Audra in the old studio down on the thirtieth floor. You're just assuming that's Audra Walker. We don't know that for sure."

"It's Audra," Mac said.

"Kind of early in the game to be making assumptions about the identity of the victim, isn't it?" Pushing his eyeglasses up on his nose, a man wearing the gold shield of a police detective stepped through the doorway. Wordlessly, he motioned for the uniformed officers to take control of the scene.

Already by the detective's side, Jim Wiehl was quick to introduce him. "This is Lieutenant Wayne Hopkins with the homicide squad."

A cocky grin crossed the lieutenant's face when he shook Mac's hand. "I work on the major case squad." Mac quickly noticed that the detective was clad in a tailored suit with an expensive fitted shirt, which was not the way Mac had dressed when he'd been a detective. Every strand of his thin blond hair was in place.

"That means he worked on the investigation into Audra Walker's disappearance," Yvonne said, "and apparent murder."

"I'm glad to see you remember me, Yvonne." Lieutenant Hopkins smiled, revealing a mouth full of bright-white straight teeth. "You look stunning, as always."

"Thank you, Lieutenant." She stepped back toward Ali's desk.

"Please, call me Wayne," he said.

Stepping between them, David gestured to the wall behind the police detective. "*Wayne,* the dead body is over there."

Seeing Gnarly, who had stood up to place his front paws on Ali's desk in order to lap up the then cold coffee, Lieutenant Hopkins asked, "Is that a dog?"

"Very good," David said. "I see your investigative skills are top-notch."

"I hate dogs," Lieutenant Hopkins said. "They can't be trusted."

"I'd trust that dog with my life. As a matter of fact, that very dog has saved my life." David jerked his thumb over his shoulder to where Gnarly had finished the coffee and had sat down between Ali's legs to be petted. "So I trust him more than I trust some humans."

"I don't care if he saved you and your whole family. He's contaminating my crime scene," the detective said. "So get him out of here."

Taking the cue from the police lieutenant, Ali took Gnarly's leash and led him to the doorway. They waded through the crowd to go down the hallway.

Turning to where Mac was showing the skeleton wrapped in plastic wrap to a member of the crime-scene investigative team, the police lieutenant said, "As I was saying, we don't know that that's Audra Walker. Not until our medical examiner does the autopsy."

"How many women connected to this building have disappeared in the last two years?" David asked.

"And how many wear a cameo locket with their children's baby pictures in it?" Mac added while using a pen to point to the area that had once been the skeleton's chest.

"I don't care if you are Mac Faraday," Lieutenant Hopkins said. "This is not Spencer, Maryland. You're in New York, and this is my crime scene—not yours."

Mac held up his hands to indicate he was wearing evidence gloves. "I saw the locket, which is still around her neck, and recognized it." He stepped aside to allow the investigators to peer into the hole in the wall at the skeleton.

"Recognized it?" Jim Wiehl repeated what Mac had said.

Behind her husband, Pam seemed to be holding her breath as she gazed at the skull peering out at them from the hole in the wall.

"Audra Walker always wore that cameo locket," Mac said. "She was wearing it every time I saw her."

"When was the last time you saw her?" Lieutenant Hopkins asked Mac with a wicked grin.

Mac paused to think a moment. "At least six years ago."

"How close were you two?" the lieutenant asked.

"We worked together for several weeks," Mac replied. "We became friends."

"Close enough friends for you to know about a locket she never took off," the detective noted.

"Mac Faraday had never been in this building until today," David said. "He didn't have access to the crime scene." With a wide sweep of his arm, he indicated Yvonne, her producer, and the other news journalists who were crowding in the doorway to get a view of the scene. "They all did. *They* are your suspects."

"Did you get the papers signed?" Mac asked David in a low voice after they'd been ushered out of Yvonne's office and into a conference room.

Gnarly had climbed up into a chair at the head of the conference table. Draping his head over one of the chair's arms, he proceeded to take a nap.

"Yvonne didn't have a pen," David answered Mac's question.

Mac looked over his shoulder at a box of pens resting in the middle of the conference table. Each pen was marked with the name, logo, and address of the ZNC news network. "Seriously? We're in an *office* building, and Yvonne couldn't find a *pen*?"

"We're going to go have lunch together," David said. "She wants to catch up—though I don't know if we'll be making lunch now. Don't worry. I'll get her to sign the papers."

"David," Mac said, "take my advice. It's never a good idea to play with fire—especially with old flames less than a week before you're supposed to get married."

"I'm not going to cut all of my old friends and acquaintances out of my life simply because Chelsea has trust issues," David said. "I'm not going to sleep with Yvonne. We're just going to have lunch together—unless she blows me off for this story and that idiot police lieutenant."

"Oh," Mac chuckled. "Am I picking up a hint of jealousy?"

"Why would I be jealous of that moron?"

"Because he's sniffing around your wife."

"She is not my wife."

"She is until you get her to sign those papers," Mac said. "The sooner you get her to sign them, the sooner we can get back to Deep Creek Lake."

David chuckled.

Confused, Mac asked, "What?"

"You want to leave? I fully expected you to get wrapped up in Audra Walker's murder, and I figured that I would be the one dragging you back to Deep Creek," David said. "You knew Walker. You said she was your friend."

"Considering that the body was hidden in Yvonne's office, I'm sure she'll keep up on the case," Mac said.

"Are you ready to go, my love?" Making an entrance, Yvonne swung open the door and breezed in.

"You mean we're still on for lunch?" David rose from his seat at the conference table. "I thought for sure that you'd take down Pam Wiehl for this story."

"I tried, but I lost," Yvonne said. "Pam Wiehl is married to the executive producer and is the headliner for *Crime Watch*—that trumps my legs hands down."

"How long has she been married to Jim Wiehl?" Mac asked.

"Like, forever." Yvonne added with a grin. "They were high school sweethearts from a small town in Montana and ran off to come to New York the summer after they graduated from high school. He went to film school, and she went to journalism school while working her way up from receptionist here at ZNC." She grasped David's arm with both hands. "I know of a lovely place for us to have lunch."

Mac saw a flicker of concern cross David's face. "Don't take too long with all of your catching up. We need to get back to Spencer tomorrow. There's a lot left to do for the wedding *this* weekend."

Without acknowledging his statement, Yvonne led David toward the door, only to have Mac stop her with a question. "Do you have any idea of how Audra ended up back here at the studio?"

With her hand on the door, Yvonne stopped to turn back to him. "Huh?"

"You interviewed Audra Walker the night she disappeared," Mac reminded her.

"About her book *The Night Jolene Died*," Yvonne said. "Then she went back to her hotel—the Four Seasons. The next morning, she was gone. Hotel security cameras recorded her arrival. Her key cards confirmed that she'd gone to her room. Hotel security also showed her leaving again shortly after midnight and taking a cab—"

"That brought her back here to midtown Manhattan," Mac said. "Why did she come back after midnight?"

"According to the police," Yvonne said, "her cell phone records showed that she received a text from someone using my name, claiming that I had some information about the case she'd told me about, and saying that we needed to meet in private. Whoever it was said it would be too dangerous for me to be seen talking to her about it. It ended up being a burner phone."

"So she was lured away from her hotel," David said.

"That's what it looked like to me," Yvonne said. "For a while there, the lead detective thought I had sent her that text. It was only because I had an alibi that they stopped questioning me."

"If she was lured back here by a text supposedly sent from you, why would the police have thought she just took off because she was distraught over her husband's death?" Mac asked.

"Some people think she set it up to look that way," Yvonne said. "Audra was a public personality. Her disappearance jacked up her book sales—it made her a legend. If she had just retired, she would have faded off into the landscape. As it is, she went out with a bang."

"That's for sure," David said.

"The police didn't close the case and decide it had been a voluntary disappearance until last year, when one of Audra's friends received a postcard from Australia saying that Audra had met a man and ran off to start a new life," Yvonne said.

"Obviously, that postcard was a fake," Mac said. "Audra Walker's murder was planned—premeditated. Who were Lieutenant Hopkins' suspects before he closed the case?"

"He inherited the case from Sergeant Caleb Roberts, who retired last year," Yvonne said. "Hopkins worked under him. Roberts retired. Then Hopkins made lieutenant." She chuckled. "I'm sure you noticed his kowtowing to the Wiehls."

"That I did," Mac said.

"The camera loves Hopkins, and Hopkins loves the camera," she said. "Pam asked him to come on the show as an expert on a story she was working on. He did okay, and now he's on ZNC's list of people to call in when we need to interview a law-enforcement expert. Hopkins never passes up a chance to be on camera."

"Isn't that a conflict of interest?" Mac asked. "Someone with access to this building and these floors lured Audra Walker here to kill her and seal her in that wall."

"They would have had to get through security," David said. "There are metal detectors down in the lobby. Mac and I both had to show our police badges and gun permits and log in our weapons with the building security."

"Practically every journalist I know is packing," Yvonne said, "including me. Believe it or not, even I've received threats from suspects I've profiled on our show. After that magazine was attacked in Paris, this building doubled its security. Jim always has a gun on him. Pam has had a few stalkers during the course of her career, and"—she lowered her voice—"I heard a rumor, unsubstantiated, that their daughter was kidnapped in Europe the year before I came to ZNC. According to my source, that's why they do *Crime Watch*—so that they don't have to travel as much and can stay here in New York with their children."

"Wouldn't Pam Wiehl's daughter being kidnapped make big news?" Mac said.

"My source says they never reported it and used a mercenary or something like that to get her back," Yvonne said. "I have no idea how true that story is. I do know that she still lives with her parents. In the back of my mind, I sense a big story there."

"If you sense a story," David asked, "why aren't you digging into it?"

"Because the Wiehls could kill my career with one phone call," Yvonne said. "As far as security here, you can only keep your weapon on you if you have a permit and have registered your gun with the building security."

"But security was doubled *after* Audra Walker disappeared," Mac noted.

"It was still heavy back when she went missing," Yvonne said.

"Did the Wiehls have access to the floors that were under renovation?" Mac asked her.

"Yes, but they had no motive to kill Audra," Yvonne said with a laugh. "I interviewed Audra that night, which was an honor because Audra Walker was big in investigative journalism circles. She and the Wiehls seemed very cordial to one another. Why would they kill her?"

Unable to come up with an answer, Mac looked over at Gnarly, who was resting his head on the tabletop. The dog looked imploringly at Mac. Narrowing his eyes, Mac mentally told Gnarly, *Don't tell me you have to go out now.*

Lifting his head, Gnarly uttered a whine.

"What book would Audra have thought you had information about?" David asked Yvonne.

Yvonne shrugged her shoulders while lifting her arms in an exaggerated I-don't-know gesture. "*The Night Jolene Died* was already published. She was on the book tour selling it. I asked her at the end of my interview what she would be working on next. She said she was going back to work on a book about Romeo and Juliet."

"Romeo and Juliet?" Mac asked.

"The Texan version," Yvonne said. "You are aware that Audra was from Texas?"

"I didn't know that," David said.

"Born and raised," Yvonne said. "Apparently, there was a young couple out in the small town where she was raised who were like a modern-day Romeo and Juliet. Their parents hated each other, and they made a suicide pact and killed themselves by driving his car off a cliff into a rocky canyon, like the final scene in *Thelma and Louise*. Only this was on a still, starry night, and they drove off the cliff at a lovers' leap on prom night. The car burst into flames as it sailed over the cliff and lit up the whole sky."

"How tragic," David said.

"Audra was working on the story behind the story," Yvonne said. "She had a real talent for digging far beneath the surface to get to the truth. Her murder is a real loss for our whole field."

"She was a great lady," Mac said. "A great talent."

"Well," Yvonne said. "I'm sure that with you on the case, we'll find out who did this awful thing."

"After I get David back to Deep Creek Lake and get him married," Mac said.

"Why, of course," Yvonne said while leading David back to the door.

"David, wait!" After grabbing a pen from the box on the table, Mac rushed over to him, opened his sports coat, and tucked the pen into his inside breast pocket. After closing up the jacket, Mac patted the pocket containing the pen. "No excuses."

Chapter Five

"I'm surprised," David said while walking with Yvonne to the elevators. "Four years ago, you would have fought tooth and nail for the Audra Walker story."

At the elevators, Yvonne pressed the call button to take them down to the lobby. "My contract is up for renewal, and ZNC is offering me my own show following Ryan Ritter's to keep me from going to another network. Considering how big Ryan's audience is, my show is almost a guaranteed hit if even half of them don't bother switching the channel. But none of that is going to happen if I buck the Wiehls."

"Hey, Harding," a male voice called from up the hall. A man who David recognized as one of Yvonne's cohosts on *Crime Watch* trotted up to them. "Have you heard the news?" Offering his hand to David, he introduced himself as Ian Griffith.

"Of course, it was happening in my office," Yvonne said. "How could I not have heard about it?"

"Not Audra Walker," Ian said. "I'm talking about Ruth Rubenstein. She was murdered last night."

Yvonne's mouth dropped open. "Seriously?"

"Who's Ruth Rubenstein?" David asked.

Ignoring David, Ian replied, "The media is already at the scene, and her husband has announced that he's filing a wrongful death suit against ZNC and you."

David repeated his question to Yvonne. "Who is Ruth Rubenstein, and why would her husband be suing you?"

Ian scoffed at him. "I take it you've been living under a rock."

"Ruth Rubenstein is an Internet troll," Yvonne said.

"Who Yvonne outed on the air Friday night," Ian said. "Since then, the Internet worldwide has gone crazy. Ruth Rubenstein became the most hated woman on the planet." He smirked in Yvonne's direction. "Now she's dead."

Looking at Yvonne in disbelief, David took a step back from her.

"She drove a young woman to suicide," Yvonne said. "Melissa O'Meara. Twenty-five years old. Always dreamed of being an author. Her first book, a romance published by a small press, was scheduled to be released next week. Rubenstein and her troll friends panned it on a huge book readers' site without even reading it. When the author tried to defend herself—"

"That was O'Meara's first mistake," Ian said. "Never feed the troll."

"Rubenstein responded in the most vicious virtual way possible," Yvonne said. "Then all of the rest of the trolls piled on. These creeps were posting one-star reviews and ugly comments about a book they hadn't even read. The book's ratings were at rock bottom before it was even released."

"Mob mentality is just as strong in the virtual world as in real life," David said.

"The book got a ton of negative publicity because of the troll attack, not because of its content at all," Yvonne said. "Melissa ended up taking a bottle of sleeping pills and killing herself. She said in her suicide note that with the death of her dream, she had nothing to live for. It was heartbreaking. None of these people had ever met Melissa. Not one of them had read her book. I was so outraged that I hunted down the troll who started and led the attack on Melissa and outed her on the air."

"Real name and picture," Ian said. "The Internet did the rest. Folks on Twitter published her home address, and within an hour Rubenstein was getting death threats." He shook his head at David. "I can't believe you didn't know anything about this."

"I've been busy in the real world," David said.

"Well now Rubenstein is dead—murdered—and her husband's planning to sue for ten million dollars." A cocky grin came to Ian's lips. "I wonder if the other networks will still be courting you for your own show if you end up costing ZNC millions of dollars."

"You know what they say, Ian," Yvonne said. "There's no such thing as bad publicity."

"Publicity is one thing," Ian replied. "Money is another. Look at Jenny Jones. Her pursuit of ratings got one of her guests murdered. Where is she now?"

"Ruth Rubenstein was a bitter old hag collecting disability who did nothing but sit around in her bathrobe and use the Internet to prey on innocent people pursuing their dreams," Yvonne said. "What grounds does her husband have to sue us?"

"Because you set his wife up to be murdered by a fellow sicko with a warped sense of revenge," David said.

"If I were you, I'd call legal ASAP." Ian smoothed his hair with both of his hands. "In the meantime, I'm going to lunch at Finnegan's. One of my spies told me that Charles Weller is having lunch there with some of his vice presidents, and I hear their network may be looking for another journalist to head up their new show … one who's not so passionate about getting ratings that they get people killed." He hurried on his way.

"You actually *like* working with these people?" David asked while the elevator doors opened.

"Forget about them."

"Yvonne!"

Before they could step onto the elevator, a middle-aged man whose distinguished appearance was made even more sophisticated by his expensive tailored suit trotted down the hall toward them. Holding the elevator doors, David noticed a young man following a few steps behind him.

"I thought that was you," the older gentleman said with a broad smile. Clasping both of Yvonne's hands in his, he greeted her with a kiss on the cheek. "How are you? I heard a dead body was found in your office. Are you okay?"

"I'm fine, Preston," she replied. "Thank you for asking." She introduced David to Preston Blakeley, the CEO of ZNC, whose office suite was on the fortieth floor of the building. Wrapping an arm around David's waist, she ushered him forward. "This is my very good friend from back home, David O'Callaghan."

Sensing that this would take a while, David allowed the elevator to continue on its way.

Preston paused to look David up and down before offering his hand to him to shake. "Pam Wiehl told me that it was Mac Faraday, Robin Spencer's son, and a friend of his who found the dead body in Yvonne's wall. I assume that's you."

"We grew up together in Spencer," she said.

"Ah," Preston chuckled. "High school sweethearts."

It was Yvonne's turn to grin. "Something like that." Her giggle took on a naughty tone that made David's cheeks warm.

"Well, Yvonne," Preston said. "I can see that you and your friend were on your way out—"

"I do have a flight to catch," David said, lying to hurry the executive along.

"If you need another place to work while the police do their thing in your office, Yvonne, please let me know," Preston insisted. "We'll make room for you on the fortieth floor." He turned to his assistant. "We have a vacant office upstairs, don't we, Howard?"

"Certainly, sir," Howard replied.

Preston shot Yvonne a wide, white smile. "We can't deny ZNC's darling of crime a place to work, can we?"

"No, we can't."

With a chortle, Preston said, "I was just talking to Jim about the Audra Walker story. We got Hopkins to agree to an exclusive interview tonight with Pam. She's taking the lead on this story." With a cock of his head, he studied her. "Are you okay with that?"

"Sure, I'm fine," Yvonne said. "I have my own breaking stories to keep up on."

"I was just wondering, since you've been investigating Walker's disappearance."

"No," Yvonne said with a shake of her head. "That was always Pam's story." As if to reassure him, she flashed him a broad grin. "Of course, as has always been the case, if a big lead happens to land in my lap, you know me … "

It took a full moment for a slow grin to cross Preston's face before he replied, "Yes, I do know you, Yvonne. No one has ever forgotten about your scoop on the Hilton case—the one you got after Jim told you to back off."

She giggled. "A good news journalist doesn't stop following the evidence just because it leads her in an unpleasant direction."

"Even if that direction leads her into a major shareholder's backyard?"

"If I hadn't broken the story, one of our competitors would have."

"Not necessarily," Preston muttered.

David watched Yvonne and the CEO lock gazes until Preston allowed a smile to force its way across his face. "Howard will set up office space for you on the fortieth floor, Yvonne. It will be ready by the time you return from lunch."

After shaking his hand, Yvonne allowed him to once again kiss her cheek before she and David continued to wait for the elevator.

"Quite a friendly CEO," David noted.

"Preston does have a weakness for the fairer sex," Yvonne admitted. "But he's also a perfect gentleman. He's got a ton of influence in the biz."

"I can see that he's quite fond of you, even if you do disobey orders by breaking unpopular stories."

"Hey, like I told him, I don't make the news—I only report it," she said. "It wasn't my idea to kill the shareholder's wife's lover and cut him up into little pieces. How was I supposed to go on the air and totally ignore the story while all the other networks he wasn't on the board of covered it?" With a smug grin, she added, "Blakeley and Jim can't complain. Our ratings soared when I broke that story. I'm bringing in a lot of advertising revenue and big numbers in viewers and e-mails. Now if any of that stops, Jim will put me on a short leash, and Blakeley won't remember my name."

"Will he remember your name if you end up costing the network millions of dollars due to a huge lawsuit for getting a troll killed?" David asked while watching the numbers above the doors indicate that the elevator was on its way back to their floor.

The elevator chimed to announce its arrival. Once inside the car, Yvonne wasted no time in revealing her intentions for their lunch date. She threw her arms around him, and she and David fell against the back wall of the elevator, where she pressed her body against his. Locking her mouth over his, she pressed her tongue into his mouth while groping for his belt.

Turning his head to break the lip-lock, David gasped for breath and fought her hands. "Stop it."

"I thought you loved it when I take charge." She turned his head to search for his lips.

The elevator stopped and chimed.

Instantly, Yvonne whirled around and took a step back to stand next to David.

The doors opened.

Seeing Yvonne and David on board, Lieutenant Wayne Hopkins and Pam Wiehl paused before stepping on. The detective pressed the button for the ground floor, even though it had already been pressed.

"I see your friend has made himself right at home, Yvonne," Pam said.

David fought the flush he felt rising in his cheeks. Hoping Yvonne had not left lipstick on his face, he wiped his mouth.

Before the doors could shut, a hand abruptly reached out to block them. When the door reopened, Ali Hudson grinned. "Just in the nick o' time." Stepping onboard, she greeted each of them with a nod. When her eyes met David's, their gaze locked for a moment longer than necessary until Yvonne's voice broke their electricity.

"I see you're feeling better, Ali," Yvonne said.

"Much better, ma'am," she replied from over her shoulder toward where David and Yvonne were standing behind her. "Sorry for gettin' all choked up a bit ago. Just needed some time to pull myself together. Now I'm fine as frog fur again."

"Frogs don't have fur," David whispered to Yvonne. "Do they?"

Turning back to face the front of the elevator, Ali noticed the detective. "That's a mighty purdy tie you're wearin' there, sir. Makes you look as cute as a possum."

Unsure of whether the attractive research assistant had paid him a compliment, Wayne Hopkins patted the tie.

Equally unsure of what she'd meant, David silently asked himself if possums were considered cute. Repeating Ali's statement in his head and taking note of her low, sensual voice heavily laced with a Southern dialect, he concluded that he'd enjoy anything she told him—even if he didn't understand half of what she said.

After hesitating, Lieutenant Hopkins thanked her. "Got it at Macy's," he said while stroking the tie as though it were a prized possession. "Cost four hundred dollars."

David's ears perked up. *Four hundred dollars for a tie? Most expensive tie I ever bought was forty bucks.*

"It brings out the green in your eyes," Ali said.

Watching her, David felt the corners of his lips curl. He sensed what was coming next.

"Did y'all find an apparent cause of death for the victim?"

Between her thick Southern accent and the speed in which Ali spoke, David had to repeat what she had said over and over again in his mind in order to decipher her question to the detective.

"Two bullet wounds to the back of the head," Hopkins said. "One to the back. Looks like it could be a forty-five caliber."

"Did y'all find the slugs with the body?" she asked.

"I'm taking the lead on this story, Ali," Pam announced. "So you have no need to research this case."

"Sorry, ma'am. You can't blame a girl for being curious," Ali said. "After all, she was found only a few feet from my desk."

"If you want to know what's going on with the case, you can watch my interview with Lieutenant Hopkins on *Crime Watch* tonight," Pam said.

"Are y'all invitin' Sergeant Roberts to be interviewed too?" Ali asked.

"Sergeant Roberts?" Lieutenant Hopkins asked.

"He was the lead investigator in Audra Walker's disappearance, sir," Ali said. "I'd expect 'im to be contacted about her body being found. Y'all call 'im yet?" She turned to Pam. "You gonna interview 'im too, ma'am?"

Much to David's disappointment, the elevator doors opened. He found Ali Hudson's spunky pursuit of the case intriguing.

"We don't even know if the body is Audra Walker's," Lieutenant Hopkins said while following Pam Wiehl off the elevator.

Refusing to give up, Ali Hudson pursued them across the lobby toward the street. "The news is already reportin' the discovery of a body. They're figurin' it's Audra Walker. Have y'all contacted her family yet?"

"We will when we get a positive ID," Lieutenant Hopkins said as he buttoned up his coat.

"Yvonne Harding!" came a voice from the street in front of the News Corp Building.

Before Yvonne could react, an older man dressed in a worn coat and shabby clothes hurried toward them. A pack of news camera operators and journalists followed to surround him and Yvonne Harding.

"You killed my wife," the man announced into the microphones thrust in front of him.

Having never been the target of the news journalists before, Yvonne stared into the cameras like a deer caught in headlights in the middle of the night. Immediately, David reached out, grabbed her by the arm, and stepped in between her and the mob.

"Ruth Rubenstein!" the man announced her name. "You have no idea who she was, do you? You never even met her. Talked to her. Tried to understand what type of lovely person she was."

Yvonne found her voice. "She ripped away a young woman's dream! A young woman who put everything she had—her heart and soul—into pursing her dream. And then, just when she was on the brink of making it a reality, your wife attacked her in a very public manner, ripping at her in the most vulgar and public way until she killed herself."

"Ruth was a person, too!" the man said. "Yes, she might have been cruel, but did you even try to understand why she was the way she was?"

"Oh, you mean she was a victim?" Yvonne laughed.

"Is that to say that you don't feel responsible for Ruth Rubenstein's murder?" one of the journalists asked.

"I am not responsible for the actions anyone took against Ruth Rubenstein for her own behavior," Yvonne said over the voice of Ali Hudson, who was trying to shush her while David attempted to block the cameras' view of the news journalist.

"Someone murdered my sweet wife—"

"Sweet?" Yvonne laughed.

"Because you told the world who she was and blamed her for Melissa O'Meara's suicide." Turning his beard-covered face to the camera, he pointed at the famed journalist. "Well, Yvonne Harding, it is your fault that someone took my wife from me, and for that, you're going to pay. I'll see to that!"

Grabbing Yvonne by the arm, David dragged her through the mob and down the street, leaving Ali Hudson, the distraught husband, and a horde of news journalists behind.

Chapter Six

"I've had finer moments—much finer." Cringing, Mac squeezed the plastic baggie filled with Gnarly's still-warm poop, searching for the wedding bands. Even with his hands encased in evidence gloves and the barrier of the plastic bag, he was disgusted. "Picking through garbage for evidence back when I was a newbie in homicide was better than this."

With a curious expression on his face, Gnarly cocked his head at him.

Finding nothing, Mac tossed the bag into the trash bin. He then slipped off the evidence gloves and threw them in as well before washing his hands with a sterilizing disinfectant he carried in his pocket. Grateful that there was no one in the alley to see him searching through the canine's discharge, Mac picked up the dog leash and led Gnarly back out to the street.

Rounding the corner of the News Corp Building, he bumped into Ali Hudson, who was rushing down the front steps. After apologizing, Mac asked her, "Are you okay?"

"No matter, sir," she replied. "My fault. I saw that police lieutenant leavin' and wanted to talk to him, so I went runnin' out like the dogs were chasin' me." She knelt next to Gnarly to stroke him on the top of his head. "I was in such a dag-nab hurry that I forgot my bag and my money for lunch." She showed Mac the oversized bag she'd hung from her shoulder and tucked under her arm.

"Did Hopkins give you any information about Audra Walker's murder?" Mac asked.

After tossing her head to brush away the long, dark tendrils that had fallen into her face, she looked up at him from where she was kneeling next to Gnarly. She held up a slender hand to shield her eyes from the sun. "She was shot twice in the back of the head and once in the back."

"How ironic that you were investigating Audra Walker's disappearance, and there she was, only a few feet from you."

"How—"

"I heard you on the phone setting up a meeting with Sergeant Roberts—the lead investigator in the Audra Walker case. Remember? I was waiting with David to see Yvonne, and Pam Wiehl came in. She seemed to think Audra Walker's disappearance was voluntary."

"Of course," she said. "I should've expected y'all to remember that. You've got plenty of notches in your gun when it comes to solvin' murders."

"Audra Walker said the exact same thing to me when we first met."

Ali swallowed before saying, "I saw your brother leavin' with Yvonne. Why didn't you go with 'em?"

"They're—" Stopping, Mac chuckled. "How did you know?"

"Y'all have the same eyes and jawline," she replied. "Different last names. So my guess is you're *half* brothers."

"Same father, different mothers."

"But you're *friends*. That's the important thing." Hesitantly, she asked, "Is he …"

"Getting married this weekend."

"Figures." She shrugged her shoulders. "I'm probably not his type anyway."

"Why do you say that?" Mac asked.

"He seems pretty tight with Yvonne," she said. "Granted, she doesn't know a bit from a butt—"

"Excuse me?"

"A bit," she said. "As in a bit on a bridle ... for horses? I figure you know what a butt is. She's completely citified."

"Gotha."

"But I'll give her this—she's so good-lookin' that she'd make a man plow through a stump." She frowned. "I'm just not in the same league as her."

"Just because you're not in the same league doesn't mean you're not in the game," Mac said.

"Your brother's getting married," she said. "That means the game's over."

Not knowing what else to say, Mac asked, "What progress did you make in your investigation into Audra Walker's disappearance-turned-murder?"

"Why do y'all care 'bout our investigation?"

"Audra Walker was my friend," Mac said. "That's my interest. What's yours?"

"It's my job," she explained. "Yvonne told me to research the case. I'm her assistant—"

"Yvonne couldn't care less about the Walker case," Mac said. "After Audra's body was found and Pam Wiehl called dibs on the case, Yvonne went to lunch. So"—he moved in closer to her—"I think your interest in Audra Walker is personal."

"Okay, I'll fess up," she said with a shrug of her shoulders "Yvonne is interested in the case, but she cares more 'bout bein' a celebrity journalist, with the emphasis on 'celebrity.' That's why she hired me to be her research assistant." She glanced around to ensure no one was in hearing distance. "I investigate the cases and write up the copy, and she gets in front of the camera to report the case while lookin' pretty."

"But you're the one with the fire in your belly to find Audra Walker's killer," Mac said. "Not Yvonne."

"I'm an investigative journalist," Ali said.

"So is Yvonne."

With a chuckle, she replied, "Used to be … till she made *People's* list of the hundred-most-beautiful people in the world."

"Funny how that happens," Mac noted.

"Sad, really." She had her arm wrapped around Gnarly, and she was lovingly scratching him on his chest. With a dewy expression in his eyes, the dog tilted his head back and pressed it against her cheek. She seemed to have hypnotized him.

"Gnarly likes you," Mac noted.

"I like Gnarly." She hugged the dog while he kissed her on the cheek. "I really miss my dog, Storm. She's stayin' with my brother. He calls her 'Princess Storm' because she's so spoiled."

"What kind of dog is she?"

"Belgian shepherd," she replied. "She's 'bout as big as Gnarly and has tall ears like him. I guess that's why he's makin' me miss 'er."

"I imagine a big dog like that would be kind of hard to keep in a Manhattan apartment," Mac said.

"Which is why she's back in Texas," she explained. "But one day, I'll go back and …" Her voice trailed off.

"I thought every investigative journalist strove to live in New York or LA," Mac said.

"That's if you wanna be a star," Ali said. "There's a difference. There are those in the business who wanna chase the story. They go where the story takes them. Yvonne Harding used to be that way. But somewhere along the line, the thirst for justice fell to the wayside ... which opened the door for her ambitious research assistant to make a name for herself by chasin' down the killers of a legendary investigative journalist."

Mac was having a hard time buying Ali's claim that pure ambition was driving her pursuit of the Audra Walker case. "Have you had lunch yet?"

"I'm so hungry I could eat the sign off a hamburger stand."

With a laugh, Mac said, "I take it that means you want lunch. Where's a good place that will allow dogs?"

"The park." As if to enter his plea to join them, Gnarly turned his head to plant a kiss in her ear, which prompted her to giggle. "I guess we have a date."

With Gnarly between the two of them, Ali and Mac strolled down the sidewalk in the direction of a small park that included a playground and a diner truck.

"What've you uncovered so far?" Mac repeated his question.

"Audra Walker did three interviews in the News Corp building on the day she disappeared," Ali said. "Her second interview ended up bein' with a journalist who was close friends with Senator Brennan and his family. He accused her of everythin' from character assassination to bein' a domestic terrorist."

"Slight exaggeration, but I get your point."

"Patrick Brennan, the heir to the Brennan dynasty, does have an alibi for her disappearance," Ali said. "But I don't put much stock in that. He's so crooked he has to unscrew his britches at night."

The visual she had created brought a smile to Mac's face. "Brennan would have hired someone to do it."

"Just like his pa did to get rid of Jolene Fitzgerald," Ali said.

"However," Mac said, "considering all the attention Audra and the book got after her disappearance, I don't see what he would've gained from it."

"Maybe he's not as bright as his father," Ali said. "Anyways, Audra's interview with Yvonne Harding was the last one that day."

"Being a journalist, she had to have had friends and acquaintances in New York," Mac said. "Have you interviewed any who talked to her during her trip?"

"Sure 'nuff," Ali said. "They say all basically the same thing. She was fat and sassy."

"Audra Walker wasn't fat ..."

"No, she wasn't by any means." Ali sighed. "It's a sayin'. You folks who are raised on concrete—by all accounts, Audra Walker was happy."

"Gotcha," Mac said. "But her husband had recently died."

"Bull!" Pausing, Ali shook her head at him. "Of course, she felt lower than a gopher hole 'bout that. She loved her husband and missed him a ton, but folks keep forgettin' that Audra Walker was an independent woman. He'd been dead two months, and she was gettin' on with her life."

Struck by her passion, Mac asked, "Did you ever meet Audra Walker?"

Seeming to consider the reason behind his question, she gazed at him. After a long pause, she said, "Not personally. I saw her speak where I went to school. She inspired me." Hurrying toward a street vendor, she asked, "Do you like hot dogs?"

After they had purchased their lunches, which included a plain hot dog on a bun for Gnarly, they sat on a bench. While Mac settled for simple mustard and catsup on his, Ali's hot dog was slathered in extra chili, cheese, and onions. She ordered an energy drink with which to wash it down.

"What do you know about the Texan Romeo and Juliet?" Mac asked.

"Do y'all mean the book that Audra Walker was a-fixin' to work on next?" Ali asked. "I saw in that last interview that she told Yvonne that that was her next project. She'd been workin' on it for years but wasn't makin' a lot of progress."

Noticing that Mac had stopped eating to watch her, she said, "That's what Walker's assistant told me."

"What's the story behind the Texan Romeo and Juliet?"

Seeing that Gnarly had finished his hot dog, she picked up his wrapper, got up, and went to throw it away. The chilly autumn wind had blown locks of her long, dark hair loose from the updo, and they fell down past her shoulders.

After sitting down on the bench to continue her lunch, she said, "It 'appened a long time ago in a small desert town. There was this couple—a boy and a girl. They were high school sweethearts."

"But their parents hated each other," Mac said.

"That's why they were Romeo and Juliet," Ali said with a smile. "From what I heard, they actually played Romeo and Juliet in the high school play. Romeo was from a middle-class family. His pap had died in a farmin' accident while workin' on a ranch that was owned by Juliet's father, who was a brutal man by all accounts. Romeo's mom sued Juliet's pappy for wrongful death, but she lost the suit."

"Which explains why the two families hated each other," Mac said.

"Juliet's pappy ordered her to stop seein' Romeo, and when she refused, he decided to send Juliet away to college. They were gonna be separated."

"So they killed themselves?" Mac asked.

"The night of the senior prom. They drove off a cliff together." Ali held up her hand in a signal to halt. "But that's not where the story ends."

Seeing that she had his attention, she stopped to crumble up her used paper plate and throw it away before reaching up to remove her hair clip and running her fingers through her thick, dark mane. Her expression was a mixture of playful and curious.

For the second time that day, something about her struck Mac as familiar. "There's more?" he finally asked.

She nodded her head. "The day of their funerals, Juliet's brother went home after the memorial service, before goin' to the grave site. I don't remember why. He walked in on a burglary and was murdered—along with his girlfriend, who happened to be with him."

"That's a real tragedy."

Ali said, "Juliet's pap lost both his son and his daughter, his only children, in one week. He died of a coronary fewer than six months later."

"Did they ever find the burglar?" Mac asked.

"Yes, sir," Ali said. "A ranch hand who had a criminal record. They found the tire iron—the one he'd used to bludgeon the son and his girlfriend with—behind the seat of his truck."

Perplexed, Mac stared ahead while Ali continued to stroke Gnarly, who was sitting between her legs with his head resting on her thigh.

"What are you thinkin' so hard 'bout?" she asked.

"I don't understand the story," Mac said. "Why would Audra Walker be interested in that case? I knew her well enough to know which cases interested her and which cases didn't. She loved a good mystery. She loved to dig deep beneath the lies on the surface and would continue digging until she grabbed the truth by the roots and brought it up to the surface for the world to see. There's no mystery to Romeo and

Juliet. A boy and a girl fall in love. Their families are at war. They make a suicide pact and kill themselves, and then, to add to the tragedy, the girl's brother is killed when he walks in on a burglar who seizes the opportunity to rob the father's house during the funeral. Murder weapon is found in the bad guy's possession, and he goes to jail. Case closed."

"That's why I don't think it had anythin' to do with Audra Walker's murder," Ali said.

"Unless it's not the whole story, and Audra knew it." Mac tossed his wrapper into the trash can located on the other side of the path. "*That*, I can see Audra Walker digging into."

David had expected Yvonne to take him to a Manhattan restaurant for their lunch. When she led him by the hand into the lobby of a luxurious apartment house complete with a doorman, he thought that there was possibly a restaurant on the top floor.

Once they were in the elevator, Yvonne explained that the building had once been a department store, and it had been converted into elegant, spacious apartments. Hers was on the tenth floor.

David felt his stomach tie into a knot. Lunch together in her apartment—alone. "Yvonne, I really need for you to sign these papers."

The elevator doors opened. With a wicked grin, she took him by the hand and led him to the corner apartment at the end of the hallway. "Wait until you see this." Using a keycard and a number combination on the security lock, she opened the door and pulled him inside.

Suspecting what she had in mind, David almost pulled her back out into the hallway.

"There's nothing to be afraid of," she said with a giggle.

Keeping his hand on the doorframe and refusing to cross the threshold, David said, "I think there's a lot to be afraid of."

"Do you not trust yourself with me, David?" Yvonne shook her head. "If not, then you should think twice about marrying Chelsea." With a toss of her head, she tugged on his hand.

Taking one step at a time, David eased across the threshold into the spacious great room. Floor-to-ceiling, wall-to-wall windows looked out across the metropolitan outside. The room was furnished with modern urban textures and abstract art pieces. The furnishings were stark steel and leather pieces.

A platter of oysters, crackers, cheese, and appetizers filled the dining room table, along with a couple of bottles of chilled champagne on ice.

Yvonne closed the door behind him and locked the dead bolt. "Hungry?"

"Not really," David said.

"Neither am I." Throwing her arms around him, Yvonne pushed David up against the wall and smashed her mouth over his.

Fighting to keep her from tearing at his clothes, David peeled her hands away. Desperate to escape, he pushed her back by placing both of his hands on her shoulders. "Stop it, Yvonne!"

Stunned by the outburst, she fell back.

Wiping her taste from his lips, David pushed up off the wall and went into the living area. "I told you. I'm marrying Chelsea on Saturday. I fought to make it up to her when I messed up, and I'm very, very lucky that she gave me another chance and agreed to marry me." Yanking the divorce papers out of his pocket, he tossed them down onto the coffee table. "I want you to sign these papers." He held out the pen to her. "Sign them now, and I'll be leaving."

Yvonne's eyes narrowed. "You told me you loved me."

"I did," David said. "I do. But I want to marry Chelsea."

A slow grin came to Yvonne's lips. "But you can't marry her until I sign those papers." She took a step toward him.

As she closed the space between them, David backed up. "Don't mess with me, Yvonne."

"I'm your *wife,* David," she said while moving in closer. "You wanted me. You loved me. You married me. We were good together."

"That's all ended." David held out his hand. She stepped into it. "Things are different now. We're not the same people we were when we went through that drive-through."

Yvonne took his hand. Slowly, she wrapped her lips around his index finger. Looking at him seductively through her eyelashes, she slowly licked his fingers, one by one.

David sucked in a deep breath.

Wrapping her arm around his neck, she moved in to kiss him on the lips and then thrust her tongue into his mouth. Locking her gaze on his eyes, she offered him a sensuous grin. "Why don't we go into the bedroom and talk about this?"

Stripping off her clothes along the way, Yvonne sauntered across the great room to the hallway leading back to the bedroom. By the time she disappeared down the hallway, all she had on were her black lace bra and her panties.

As soon as she was out of sight, David snatched up the divorce papers and pen and left.

Chapter Seven

The afternoon sun streamed in through the hotel room window, bathing Mac's face in sunlight. As much as he enjoyed the warmth of the light beam, his interest was on something else. He had a certain canine under surveillance.

Archie had a wine and cheese basket delivered to their room, along with a mushy love note for Mac. Immediately, he called Archie to thank her and to get an update on the wedding preparations in Deep Creek Lake.

"Not great," Archie said.

"What do you mean, not great?" Mac asked. "Not great as in, the caterer doesn't have enough shrimp for the cocktails? Or not great as in, the bride is still mad at the groom?"

"I don't think she's as mad as she is having second thoughts," she replied. "I don't know. She won't talk to me."

"Is she keeping her wedding appointments?" Mac asked.

"Yes, and I consider that to be a good sign," Archie said. "We went to the bridal shop for the last fitting for her gown, but ..." She uttered a deep sigh. "Oh, Mac, she was so quiet, and she does not look like a happy bride at all."

Their thoughts filling with fears for their best friends' happiness, Mac and Archie sat in silence.

After disconnecting the call, Mac returned to the sitting room to find that one of the packages of cheese was missing. He had only one suspect.

So Mac stretched out on the sofa and closed his eyes. With a fake snore, he managed to convince Gnarly that he was asleep. It was all he could do to not laugh while, through the slits of his eyes, he watched the German shepherd belly across the sitting room. Occasionally, Gnarly would stop to look over his shoulder, back in Mac's direction. When he finally reached the table, he climbed up into a chair and poked at the selection of cheeses and meat packages with his long snout before deciding on a tube of summer sausage.

Gnarly was about to jump down to the floor with the sausage in his jaws when Mac sprang up. "Drop it!" With a yelp, Gnarly staggered in midjump. The chair overturned, and the German shepherd collapsed to the floor. The sausage went flying.

Mac doubled over laughing. "That'll teach you!" His ears back flat on his head, Gnarly scurried over to Mac, who took him into a hug. "You are one sneaky rascal." Picking up the sausage from the floor, he proceeded to open it up to give Gnarly a piece.

Hearing the door unlock, Mac checked the time on the clock to see that it was not yet one o'clock. *Too early to be David.* When David stepped through the door, Mac could see by the expression on his face that something was wrong.

"You're back early," Mac said. "You two must not have had much to catch up on."

David tossed the divorce papers onto the table. Mac picked them up and saw that the signature line was still blank.

"She won't sign them," David said. "She took me to her apartment and tried to seduce me."

"Did you—"

"No," David said forcibly. "What do you think I am? I said I wanted to marry Chelsea, and I meant it. Why won't anyone believe me?"

"I'm sorry." Mac sighed. "You deserve more credit than that. Are you saying Yvonne refused to sign these unless you slept with her?"

"Pretty much," David said.

"Which puts you between a rock and a hard place," Mac said. "If you sleep with her, Chelsea will call off the wedding."

"I don't want to sleep with Yvonne," David said. "She's not the same woman I married without knowing it."

"They never are," Mac muttered. "But if Yvonne doesn't sign these papers, you can't marry Chelsea, because you'll be committing bigamy."

"Exactly," David said.

"She has you by the short hairs, and she knows it," Mac said.

David leaned over with both hands on the table. "Can Willingham force her in some way—"

"I doubt it. You can't force someone to sign anything."

"Then what am I going to do? Until she signs these papers, Chelsea and I can't get married."

Tapping the folded-up divorce papers in his palm, Mac said, "Let me think about this." Deep in thought, he strolled over to the windows that provided a view of the city. The conversations and scenes of the day replayed in his mind. In particular, he thought of one he'd had with Ali Hudson.

"She cares more about bein' a celebrity journalist, with the emphasis on 'celebrity.' That's why she hired me to be her research assistant."

A slow grin worked its way to Mac's lips while a collage of thoughts came together and formed a plan for action. He didn't notice that David had crossed the suite and was standing next to him until he said, "What are you thinking?"

A wicked grin crossed Mac's face. "She wants to play hardball … We can play hardball."

It has to be here someplace. He said he'd let me look at it.

Donning a pair of latex gloves to avoid leaving any evidence for the police, Ali scoured the titles of every book on the bookcase. She found nothing in the spare room that he used for an office.

She had to hurry. She was already on borrowed time. Eventually, someone would call or stop by the old man's apartment and find him dead from a single gunshot wound to the head.

As part of her duties as Yvonne Harding's research assistant, Ali Hudson was expected to be on the set for the recording of *Crime Watch*.

The problem was that Sergeant Caleb Roberts moved their meeting up to six o'clock—the same time that *Crime Watch* recorded their hour-long broadcast that was aired at eight o'clock. Ali had managed to beg out of the recording session by claiming she had chipped a tooth during lunch and had to make an emergency run to her dentist to get it fixed.

Luckily, Yvonne was in such a foul mood—and distracted—when she returned from lunch that she didn't seem to care enough to ask any questions, even when Ali sat down across from her to go over the details of Ruth Rubenstein's murder for her segment on the show.

"How was lunch with the beefcake?" Ali asked when Yvonne stormed off the elevator after lunch.

The glare in Yvonne's eyes was enough to answer her question. *He must have broken the news to her about his upcoming nuptials.*

"Have you researched the details of Rubenstein's murder?" Yvonne asked her.

Ali rose up from where she was leaning against the wall in the hallway outside their office, which was roped off as a crime scene. "Charmed the details outta couple of uniforms." She held out her tablet so Yvonne could see that she'd been working. "Blakeley's assistant said they have an office for you upstairs. Wanna meet up there?"

Without answering, Yvonne spun on her heels and led the way to the elevators.

"You're gonna be walkin' a fine line tonight," Ali warned after they took their seats at the table in the temporary office the CEO had arranged for Yvonne on the fortieth floor. "Even though Ruth Rubenstein could've made a hornet look cuddly and pretty much drove a young woman to offin' herself, she was murdered and—*allegedly*—her husband loved her." Ali waited for her to pick up on what she had said and respond. It took a full moment.

"Allegedly?"

"Carl Rubenstein has a mistress who he's been shackin' up with," Ali said. "Her name is Polly Langley. She's the office manager at the warehouse where Carl works as a foreman. Everyone knows that they've been pussyfootin' 'round for well over a year. He wanted a divorce, but Ruth refused to give him one."

Yvonne shot a fiery glare in Ali's direction.

Unnerved by her reaction, Ali stuttered momentarily before getting back on track. "Although Carl has been playin' house with Polly, he was still supportin' Ruth. All she had comin' in was her disability check. He made the lion's share of their income. If he'd divorced her, with New York bein' a community-property state, he would've had to pay her alimony—practically half of what he makes—and they would have had to split everythin' down the middle. Now that she's dead—"

"So he had motive." Yvonne smiled for the first time since returning from lunch.

"But he's got an airtight alibi," Ali said. "Polly is his alibi for the night of the murder. She says Carl was at her place, on the other side of Brooklyn, while Ruth was bein' strangled with a computer cord in front of her desktop."

"The mistress is lying," Yvonne said.

"They were having supper with two other couples." Ali held up her hand, spreading out all of her fingers. "He's got five witnesses who swear they were all on the other side of Brooklyn watchin' the ball game all evening."

"If he was cheating on Ruth, and she was bleeding him dry, why is he jumping all over me?" Yvonne wanted to know.

Ali laughed. "Cause somehow they killed her. Think 'bout it. You outin' Ruth as an Internet troll was the best thing that could've happened for Carl. The social media crucified her. His shrew of a wife is dead and he can blame you and the network for it. You gave him a license to slap you and the network with a wrongful death suit. The network ain't gonna want the bad publicity that'll come with a trial. They'll settle outta court for a million or two dollars, and Carl Rubenstein'll be ridin' a gravy train with biscuit wheels."

"Sometimes I have no idea what you're saying," Yvonne responded. "But I think you're telling me that I did Carl Rubenstein a favor by outing his wife."

"You might as well have handed him the winnin' lottery ticket signed, sealed, and delivered."

"But he's got a solid alibi," Yvonne said. "So it had to be some anonymous, deranged vigilante. Even if the police find him or her, Carl Rubenstein's lawsuit will stick. The vigilante would have never found Ruth and killed her for driving O'Meara to suicide if I hadn't outed her."

"Carl and his mistress did it," Ali said with certainty. "Maybe they hired someone to do it. I find it very convenient that they were eatin' supper with not one but two other couples and watchin' baseball at the exact same time that Ruth was bein' strangled." In response to Yvonne's worried expression, she smiled. "Don't worry, sugar. I'll figure it out. I always do."

Gathering up her news copy to go over, Yvonne hurried off to makeup without another question. As soon as she was gone, Ali put on her black trench coat and hat and rushed across town to meet with the retired detective who, two years before, had been in charge of the investigation into Audra Walker's disappearance.

Unfortunately, dead men don't talk.

Ali's only hope to uncover the details of Audra Walker's disappearance was to find the notebook in which he had kept his notes of the case—the one the detective had promised to let her examine.

Aware that time was ticking away, Ali gave up. Given Yvonne's foul mood, she would be furious if Ali wasn't back at the studio before they finished filming. With one last glance around the apartment, she made her way to the front door, pausing to gaze with sympathy at the old man sitting in his easy chair, his head a bloody mess.

"I'm gonna find who did this," she whispered to him. "I promise."

Silently letting herself out through the front door, she paused to turn the knob and lock the door behind her in order to leave the place the way she'd found it. For a police detective, it wasn't much of a lock. Sergeant Robert's killer had been unable to lock the dead bolt from the outside. It had taken her fewer than thirty seconds to pick the regular lock.

Turning around, she came face to face with an elderly woman moving toward her. Her arms were filled with grocery bags. Their eyes met, and Ali smiled and greeted her in Italian with a heavy foreign accent. "Buona sera." *Better to acknowledge her in a friendly manner than to hide my face and run. Less suspicious. When the police ask if she saw anyone suspicious, she'll dismiss me as not suspicious and remember me as a foreigner.*

"Hello," the elderly lady replied politely while quickly turning away to unlock her apartment door. As soon as the door was open, she hurried inside, as Ali knew she would.

The heavy foreign accent had made the neighbor, who didn't want to get trapped in an awkward conversation with someone who didn't know English, run away as quickly as possible.

Out on the street, Ali stopped at the nearest pay phone and, using her knuckle, dialed the emergency operator.

"Nine-one-one," the operator said. "What is your emergency?"

"Me gustaría informarles de un asesinato," Ali said, indicating she'd like to report a murder.

"Do you speak English?" the operator replied.

"No, no hablan inglés," Ali lied with desperation in her tone.

Chapter Eight

"What type of male homicide detective wears mascara?" Mac muttered to David as they waited in the back of the control booth while Lieutenant Wayne Hopkins prepared to be interviewed on camera by the headline host of *Crime Watch*. The police lieutenant had changed into a blue suit and had taken off his glasses. Mac noticed that he'd applied mascara to his eyelashes to make his eyes less beady.

"Is it me, or has Archie rubbed off on you?" David asked Mac with a sly grin.

"Rubbed off on me in a good way or bad?" Mac asked.

David reached over to scratch Gnarly, who was sitting between Mac's knees, behind his ears. "You're suspicious of anyone who doesn't like Gnarly."

"I'm suspicious of police officers who are camera hounds," Mac said. "And I'll admit it. Gnarly has proven to be a good judge of character. It's been proven that most of the time, if he doesn't like someone, there's an excellent reason for it."

"You'll get no argument from me," David said.

Crime Watch was recorded in one of ZNC's multiple studios on the thirty-sixth floor of the News Corp Building. The directors and producers oversaw the production in the sound-proof control room that looked out onto the set. On that set, journalists interviewed their guests or reported from a huge news desk equipped with computers and monitors built onto the desktop where viewers would not see them.

Once one was outside the control booth and facing the set, he or she would see that on the right side of it was the sound stage, which contained recording and computer equipment, chairs, desks, lights, and anything else that might have been needed on camera. The outer corners and far walls were dimly lit in stark contrast to the brightly lit stage and set. Shelving units, unused equipment, and a snack table filled with day-old pastries and stale sandwiches were stationed at the far wall.

The makeup department was located on the other side of the control room. On-air personalities and their guests could watch ZNC's newscasts streamed live on monitors and could communicate with the directors and producers via intercoms while preparing to go on camera.

In the control room, Jim Wiehl was speaking in low tones with ZNC's CEO and preparing for his wife's interview with the detective. Even before David had clued him in, Mac had sensed that the distinguished executive was someone of importance. As soon as Preston Blakeley entered and demanded Jim's attention, an air of apprehension dropped in the room.

"Most likely, he came down from the fortieth floor to watch Yvonne Harding's segment about the Internet troll's murder," Ryan Ritter said as he walked behind Mac and David.

The celebrated news journalist offered Mac his hand to shake. "I heard you were in the building today when Audra Walker's body was discovered." Spotting Gnarly, he asked, "Is this the cadaver-sniffing dog?"

"I don't know about cadaver sniffing," Mac said. "More like he simply finds things." Noticing that Ryan Ritter was also wearing mascara, he shuddered. *Take me back to Spencer. I'm just not ready for this.*

"Well, Mr. Faraday, you picked one bizarre day to stop by ZNC." Ryan offered Gnarly a cheese curl, which, surprisingly, the German shepherd refused. "Preston Blakeley doesn't make it a habit to stop by to watch the filming." He jerked his head in the direction of the network's CEO, who was engaged in a low conversation with the producer. "Clearly, he's here tonight to conduct damage control, since Rubenstein's husband intends to sue. In our business, all loyalty goes out the window when it comes to lawsuits. Yvonne Harding may be Blakeley's darling—"

"Darling?" Mac picked up on the term of affection. "Darling as in 'mistress'?"

"Maybe, maybe not," Ryan said. "No one is really very sure. Knowing Blakeley and the ZNC board, if Yvonne costs the company a couple of million dollars in a wrongful death suit, regardless of how good she is in bed or high her approval ratings are"—he jerked his thumb over his shoulder—"she's out of here."

"Knowing how people are nowadays—the wackos out there—Yvonne should have never outed Rubenstein. It was totally irresponsible of her," David said with disgust.

"Irresponsible like this police detective going on the air to answer questions for the whole world about an open murder investigation?" Mac asked. "It's like laying out all of your cards in a poker game and then wondering why you aren't winning anything."

"You would think," Ryan agreed. "Ever since Preston Blakeley got Hopkins signed on as an expert, he's been all about the camera. He hangs around these studios a lot, appearing at least once a week on one show or another to offer law enforcement's views on different cases." He lowered his voice. "Chatter is that he's getting his own show in the near future."

"Easy to see where Hopkins' priorities are," Mac told David.

"These people live for fame and forget about what's really important."

"Are you saying fame ruined Yvonne?" Mac asked.

Anger seeped into David's tone. "She's not the woman I married."

"It's that obsession with fame that's going to get you your divorce," Mac hissed.

Ryan Ritter jerked his head around in David's direction upon hearing the reference to being married to Yvonne Harding. Not understanding Ritter's perplexed expression, David asked, "What are you looking at?"

"We're shooting in five … four …" the director counted down.

In the studio, Pam Wiehl and Lieutenant Wayne Hopkins sat across from each other at the news desk. On the signal from the director, Pam opened the segment with a recap of the Audra Walker case, which included a break to show a clip from Yvonne Harding's interview, the last public appearance of the noted investigative journalist.

Audra Walker's face came up on the monitor. Seeing her, Mac was reminded of how pretty Audra Walker used to be, but not in a cosmopolitan way. Raised on a Texan ranch, Audra wore her thick, wavy dark mane loose. She also wore little makeup—less, he noted, than Lieutenant Wayne Hopkins and Ryan Ritter.

Seeing Audra's face, Mac remembered Ali's observation about there being a difference between an investigative journalist who lives in pursuit of the story and a celebrity.

Audra Walker was an investigative journalist first and always, with the emphasis on "investigative."

Mac recalled that Audra Walker could tell a bawdy joke, one laced with a Texan twang, as well as any of the men in the police department. The first time he'd encountered her sense of humor was when she'd met him at a police bar to go over the basics of the murder case she'd been researching.

Mac's captain at the time considered himself to be quite a ladies man. Upon seeing the leggy brunette with striking light-brown eyes, he moved right in and proceeded to brag about his long string of arrests, giving gruesome details, all in an effort to impress her with his masculine prowess. Finally, in need of a refill of his beer, the captain stepped up to the bar.

As soon as the captain was out of earshot, Audra turned to Mac and stated in a matter of fact manner, "Now there's a man who's all hat and no cattle."

She had to have noticed the complete confusion in Mac's expression.

"Have you ever been to Texas?" After Mac confessed he hadn't, she explained the saying. "Real Texans are ranchers. The bigger the ranch, the more cattle you got. Used to be that the more cattle you got, the bigger your hat."

"Cowboy hat," Mac said.

"Braggarts tend to go out and buy themselves big hats"—she held up her hands over her head to illustrate a big cowboy hat—"to put on a big show 'bout what big men they are, when really they have no cattle." With a wicked grin, she leaned across the table to whisper to him, "In other words, as much as your boss brags 'bout his sexual prowess, I'm guessin' he has a very tiny penis."

Mac choked on his beer.

"You know I'm right, sweetie, don't you?"

Gasping for air, Mac was still having trouble finding his voice when she leaned across the table toward him. She arched one of her eyebrows. With a cock of her head, she said, "Come on, Faraday. You've been in the men's room standin' over the urinal with him. I can see it on your face. Tell me I'm right. He's all hat and no cattle."

At that point, his captain returned to the table with his refill. Choking on his beer, Mac ran out onto the street, where he doubled over with laughter.

On the monitor replaying Audra Walker's last interview, which had been filmed two years earlier, Yvonne Harding was asking, "What's next for Audra Walker?"

"Oh, I'm now gonna finish that one project that's been doggin' me for my whole career," Audra said with a toothy grin. Mac could see the excitement on her face.

"What project is that?" Yvonne asked.

"The true story behind Romeo and Juliet."

"Why did you choose *this* clip?" Preston Blakeley demanded of Jim Wiehl. "It was an hour-long interview. This was the best you had?"

"Because legal advised us to not replay anything from the Brennan book until they had a chance to go over where we stand on that matter," Jim replied. "Brennan announced last week that he's planning another run for president. Legal claimed that if we ran any part of that interview about Jolene Fitzgerald's murder, it could bring in criticism from Brennan's party—or worse, a lawsuit from Brennan."

"Give me a break," Blakeley grumbled.

"Romeo and Juliet?" Yvonne asked in the interview. "Is Audra Walker moving into romantic tragedies?"

"Actually, it's not so much a romantic tragedy as it is the perfect murder," Audra replied with a mischievous grin. With a tilt of her head, she arched that eyebrow.

Mac's jaw dropped open. That tilt of the head. The arched eyebrow. That long, dark, wavy mane. *That's it. That's what's been nagging at me.*

The cameras returned to Lieutenant Wayne Hopkins and Pam Wiehl at the news desk. Blinking, Pam sat up straight in her seat and faced the camera.

"Hours after that interview with our own Yvonne Harding, Audra Walker disappeared," Pam Wiehl told the audience. "She was never seen again—until today, when what is believed to be her skeletal remains were discovered here in our own ZNC studios. With us now is Lieutenant Wayne Hopkins of the New York City Metropolitan Police, who is leading the investigation into Audra Walker's disappearance and the body that was discovered today. Wayne Hopkins has appeared as an expert in law enforcement many times here at ZNC." Turning to the lieutenant, she asked, "First, Lieutenant Hopkins, has the body been positively identified?"

"Yes," Hopkins said into the camera. "Dental records and DNA have positively identified the body discovered today as that of Audra Walker."

With an expression filled with compassion, Pam said, "So tragic. Audra Walker was a friend and respected colleague. Has her family been notified of this discovery?" Blinking her eyes, her face contorted.

"What's wrong with her face?" Preston Blakeley asked.

Jim chuckled. "Her eyelash is coming off. Good thing we're recording this interview, and it's not live."

"Not yet," the lieutenant said in response to Pam's question about notifying the Walker family. "Unfortunately, we've been unable to contact them. Walker's husband died shortly before her disappearance. She had a grown son and daughter. Her son, Phil Walker, who took over the presidency of his father's company, is traveling out of the country right now.

Her daughter, Dallas, has been backpacking through Europe for the last several months. According to her social media sites, she is currently in Italy."

The corner of one of Pam's false eyelashes was curling up toward her eyebrow.

"Keep going, Pam," Jim said to her through his earbud, which communicated with her on the set. "We'll rerecord your questions after the interview and edit them back in."

"Do you know yet how Audra Walker died?" Pam asked with wide eyes. The eyelash was flapping like a wing on her eyelid.

"We found one bullet wound to the back and two bullet holes in the back of her skull," the lieutenant said. "And we did recover those bullets, forty-five calibers, at the crime scene. Once we find the murder weapon, all we have to do is match up the bullets."

"Idiot," David said. "He just told the killer that he needs to get rid of the murder weapon."

"Where's Ali Hudson?" Mac asked.

"She should be here," Ryan Ritter replied while looking around the control room. "Where is Ali?"

"She's at the dentist," the assistant director sitting at the control panel in front of them said. "She chipped her tooth at lunch."

"Chipped her tooth?" Mac muttered. "On a hot dog?"

Several minutes later, they had finished recording the segment. Cursing, Pam Wiehl ripped off the bothersome eyelash.

Laughing, Jim said to the crew via the intercom, "Okay, Pam, go to makeup to get your eyes redone." His voice could be heard booming across the studio. "We're going to shoot Yvonne Harding's interview with the psychologist. Once we're done with that segment, then we'll reshoot Pam's portion of the Walker interview."

On the stage, Lieutenant Wayne Hopkins was disconnecting his body mic with the help of a sound technician. "Do you need me here for that, Jim? I have an appointment I need to get to." Clearing his throat, he puffed out his chest. "I'm following up on a lead for the Walker case." After the producer responded that the detective was free to leave, Hopkins turned to shake Pam's hand, only to find that she had already disconnected her microphone and galloped off to the makeup department.

In the control booth, Preston Blakeley patted the executive producer on the back. "Good job, Wiehl. Congratulations on getting Hopkins to give us this exclusive."

"We certainly scooped every other network," Jim said.

"You also gave Audra Walker's killer a road map on what to do to escape detection," Mac said.

"That's one way of looking at it, Faraday," Jim said. "Another way is that the more information the public has, the better equipped they are to help us identify the killer."

"Is that really what you want?" Mac asked. "Justice for Audra Walker or ratings?"

"Why can't we have both?" Preston Blakeley asked with a chuckle. Giving Jim Wiehl another slap on the back, the CEO said, "I've got a conference call to make to some board members on the West Coast. Jim, can I trust you to make Yvonne stay on point with the troll story?"

"Certainly, sir."

"I'm leaving with you, Preston," Ryan Ritter said while taking a cell phone out of his suit coat's pocket. "Need to stop at makeup. My show is in less than an hour."

"They're going to be busy," the director said. "We got a lot of new guests on schedule."

"No problem," Ryan Ritter said while scrolling through the screen on his phone. "I do my own makeup. Learned a long time ago that if you want it done right, you gotta do it yourself." Putting the cell phone to his ear, he followed Preston Blakeley out of the control booth.

The previous quiet during the recording of Pam Wiehl's segment had erupted into loud voices and equipment moving around the studio while technicians, camera operators, and a host of other members of the crew rushed around the set to prepare for Yvonne Harding's segment.

Upon exiting the booth, David and Mac found Yvonne reading her copy in preparation for her segment. Her expert, a psychologist, was in the process of having her body mic attached.

"Fifteen minutes, crew," Jim Wiehl's voice boomed throughout the studio via an intercom. "Then we'll begin recording Harding's troll segment."

"Now's your chance," Mac whispered while ushering David toward the news desk on the stage.

When David hesitated to move toward Yvonne, Mac shoved him forward.

Gnarly tugged on his leash to head toward the far wall, where an exit led out into the corridor, elevators, and stairwell. Wrapping the leash around his hand, Mac led Gnarly to the far outside wall of the control booth. Not wanting Yvonne to see him watching them, Mac kept back, hiding among the dark shadows of a lighting rack. He wanted to be close by so he could jump in to back David up if need be.

Behind her, David climbed the steps up to the stage. "Yvonne."

He saw her stand up straight. She lowered her script and turned around. Her face was void of emotion. "I'm surprised to see you here, David."

"You shouldn't be. You still haven't signed the divorce papers."

Yvonne glanced around at the dozens of crew members scurrying about. The assistant director, who was on their left, was giving instructions to the psychologist, who was on their right.

Trying to stay out of the crew's way in his spot behind the lights, Mac kept a tight hold on Gnarly's leash. When the dog uttered a low growl, Mac tore his attention away from David and Yvonne's discussion to see what had captured the dog's interest. Someone was coming into the studio. The bright light from the corridor outside spilled in through the open door to cast the scruffy-looking visitor clad in a worn tan jacket and work boots in silhouette. Because of the way the visitor was looking around the studio and moving about hesitantly, Mac assumed it was his first time in a television studio.

Wonder what show he's on?

"Excuse me, David," Yvonne said before bringing her hand to her ear. "Yeah, Fred? Okay. I'm ready." She then turned to David and said, "They need to do a sound check on my mic."

While stepping down off the set, Yvonne reached under her jacket to adjust the controls on the unit clipped to the back of her skirt. She gestured for David to follow her to the other side of the set, away from the commotion of the crew, and then she turned to him. "We could have talked about it this afternoon, but you took off."

"Because I didn't want to discuss it in bed," David said. "That phase of our relationship is over, Yvonne. You don't seem to get it. I'm marrying Chelsea this weekend."

"And then right after that, you can go to jail for bigamy." She grinned. "You're the one who has failed to get it, David. I don't want to sign those papers because I don't want a divorce. I wanted to marry you years ago. Now we're married, and I'm not letting you go."

"To what end?" David asked. "You live here in New York. I'm in Deep Creek Lake."

"We'll have two homes."

"I have no interest in living here with all these loonies."

"David, you have no idea how much money I make," Yvonne said. "When Dad died, he left me a fortune. You don't have to work. You can stay here, and I'll give you everything you ever wanted. All you have to do—"

"I'm not wired like that, Yvonne," he said. "What happened to you? You think that you can trap me, lock me up in this concrete cage called a city, and hand me a bunch of toys, and I'll be happy? You know me better than that."

"We'll make it work." Her lips curled. "You have no choice, David, because I'm not signing those papers."

"I was afraid you'd say that." He reached into his inside breast pocket and pulled out a folded sheet of paper. He held it out to her.

She refused to touch it. "I told you I wasn't signing those."

"These aren't the divorce papers," David said. "This is a copy of a publishing contract. Mac's lawyer made a few phone calls this afternoon. Right now, three publishing companies are in a bidding war for my story."

"*Your* story?"

"I'm calling it *Life with Yvonne,*" David said. "My kiss-and-tell book." He chuckled. "I am your husband, after all. Your fans must be dying to know what it's like to be married to Yvonne Harding." He leaned in to whisper, "I'm going to tell them *everything.* Since we grew up together, I have a lot of material. I know all about you … your secrets." A wicked grin crossed his face. "Wait until you read chapter seven about that weekend when we went to the Outer Banks and you—"

"That's blackmail!"

The harshness of her voice caused all action around them to cease.

David's eyes were locked on hers. "Yes, it is."

He was surprised to see tears fill her eyes. For a moment, he wavered about going through with his threat. But if he wanted to stay true to Chelsea, he had no choice. He needed Yvonne's signature.

"David," she said in a soft voice, "I love you. Can't you see that?"

"I love you, too, Yvonne," he replied in a low voice, "but it's too late for us. I'm marrying Chelsea."

"Because you love her, or because you owe it to her?" she asked.

"That's not important," David said. "The fact is that we're both different people than we were four years ago. This"—he gestured at the studio and the crew rushing around—"this is your life now. It's not mine. I don't belong here. I belong in Deep Creek Lake. It's time for you to let me go."

"And if I don't?" She blinked her big blue eyes at him. "You aren't really going to sell my story, are you?"

David clenched his jaw. "You know better than to mess with me, Yvonne." He reached inside his jacket to extract the divorce papers and held them out to Yvonne.

She gazed at the papers in his hand and then up into his face. "Oh, David, " she said in a breathy voice before falling against him.

David heard Gnarly erupt into a series of angry barks. Across the studio, he saw the German shepherd dart out from behind a bank of stage lights and charge for the snack table. The exit door was pushed open, and a dark figure rushed out of the studio.

Mac was so focused on Yvonne collapsing into David's arms that when Gnarly shot toward the far wall and exit, he ripped the leash out of Mac's hand. Before Mac could react, Gnarly leaped over the snack table, scattering the contents and the table to the floor, and took out a shelving unit before slipping out the exit door, which slammed shut after him.

"Gnarly, no!" Mac shouted at the runaway dog.

Grasping Yvonne in his arms, David tried to pull her up onto her feet, but they slid out from under her. She was like dead weight in his arms. "Yvonne, stop it! Stand up!" With his arms around her, he felt something warm and moist coat his hand. His heartbeat quickened. Looking over her shoulder, David examined his hand to find that it was coated with fresh, bright-red blood.

A member of the crew who saw the blood at the same time screamed.

"David—" Yvonne gasped out while clinging to his jacket.

Mac had both hands on the exit door and was in the process of opening it when he heard the scream followed by David's bellowing, "Somebody call nine-one-one!"

Blood gushing from her back was covering David's arms and clothes. "Yvonne, darling, stay with me," he pleaded with her as he shrugged out of his sports coat so he could use it to stop the bleeding. "You're going to be okay."

"No, I'm not," she breathed. "Hold me, David."

He cradled her in his arms. "I'm here, darling. Don't try to talk."

"You're right, David, I'm not the same woman."

Gnarly must have seen the perp! Grabbing his gun out of the holster he wore on the back of his belt, Mac spun around to go out the door that Gnarly had slipped out before it had slammed shut.

Jim Wiehl came running out of the control booth to talk to Mac. "What happened? Did Yvonne faint?" His eyes grew wide. "Is she pregnant?"

Mac was more interested in catching whomever Gnarly was chasing. He had to have had a hand in hurting Yvonne, the woman David had once loved enough to marry, even if he hadn't known it at the time.

David was hugging Yvonne close. He pressed his sports coat, which was soaked with blood, against the wound in her back. "Ambulance is on its way, baby. You got to hold on. What happened, baby?"

Her smile was weak. "Baby. That's what you used to call me."

Donning only a single false eyelash, Pam Wiehl pushed her way through the gathering crowd with Ian Griffith, one of the show's cohosts, directly behind her. "What happened?" Pam demanded to know. "We heard someone shot Yvonne?"

Blocking out the onlookers around them, David whispered to Yvonne, "We'll work this out."

"You were right," she said. "I changed. Do you know when?"

"When?"

"When you didn't ask me to stay." Her voice was weak. "Why didn't you ask me to stay?"

It didn't take Mac long to locate Gnarly. As soon as he burst into the stairwell, he could hear the German shepherd barking several flights below him. The dog's deep barks echoed up and down the stairwell. Mac could also hear voices of people, many of whom he assumed were security guards, calling to one another both above and below him in the stairwell.

"Did someone call out a K-9 unit?" Mac heard a guard call to someone.

"The dog is with me," Mac yelled while making his way down the stairs in the direction of Gnarly's barking. "He's chasing a suspect!"

"Looks like he caught him," the guard said.

Keeping his gun aimed at the floor, Mac continued to trot down the stairs. Gnarly's barks slowed down as more uniformed security guards and officers arrived at the scene down on the ground floor, thirty-six flights down to the main floor.

Oh, God, I hope she makes it. Can David marry Chelsea days after Yvonne dies?

By the time Mac made it to the main level, Gnarly was sitting off in the corner. Across from him, the dog was watching two uniformed New York police officers create a barricade to keep security guards and news journalists away from the lifeless body of the man they assumed had killed Yvonne Harding.

One of the uniformed officers was reporting the discovery of the body to his station. "Carl Rubenstein. Building security says he was outside this afternoon threatening Yvonne Harding for causing the murder of his wife."

Crumbled at the bottom of the stairs was the body of Carl Rubenstein. A black gun with a silencer still attached to the muzzle rested in the open space in the center of the stairwell.

"Is he " Mac started to ask. "Who shot him?" He took in the confused faces of the two police officers and the two security guards. He showed his police badge to one of the uniformed officers to identify himself, as well as his gun to prove that he had not fired it.

One of the security guards shook his head. "I got a call from upstairs saying that Yvonne had collapsed and might've been stabbed. Then I heard the dog barking and came into the stairwell to see if I could intercept the guy who did it." When I stepped in, I saw him rolling down the stairs." He pointed up the stairs. "The dog was, like, two flights up. I saw the gun bounce off the railing and hit the floor at about the same time as he landed there."

"He must have been turning around to shoot the dog," one of the uniformed officers said. "But then he tripped and fell on his own gun."

After being moved away from the scene by the uniformed officers, Mac took hold of Gnarly's leash and led him away from the dead body. Kneeling next to the dog, Mac peered as closely as he could at the gun. It appeared to be a three-eighty caliber pistol fitted with a silencer. But there was something different about it.

"How'd he get the gun in the building?" the older guard asked his partner. "What was he doing upstairs?"

"One of the producers put his name on the list of guests for *Crime Watch*," the other guard replied. "Surprised me too, after the way he was mouthing off outside. But he came in less than an hour ago, and we had a visitor's application. I personally watched him go through the metal detector. He didn't have a gun on him. He said Yvonne Harding herself was going to interview him on the air."

"Where did he get the gun?" one of the police officers asked.

"Don't know where he got it," Mac sighed. "But I can tell you how he got it through the metal detector." He stood up.

"How?" the guard who had watched Rubenstein go through the metal detector asked.

Mac pointed at the gun. "No way would your metal detector have picked up that gun. It's made out of plastic."

Up at the studio, Mac waded through the police officers and EMTs until he spotted David sitting off to the side. His clothes were soaked with blood. Never had Mac seen such a stricken expression on his face.

Gnarly trotted up and placed his paw and head down on David's thigh.

"David," Mac murmured, even though he knew what the news would be. David's expression said it all.

A single tear spilled out of one of David's tear-filled eyes and rolled down his cheek. "She's gone."

Chapter Nine

As soon as the police arrived, Mac, David, and every witness and potential suspect were separated so that their statements could be taken. Over and over again, Mac overheard the same thing.

"Is it true she was shot?"

"Did you see all the blood?"

"I didn't hear a shot. Did you? I think she was stabbed."

Across the studio, Mac was waiting for a detective to take his statement and watching David, who was covered with blood, stare at Yvonne's lifeless body. Her body was lying at the bottom of the steps leading up to the news desk where she was supposed to have been conducting an interview at that very minute. Gnarly was lying next to David's feet, staring mournfully while the on-scene medical examiner poked and prodded the once-beautiful young woman.

They should get David out of here. He shouldn't have to see them handling her like that. A uniformed officer had told Mac to sit in a cast chair on the other side of the set. Just as he stood up to go find the detective in charge, his cell phone vibrated on his hip.. He checked the caller ID, which read, *Willingham.*

Ed Willingham had been Robin Spencer's lawyer, and she had had him on retainer to handle her business affairs. One of the top lawyers in the country, Ed Willingham was the one who'd hunted Mac down after her death. Now he was keeping Mac's and his two grown children's legal and business affairs in order.

"Hello, Ed," Mac answered the phone.

"I just saw the news," the lawyer replied in a rushed tone. "Yvonne Harding is dead!"

"Yeah, Ed," Mac said. "It's a mess. David was standing right in front of her and trying to get her to sign the divorce papers when she collapsed. We believe we found the murder weapon. The shooter used—"

"She's *dead?"*

"Yes. That, I do know."

"Tell me David got her to sign those papers." The lawyer bit off every word.

Mac searched his memory of David's and Yvonne's movements in the minutes leading up to her collapse. He hadn't seen her sign anything. "I don't think so."

"Damn it!" After uttering an exasperated sigh, Ed growled into the phone and said, "Where is David now?"

"Waiting for a detective to take his statement," Mac replied. "He's really shaken up, Ed. I think he's in shock. I was about—"

"Mac, listen to me carefully," Ed interjected. "If Yvonne didn't sign those papers, David is going to be more than shaken up. He's her *husband!"*

"And the first suspect homicide detectives look at when someone is killed is the spouse," Mac said. "We do that for a reason. But David and Yvonne only just found out that they were married. They weren't living—"

"Yvonne Harding was a very wealthy woman," Ed said. "I was the executor for her father's estate. Man was as tight with a penny as they come. He left her *everything*. That, plus what she made since signing with the network—"

"How much are we talking about?" Mac asked.

"Millions," Ed said.

"But if she had that much money, she must have had a will. Since she didn't know that she was married, she most likely left everything to someone else, which would not give David motive to murder her."

"She was also a young woman," Ed said. "No husband or kids. If she had a standard will leaving everything to her next of kin, then that gives David, her *husband*, a very strong motive to want her dead. Does anyone know they're married?"

"We didn't tell anyone," Mac said.

"I'm getting on the next flight," Ed said. "Tell David not to talk to anyone until I get there."

"Calm down, Ed," Mac said, "David was standing in front of her when she was shot in the back, and they believe they have the shooter and the gun. Everything is fine."

"I'd feel better if the detective in charge told me that himself," Ed said before hanging up the phone.

While disconnecting the call, Mac saw Lieutenant Wayne Hopkins enter the studio and make a beeline for David. Quickly, Mac pressed the buttons on his cell phone to send a text to David.

"Say nothing. Ed on his way."

Across the studio, he saw David read the text as the detective stepped up to him.

Mac was slipping his phone back into his pocket when he felt it vibrate in his hand. Reading the Caller ID, he saw that it read "Unknown Number." Curious, he brought the phone to his ear.

"Mac," He recognized the sultry voice of Ali Hudson.

"Ali," Mac said. "How's your chipped tooth?"

"Better than Yvonne's," she replied. "Is it true? Yvonne Harding ate a bitter pill?"

"If you're asking if she's dead, yes. Where are you?"

"Outside," she said. "They've sealed off the building, and I can't get in. Do they have who did it?"

"Carl Rubenstein," Mac said. "They found his body down at the bottom of the stairwell, along with what they believe to be the murder weapon. Somehow he had smuggled a gun into the building."

"How did he get a gun past security?" Ali asked. "He's been threatening Yvonne. I called them myself to tell them not to let him in—"

"I overheard the security guard who let him in say his name was on the guest list for an interview on *Crime Watch*. He said that when they sent Rubenstein up, he was bragging that Yvonne Harding was personally going to interview him for her show."

"That's a bunch of bull hockey!" Ali continued cursing under her breath.

"I'm sorry," Mac said. "I knew Yvonne, and—"

"Rubenstein did not kill her," Ali said forcibly. "He wouldn't have."

Across the studio, Mac saw Lieutenant Wayne Hopkins stepping toward him. "Listen, Ali, I have to go. Can you meet us somewhere to talk about this? We're staying at—"

"I'll find you."

Click!

"Mr. Faraday," Lieutenant Hopkins said, greeting Mac with a smug grin. "Second time in less than twenty-four hours that I find you standing over a dead body."

"Yvonne Harding was a friend," Mac said. "She was a dear friend to David O'Callaghan, so I strongly suggest you talk about her with respect."

"I had nothing but respect for her as a woman and as a journalist," the detective said. "First, tell me what happened. Where were you?"

"Over by the control booth." Mac pointed in the direction of the stage lights he had been waiting behind when he saw Yvonne collapse.

"Inside or outside the control booth?"

"Outside," Mac said. "Behind the stage lights."

"Hiding?"

"*Watching* David and Yvonne Harding."

The annoying smirk filled the detective's face. "What were they doing?"

"Talking."

"What about?"

"They were old friends," Mac said with a shrug. "They grew up together. Used to date a few years back. Most likely, they were talking about old times. I was too far away to hear anything specific."

"Date?" the detective said. "Are you sure all they did was date?"

Mac chuckled. "Listen, Hopkins, I've conducted more interrogations than you ever will. I know you need to dig deep and find out everyone's secrets to uncover the reason for this murder. But you're digging in the wrong spot right now. If you want to know the personal details of David's relationship with Yvonne Harding, you talk to his lawyer, who is on his way here now."

"Lawyering up already, huh?" Lieutenant Hopkins chuckled as if he had succeeded in scoring a goal in a nasty game of one on one. "And I'm sure, as a former homicide detective, that you know that nothing spells 'guilty' like lawyering up."

"David has over a dozen witnesses, me included, who saw him standing *in front* of Yvonne Harding when she was seemingly shot *in the back*," Mac said. "Is that what the on-scene examiner found? A bullet entry wound in the back?"

"Yes," Lieutenant Hopkins said. "Shooter had to have been several feet away and must have used a silencer."

"And a three-eighty caliber pistol with a silencer was found at the bottom of the stairwell," Mac said, "along with Carl Rubenstein, who had threatened Yvonne earlier today."

"Who is conveniently dead and unable to defend himself," Lieutenant Wayne Hopkins said. "As you are aware, we need to know where everyone was and what they were doing at the time of Yvonne Harding's death. Problem is"—he grinned—"no one seems to know where *you* were. You just told me that you were *hiding* over there"—he pointed—"behind the stage lights, with a perfect target of Yvonne Harding's back."

Mac held out his hands. "Your crime-scene people are here. Do a paraffin test on my hands. You'll see I haven't fired any weapons in the last few days." He took his gun out of its holster and handed it to the detective. "You'll also see that my weapon has not been discharged recently."

As Mac had expected he would, Lieutenant Hopkins took his gun and inspected it. With a nod of his head to show his agreement, he handed it back to Mac. "How about your backup weapon?"

Mac knelt down to extract his thirty-two caliber semiautomatic from his ankle holster and handed it to the detective, who sniffed it and checked the magazine to see that no rounds had been discharged from it before giving it back to him.

While returning the gun to his ankle holster, Mac reminded Hopkins about the gun found in the stairwell. "That was fired."

"And we're assuming it was used to kill Rubenstein until forensics gets a chance to examine it," Lieutenant Hopkins said. "They'll also check to see if it was used to kill Harding.

Funny thing about that gun—besides the fact that it's plastic—is that it was wiped clean. Has no fingerprints. And forensics says Rubenstein wasn't wearing gloves and hadn't fired a weapon. No gunpowder on his hands or clothes. Plus, he didn't land on a gun. He was shot from several feet away at an upward angle."

"The gun was fired from down the stairs below him?" Mac asked.

Hopkins' eyes locked with Mac's.

"The uniformed officers found Rubenstein at the bottom of the stairs and saw me when I reached the ground floor," Mac said. "No way could I have gotten down to the bottom of the stairwell ahead of Rubenstein to fire up at him."

"You're a rich man," Lieutenant Hopkins said.

"What does that have to do with anything?"

"I'm sure if you wanted to hire someone to take out your brother's rich wife so that he could inherit her fortune, you would have all the resources necessary to make it happen."

Mac gritted his teeth. "Are you arresting David or me?"

"Not yet."

"Then we're leaving." Mac stepped around the detective. Mac had managed only to get around him before Lieutenant Hopkins stopped him with a warning that he had used many times himself.

"Don't leave town."

The street outside the News Corps building was mobbed with journalists and paparazzi trying to get pictures and information—anything to post on the news or the Internet about the death of Yvonne Harding. Unidentified sources from inside ZNC had already leaked that she had been shot in the back.

As she headed down Sixth Avenue, Ali Hudson took out her cell phone and pressed the speed-dial button to connect her to the Four Season. While Manhattan contained a host of grand hotels, it had been her experience that most of the rich and famous opted for the Four Seasons, which sported the most fabulous view of Central Park, or the Plaza, which was a couple of blocks away. From East Fifty-Seventh Street, it was only a twenty-minute walk to the Four Seasons, which was the closer of the two hotels.

"Four Seasons Hotel," the operator answered.

"Mac Faraday's suite, please?" Ali requested while taking note of a man in dark clothes and a red hoodie who had broken away from the mob in front of the News Corp building at about the same time she had. In the reflection of the shop windows, Ali could see that he was heading in the same direction as she was.

A moment later, she was connected to a guest room's voice mail. As she had expected, it did not say which room Mac Faraday was staying in.

At least I know the hotel. Slipping the cell phone into her jacket pocket, Ali turned the corner onto Fifty-Third Street. Casually looking up at the buildings towering above her, she took note of the fact that the man in the red hoodie had turned on the same corner.

Reaching into her jacket pocket, she wrapped her fingers around the ninja spike that she used for a key chain. The weapon's unique shape and compact size disguised its true nature. She carried it with her everywhere. During the five months that she had worked for ZNC, not once had any of the security guards given the weapon, with its sharp spikes that extended more than an inch beyond her fingers, a second look when it passed through the X-ray machine.

She quickened her pace, and she was approaching an alley between two restaurants when she sensed someone rushing up behind her. Before she could turn around, a leather strap was dropped over her head and wrapped around her neck, and she was jerked backward into the alley.

"This is going to be fun," she heard someone whisper harshly into her ear.

Her attacker's laughter was cut off by a gasp followed by a gurgling sound when Ali, instead of lunging forward to fight the strap meant to control her, spun around on her high heels and punched him in the throat.

Two of the spikes punctured her attacker's vocal cords. Stunned by the unexpected assault, he dropped the strap and clasped his neck. Blood squirted out between his fingers.

Instead of running away, Ali continued her attack with a knee to the groin and another blow to his ribs. The spikes ripped through the jacket. Her attacker fell back against the wall. She dropped him to the ground with a high heel to his knee.

Before her attacker had time to collect his wits, she hurried back out onto the street and trotted on to the Four Seasons.

Chapter Ten

"It's all over the news," Mac said to David, breaking the silence in the back of the taxi. "You should call Chelsea to tell her what's happening."

Looking around Gnarly, who was seated between them, to where David was sitting on the other end of the backseat, Mac wondered if David had heard him. His expression was one of being completely stricken.

"I could call her for you," Mac offered.

"No," David said in a soft voice. "I'll call."

"Has she spoken to you since—"

"No," David replied. "Did you hear the shot?"

"No, but it was so noisy in that studio, with the director calling out to people over the intercom and sets being moved and lights—"

"When I'm doing my reserve duty, I can always pick out gunshots."

"The gun they found had a silencer."

"You know as well as I do that silencers only suppress the sound of the gun shot. They don't complete mute it. I should have heard the shot."

"What if you had? Yvonne would have still been shot. Your hearing it would not have saved her." Trying to be as gentle as possible, Mac asked, "When was the last time you tried to call Chelsea?"

"None of your business," David shot back.

"It is my business," Mac said. "I'm your best man. If there's not going to be a wedding, I have a right to know. Maybe I'd like to do something else this Saturday instead of making sure another one of your old girlfriends doesn't cross paths with—"

"Four Seasons," the cabdriver said, interrupting Mac.

David sat up to reach for his wallet, only to see Mac handing money to the driver with instructions to keep the change. Seeing a wide grin cross the driver's face, David concluded that Mac had given him a hefty tip. Throwing open the door, David climbed out and took Gnarly's leash. "You don't have to take care of me," he told Mac when he joined him at the front entrance.

A doorman held the door open so they could enter the lobby. He seemingly did not notice that David was dressed in what appeared to be blue hospital scrubs. The crime-scene investigators had confiscated David's blood-covered clothes for evidence. They had supplied him with a blue cotton top, drawstring trousers, and cloth slippers to change into.

"Next cab, I'm paying for," David told Mac while he led Gnarly across the hotel's elegant marble lobby.

Without a word, Mac followed them past the throngs of guests, a few of whom took notice of David's less than sophisticated attire, to the elevators. David waited until they were on the elevator and Mac had pressed the button for the twenty-third floor to slump over. "Sorry," he muttered.

"Don't be. You've been through hell today." Mac shot a grin in his direction. "I'd say you even have a pass to get drunk tonight."

"I'd settle for a nice hot shower and a good night's sleep." David sighed. "But I don't think it's going to happen … ," he said, his voice trailing off.

The elevator doors opened, and Mac led David and Gnarly down the hallway to their suite. After using the keycard to enter it, Mac stopped inside the door. Seeing a dark figure sitting at the table in the window that provided a brightly lit night view of the New York skyline, he grabbed for the gun on his hip.

"There's no need to get your boxers in a bunch, Mac!" she yelled while holding up both hands. "Don't shoot!"

Yanking the leash out of David's hand, Gnarly bounded across the suite to plant both front paws in Ali Hudson's lap and lick her face. After that, he grabbed the food that she had had room service deliver while she'd been waiting for them.

When Mac started to chastise the dog, she cut him off with a wave of her hand. "That's okay, hon. I was done anyway. That burger was big enough to feed an army." She set the plate down on the floor for Gnarly. Holding up a bottle of beer, she added, "I broke into the minibar. I hope you don't mind."

"How did you get in here?" Noticing a fresh floral arrangement in the center of the table, Mac extracted the card to read the name of the sender. The card read, "Thank you for last night, Bubbles." Furrowing his brow, Mac tossed the card to the table.

The corner of her lips curled. "Once I determined that you were here at the Four Seasons, I went to the gift shop and ordered a flower arrangement to be sent up here to your room. Then I waited in the lobby for them to deliver them, at which point I followed the clerk. When he came out of your suite, he ran into me as I was just 'bout to insert my key card into the lock—or so he thought. So, like a gentleman, he held the door open for me to come in." Pleased with herself, she smiled up at him.

Mac turned to exchange glances with David, only to find him studying his cell phone. He seemed to be weighing his options in regard to calling Chelsea.

"I'm sorry 'bout Yvonne," Ali said to David. "From what little I know, I saw that she really cared 'bout you—a lot."

"Thanks," David murmured before excusing himself to go into his room. "I'm going to call Chelsea and take a shower."

"Is Chelsea his—" she started to ask Mac.

"Fiancée." Mac saw a shadow of disappointment cross her face. Crossing to the minibar, he took out another bottle of beer, which he handed to her, and two minibottles of scotch. He emptied each one into a glass. Then he took one into the bedroom where he found David, his back to him, speaking into his cell phone.

"The detective in charge of the case told us not to leave town," he said. "No, we aren't suspects." He turned around to find Mac holding out the glass to him. "We're witnesses. Willingham is on his way up now. He should get everything sorted out so that we can come back to Deep Creek tomorrow. Mac has the charter jet company on standby, so we can leave as soon as we're free to go. We'll get our license first thing when I get back, and we'll be ready to get married on Saturday."

About ready to turn around and leave David alone to talk to Chelsea, Mac paused when he saw a flicker of worry cross David's face. "Did they say what they wanted? Sure. If they need to talk to someone—I'll call them tomorrow morning to give permission for them to talk to you. Take Bogie with you. He's got that magic touch with Mom. He'll be able to calm her down."

The reference to Bogie, the deputy chief of Spencer's police department, was all the evidence Mac needed to understand that Chelsea had received a call from the nursing home where David's mother, an Alzheimer's patient, was living.

Of course, everything has to hit the fan at once—the week before David's wedding. First he finds out he's married and didn't even know it. His wife is gunned down in front of him. His bride is not speaking to him. Now his mother, who's been suffering from dementia for years, is having some sort of relapse while we're being held as witnesses, if not suspects, for murder.

Deciding to make his own drink a double, Mac went back into the sitting room, where he found Ali Hudson lounging on the sofa with Gnarly stretched out next to her. He was resting his head on her chest. She was drinking her second beer straight from the bottle.

"Have the police contacted you yet?" Mac asked her while pouring the second bottle into his glass. He quickly took a healthy gulp of it. It felt good flowing down his throat.

"Ryan Ritter called me right before I called you," she said.

"Ryan Ritter?" Mac repeated. "Why would—"

"He told me 'bout Yvonne gettin' shot and was worried 'bout me since I wasn't there," she said. "I'm usually in the studio during shootin' to assist Yvonne."

The corners of Mac's lips curled. "Why weren't you there tonight?"

"I had a dental appointment."

"Because you chipped your tooth on a hot dog at lunch." Cocking his head at her, he chuckled.

"Why, sir, I do declare," she said with a heavier drawl than usual. "Don't you believe me?"

"No."

Her eyes grew wide.

"Where were you?"

"I wasn't in the buildin'," she said. "Security'll tell you. If they can't, the security cameras—"

"I know you didn't shoot Yvonne," Mac said. "I'm simply interested in where you were. My gut is telling me it had something to do with Audra Walker's murder, and she would have wanted me to do everything I could to keep her daughter safe."

All the undertones of playfulness evaporated from Ali's expression. With her big brown eyes, she stared across the sitting room at him. The light from the lamp was shining on her face, and he noticed that her eyes were the same color as her mother's had been.

Silence stretched between them.

"Lieutenant Hopkins said Audra Walker's daughter, Dallas, was backpacking across Europe," Mac said. "Her social media site says she's in Italy … but that's not true … is it, *Dallas?*"

"What gave me away?"

"First it was your fondness for colorful Texan sayings," Mac said with a chuckle. "I even recognized a few of them from when I worked with your mother. At first, I dismissed it. Then I noticed that you had her eyes—the lightest brown."

"Pap used to say they were the color of the finest cognac," she recalled with a hint of melancholy.

"He was right," Mac said. "But that's not all. You've inherited her mannerisms—the way you cock your head and arch that eyebrow—not to mention her biting wit and wicked sense of humor."

"You were right, Mac," she said. "She *never* would've walked away from Phil and me. I knew from the very first day that somethin' was up. Someone killed her, and that idiot Hopkins insisted she left voluntarily."

"What about the lead detective before him?" Mac asked. "You were on the phone with him when we came into Yvonne's office this morning."

"Caleb Roberts," she said. "He believed me when I said that somethin' happened to her. But after he retired, Hopkins took over. He said a friend of Mom's—she was really more of an acquaintance than a friend—got a postcard from Mom sayin' she had met a man who she knew we would disapprove of and had decided to take off with him. This friend gave the postcard to the police, and their expert said the handwritin' was Mom's, so they closed the case. Our expert said it wasn't—that the handwritin' was a forgery."

"Now that your mother's body was found in Yvonne's office," Mac said, "I wonder what that expert has to say."

"No one would tell Dallas Walker anythin'," she said. "But Ali Hudson, investigative journalist, is another thing."

"The media does background checks," Mac said. "How did they not know—"

"Ali Hudson was my roommate in college," Dallas explained. "She studied journalism. I studied criminology. When Hopkins closed the case on Mom's disappearance, I decided it was time to go undercover. Ali got married, and they started havin' babies right away. Since she was changin' diapers instead of investigatin', I offered to buy her identification to land a job with ZNC. I bought her social security number, driver's license—everythin' in her name. While I've been here in New York, she's been on the Internet as me, postin' stuff on my sites, checkin' my bank accounts, and makin' it look like Dallas Walker is backpackin' through Europe. She's even been texting folks as me."

"Even if you are Audra and Buddy Walker's daughter," Mac said, "don't you see that going undercover in New York City is taking a big chance? What if someone, like your mother's killer, recognized you as Buddy Walker's daughter?"

"I'm a Walker," she said. "Not a Kardashian or a Hilton. My face is not all over the Internet, and I don't tweet every time I take a trip to the outhouse." She sat up in her seat. "Look, Mac, I understand where you're comin' from. I admit I come from a long line of proud Texas ranchers who'd think nothin' 'bout chargin' into hell with a bucket of ice water, but we got smarts, too. Our folks made sure Phil and I never forgot what stock we came from or who we really were."

"Your mother considered herself a renegade cowgirl who liked to chase down bad guys," Mac recalled with a fond grin.

Draining the last of her beer, Dallas moved forward to sit on the edge of the sofa. "And now I'm chasin' down the bad guys who killed her."

"Was it just a coincidence that you ended up working for Yvonne Harding, the last reporter to interview your mother before she disappeared?"

She shook her head. "I called in a few favors from friends of Mom's to get me up close and personal with Yvonne. I was very lucky. Once she saw my talent for diggin' up the facts behind a story, which allowed her the freedom to be the celebrity, she gave me free rein, which allowed me to use her name and contacts to dig into Mom's disappearance."

"Is it possible that your investigation got Yvonne killed?" Knowing then that she was the daughter of Audra Walker, Mac recognized the intense concentration in her eyes. "You said it couldn't have been Rubenstein. What makes you so certain it wasn't him?"

"Rubenstein had no reason to want Yvonne dead," Dallas murmured in a low voice.

"They said at the studio that Yvonne outed his wife—"

"Who *he* wanted dead," Dallas countered. "Listen, I spent less than an hour workin' on the Rubenstein murder before learnin' 'bout her devoted husband's mistress, who he's been wantin' to marry for well over a year. When Ruth gave up her guitar for a harp, it was his lucky day." She went over to the minibar.

"Guitar?" Mac muttered. "Harp? Was she—"

"Ruth Rubenstein traded in her guitar for a harp," Dallas said, "to play while singin' with the angels."

"Ah," Mac said with a nod of his head. "Now I understand."

After yanking open the door, she took out another beer and a bottle of scotch. "Plus, Carl Rubenstein had every intention of suin' Yvonne and ZNC for wrongful death, knowin' ZNC would settle in order to avoid the bad publicity. Why would Rubenstein screw all that up by whackin' Yvonne, who he had threatened in order to publicize his case?" She tossed the bottle of scotch to Mac from across the room.

Catching the bottle, Mac said, "And mess up his chances for a million-dollar windfall."

"He was set up." Taking a gulp of her beer, Dallas sat down across from him.

Mac stood up. "By someone who contacted Rubenstein to invite him down to ZNC for a phony interview with Yvonne and then called down to security to put his name on the list of people allowed up to the studio. Our killer also had access, after hours, to the floors that were being renovated two years ago, when your mother was lured up there, murdered, and hidden inside the walls."

"Someone connected with that building," Dallas said in a low voice.

"Any names pop into your mind?"

"Do you think the same coward who murdered Mom killed Yvonne?"

"Yvonne was shot in the back the same day Audra Walker's body was discovered. You've been using Yvonne's name to dig into Audra Walker's case."

"And the lead detective in Mom's disappearance was killed today," Dallas said. "I went to meet Sergeant Roberts at his place this evening. He was gonna give me his case folder on Mom and his notebook with his personal notes on the case. But someone had shot him deader than a doornail before I got there."

Mac lowered himself back into his seat. "It all has to be connected."

"Then," she continued, "after I talked to you on the phone in front of the News Corp and started comin' this way, I noticed a guy break from the crowd to follow me. As soon as I hit an alley, he attacked me."

Mac jumped to his feet. "Attacked you? Why didn't you tell us when we got here?"

"I'm tellin' ya now."

"This is why your mother would not have wanted you to be here," Mac said. "David is a chief of police. I was a homicide detective. We walk in, and you're sitting there, eating a cheeseburger as calm as you please, and now I find out that that was shortly after you'd been attacked."

"He didn't hurt me," she said with a casual shrug of her shoulders. "He ended up gettin' the raw end of the deal. I left him bleedin' in the alley. I thought he was just a common, everyday, gutter snipe lookin' to mug me or rape me, but now I'm not so sure."

"In light of Yvonne's and the lead detective's murders, I think maybe whoever killed your mother was tying up loose ends. Since you're Yvonne's assistant, he or she didn't want to take a chance on you knowing too much. Who knew you were meeting with Sergeant Roberts tonight?"

"No one was around when I set up the meet," she said. "I did talk to him this mornin', before y'all found Mom's body. Ryan Ritter was there when the call came in, but he left as soon as I answered the phone. I'm sure he didn't hear our conversation. You, David, and Pam Wiehl were there while I was talkin' to him. I know Pam told Jim. After the fact that Mom's body had been found hit the news, Roberts called and I told him who I really was. That was when he suggested we move up the meetin'. He promised to give me everythin' he had. But by the time I got there, he was already dead."

"Did Preston Blakeley know about your investigation?" Mac asked. "He was there this evening and was very interested in the Lieutenant Hopkins' interview with Pam Wiehl."

"He set that interview up," she said. "Lieutenant Wayne Hopkins has designs on havin' his own show and Preston Blakeley seems to be more 'an willin' to make it happen."

"There's our list of suspects," Mac said. "Preston Blakeley and the Wiehls. They all had access to the murder scene, know about you talking to Roberts, and had the means to set up Carl Rubenstein."

"Now all we have to do is identify which fox got into the henhouse and killed my mom," she said.

Chapter Eleven

As sleep was giving way to consciousness, Dallas Walker could feel someone watching her. She became aware of the gentle touch of Gnarly's fur while brushing her fingers across his shoulders.

The pleasant feel of his soft fur was overtaken by the noise of the city outside. After five months of living in Manhattan, Dallas still was not accustomed to the continuous bombardment of the sounds and smells of the metropolis. She so longed to wake up to the sweet scent of the magnolias and wisteria that grew outside her bedroom window and the lovely melody of the birds dancing in the trees.

Smelling coffee, she rolled over onto her back. Becoming aware of a blanket draped across her, she pulled it up to her shoulders and turned her head.

As her vision cleared, she saw him studying her from the sofa across from her. Her heartbeat quickened when her eyes met his, which still held a hint of sadness from his loss.

"Good morning." Sleep made her sultry voice more raspy than usual.

She gazed longingly at the coffee mug he brought to his lips. Shoving away the question that sprung to her mind—

"What would it feel like to touch those lips with mine?"—she sat up. *That was so inappropriate, Dallas. He's getting married in a few days.*

He startled her out of her fantasy by saying, "Want some coffee?"

Afraid her voice might give away her thoughts, she wordlessly nodded her head.

He went over to the suite's breakfast bar, where he poured a mug for her. "Cream and sugar?"

"Both. Make 'em double." Shivering against the autumn morning's chill, she pulled the blanket up and wrapped it around her shoulders. She sat up and tucked her feet under her.

Interpreting the opening on the sofa as an invitation, Gnarly curled up next to her and lay his head down in her lap. She greeted him by stroking his head.

David held out the mug to her, and her fingers brushed against his when she reached for the cup. That time, instead of pulling his hand away, he allowed her fingertips to touch his knuckles. Slowly, he dragged his gaze to meet hers before allowing her to take the mug.

"Thank you," she murmured. After taking a sip, she added, "I'm sorry."

"I know you are," he said while retaking his seat. After picking up his mug, he asked her, "Why'd you spend the night?"

"I fell asleep, and I guess Mac didn't wake me up to send me home," she said. "Besides, I don't feel very safe at my place—"

"I wouldn't either," David said. "An off-duty cop was killed just a couple of blocks from here last night."

"Really?" she asked. "Some guy tried to attack me while I was walkin' here from the News Corps building."

David sat up. "Are you okay?"

"Yeah," she said. "I punched him in the throat. He obviously didn't see that comin'."

"Punched him in the throat?" David repeated. "With what?"

She paused. "What does it matter?"

"This police officer was found in the alley only a few blocks from here, and he had a stab wound in the neck. He bled out in the alley, and you just told me that you punched your attacker in the throat."

"Why would a *police officer* try to strangle me?" she asked.

"Good question."

"Don't ask me! Ask him!"

"*Can't!* He's *dead!*"

"What's going on?" Lured in by the raised voices, Mac threw open the door leading into his room. Having forgotten that Dallas had spent the night, he was dressed only in his boxer shorts. Upon seeing her look up at him, he rushed back into the bedroom for his pants.

Amused, Dallas called out to him. "Come on, Mac! I'm sure you don't have anythin' I haven't seen before!"

David leaped off the sofa and followed Mac into the bedroom. "Did Ali tell you that she killed a cop last night?"

"Dallas," Mac corrected him.

"What?"

"Her name is Dallas." After zipping up his pants, Mac grabbed a shirt and returned to the sitting room.

"I thought her name was Ali."

"That was her alias," Mac explained.

"Oh, alias." David turned his attention back to her. "So you're using an assumed name—a fake identity—and you're killing cops? Give me a reason not to turn you into the police."

"It was self-defense, and he was still alive when I escaped." She dug through her jacket pocket to extract her keys and held the ninja spike out to David. "This is what I used. The spikes are only a little over an inch long. While they're sharp, they aren't long enough to be lethal. He was bleedin', but if he had gotten to a doctor, I'm sure he would have survived."

David wrapped his hand around the ninja spikes to test out her assessment.

"Dallas told me about it last night," Mac told him. "She was attacked *after* Yvonne was killed."

Slowly, David asked, "Are you thinking—"

"Just seems like an awfully big coincidence for her to be attacked the same evening Yvonne was killed," Mac said. "And the same day that Audra Walker's body was found in the News Corps Building. That's why I let her stay last night."

"Everyone at ZNC knew I investigated Yvonne's cases for her. Anythin' she knew, I knew."

David handed the keys back to her. "I thought Carl Rubenstein killed Yvonne because he blamed her for his wife's murder."

"You have a lot of catchin' up to do, darlin'."

Mac picked up the dog leash from the coatrack. "Dallas, you fill David in while I take Gnarly for a walk."

"I already walked him," David said. "We went for a run first thing this morning."

"No." Mac stared at him.

"Yes," David said. "That's how I found out about the police officer getting killed. The doormen were talking about it."

"What did Gnarly do?" Mac asked.

"He sniffed the doorman, who gave him a biscuit." Seeing that Mac wanted more information, David elaborated. "Then we went over to Central Park."

"Did Gnarly do anything else?"

David frowned. "What else would he do? Dog stuff. That's what he did."

"You know it's illegal to leave it," Dallas said.

"I put it in a baggy and tossed it," David said.

"Where?" Mac blurted out before he could stop himself. Seeing their puzzled expressions, he cleared his throat. "I need coffee."

When he heard the knock on the door, Mac bypassed the coffee maker to peer through the peephole. It wasn't even seven thirty, and Ed Willingham was already sweating.

"I hope you have coffee," Ed said when Mac threw open the door.

"Help yourself." Mac gestured to the coffee maker. When he saw Ed drain what was left in the carafe, he called down to room service to order a fresh pot.

While preparing his coffee, Ed directed his attention to David, who was seated across from the brunette eying the city out the window. "Mac tells me you didn't get Yvonne Harding to sign the divorce papers."

Jerking, Dallas turned her attention back to David. "Divorce? You two were *married?"*

"Four years." Then Ed turned to David. "Who's this?"

"Dallas," David said.

"As in Texas?"

"After Dallas, Texas," she said with a grin. "It's where I was conceived. My brother's name is Phil. He was named after—"

"Philadelphia," Mac finished with a grin. "Her parents had a sense of humor."

"You're Audra and Buddy Walker's daughter, Dallas." He patted his chest. "I'm Ed Willingham. I defended your mother twenty years ago when she went to jail." With a wide grin, he hurried over to shake her hand.

"I barely remember that," she said. "I was just a little girl. But I heard all about it."

"I heard on the news that you were in Italy," Ed said.

"No," Mac said. "She's been working undercover at ZNC for the last five months."

"As stubborn as your mother, I see."

"Pap used to say that the nut doesn't fall very far from the tree in our family, which was his way of sayin' we were all nutty."

"You need to keep an eye on this one," Ed said to Mac over his shoulder.

"I know that already," Mac replied.

Ed turned back to David. "We have to talk about Yvonne's murder."

"I'm not a suspect, Ed. I was standing in front of her when she was shot in the back. Over a dozen members of the cast and crew saw me."

"And not one member of that cast and crew saw where *Mac*, your best man, was." Ed jerked a thumb in Mac's direction. "With her dead, not only can you marry Chelsea on Saturday, but you can also give her a very wealthy husband."

"Wealthy?" David muttered. "She did tell me that her father had left her a lot of money, but I wasn't really paying attention."

"But if she didn't know she was married to David," Mac asked, "then why would she have put him in her will?"

"I contacted her lawyer last night after I talked to you," Ed said. "He was as surprised as everyone else to find out that Yvonne had been married. He told me that Yvonne didn't really have anyone, but since she was worth so much, she'd had a standard will drawn up." He glared at David. "Everything goes to her next of kin, which gives you, David, a very strong motive—about nine million motives—

to want Yvonne to die, and not to sign those divorce papers. Plus, we haven't even talked about the life insurance policy she had with the network—a million to her next of kin, and double indemnity since she was killed on the job."

"But David didn't do it," Mac said. "He's got witnesses."

"The police are thinking *you* did it for David," Ed said. "Can you think of anyone else who would want Yvonne Harding dead?"

"Ian Griffith," Dallas said. "He was so jealous of Yvonne that he couldn't see straight. Another network was offerin' Yvonne her own show. ZNC was in a biddin' war with them to keep Yvonne and was gonna give her more money and her own show with Ryan Ritter as the lead-in. When Ian got word that Ruth Rubenstein had been murdered and that her husband was plannin' to sue Yvonne and ZNC, he was practically dancin' with joy."

"How about Pam Wiehl?" Mac asked. "She overheard you talking to Sergeant Roberts."

Dallas shook her head. "I can't see Pam killin' anyone. Professionally, she's fat and sassy. *Crime Watch's* executive producer is her husband, who loves the daylights out of her. The show is secure in its ratings. Really, they're a couple of homebodies. They spend every weekend home with their daughters."

"But she's getting a little long in the tooth," Ed said. "In her business, you're over the hill after forty. It would be very easy for the CEO and board to decide to go for a younger audience by replacing her with a younger host—like Yvonne."

"Yvonne didn't want *Crime Watch*," Dallas said, "because even as the lead host, she'd share the spotlight with three other hosts. She wanted to be the one and only host of her own show and ZNC was gonna give her that."

"Unless she cost them a million or so dollars in a lawsuit," David said. "Ian told us that yesterday."

"With Yvonne and Rubenstein dead, both ZNC and Ian Griffith scored," Mac said. "We need to take a look at him."

"Ian Griffith isn't smart enough to pull off a murder," Dallas said with a laugh. "The only reason the Wiehls keep him on *Crime Watch* is because the lady viewers think he's pleasin' to the eye and he's got a great sense of humor. But when it comes to competence, he couldn't knock a hole in the wind with a sackful of hammers."

"Not only that, but wouldn't Ian Griffith be taking a big chance committing murder?" David asked. "If he expected Yvonne to get fired, why didn't he just wait for Rubenstein's lawsuit to run its course and then make his move for the top spot on the show?"

"Maybe Blakeley offered Ian his own show in exchange for eliminating Yvonne and the lawsuit," Ed said. "With both of them dead, everyone wins."

Tossing the blanket aside, Dallas stood up. "I'll check out Ian and Mr. Blakeley when I get to the office."

"David and I are coming with you," Mac said. "I have a bad feeling about that man who attacked you last night. If he did turn out to be a police officer, then we need to check out his connection."

"What man attacking—" Ed asked, only to have Dallas cut him off.

"Do either of you have a button-down shirt? People'll talk if I go in wearin' the same clothes I wore yesterday. I don't have time to go back to my place."

"I only packed for overnight," David said, "and the police confiscated my clothes last night."

"I have a button-down shirt." Ed tossed his suitcase onto the coffee table and opened it up. "Is white okay?"

"White'll be perfect," she said while unbuckling the belt on her pants. "I'll also need a white undershirt. Otherwise, everyone will see my chocolate-brown Fleur Turner."

"Whatever that is." David rose from his seat. "I do have an extra white T-shirt I can lend to you."

After she followed David into the bedroom, Ed turned to Mac. "If Dallas is anything like her mother, which I can already see she is, you and David need to stick real close to her."

"Audra was spunky, but she wasn't stupid," Mac said.

"The woman spent ten days in jail rather than give up her source for *Sleeping with the Enemy*," he said. "That's takes more than spunk. My lawyers have represented more than one journalist that the police and feds have gone after for sources. With most of them, you threaten to send them to jail, and they cave. Not Audra Walker."

Mac quickly said, "*Sleeping with the Enemy* was about the murder of Zachery Bailey, the doctor-husband of a superior court judge in Washington State. Everyone thought he was killed in retaliation for some mob cases she had presided over. Walker's book said the judge hired a hit man to kill her husband, who came from a wealthy family, so that she could inherit his fortune and be with her lover."

"Walker's book had so many details in it that the feds knew her source had to have been the hit man Judge Bailey hired, but she had given her word that she wouldn't give away the assassin's identity, and"—he sighed—"she kept that word."

"I never understood how she could go to jail for not divulging her source," Mac said. "What about her First Amendment—"

"Justice department argued that since she wrote books freelance, not for any news organizations, she could not hide behind the shield law," Ed said. "I got that overturned pretty easily. Even so, she spent ten days in jail protecting this professional killer and was tough enough that she was prepared to stay even longer." He chuckled. "She probably wanted to stay longer. She came out of jail with another award-winning book—a story she got from her cellmate. She made about three prison pen pals. Audra Walker was one tough cookie."

"So's her daughter," Mac said. "Someone put three bullets into Audra Walker and sealed her body in a wall, killed the last journalist who interviewed her, and tried to kill her daughter last night. My gut is telling me that all of this is connected. Can you call your contacts in the police force to find out about this off-duty police officer who was killed last night? Dallas says someone tried to mug her. We suspect that attack is connected."

"Could she have blown her cover?"

"I doubt it," Mac said. "Since Dallas was Yvonne's research assistant, the killer would have wanted to eliminate her to avoid risking any loose ends."

Ed was nodding his head. "I'll make a few phone calls about that off-duty cop to see if he's dirty."

David was aware of Dallas's following him into the bedroom and closing the door, but he didn't think anything of it. After all, she needed his undershirt and a place to change her clothes.

Taking the white undershirt out of his suitcase, he said, "This may be a little big in the shoulders, but it should do."

He turned around to find her standing on the other side of the bed. She had taken off the double-breasted top of her pantsuit. Above the waist, she wasn't wearing anything but a chocolate-brown silk-and-lace bra. The hue of her underwear matched the brown in her eyes. With a toss of her head, she shook her hair back behind her shoulders, letting it spill down her back, and held out her hand to take the shirt.

Stunned by her lack of modesty, David made no move to give it to her.

"Let's see how this looks." She snatched the shirt from his hand. After pulling it on over her head, she unzipped her pants to tuck it in. Frowning at her image in the mirror, she put on the stark-white button-down shirt and fastened the bottom buttons. Cocking her head, she studied her reflection. "Whatta ya think?"

She turned to David, who was trying to get the image of her perfectly toned body out of his mind.

He swallowed. "Good."

Turning back to the mirror, she furrowed her brow. "You can see my bra underneath."

With her calling it to his attention, David had to agree she was right.

"That won't work." In one movement, she pulled both white shirts off over her head. While David's mouth hung open, she undid the bra's clasp between her breasts and shrugged out of it.

As much as he did not want to take in her beautiful, plump breasts, he couldn't resist uttering a gasp of surprise. "Obviously, they don't teach modesty in Texas."

"I grew up surrounded by rough and burly ranch hands. I would've never survived being prissy and modest." With a naughty grin, she tossed the bra to David, who caught it with one hand. "Souvenir of your trip to New York," she said with a wink.

"And all I was looking to take back to Deep Creek Lake was a divorce." David tossed the bra into his overnight bag.

She had already pulled both shirts back on over her head. "How is it that Yvonne was married to a hunk like you and never told anyone?" While tucking the undershirt into her pants, she turned to David and looked him up and down. "If I was your wife, I'd shout it from the rooftop."

"Neither of us knew."

Hands on her hips, she cocked her head at him. "Dude! How do you get married and not know it?" Her tone was filled with doubt.

"Picture it," David said. "Drunk in Vegas."

Her hand shot up. "'Nuff said!" She strapped the belt that she had previously worn on her pants around her waist to cinch in the men's white button-down shirt that hung down low enough to cover her hips. She left the top four buttons undone to show the white undershirt beneath.

With only a few pieces of clothing, she had transformed her look into stylishly casual. Without asking, she picked up David's comb and ran it through her thick locks. "Wish I had time to wash my hair. Do you have a rubber band?"

David went into the bathroom to go through his shaving kit. He returned with an old, worn rubber band to find that she had begun French braiding her hair from the crown. "I have no idea where this came from." He held out the band to her.

Because she was using both hands to work the braid, she was unable to take it. "Take a tater and wait, sweetie."

"What?" David asked her.

"It means don't get your boxers in a wad," she said to his reflection in the mirror.

He stared back at her reflection for a moment before shaking his head. "I don't understand half of what you say … but you sound good saying it."

"I'll take that as a compliment, sir," she replied to his reflection in the mirror.

Their eyes locked.

Guilt washing over him, David turned around to break the connection, leaned against the dresser, and focused his attention on the rubber band.

"Did you love her?" she asked. "Yvonne, I mean."

"Yes," David replied.

"But you're marryin' this other woman."

David nodded his head.

She noticed a dark shadow cross his face. When she finished braiding, she reached for the rubber band, allowing her hand to rest in his. "Do you *want* to marry this other woman?"

"I wouldn't have asked her if I didn't," David said.

"Didn't. You're speakin' in the past tense, sugar." Taking the rubber band, she turned back to the mirror. "Maybe you wanted to *then*, but you aren't so sure *now.*"

"Why would I not be sure now?" David's tone was sharp. Turning away from her, he went to the nightstand and opened the drawer.

"I don't know." Through the mirror, she watched his reflection as he picked up a gun from the drawer. "How does she feel 'bout your gettin' drunk and marryin' Yvonne Harding in Vegas?"

"None of that was Chelsea's fault." David slipped the gun into a holster he wore on his belt behind his back. "She has a right to be upset."

"Yes, she does," Dallas said. "If it was me, I'd raise hell and stick a chunk under it."

David turned around to face her. Placing his hands on his hips, he asked her, "What does that even mean?"

"She has every right to be mad at you," she said. "What I don't understand is why you're mad at her."

"I'm not." David extracted a smaller handgun that was still tucked in its holster from the overnight bag.

She folded her arms across her chest. "Are so."

"Am not." He propped his foot up on the bed and lifted a leg of his blue jeans.

"Is she talkin' to you yet?" she asked while watching him fasten the holster around his ankle.

"As a matter of fact"—he tightened the holster's fastener with a sense of vengeance—"she is." He dropped his foot to the floor so hard that it caused a stomping sound.

"I stand corrected." With a shrug, she whirled on her heels and sauntered to the door. "Before you go back home to marry your second wife, whatta ya say we go catch your first wife's killer?"

"I can't believe you haven't visited Violet since coming back to Spencer," Deputy Chief Art Bogart told Chelsea during their drive to the nursing home in Oakland, Maryland, where David's mother lived. Molly, Chelsea's white German shepherd, was sitting in the backseat of his SUV.

Bogie, as everyone called him, had spent his entire law-enforcement career working for the Spencer Police Department. Sixty-five-year-old Bogie had been Patrick O'Callaghan's best friend and was David's godfather. His hair and bushy mustache were gray, but he had the huge muscular build of a man half his age. More than once, young police officers had tried to challenge the older officer to a bout, and every time they ended up eating mat in less than a minute.

"I think David preferred that I not see her," Chelsea said. "That I remember her the way she was, which was pretty mean and nasty anyway. David used to be ashamed of letting his friends meet her."

Unsure of how much David had revealed about his personal family situation, Bogie simply said, "Violet has her own personal demons. Problem with demons is that some people like to hang onto them and refuse to let them go, not realizing that if you hang onto them too long, they'll consume you—and drive you mad."

Unsure of what Bogie was trying to tell her, Chelsea looked at him from out of the corner of her eye.

"I visit Violet pretty regularly," Bogie said while keeping his eyes on the road. "I'm one of the very few people she still recognizes. She's convinced David is his dad. Sometimes she'll get violent when he comes to see her. The nursing home told him that he shouldn't visit her alone anymore. That's why I come."

"Why would she get violent with David if she thought he was his dad?"

"I'm sure you heard all those rumors about him and Robin Spencer."

"Well, it turns out there was some truth to the rumors," Chelsea said. "They had a baby together."

"That was long before Pat even met David's mom," Bogie insisted. "It was ancient history. Even though he married her and started a family with her, Violet never felt secure in their marriage. Instead of letting Pat's past go, she let it get to her and destroy everything she had—not the least of which was her mind."

At the nursing home, Bogie reminded Chelsea of a beloved politician as he shook hands, slapped backs, and asked this resident or that one about this daughter or grandson. He welcomed everyone by name. Obviously, he didn't visit just Violet regularly. They stopped in three different rooms before they finally made their way to their intended charge.

When they stepped into the lounge where the television was on, the face of every resident in the room lit up, and there was a chorus of "Hi, Bogie!"

While the big deputy chief made his way around the lounge, Chelsea managed to pick Violet O'Callaghan out of the residents. Thinking back, she concluded that it had been over fifteen years since she had seen David's mother. In that time, she appeared to have aged fifty.

Her thick blond hair was disheveled. Sunken into her skull, her small eyes darted about the lounge while her lips worked. Slumped over in her wheelchair, she resembled a nasty predator looking for someone to attack—not because it was hungry, but simply because it wanted to.

No wonder David never brought me to visit her.

"Hello, Violet, how are you today?" With a jolly greeting, Bogie pulled up an ottoman and sat in front of her. "They tell me that you had a really bad day yesterday." With a wave of his hand, Bogie beckoned Chelsea to join them.

Like a mouse approaching a lion, Chelsea made her way across the lounge in their direction. In a flash, she recalled an afternoon when she had visited the O'Callaghan home not long after she had started officially dating David. Chelsea's older brother, Riley, and David had grown up together. Even though they were best friends, visits to the O'Callaghan home had been few and far between.

Chelsea learned why that afternoon. She and David were on their way to a cookout when they realized they had forgotten a cooler for drinks. They were in the kitchen, putting ice in the cooler and giggling like the crazy teenagers in love that they were, when David's mother walked in.

"Who's the strumpet?" she demanded an introduction.

"Mom—"

With mocked embarrassment, Violet covered her mouth with her hand. "Excuse me." That was when Chelsea realized David's mother, the wife of Spencer's chief of police, was intoxicated.

"Mom," David said, "this is Chelsea. She's Riley's sister. You've met Riley."

Pleased to meet the mother of the man she loved, Chelsea extended her hand. "Pleased to meet you, Mrs. O'Callaghan."

Ignoring the girl's hand, Violet took her time looking Chelsea up and down. Her gaze stopped on Chelsea's miniskirt and long legs. "I see you're a leg man. I'm surprised—your father's into boobs."

Chelsea's mouth dropped open.

The cooler was only partially full, but David slammed the lid shut. "We have to go. We're going to be late." He picked up the cooler. "The cookout is going to run late, so don't wait up, Mom."

"I stopped waiting up for you and your father years ago," Violet said.

Chelsea wanted to get out of that house as much as he did. "Let's go, David." Then, instinctively, she gave him a peck on the lips.

The show of affection prompted an explosion from Violet O'Callaghan like none that Chelsea had seen in her young life. "How dare you!"

With no idea what she had done, Chelsea was startled. She felt her heart jump, and it felt like it was in her throat.

David appeared equally surprised by the outburst.

"Who do you think you are, coming into my home and nuzzling my man!" When Violet advanced on them, David reached out his arm to guide Chelsea behind him. "Have you no shame! It's bad enough that you think you can just take whatever you want, whenever you want—"

Fear made Chelsea stop paying attention to what the woman was raging about. All she wanted was to get out of that house. David stayed between her and his mother, and then, clutching the cooler like a shield, he and Chelsea backed out of the house and ran for the car.

Almost two decades later, Chelsea still vividly remembered the image of Violet O'Callaghan cursing at the two of them from the front door while they made their escape. Among the accusations that Chelsea heard that day was one of betrayal.

Bogie reintroduced the two women. "Violet, do you remember Chelsea Adams?"

"Adams?" Violet asked. "I … don't …"

Chelsea recognized the penetrating glare in Violet's eyes as she looked her up and down. Her eyes fell on Molly, who stepped forward to place herself between her master and the withered old woman. Clinging tighter to Molly's leash, Chelsea edged over to hide behind Bogie.

A slow grin worked its way to Violet's wrinkled lips. "I know who you are."

Bogie sighed with pleasure. "She must be having a good day today," he whispered over his shoulder at Chelsea.

"You thought I wouldn't recognize you." Violet uttered a string of curses. "You did this!" She beat the arms of her wheelchair. "You! You think that since I'm not a Spencer—since I didn't grow up with a silver spoon on Spencer Point—that I'm simpleminded and don't know what your plan is!" she cackled.

Bogie stood up and turned around. "Maybe you'd better go, Chelsea."

Molly was more than anxious. Whining, she pawed at Chelsea, whose eyes were locked on the beady blue eyes of the old woman in the chair, David's mother—the woman who had borne the man she loved.

"Drive me crazy and have me locked up—aye? Well you may have his heart, but I have his soul! He's never going to leave me, because he owes me!" She pounded her bony chest with one of her claws. "Me! He owes me, and I'll never release him from that debt!"

"Go, Chelsea!" Bogie was pushing her out of the lounge.

The old woman was advancing in her wheelchair. "Till death do us part! That's what he said, and I'm holding him to it—no matter how much he yearns for you! He's mine! Body and soul! I'm not giving Pat up—ever!"

Nurses were rushing from every direction. One was carrying a syringe.

"Do you hear me, Robin Spencer?" Violet cackled. "Patrick O'Callaghan is mine, until death do us part—body and soul! I'm holding him to it!"

The rest of the old woman's curses roared in Chelsea's ears. Up on her hind legs, Molly was pawing at her. She recognized the German shepherd's cries.

"Chelsea, you need to lie down," she heard through the roar in her ears. "You're going to have a seizure." Bogie's face was spinning before her eyes. "Where's your medicine?" She felt her handbag ripped out of her grasp right before everything went black.

Chapter Twelve

Even though Mac wanted to go back to the News Corp Building, Ed Willingham insisted he go to the police station to find out the status of their investigation into Yvonne's murder. There was nothing the lawyer hated more than surprises. If he had to personally climb the ladder up to the police commissioner's office to uncover what evidence the detectives had and the name of their suspects, Ed Willingham was willing to do it.

Fearing for Dallas' safety, Mac suggested that David, who apparently was in the clear as a suspect, escort her to ZNC's studio with the excuse that he had a right to go through Yvonne's office since he was her husband. He could possibly identify any suspects not on their list.

To Mac's surprise, when he made his suggestion in the lobby of the hotel, David's face turned pale. His eyes darted over to where Dallas was speaking to her brother on her cell phone. "I'm sure Hopkins is going to want to talk to me again. I should go with you."

"If the police want to talk to you, I'll call you to come down to the station," Ed said. "But since you're not a suspect—"

"They think I arranged for Mac to kill her," David said.

"Someone attacked Dallas last night," Mac said. "It could be the same person." Noting that David's eyes were flicking in her direction, he asked, "What's wrong?"

"Nothing." David paused before whispering, "I can't understand half of what she says."

Mac chuckled. "You'll get used to it."

"That's what I'm afraid of."

When David reached for Gnarly's leash, Mac yanked it out of his reach. "He's coming with me."

"To the police station?" David asked. "You've been sticking to Gnarly like glue lately. I don't even know why you brought him to New York."

"David's got a point," Ed said. "Why did you bring Gnarly?"

Holding the German shepherd close to him, Mac said, "I've grown quite fond of Gnarly."

Dropping her phone into her oversized bag, Dallas turned to rejoin them. "Well, I'm ready to go, puddin'. Let's blow this pop stand." After tightening the belt to her black trench coat, she slipped her hand through David's arm. "Phil talked to Lieutenant Hopkins this mornin'. He says Hopkins told him that they have a suspect for Mom's murder."

"Who?" Mac asked.

"The mob. That's all Hopkins would tell him."

"Why would the mob want to kill your mother?" Ed's expression was doubtful. "I know for a fact that they had a high regard for her."

Dallas smiled. "Phil said the same thing—only he didn't use such polite language."

"I don't trust Hopkins," Mac said.

"Neither do I," she said. "He's as crooked as a barrel of fish hooks. He's more interested in gettin' his pretty face on TV than in findin' Mom's killer, which makes for a very dangerous conflict of interest if you ask me."

"Especially since all of our suspects work in television," Mac said. "Any one of our suspects could help Lieutenant Hopkins with his ambitions to be famous."

"Which makes it harder to prove," Ed said. "There's no money trail to follow from Hopkins to the killer."

"But maybe there's another type of trail," Mac said. "Sergeant Roberts, the original lead detective in Audra's disappearance, was killed yesterday. While we're at the police station, let's see if we can find out if he got any calls from his old partner, Hopkins, shortly before his murder."

"But we don't have any proof that Lieutenant Wayne Hopkins is dirty, except that he's a jerk," David pointed out. "I've known lots of jerks in my time, but that didn't necessarily mean they were crooked."

"Yes, that's true," Mac said. "But then I've never met a dirty cop who wasn't a jerk."

Mac was so focused on getting Gnarly out onto the street and into the taxicab that he didn't notice until they were in the backseat with the German shepherd draped across Ed's lap, that Dallas was leading David down the street with her hand in his. When the cab drove past them, Mac turned around in his seat to watch the two of them, hand in hand, hurrying along with the morning pedestrians on their way to work.

His eyes narrowed to slits. *What's that about?*

"Show me when we get to the alley where you were attacked," David said.

"It's a couple of blocks from the News Corp Building," she said.

"What time was it?"

"I got to the buildin' a little after seven o'clock," she recalled. "I decided to give up tryin' to get in 'round twenty to eight and started walkin' to the Four Seasons. Had to be 'bout quarter to when I passed that alley."

"Yvonne collapsed around five minutes to seven," David said. "The whole building was locked down immediately. No one, except emergency crews, could get in or out. Mac and I weren't able to leave until right before eleven. I think they allowed people on the other floors to go a little after nine."

"Maybe the killer got out before the buildin' was locked down." She stopped at an alley running between two restaurants. The entrance was roped off with yellow crime-scene tape.

"From the thirty-sixth floor?" David followed her line of sight into the alleyway. Two members of a New York crime-scene crew was scouring the dirty pavement for evidence, while two uniformed police officers were standing guard to keep spectators out.

It was only when David tried to step over to speak to one of the uniformed officers that he realized he was clutching Dallas' hand in his. Startled, he turned back to her and looked down at their hands. Their fingers were entwined. *How long—when?* He dropped her hand as if it were on fire. Confusion crossing her face, she cocked her head at him.

David turned back to the uniformed officers. "Excuse me," he said while taking his police chief's badge out of his pocket to show them. "I heard an off-duty police officer was killed here last night."

"Yes—" the younger officer said.

The older officer interrupted him. "We're not able to comment on an open murder investigation. What interest would an out-of-town police chief have in one of our cases, anyway?"

"A news journalist was killed just two blocks from here," David explained.

"Yvonne Harding," the younger officer said with a nod of his head. "I'm a fan. She had legs—"

"Her assistant was attacked not long after her murder," David said, "in this area. We're trying to determine if it was the same perp. Maybe your police officer ran into him. All I want to know is the approximate time he was killed."

The two officers regarded each other before the older one shrugged his shoulders. "Off the record?"

"Off the record will work," David replied.

"Tate was not only off duty," the older officer said, "but he was also on suspension. You didn't hear it from me."

"What for?" David asked.

He answered him in a low voice. "Female suspects complained that he was too touchy with them. Word is that a prostitute managed to get something on tape, and he was suspended without pay pending a hearing."

"Maybe one of his victims got revenge," the younger officer said.

"Did the on-scene ME have an approximate TOD?" David asked.

"The scuttlebutt says it was between eleven and midnight," the older officer said. "But I doubt if he had anything to do with the Harding murder. Tate made a lot of enemies, and a lot of people are saying he was dirty. How could a dirty cop and pervert be connected with an uptown journalist like Yvonne Harding?"

"Good question," David said before thanking them for their help and ushering Dallas back out toward the street with his arm around her waist.

"That TOD is at least three hours after I got dragged back into the same alley," Dallas said. "Proves that I didn't kill him and that, most likely, it's not the same guy."

"Maybe," David said. "Maybe not."

"What's that dog doing here?" Lieutenant Wayne Hopkins asked when he looked up from his pristine desk among the maze of cubicles that made up the squad room and found Gnarly sitting in front of him, his dark eyes focused directly at him.

"Looks like he's staring at you," Mac replied. "Thought maybe you'd have some additional questions or information for me about Yvonne Harding's murder, so my lawyer and I decided to be proactive and stop by."

"And you had to bring the dog with you?" the detective replied. "How'd you get him in the building anyway?"

"He's a trained military and law-enforcement officer." Mac neglected to mention that Gnarly was the only army K-9 that had been dishonorably discharged from the US Army. His case file was sealed, and to date, no one had been able to get it opened to find out why he was kicked out.

Lieutenant Hopkins looked down to where Gnarly was crawling on his belly to snag a breath mint that had bounced under a chair. His eyes narrowed. "Yeah. Right."

Moving around the desk to refocus the detective's attention off of Gnarly, who was in the midst of standing up and knocking over the chair after capturing the mint, Ed Willingham said, "My client came down here voluntarily to offer any assistance he can and to find out who killed Yvonne Harding, a good friend of his and the wife of his best friend."

"You should have called first," Lieutenant Hopkins told them with a chuckle. "Would have saved you and your attorney a trip. We got this case all wrapped up a few hours ago, and you, Faraday, are in the clear. So you can take your pooch and go home."

Gnarly's head snapped up from where he was sniffing the floor for more goodies, and he cast a glare at Hopkins. Clearly, he did not like being referred to as a "pooch."

Mac glanced around the noisy detective squad room. In his tailored suit and tie, Lieutenant Wayne Hopkins appeared out of place among the dozens of other detectives in their off-the-rack attire.

In spite of the grin that had come to Ed Willingham's lips when he heard the news, Mac was suspicious of how quickly Lieutenant Hopkins had switched suspects and closed the case.

"You got the shooter?" Mac asked.

"Yeah, we got him," Hopkins said. "He's in the morgue. Carl Rubenstein."

"But you said last night that he had no gunshot residue on his hands or clothes," Mac reminded him.

"Because he was wearing gloves," Hopkins said. "We found his gloves in the stairwell where he'd tossed them."

"Where in the stairwell?" Mac asked. "I was maybe a minute behind Rubenstein and ran all the way down the stairwell from the thirty-sixth to the ground floor. There were no gloves."

"Guess you're not as observant as you thought, Faraday."

"Even if you found gloves with gunshot residue on them, how about Rubenstein's clothes?" Mac asked. "Last night you said forensic found nothing on his clothes to indicate that he had fired a gun. He may have had time to toss the gloves, but he certainly didn't have time to change his clothes."

Behind his eyeglasses, Lieutenant Hopkin's eyes narrowed into a glare.

"Mac," Ed Willingham whispered in a warning tone.

"And the gun?" Mac asked. "The gun was found all the way down on the ground floor—thirty-six stories down."

"He threw the gun over the bannister, and that was where the gun landed," Hopkins said with a sigh of exasperation. "Ballistics proved that the bullets that killed both Yvonne Harding and Carl Rubenstein came from the three-eighty caliber handgun we recovered in the stairwell."

"Who fired the shot that killed Rubenstein?" Mac asked. "Don't tell me he fell on it, and it went off. I saw the body. It was not a contact wound."

"Mac, stop while we're ahead," Willingham said in a low voice.

"Not that this is your case, Faraday," Hopkins said with a glare. "But I'll tell you what our crime-scene people uncovered. Rubenstein killed himself by accident. As soon as he entered the stairwell, knowing that you and the dog were behind him, he tore off the gloves he was wearing when he shot Harding and tossed them on the landing at the thirty-sixth floor. Then he started making his way down the stairs, flight by flight. When your dog started gaining on him, he realized he needed to get rid of the gun so he wouldn't get caught with the murder weapon on him, so he tossed it. But the gun didn't go straight down through the stairwell. It hit the railing on one of the flights, causing it to go off, and the bullet ricocheted and hit Rubenstein in the chest, killing him. Ain't it ironic?"

"Quite," Mac replied.

With a dare in his tone, Lieutenant Hopkins asked, "Any other questions, Faraday?"

"No." Willingham grasped Mac firmly by the arm and turned him away from the police detective. "Thank you for your time, Lieutenant."

Looking over his shoulder back at the police detective, Mac's eyes locked with Hopkins before his lawyer managed to usher him and Gnarly outside the squad room.

"What was that all about?" Willingham asked. "Do you *want* to be a suspect in Yvonne's murder?"

"There were no gloves in that stairwell," Mac said, "and Hopkins didn't answer my question about gunshot residue on Rubenstein's clothes."

"Maybe Rubenstein was hiding behind a piece of scenery when he fired the shot and the residue didn't get on his clothes," Willingham said. "As for the gloves, you simply missed them. You were looking for a killer, not gloves."

"Dallas says Rubenstein had no reason to want Yvonne Harding dead. He was suing both her and ZNC for wrongful death in his wife's murder," Mac said. "With Yvonne dead—"

"He can sue her estate," Willingham said.

"But why kill Yvonne for causing the death of a woman he wanted rid of anyway?" Mac asked. "This whole investigation stinks. Hopkins knows who killed Yvonne and is covering it up. Whoever killed Yvonne has the power to make Hopkins a star, so he's crawled into bed with her murderer to cover it up." He shook his finger at his lawyer. "I'm going to find out who that is."

"Find out next week, after we get David back to Spencer and married." Willingham took his cell phone out of his pocket. "I'm calling the airport to schedule your flight. You and David are going to be back in Deep Creek Lake by dinner."

"What about Dallas?" Mac asked. "She's going to continue to dig into Audra's murder. We can't leave her here alone. My gut is telling me that they're going to go after her next. Didn't you say you had someone you could call to find out about that off-duty cop who was killed last night?"

With a tired sigh, Willingham slipped his phone into his pocket. "If I get you information on that murder, will you call in David, get on the plane, and go back to Spencer like a good boy?"

His face filled with innocence, Mac held up two fingers in a sign of scout's honor.

"I happen to know you were never a boy scout." His lawyer punched the elevator call button to take them up to the top floor of the police station.

Chapter Thirteen

"Are you okay, puddin'?"

In the confines of the elevator silently speeding up to the thirty-fifth floor, Dallas' question to David came out of the blue.

David was immersed in thoughts about Chelsea's continued cold shoulder toward him. The only time she had spoken to him since the news of his marriage to Yvonne had been when she'd answered his call the day before. That was because the nursing home had left a message for him on his voice mail about his mother becoming increasingly difficult to manage. Chelsea should have been relieved to hear the news that he was free to go through with the wedding due to Yvonne's death. But how could she have been happy without coming across as cold hearted? Chelsea had known Yvonne. She hadn't hated her, even though Yvonne had been friends with Katrina, who had broken him and Chelsea up.

Talk about ancient history!

Still, Chelsea had not answered the phone when he had called that morning to wish her a good day, which he knew would be especially needed since she was visiting his mother.

How can I marry a woman who won't even speak to me? How can I be married to a woman who doesn't trust me? Thoughts of his own parents' relationship made him shudder.

"Havin' second thoughts 'bout tyin' the knot?" Dallas' low, sultry voice sounded almost unearthly to him.

Lost in his thoughts, he replied in a low voice, "Yes."

"That was easy."

Realizing that the voice was coming from the lanky brunette standing next to him, David jerked his head to see Dallas was gazing at him. He saw an extra sparkle in her light brown eyes that brought an involuntary smile to his lips.

"Would you've still married Yvonne if you hadn't been drunk in Vegas?"

"Probably not," he said with a shake of his head. "You can love someone with all your heart, even if they'd be the worst person for you to marry."

The elevator chimed to signal that they had reached their floor. David held the doors open so Dallas could step out.

"What made Yvonne the worst person for you to marry?" she asked while slipping past him.

Within the space of the elevator doorway, she stopped to face him, her body close to his, her eyes locked with his, for only a few seconds—long enough for David to feel the electricity of her body drawing him to her.

"Hold that elevator, please!" called out a woman galloping down the corridor in high heels.

Breaking his gaze from Dallas', David slipped his arm around her waist to usher her off the elevator so the speeding woman could rush on. After releasing the door for her to descend, he hurried Dallas in the direction of Yvonne's corner office.

"We wanted different things," David explained. "I'm happy being a small-town police chief in Maryland. She wanted to be a star in the big city. The two lifestyles can't exactly sync with each other."

A grin came to her lips. "You're pretty young to be a police chief. You must be darn good."

"It's a small police force," David said. "I only have a dozen officers under me."

"My grandpappy on my mother's side was a Texas Ranger," she said. "*His* pappy was a county sheriff. Another great-grandfather was a Pinkerton. He was part of the posse that chased Butch Cassidy and the Sundance Kid into Mexico."

"With all that in your genes, why didn't your mother become a police officer?"

"Grandpappy wouldn't let 'er," she replied before stepping into the office. She stopped to look at the gaping hole where her mother's body had been discovered only the day before. "Said she'd get 'erself killed."

"I guess that's where your mother's and your thirst for justice came from." David went over to where the yellow tape was marking off the closet. The crime-scene investigators had done all that they'd needed to do. Now the tape served to warn people of the debris left behind.

After taking off her trench coat and hanging it on a coat hook, Dallas stepped over to the coffee maker to pour water into the carafe and prepare a pot. "Coffee?" she asked him while filling the pot from a jug of filtered water.

She was standing so close to where he was studying the closet as best he could without moving beyond the yellow tape that she could feel the heat from his body. Involuntarily, she swallowed down the excitement she was feeling.

Too quickly, he turned around and collided with her. The water in the pot spilled down the front of David's jeans.

Startled, Dallas dropped the pot, and it clattered to the floor, spilling the rest of the water at their feet.

"Oh, I'm so sorry!" She grabbed several paper towels from a roll on the break table and pressed them against the wet spot on his pants.

"Ali, are you okay? I heard you scream!" Ryan Ritter rushed into the doorway in time to see her pressing her hands against David's privates.

"I'll do that!" David snatched the paper towels out of her hands and turned away from her.

"But—"

"I've got it!" He hurried past her to go in search of the men's room, only to find Ryan Ritter blocking his escape.

Folding his arms across his chest, the noted journalist said, "David O'Call—is it O'Callaghan?"

"That's right, Mr. Ritter," David replied. "We met last night."

Instead of moving out of the way, Ryan offered David his hand. "I overheard you and Faraday talking last night. About you and Yvonne being married?"

"Which you, of course, told the police," David said.

"As a police chief, I'm sure you understand the importance of witnesses being straightforward with information they have. I couldn't not tell Hopkins."

With a sigh, David had to admit that Ryan Ritter was right.

"I'm so sorry for your loss." As they shook hands, Ryan chuckled. "Why she kept you a secret from everyone, I'll never know. Maybe she thought she'd go further in her career if everyone thought she was single. I knew her since her first day here at ZNC and had no idea. She certainly didn't act married."

"Yvonne was very good at keeping secrets." Gesturing in the direction of the hallway, David excused himself and hurried out.

Once David was gone, Ryan turned to Dallas, who had just pressed the button to get the coffee brewing. "You really had me worried last night, Ali."

After spending the morning with Mac and David, who had been calling her by her real name, it took a full moment for Dallas to recall that everyone at ZNC still knew her as Ali Hudson.

"My dentist was backed up with appointments," she said. "By the time I got here, the buildin' was in a lockdown. I told you that when you called."

"I mean after that," Ryan said. "I tried calling you later, but you didn't answer. I thought whoever killed Yvonne had gone after you."

"Because I turn my cell phone on to airplane mode at night so I don't have to listen to it beepin' and dingin' all night long." She fought to keep the annoyance she felt out of her tone. When she had turned her phone on earlier to call her brother, immediately several missed phone calls from Ryan Ritter spilled into the log. She grit her teeth to keep from pointing out to him that he was old enough to be her father.

He stepped up behind her. "I almost called the police," he said softly into her ear. "I worry about you—young small-town girl in the big city. Bad things could happen. Look at what happened to Yvonne."

Dallas scurried around her desk to move out of his reach. "Sir, I can take care of myself."

"I can see that." Ryan stood up straight. "You may not be aware of it, but you have a problem now that your boss is no longer with us." A slim smile crossed his face.

Trying to figure out his angle, Dallas stood up straight and studied him with her eyes narrowed.

"Ms. Hudson," said the chief of building security as he stepped through the open doorway and up to Dallas' desk. "I'm sorry about Yvonne Harding's death, ma'am. From what I've seen on *Crime Watch*, you two made a good team. She really appreciated your go-get-'em attitude."

"Thank you, Hank." Dallas eyed the official-looking envelope he was clutching in his hand. She had seen the security chief deliver identical envelopes in the past. Between the envelope and Ryan's comment about her being in trouble, she sensed what was coming next. "I believe you have something for me." She held out her hand.

Clearing his throat, Hank placed the envelope in her open palm. "I'm sorry, Ms. Hudson."

With one quick motion, Dallas ripped open the envelope and extracted the single sheet of paper. The language was formal and to the point. With the death of her supervisor, Yvonne Harding, who had hired her as her assistant, Ali Hudson's services were no longer needed.

She'd been fired.

"I'm to escort you out of the building," Hank said. "I'll give you twenty minutes to collect your personal items." He turned to leave only to have her stop him.

"I don't need twenty minutes. I can have my stuff together in one-half less than no time."

"Huh?" Hank looked over at Ryan.

"She's telling you to wait."

Dallas yanked open the side drawer of her desk and tossed her belongings into the bag. "Is Ian Griffith in yet?"

Hank shook his head.

"I wouldn't be expecting him in until this afternoon," Ryan said. "I saw him walking out with Preston Blakeley around eleven last night. They were going out for drinks to calm their nerves about Yvonne's murder." He added with a shake of his head, "Ian's not letting any grass grow under his feet as far as campaigning to host that new program ZNC was planning for Yvonne."

"The incompetent snake," Dallas said. "Ian Griffith doesn't have enough sense to spit downwind and Blakeley knows it."

"What does that mean?" Hank asked.

David stopped in the doorway when he returned to find Dallas packing and Ryan Ritter and another gentleman standing over her. "Is everything okay in here?"

"Looks like we can have that brunch you offered me, sugar," she said with a wide grin. "I've been *fired.*" She grabbed her coat off the hook.

"Not necessarily," Ryan said. "Ali, I can have you back on staff by lunch. I've been needing an executive assistant."

"You have Betty," Dallas said with a laugh while David helped her put on the trench coat. "She's been with you for over eight years."

"I could use two." Ryan scoffed. "In case you haven't noticed, *Ryan Ritter* is ZNC's top-rated show and has been for the last ten years running. If I need two executive assistants to keep me happy, ZNC will approve it like *that.*" He snapped his fingers. "Yvonne claimed that you were the best in the business, and from what I've seen, she wasn't lying. I'd be a fool to let you get away." He held out his hand for her to grasp. "Now you just come along with me upstairs, and we'll have a little talk with Preston."

Dallas refused to take it. "Thank you for the offer, Mr. Ritter, but I've already got a new job." Casting a glance in David's direction, she added, "Mac Faraday offered me a job this mornin'. As a matter of fact, I was comin' in to give my notice to Mr. Blakeley."

David's eyes grew wide at the news, which he knew was a bold-faced lie—a lie that Dallas had said as effortlessly as if it had been the truth. She was convincing enough that he had to pause to replay the events of the morning to see if he had indeed missed Mac's hiring her.

"Mr. Faraday hired me to be *his* executive assistant."

David jumped in. "Yvonne was raving about how thorough Ali is and about how she pays attention to the most minute details. So he called her this morning to offer her a job with a significant increase in pay and full benefits."

Ryan's eyes narrowed. "Looks like you made out with Yvonne's murder. Better hope the police detective investigating the case doesn't find out."

Dallas slung the strap for her bag over her shoulder. "I have no doubt that he will." She reached out for David's hand. "You ready to go tie on the feed bag, lamb chop?"

"Sounds good to me, dear." David took her hand into his. "It was nice seeing you again, gentlemen." With that, they left the office.

In the corridor, Hank hurried to pass the two of them and to call for the elevator. Making his way toward them, a clerk was pushing a mail cart filled with stacks of bound envelopes and packages.

Dallas was eying the cart.

Grasping Dallas' hand, David was aware of Ryan Ritter following close behind them.

"Are you moving to Deep Creek Lake to work for Mac Faraday?" Ryan asked her.

"That is where he lives," Dallas replied as they closed in on the cart.

"Exactly what does he need you to do for him?" Ryan asked while the three of them passed the cart.

With a cry, Dallas toppled to the side directly onto the mail cart. On her way to the floor, she grabbed the end of the cart, which rolled over and landed on top of her.

David was the first one to reach her. "Are you okay?" Tossing the mail cart aside, he bent over in time to see Dallas shoving something into her oversized bag. Ryan, Hank, and the mail clerk hurried to offer Dallas their hands to help her to her feet.

"I'm fine," she gasped out while rolling over onto her knees. "I fell off my heels. Lucky thing this cart was here to catch my fall." She tossed her purse strap over her shoulder before holding out her hand to David.

Wrapping his other arm around her waist, he lifted her to her feet. While helping her straighten her clothes, he took notice the large brown padded envelope she had shoved into her bag. The return address read "Roberts."

The mail clerk didn't see that she'd taken the envelope—he was too busy eying the mess of letters scattered all over the floor like fallen leaves in the autumn.

"Sorry 'bout the mess, hon," Dallas apologized while David ushered her onto the elevator.

On the ground floor, Dallas quickly turned in her building security badge and the key to Yvonne's office. Then, amid good wishes from the security staff, she trotted out of the building as fast as she could without attracting attention.

"What did you just steal off that mail cart?" David asked her in a hushed voice once they were out onto the street.

Her hand still in his, Dallas continued up the street at a brisk pace. "Just keep walkin', darlin', an' don't look back."

The last place Archie Monday had expected to be three days before David and Chelsea's wedding was the emergency room at Garrett County Memorial Hospital. She and Chelsea were supposed to be meeting with the music director at the church to go over the final music selection for that Saturday.

Thinking about the meeting, Archie grumbled. Actually, it should have been Chelsea and David meeting with the music director, but since David was in New York … Her grumble turned into a growl.

Archie had worked herself up to a full-fledged mad by the time she got to the waiting room, where she found Bogie playing patty-cake with a little girl who was there with her mother. "How's Chelsea?"

"She had a grand mal seizure." After accepting a hug from the child, Bogie stood up from the old, faded sofa and turned his attention to Archie. "She's come out of it already and is resting. The doctor is with her now."

"Didn't Molly warn her so that she could take her medication?" Glancing around, Archie noticed that Chelsea's service dog was missing. "Where's Molly?"

"She's with Chelsea in the examination room," Bogie said. "Molly did warn her, but I think Chelsea was too upset to notice."

"Upset about what?"

Bogie sucked in a deep breath. "Violet went ape on her. Thought she was Robin."

"That's the last thing Chelsea needs right now," Archie said. "She's already mad at David for getting married without knowing it. The last thing she needs is his crazy loon of a mother attacking her."

"I know." Bogie nodded his head in the direction behind her. "Doc's on his way now. I've been trying to think of where I know him from. He looks familiar."

Archie spun around on her heels to watch a huge man in green doctor's scrubs making his way toward them. He was clearly as tall as Bogie with broad shoulders and a barrel chest. In contrast to his intimidating size, he had a welcoming smile that—even from down the hallway—made Archie feel at ease. As he approached them, he stuck out his hand to Bogie. "Deputy Chief Bogie, good to see you again."

Suddenly recognition filled the deputy chief's face. "Blanchard! Seth Blanchard!" He turned to Archie. "That's why I know him. Seth grew up in Spencer. Swept the science fair every year. His mother is chief of staff here at the hospital." He turned back to Seth. "I thought you moved out of the area—thought you were working at Johns Hopkins?"

"Now I'm back," he explained. "Garrett Memorial made me an offer I couldn't refuse. Head of ER." He looked down at Archie. "You must be Chelsea's friend Archie. She was worried about upsetting your schedule—something about a wedding?"

"She's getting married this weekend," Archie said.

"To David O'Callaghan." Bogie told her, "Seth went to school with Chelsea and David and all of them."

"So Chelsea and David are finally getting married?" Seth mused. "She didn't tell me she was marrying *David* … only …" His voice trailed off.

"How is she, Doctor?" Archie asked.

Seth paused before replying. "She's resting right now. Grand mal seizures can really wipe you out. It's best if she takes it easy." Looking around, he asked, "Where's the groom, by the way?"

"He's out of town," Bogie said.

"Investigating a murder. He's the chief of police in Spencer. When can we take Chelsea home?"

"I'd like to keep her overnight to run some tests. An MRI—"

"But we have a wedding this weekend," Archie objected. "Over two hundred guests."

"It wouldn't be a very nice wedding if the bride collapsed in front of over two hundred guests, would it?" Seth asked with a slightly smug grin.

Archie placed her hands on her hips. "When can we see Chelsea?"

Seth gestured down the hallway. "Examination room one. I'll go arrange for her to be checked into a room and join you shortly."

"This is not good," Archie told Bogie. "First, David has to go to New York to divorce a wife he didn't know he—" Watching the doctor make his way to the nurse's station to check Chelsea in, she punched Bogie in the chest. "Did you see that?"

Grabbing the gun he wore on his hip, Bogie whirled around to see the threat he assumed Archie had identified. "See what?"

"That doctor!" She jerked her head in the direction of the nurse's station. "Just now! Did you see the bounce in his step?" Grabbing Bogie by the front of his shirt, she hissed, "I think he's interested in more than Chelsea's medical condition."

Looking down the hallway to where Dr. Seth Blanchard was joking with two nurses while completing the necessary forms, Bogie said, "Oh, I wouldn't doubt it."

Archie's eyes widened. "Then I'm right?"

"Seth always had a thing for Chelsea," Bogie said. "Everyone knew about it."

"Then he's keeping her here in the hospital so he can make a move on her while David's out of town," she said.

"That's what I'd do if I were in his shoes."

"Not on my watch!" Archie whipped out her cell phone.

Chapter Fourteen

With a growl, Mac tossed the poop-filled baggie into the garbage and yanked off the evidence gloves after it. "You better not have left them in Central Park this morning. You wouldn't have. Would you have?"

Innocence filled the German shepherd's face. He cocked his head at Mac.

"Look, Gnarly," Mac whispered at him. "You only have two days left to cough—I mean, give them up."

Gnarly's ears fell back. Hanging his head, he uttered a whine.

Squatting down in front of him, Mac stroked the top of his head. "You can do it, buddy. I know you can. Not for me. For David and Chelsea and Molly … Do it for Molly. You like Molly." Grinning, Mac nodded his head while picking up the leash. "Next one's for Molly." He held out his hand. "Deal?"

Gnarly placed his paw into Mac's palm to shake.

Feeling the phone vibrate on his hip, Mac checked the caller ID on his cell before bringing it to his ear. "Hey, hon, what's going on there?"

"Everything's falling apart," Archie said. "David needs to get back ASAP."

Mac rose to his feet. "Why? What's going on?"

"Violet went ape on Chelsea, she had a seizure, and now she's stuck in the hospital with Dr. Love, who's planning to put the moves on her. So David's got to get his butt on a plane and get back home, or there's not going to be any bride for him to marry."

Lost, Mac asked, "What? Is Chelsea okay?"

"No," Archie said. "She's in the emergency room, and Dr. Love is checking her in so he can lure her away from David and the wedding. Yvonne's dead, right? That means David's free to marry Chelsea. So get him on a plane and back down here to fight for the woman he loves—ASAP."

As if Archie were there in front of him, Mac held up his hand in a gesture for her to calm down. "Okay, I understand. David's doing something for me right now, but he's been cleared as a suspect. So as soon as he gets back to the hotel, we'll check out and fly back home. We should be there by dinnertime."

"Good," Archie said. "Tell him to hurry up. This doctor looks way too happy."

"He's a nice guy," Mac heard Bogie say in the background.

"I don't care," Archie replied to Bogie. "Let him get his own girl!" Abruptly, her tone went up an octave. "Oh my God, he's bringing her flowers!" Returning to her conversation with Mac, she hissed, "Tell that pilot to step on it!" As an afterthought, she added "I love you" before disconnecting the call.

Stunned at how quickly everything had changed—it had only been one day—Mac looked down at Gnarly, who was gazing back up at him. "Maybe we're not going to need those rings after all."

"Mac, what are you and Gnarly doing out there?" Ed Willingham called to them from the back door leading into the police station. "Never mind, I don't want to know.

You wanted information about that dead police officer? I've got someone who'll talk to you. But not here." He checked the time on his watch. "We've got five minutes to get there." He gestured at Gnarly. "Are you through here?"

Mac's sigh was filled with exasperation. "Yeah, we're done here." He led Gnarly out of the alley to join Willingham at the curb, where the lawyer hailed a taxi.

"Lucky for you, I know people," Ed said once they were settled in the backseat of the cab with Gnarly sitting in between them.

"I know you know people," Mac said. "That's why you're my people."

"Person," Ed corrected him.

"Huh?"

"I'm not a people," Ed said. "I'm a person. Singular. One people is a person, not people."

"I know that," Mac said.

"Then why did you call me your people?"

"I was following—" Disgusted, Mac noted that the cab was pulling over in front of a corner diner. "Forget it. We're here. Let's go meet your *person*."

In Spencer, Maryland, a diner would find itself in the midst of a lull during the midmorning hours between breakfast and lunch. That was not the case at the midtown Manhattan diner and delicatessen. Customers shopping for fresh lunch meat, cheeses, and salads were lined up in front of the deli case, where two clerks were hurrying to fill their orders and dodging the two cooks preparing meals for patrons in the diner section of the establishment. Practically every table was filled with customers enjoying either late breakfasts or early lunches.

When Mac, Ed, and Gnarly entered the diner, one of the servers who was carrying a tray filled with luncheon plates stopped when she saw Gnarly. Before she could chase them out, Mac said, "He's a service dog."

"Where's his vest?"

"He was mugged," Mac replied. "In the park ... this morning. The guy had a poodle—it was awful." He stroked Gnarly's head.

With his ears laid back flat on his head, Gnarly gazed up imploringly at the server.

Seeing the server soften in response to the dog's pleading eyes, Mac said, "He was totally traumatized."

"We just came from the police station," Ed added.

Without saying a word, she continued on her way to deliver her order.

Ed led them back to a table in the far corner where a thin woman with ultrashort dark hair was drinking a cup of coffee. Ed quickly introduced her as Lieutenant Abby Gibbons. "She's an investigator with internal affairs."

Even while he shook her hand, Mac felt the hair on the back of his neck stand up on end. Sensing the tension, Gnarly shot out from under the table where he'd just lain down between Mac and Abby.

"Believe it or not, I'm on your side," she said in response to seeing Mac almost back away from the table. "I know your background, Faraday. You were a good cop. But don't tell me that during your career you never once encountered bad cops. It's my department's job to get rid of them. The way things are nowadays, one bad cop ruins the reputation—and threatens the lives—of thousands upon thousands of the good cops who go out every day to literally lay their lives on the line for the public, many of whom don't appreciate it."

"I know exactly where you're coming from," Mac said. "It's just been my experience that sometimes in internal affair's quest to weed out the bad cops, the reputations of good cops get ruined along the way—"

"And you never once accused someone of murder who ended up being innocent?" Lieutenant Gibbons shot back. "All we care about is getting at the truth—just like you." With a shake of her head, she took a sip of her coffee. "The media never tells the public about the good white cop who took a bullet for a black mugging victim. That happened just last week. The officer survived but will be in the hospital for another week and in physical therapy for months. But let a journalist find out about a white cop who shot a black heroin addict choking his partner to death and refusing to let go, and suddenly the whole country hears about it, and we have riots and looting. Last year, we lost two good cops in an ambush in retaliation for one white cop who'd shot a black kid whose rap sheet for violence was as long as your arm."

"And I'm sure that the politicians and members of the media fanning the flames had nothing to do with those two cops being ambushed," Mac said with heavy sarcasm.

"I totally agree," she replied. "Better for IA to keep a heavy finger on the pulse of the police to weed out the bad ones before things reach that point."

Mac could see by the set of her jaw as she took a sip of her coffee that she was bitterly angry. It was more than a matter of bad publicity. Many good officers had died in the line of duty without so much as an acknowledgment from the same media and politicians who jumped to politicize incidents that could be easily spun to serve their own agendas.

Mac's perception of her as the enemy shifted. Swallowing, he asked, "What can you tell me about the off-duty police officer who was killed a couple of blocks from the News Corp building last night?"

Her forehead wrinkled when she furrowed her brow. "Why do you want to know?"

"A friend of mine was attacked. She didn't report it, because she got away. I'm suspicious because it was shortly after

Yvonne Harding was murdered, and this friend of mine was a close associate of hers. I want to know if the attempted attack could be connected to Harding's murder."

"Officer Warren Tate wasn't an off-duty police officer," she said. "He was on suspension for sexual harassment of female suspects and police brutality. His last victim was a prostitute who recorded him threatening to arrest her for solicitation unless she serviced him for free. On top of all that, units have made several domestic abuse calls to his home, but they've kept them off the books. After he was suspended, his wife got a restraining order."

"So he has a violent history," Mac said. "Do you have any idea why he would try to mug a woman—or maybe worse?"

He had half expected her to shrug her shoulders and answer that she didn't. Instead, she looked directly across the table at him, studying him and apparently weighing her options.

"Well?" Mac prodded her.

"Off the record?" she asked Ed Willingham.

"That's why we're meeting here instead of in your office, Abby," Ed said.

"Tate was one of a group of officers who have been on my radar for quite a while," she said. "It started out as little things. A suspect would claim the officer roughed him up—that type of stuff. But then the incident reports involving these particular officers gradually became more serious. A defense attorney would tell me, off the record, that his client claimed he'd had twice as much cocaine on him as what was written in the arrest report. A couple of times, defendants swore evidence had been planted."

"Those claims always happen," Mac said.

"I know, but there's something about these cases that makes me believe the suspects filing the claims," she said. "When I put pressure on the detective in charge of the case where the defendant claimed the evidence had been planted, he found evidence proving the suspect was indeed innocent. The evidence against him had been planted and the only one who could have done it was Officer Warren Tate. Lately, cases like these always involved one or more of this particular group of officers, who I now refer to as the 'Dirty Six.' When I looked into their backgrounds, I found that they'd all originated from the same precinct in the Bronx. Found out that they all hung out together. Drank together at the same cop bar. One of them has a very expensive boat. Another one just put in a new swimming pool." She sat back in her seat. "Warren Tate was one of the Dirty Six."

"What about the remaining five?" Ed asked. "Are they all still on the force?"

"Yes, and I can't get anything concrete to use to move on them," she said. "Wish I could. In the last couple of years, they've become more organized."

"Wouldn't that be normal?" Mac said. "If they're going to pull off bigger stuff, they have to plan better."

Slowly, she shook her head. "I think someone realized what they were doing and decided to recruit them for bigger things. I suspect they now have a leader—one who's not on my radar."

"What type of bigger things?"

"Paid muscle, or maybe even worse," she said. "Six months ago, a witness for a major murder case involving the son of a heavy hitter on Wall Street was killed in a home invasion. He, his wife, and two of their three children were killed. The murder case got tossed out of court. The witness's teenaged daughter survived. She gave a description of one of the men who broke into the house. When we got a suspect and put him in the police lineup, she didn't pick him. She picked one of the officers standing in—Warren Tate. The witness swears up and down it was him. One hundred percent certainty. The prosecutor came to me, and I dug into Tate. Found that he was off duty that night, as were three other members of the Dirty Six. The victim says four men broke into the house."

"Why would cops kill a witness?" Ed asked with a catch in his throat.

"That's the thing," she said. "*They* had no motive. But the defendant in our murder case comes from a family that believe firmly in bending, if not breaking, the rules. Their pockets are deep enough to pay for it."

"Cops moonlighting as paid assassins," Mac said.

"And I believe they have a ringleader within the police department," Abby said. "Has to be someone on the inside. In spite of all the work I've done investigating them, digging into their stories, and interviewing them, every time I think I'm on the verge of nailing them, they slip away. None of the six is smart enough to do that. There's another member of their group who I haven't identified, and he's leading them."

Mac sat back in his chair. "Then Warren Tate has to be involved in Yvonne Harding's murder. With his police identification, he could have easily left the building even after the lockdown."

"In that case, we're talking murder for hire," Ed said.

"Whoever hired him had Yvonne's assistant on the list to make sure there were no loose ends." Mac turned back to Abby. "What's the estimated time and cause of death for Tate?"

"His throat was slashed between eleven and midnight," she replied.

"Throat slashed?" Mac asked. "Are you sure about the time?"

She nodded her head. "That's what the preliminary autopsy report says. Why?"

"Harding's assistant says she was attacked shortly before eight o'clock, and she got away by jabbing him in the throat with ninja spikes."

"He did have bruises and small puncture wounds on his throat, but nothing fatal. The ME says those were at least a couple of hours old. What killed him was a deep cut across the throat that sliced through his jugular."

"Then it wasn't her," Mac said. "Someone else killed him." He sighed. "Maybe whoever hired him felt he was too much of a liability."

"If the murderer has cops working for him, how can you investigate Yvonne's murder without the killer being one step ahead of us?" Ed asked.

"You can't," Mac said. "Who better for a criminal to have working for him?"

Ed agreed. "Even when the media is against the cops, generally, people trust them."

"Cops can get in and out of places that others can't," Mac said. "Like police evidence lockers. And then they can remove evidence. Pull up to a witness in a cop car and uniform, and say the detective downtown needs him—" He shrugged his shoulders. "Most people would just climb in without a second thought."

"You scare me," David told Dallas after they had trotted across the first street on their way back to the Four Seasons.

"Really, O'Callaghan?" She batted her long eyelashes at him. "A big ol' man like you, scared by a little ol' girl like me?"

"You just shot off a lie back there at Ryan Ritter as smooth as they come," David said. "I know most of the tells for lying, and I didn't see one. You're either a con woman or a pathological liar."

"Maybe I'm both." She stopped at the curb to allow traffic to speed by, even though the walk light was on. Keeping pace with her, David stopped short, but not before almost getting clipped by a taxi. "Here in New York, sweetie, walkers don't have the right of way," she told him while brushing away an imaginary speck of dirt on his sports coat. She admired the sweater he wore underneath. "I like that color on you. It brings out your baby blues."

David remained serious. "Why did you lie to Ritter? He was offering you a very good job. From what I see, he's huge in your business. He could really help you."

"Help me right into bed." Stepping off the curb, she hurried across the street, with David rushing to keep up. In spite of her high heels, Dallas had no trouble moving quickly when she wanted to. "He's been chasin' me ever since I stepped foot in ZNC."

"Well, you are an attractive woman."

She stopped so abruptly that David had continued several feet before he realized she was no longer walking in step with him. When he turned back to her, a slow grin worked its way across her face. "You almost had me convinced you hadn't noticed."

"You're kind of hard not to notice," David said.

Sauntering up to him, she said, "A man doesn't tell a woman that she's *attractive* unless he's *attracted* to her." She gazed up into his eyes.

Standing toe to toe with her, David noticed that she was much taller than Chelsea. With her high heels, her forehead came up to the bridge of his nose.

"Honey, I do believe you *are* attracted to me," she said in a low voice.

"I notice every woman who shows me her breasts." Tearing his gaze from hers, he grabbed her hand, and they continued down the street. "Was Ritter chasing after Yvonne?"

"I think they had a fling a while back," she said. "I don't know that for a fact. It was just a feelin' I had. A sort of familiarity between the two of them, but not from somethin' recent. Like they had a past together."

"What's in the package you stole from the mail cart? Nice move, by the way."

"Thanks," she said. "I learned long ago that when an *attractive* woman falls down, men are so anxious to help her up that they don't notice anythin' besides her T and A—especially when she manages to spill stuff out of her bag. They're so afraid they might lay eyes on her diaphragm that they purposely don't look to see what she's shovin' into her bag."

"Well, I did notice you stuffing a brown envelope into it," David said. "What's in the package?"

"I'm hopin' somethin' that'll lead me to Mom's killer."

They stopped short when a police car tore around a corner to block their path across the next intersection. They were only one block from the Four Seasons Hotel. Two police officers climbed out of the cruiser.

"Ms. Ali Hudson?" the police officer who had been sitting in the passenger seat said.

Dallas clutched her shoulder bag. "Yes."

David noticed the driver talking into his cell phone, not the radio he was wearing on his belt.

"We've been asked to bring you into the precinct for questioning."

"Is this about Yvonne Harding's murder?" Dallas asked.

"Maybe. They just told us to bring you in." The police officer, whose nameplate read "Sauer," reached out for her arm.

"Not without me." David stepped between them.

The officer turned back to his partner, who nodded his head. "Sure. But you'll have to turn over your weapons." Sauer grinned. "I don't know how they do things in your little police department in Maryland, but here we don't allow people packing firearms in the cruiser." He held out his hand for David to turn over his gun.

While David understood the safety procedure—his department had the same rule—he felt apprehensive about turning over his weapon to Officer Sauer.

Maybe it's paranoia. Something just doesn't feel right. But they are officers driving a real cruiser.

Slowly, David reached behind his back and under his sports coat to extract his gun from its holster. Holding it by only two fingers, he handed it to the officer.

While tucking David's gun into his front waistband, Officer Sauer said, "Your backup weapon, too."

David felt as if the officer were asking him to strip down to the skin on the street. The hair on the back of his neck was saying that the last thing he wanted to do was get into that cruiser totally unarmed. His eyes narrowed while he peered at the barrel-chested officer smirking at him.

"You were the one who said you wanted to come along," Officer Sauer said. "No ticket, no ride. Who knows? I suspect they'll have some questions for you, too. So hand it over."

With a sigh of disgust, David knelt down to lift his pant leg and remove the weapon. He could feel Dallas gazing at him from where the driver was ushering her into the backseat of the cruiser. Even with Officer Sauer standing between them, he could feel her fear.

Feeling like he was making a fatal error, David slapped his weapon into Officer Sauer's open palm.

Chapter Fifteen

Ed Willingham studied the room-service menu for an item that would be sufficiently sinful—that is, something he wouldn't be allowed to eat at home in front of his wife—yet not so naughty that it would raise his cholesterol.

Across the table, Mac was pressing in the phone number for Audra Walker's former executive assistant, Letty Bolger, whose number Ed had managed to get from his contacts.

"What are you hoping to get from Audra's assistant?" Ed asked.

"She was traveling with Audra on that tour," Mac said. "She most likely would have accompanied Audra to ZNC for her interview. That makes her a witness. She can tell us who Audra talked to and what they talked about."

Mac sat up straight in his chair when an elderly woman answered the phone.

"Is this Letty Bolger?" Mac asked.

"May I ask who's callin'?" she replied in a hesitant tone.

"This is Mac Faraday. I was friends with Audra Walker. I'm sure you heard that her body was found yesterday here in New York ... in the News Corp Building." He listened to the silence on the other end of the line before adding, "Audra

Walker worked with me on a homicide case that I investigated years ago."

"I remember," she replied. "In Washington, DC. We never met, but she spoke about you. Very sharp … and a great tush."

"Excuse me?"

"Butt," Letty clarified. "If you're the one I think Audra was talkin' 'bout, she ranked yours a nine."

What is it with these Southern women? Mac felt the blush go all the way up to his hairline.

"Are you okay, Mac?" Ed asked, "You look flushed."

With a shake of his head, Mac returned to the reason for his call. "Letty, Audra and I were friends. I'd like to find out who killed her. Now it looks like she was murdered in the News Corp Building, which was near where the cab dropped her off when she went back to Midtown. That was the same building where Yvonne Harding interviewed her."

"I saw on the news that Yvonne Harding was shot last night," Letty said.

"Exactly," Mac said. "Am I right in assuming you went with Audra to the News Corp Building for her interview with Yvonne Harding?"

"The last time I saw Audra was at the hotel after the interview," Letty said. "I told the police that. I didn't even know she'd left. She was workin' when I went to bed."

"But for some reason she went back to the News Corp Building."

"The police said she got a text from Yvonne Harding, but Yvonne said it wasn't her."

"That text came from a burner phone that was never located," Mac said. "Did you go with her to the Yvonne Harding interview?"

"I always went to interviews with Audra," Letty said.

"What happened at that interview?" Mac asked. "Did anything strike you as unusual? Even if you don't think it has anything to do with her murder, I want to hear it."

There was a long silence before Letty answered him in slow, measured words. "Somethin' inspired her—at least, that's the only way I can put it."

"Inspired her?"

"There was this book that Audra had been workin' on for as long as I knew her," Letty said. "And I worked for her for fifteen years before she disappeared—I mean died."

"The Texan Romeo and Juliet," Mac said. "Dallas told me about it."

"You know Dallas?"

"Yes." Not wanting to reveal that Dallas was in New York, he rushed on. "What about this book?"

"Audra hadn't done any work on that book for years," Letty said. "I thought she'd given up on it. Suddenly, when we were leavin' the News Corps Building and were in its elevator, she called Joyce, her office assistant back here in Texas. She told her to get the folder on her desktop at her office and to send it to her laptop. She didn't even want to stop to eat. She jumped on it as soon as we got back to the hotel and was still workin' on it when I went to bed at ten o'clock." She paused and then added, "Audra told me she'd had a breakthrough."

"What kind of a breakthrough?" Mac asked.

"She didn't say."

"So she talked to someone," Mac said. "Or something someone said provided a breakthrough on this Romeo-and-Juliet story that she had basically abandoned years before?"

"Oh, she never abandoned the project," Letty said. "Audra would have never abandoned it. It was too important to her. The real-life Juliet was Audra's best friend in high school. Audra always felt there was somethin' weird about their suicide pact. She believed it was murder, but she couldn't prove it. She didn't have all the pieces. But that night ... somethin' happened."

"Can you e-mail me everything she had for the project?" he asked her.

"Sure. The police have it. Dallas has it. I can send it to you, too, I guess. Maybe you can figure out what got in her craw at ZNC. No one else seems to have been able to."

"Maybe a pair of fresh eyes can make sense of it. Who did Audra talk to that night?"

"Everyone," Letty said with a sigh. "All four hosts on *Crime Watch*. Very nice people. Pam Wiehl struck me as rather distant. She didn't talk much to Audra."

"Any idea why?"

"I assumed professional jealousy. Pam and Audra had the same publisher. Pam had just released a book 'bout white slavery and sex crimes against young women, particularly young American girls travelin' in Europe. Young women were bein' lured to Europe with promises of good jobs and travel, only to be abducted and forced into prostitution. Pam considered that to be a very important subject. Both Audra's and her book made it onto the *New York Times* best-sellers list, but Audra's was higher on the list, and she was gettin' more media attention."

"Because her book was about the murder of a sex symbol who was having an affair with a US Senator," Mac said. "Juicier and sexier topic."

"Audra was used to it," Letty said. "Pam Wiehl considered her to be a sensationalistic journalist and was jealous that she was makin' more money and gettin' more awards and publicity than she was. That's why Yvonne Harding was interviewin' her. Pam Wiehl considered herself to be above interviewin' a muckrakin' journalist like Audra."

"Did she actually say that?"

"No, but I could feel it," Letty said. "She hardly said anythin' to Audra. Audra would walk into the room, and Pam Wiehl would leave. At one point, in the control booth, I overheard her husband, Jim, tell her that she had to talk to Audra. Well Pam said she couldn't because she was afraid she'd say somethin' that she'd regret, and if that happened, everyone would know."

"Know what?" Mac asked.

"I have no idea," Letty said. "Obviously, the Wiehls had a secret that they were afraid Audra knew 'bout or would find out 'bout and make public, and that was why Pam was steerin' clear of her."

"Had Audra ever met the Wiehls before that night?"

"Sure. Audra always did interviews with ZNC when she had a new book released, which was 'bout once a year. Pam Wiehl had interviewed her quite a few times. But for that last tour, Pam refused to interview her and pushed her off on Yvonne, who considered it to be a huge opportunity. Audra was a Pulitzer Prize–winnin' author, you know."

"Anyone else?" Mac Asked. "Do you remember anything else from that evening?"

"Ryan Ritter flirted with her," she said with a smile in her voice. "I think they even made a date. He's so handsome and charmin', and he's got this sexy New England accent. He asked Audra to appear on his show the next week. She said she would, and we made arrangements for his assistant to call me the next morning to set up the interview. I think she took a likin' to him, because when we were leavin' the studio after the interview, he stopped her at the door and asked if he could call her later. She told him that she would be expectin' his call. And then she winked at him and called him Tex."

"Tex?" Mac repeated the name while noting that Ryan Ritter hailed from Boston. *Most likely a term of endearment.*

She used to call me Slim. Of course, I was slimmer then. He groaned while he thought of the fifteen pounds he had put on since receiving his inheritance.

"Oh, I just remembered somethin'!"

Her gasp caught Mac's attention.

"The CEO, Preston Blakeley," Letty said. "Audra and he got into a real row."

"What about?"

"Because Audra does her homework," Letty said with a grin in her voice. "She found out that Preston Blakeley was a big supporter of and had made huge donations to Senator Brennan's campaign. On the way to the studio, she predicted that he would cause trouble. Sure 'nuff, as soon as we got there, one of his minions met her in the studio to tell her that they were pullin' the plug on the interview. Well, if you really knew Audra like you said you did, then you know that it's not a good idea to try to pull a fast one on her. Why, when Audra Walker got riled up, she made a hornet look cuddly. She followed that minion back up to Blakeley's office, slammed the door, and had a private one on one when him. Five minutes later, when she walked out, the interview was back on. I looked in the office at that CEO, and he looked like she'd given him the wire-brush treatment."

"What did she say to him?"

"I have no idea," Letty replied.

"I wonder if that got her killed."

In the back of the police cruiser, Dallas jumped in her seat when she saw it turn left instead of right. "Aren't you taking us to the Tenth?"

"No, the Thirteenth," the driver replied.

Her eyes wide, Dallas glanced over at David, who said, "But the detective investigating Yvonne Harding's murder came from the Tenth."

"The detective investigating Yvonne's murder came from the Tenth, Stan," Officer Sauer said in a mocking tone.

"Stop the car!" Dallas ordered. "Now!"

"Stop the car!" Officer Sauer cackled. "Now!"

"We'll be stopping soon enough," Stan said in a low, steady tone.

David looked out the window. The cruiser rolled past a line of police vehicles parked in front of a police department with a sign on it that said Thirteenth Precinct. He felt Dallas curl her long fingers around his hand. She was trembling.

She moved over close to him to whisper in his ear. "They're taking us to the East River."

Keeping his eyes locked on the two officers in the front seat, David whispered, "When we get there—no matter what happens—stay in the car."

He turned his head slightly to look into her eyes and squeezed her hand in an effort to transmit courage to her. Her chest was heaving up and down with quick, nervous breaths.

The cruiser made its way down an alley between two old warehouses. The East River came into view straight up ahead.

As Dallas stared into David's eyes, her breathing steadied. She reached into her bag and extracted the ninja spike, which she placed in David's hand. While wrapping his fingers around the spikes, David looked up into the rearview mirror and saw Stan watching them.

The cruiser came to a stop.

"End of the line for the lovebirds." With yet another laugh, Officer Sauer unlatched his seatbelt and threw open the door.

In contrast, his no-nonsense partner, Stan, turned off the police car and opened the car door like he was making a routine call.

Officer Sauer yanked open David's door. "Ever seen the East River before, Chief? Now's your chance." He grabbed David by the right arm to drag him out.

"Don't move," David hissed at Dallas.

Laughing like a hyena at the slow, deliberate pace in which his latest victim was climbing out of the safety of the police cruiser, Officer Sauer was unprepared when David spun around to deliver a spiked blow with his left fist to the right side of his throat. Two of the spikes punctured his neck. He was still reeling from the shock when David reached down to the officer's midsection to grab the grip of his gun, which was still tucked in his waistband, and pulled the trigger, firing a shot through Sauer's lower abdomen.

In one smooth movement, David ripped the weapon from Officer Sauer's pants and fired off three shots across the roof of the cruiser at Stan, who was still in the process of drawing his weapon in response to David's attack. One of David's shots hit Stan in the neck, and another hit him between the eyes—but not before the officer managed to get one shot off.

David felt a burning sensation not unlike that of a branding iron across his left upper arm. Aware of movement at his feet, he turned to see that although Sauer was wounded, he was struggling to extract his gun from his holster.

"No, you don't," David said before firing two shots into his head.

Officer Sauer dropped down to the pavement. Blood flowed freely from his wounds and pooled around him.

All David could see was the badge pinned to the officer's chest. *I shot a cop. One of my own. A brother. Two brothers.*

"This one's buzzard bait," Dallas said, her announcement breaking through his thoughts. "How 'bout that one?"

Stunned at what he had done, David could only stare down at the police badge shining off of the late morning sunlight. Later, he would not remember seeing Dallas come around the car, extract the ninja spikes from his hand, and kneel down next to Officer Sauer to check for a pulse.

"They're both dead." She took Officer Sauer's gun from his holster and handed it to David. "You're gonna be needin' this."

His hands were so numb that David could barely feel the cold metal when he took the weapon. He tucked it into the waistband of his pants and covered it up with his sweater. "Take his spare magazines, too." His own voice sounded like it was in a fog.

She was already handing him the magazines, which he slipped into his pockets. Seeing the bloody tear through the left sleeve of his sports coat, she gasped. "You've been shot."

Squinting at her, David shook his head. He didn't understand what she'd said until she started poking through the hole in his sleeve to examine the wound.

"Looks like Stan managed to clip you before you took him out," she said. "You might be needin' a couple of stitches. Right now, we need to get outta here."

She dropped back down next to the dead police officer to search his pockets. She extracted the backup weapon that he had taken from David earlier. While David placed his weapon back in his ankle holster, Dallas removed Officer Sauer's backup weapon and placed it, holster and all, around her own ankle.

"Do you know how to use a gun?" David asked.

With a grin, she unholstered the thirty-two semiautomatic, extracted the magazine to check the rounds, shoved the magazine back into the grip, and then checked the sights.

"I wouldn't be a real Texan if I didn't know how to shoot a gun." She slipped the weapon into its holster and pulled down her pant leg. "Sugar, police are gonna to be here faster than a prairie fire with a tail wind," she said while urging him to his feet. "Since we don't know which ones are the bad guys, we need to go underground till we get it figured out." Clutching her shoulder bag close to her with one arm, she tugged his arm with the other.

David took one last look at Officer Sauer. "I'm sorry," he murmured.

Grabbing him by both arms, Dallas forced him to look at her. Her tone was gentle yet firm. "You had no choice, hon. They were gonna *kill* us."

Far in the distance, David heard police sirens growing nearer.

"It's time to blow this pop stand, partner," she said. "Now!"

Forcing one foot in front of the other, David allowed her to lead him down the river and through an alleyway back toward the city—away from the approaching police sirens.

Chapter Sixteen

"Mac, are you going to finish those fries?" Ed Willingham eyed the untouched pile of fries on the plate across the table from him.

Absorbed in the research notes that Letty Bolger had e-mailed to him, Mac had only eaten half of his BLT sandwich and hadn't touched the fries that room service had brought up for their lunch.

Like a couple of vultures, Ed was eying the uneaten fries while Gnarly was focusing his attention on the leftover sandwich.

"Take them." Without taking his eyes from the laptop, Mac shoved the plate in Ed's direction.

Not to be ignored, Gnarly jumped up to put his front paws on the table and snag the sandwich, leaving the fries for the lawyer.

"Did you see what he did?" Ed gasped.

"You need to learn to move faster, Ed," Mac said. "How old was Audra when she disappeared?"

"Forty-eight," Ed answered without hesitation. The information he had acquired from his sources in the police department was still fresh in his mind. Although he was unable to get access to the nitty-gritty details of the case until a client of his was charged, he was about to get enough details to help Mac. "She would have been fifty this year. Phil is twenty-eight. Dallas just turned twenty-four."

"My daughter is the same ages as Dallas."

Mac recalled many discussions with Audra Walker in which they'd compared notes on the two girls who, at the time he worked with Audra, had both been young women yearning to spread their wings and fly from the nest. Audra was worried about Dallas, who, she confessed, had inherited her independent spirit. "I swear that if her pappy didn't keep a tight rein on that girl, she'd be wilder than an acre of snakes," Audra had said.

"Finding anything in that file, Mac?" Ed asked him.

"Audra's Romeo and Juliet are Clint Brown and Kimberly Castillo," Mac said. "She actually managed to get copies of the police reports for their suicides. It happened thirty-two years ago in Marfa, Texas—that's in Western Texas, near Big Bend. Kimberly Castillo's father owned a huge ranch outside of Marfa. Clint's father was crushed to death when a tractor rolled over on him. Brown's widow claimed it was faulty equipment. She filed a wrongful death suit and lost. There was bad blood ..." His voice trailed off, and he clicked the arrow key to move on to the next page. "Dallas already told me all this."

He continued clicking until he came to more witness accounts. "Here it is."

"What is?" Ed stopped eating to ask.

"A witness statement from Audra Sinclair," Mac said. "Sinclair was Audra Walker's maiden name. She was there. It happened up at Miner's Bluff, a lover's lane that the kids used to frequent to make out—"

"Nobody uses that term anymore, Mac," Ed said. "Now it's 'hooking up.'"

"Whatever," Mac replied. "Anyway, it was after midnight, after the prom, and the place was jammed full of kids—couples—otherwise engaged. Audra says in her statement that she was there with her date, Dan Something, when suddenly they heard this loud screaming. Audra claims she jumped up to see what the screaming was about and saw Clint's car, engulfed in flames, going over the cliff."

"What a way to remember your prom," Ed said.

"When the parents were notified, they found notes in both Clint's and Kimberly's bedrooms stating that they had a suicide pact. Since they couldn't be together in life, they wanted to be together in death."

"What a nightmare," Ed said.

"It gets worse for Horace Castillo, Kimberly's father," Mac said. "A week later, after the memorial service for his only daughter, his only son and his girlfriend were murdered when they walked in on a burglary at their home. Bludgeoned to death." He pushed the image of losing both his grown son and daughter in such a horrific manner from his mind. "Horace Castillo died of a heart attack less than six months later."

Mac clicked to the next page. "Crime-scene report. Both bodies were burnt beyond recognition. Kimberly was found in the car. Clint's body was found at the bottom of the cliff, seventy-five feet from the vehicle." He paused and then muttered, "Pretty far away, if you ask me." He continued to read from the report. "Identification was based on eyewitness reports from their friends who saw the car going over the cliff with Kimberly and Clint inside."

"Not DNA?"

"This was over thirty years ago, Ed," Mac reminded him. "DNA wasn't available to a small town in a rural Texan county. Small sheriff's department." He double-checked the report. "They didn't use dental records for either one of them."

Looking across the table at Ed, Mac said, "That's what drew Audra to this story. Suppose it wasn't a suicide pact? All these teenagers were focused on what teenagers are focused on at prom night. The witnesses know that these young lovers are going to be apart and that they're upset about it. Kimberly screams to get their attention so they'll see Clint's car going over the cliff." Raising his voice, he asked, "Why was the car on fire *before* it went over the cliff?"

"If the gas tank ignited due to the crash, it would have caught fire after the car had gone over," Ed said with a nod of his head.

"They set it on fire because they needed the bodies to be burned beyond recognition," Mac said. "Two bodies, a young woman's and a young man's, are found at the crime scene. Suicide notes are found. Between the notes and the kids' statements, no one questioned that it was Kimberly and Clint. Kimberly comes from a wealthy family. She knows the combination to her father's safe. During the service, they break in to steal the money, planning to blame it on a burglar taking advantage of the family's being away. And then her brother walks in."

"They had already killed two people," Ed said. "The young man and woman found at the bottom of the cliff."

"They kill Kimberly's brother and girlfriend, plant the murder weapon to blame a field hand, clean out her father's safe, and run away to start a new life," Mac said.

"If Audra believed they weren't dead, why didn't she ask to have the bodies exhumed and then check the dental records?" Ed asked.

"Based on what I just told you, did she have enough to warrant a subpoena to do it?" Mac asked. "If someone came to me asking to exhume my dead son's body to prove he'd killed four people in order to fake his death and pull off a burglary, I'd say no. I wouldn't want to know."

"They were Audra's friends," Ed said. "If they're still alive—"

"She had to have picked up their trail at ZNC." Mac slapped the laptop shut. "That's where we're going to start." He picked up his cell phone. "I'm going to call David and tell him and Dallas to meet us in the lobby."

David lost track of how many blocks Dallas had led him down. Since he was unfamiliar with New York City, he allowed her to lead him block after block, turning one corner after another and crossing multiple busy intersections. Once they were out of earshot of the emergency vehicles and among the crowds of the city, Dallas yanked David into an alley between two shops.

"We need to get you cleaned up." Dropping her handbag to the filthy ground, she stripped off her trench coat and proceeded to unbutton the white shirt Ed Willingham had given to her. "Take off that sweater. That bullet hole and blood'll be drawin' attention to you."

Her reference to his wound made the sting from where the police officer's bullet had grazed his arm register with his brain. Involuntarily, he grabbed his arm.

With the white shirt Dallas was wearing hanging open and revealing David's undershirt underneath it, she knelt down to rummage through her bag. "I have a first aid kit in here. Nothing fancy, but it should have an antibiotic to clean you up and a bandage to stop the bleeding." Opening up the plastic case, she extracted a tube and a bandage. "Don't be shy, sweetie. We need to clean up your jacket and ditch that bloody sweater."

After shrugging out of his sports coat, David pulled the sweater off over his head and tossed it to the ground.

Taking in his firm, slender build, she rose to her feet and began tending to the deep cut across his bicep. The rubbing of the sweater across it had made it start bleeding once again. She ripped open an antiseptic towelette with her teeth, spit the torn paper out on the ground, and went to work cleaning the blood from in and around the wound.

"I forgot to thank you"—she said in a low voice—"for back there. For savin' me."

Looking over his shoulder into her light-brown eyes, he shrugged. "They were going to kill me, too."

"Not if you had just let them take me away, which I was gonna let them do. I had no idea they weren't real cops."

"They were real cops," David told her from over his shoulder. "Real and dirty. The worst kind."

Pressing up against him, she wrapped both hands around his arm. "Thing is, darlin', you saw that somethin' was fishy from the beginnin'. I didn't. What clued you in?"

"Stan was talking on his cell phone, not on his radio."

"Could've been a personal call?"

"Yeah, but his body language told me that it was all business," David said. "It struck me that things weren't right." He shifted away from her and pulled his arm around his body in an attempt to look at the cut. "I think it's clean enough."

Reminded of his wound, she tore her gaze from his blue eyes to put the ointment on the cut and to bandage it. "I have a sewin' kit in my bag."

"Is there anything you don't have in that bag?"

"Nope." With his sports coat tucked under her arm, she knelt down to dig through her bag for the kit. "All we need to do is tape up the bullet hole in the sleeve then it won't be so noticeable." Uttering a cry of success, she extracted the kit from the bag and held it up for him to see. "This'll do us for now."

While David dressed in Ed's white button-down shirt, she mended the tear in his sports coat. She then searched for a way to dispose of the bloody sweater. Spotting a trash bin, she fished multiple shopping bags out and hid the sweater inside one bag after another before burying it under several large green garbage bags.

By the time she had finished, David had redressed and was working on a plan of action. "First thing we need to do is change our appearances." He took out his cell phone and removed the battery. "Security cameras in the cruiser will show them exactly what happened. Our pictures are going to be all over the news, and everyone in the city is going to be looking for us."

Looking up from where she was fastening up her trench coat, Dallas nodded her head to tell him that she understood.

"Once they identify us, they're going to try tracking us by the GPS in our cells," he said. "Take the battery out of your phone, and put it in your purse." He slipped his phone's battery into his pocket. "We need to get a burner phone so I can call Mac and let him know what's gone down."

Dallas was already digging through her bag.

"Unfortunately, I only have about forty dollars in cash," David said. "We can't use our credit cards, and forty bucks isn't enough for us to buy—"

"Will ten thousand dollars be enough?" She pulled her hand out of the bag and held up a thick wad of bills.

"Where did you get ten thousand dollars?"

"It's part of my runaway kit. I keep it in a secret compartment in my shoulder bag." She held open her bag to show him a side compartment that had been tightly sealed with Velcro so that it appeared to be an inside side seam. "Cash, alternate identification, credit cards"—she slapped a phone into his hand—"and a burner phone. Already activated. Everythin' I need in case my cover gets blown or somethin', and I need to hit the road in a hurry."

While she explained her runaway kit, David counted out the cash. As she had said, she had ten thousand dollars in used mixed bills. "Ten thousand dollars. Where were you planning to run away to? The Antarctic?"

"Who says that when you're makin' a quick getaway you can't do it in style?" She snatched the money back, bound it together with a rubber band, and placed it in her bag. "I also have a driver's license and two credit cards—a MasterCard and a Platinum American Express under a new identity. Unfortunately, I only have one ID, and it's for a woman, so I guess it's mine. But that's okay."

Without missing a beat, she switched to a heavy New Jersey accent, which, combined with her low, sultry voice, made David suck in his breath. "I'll be Angelina Rosetti from Joisey, and you can be my boy toy, Tony"—she wrapped her arms around his neck and batted her eyelashes—"caterin' to my every de-si-re."

While he and Ed were taking the elevator down at the Four Seasons, Mac squinted at the screen of his cell phone and thumbed the "end" button.

"What's wrong?" Ed asked him.

"David's phone keeps going straight to voice mail."

Mac tightened his grip on Gnarly's leash when the elevator doors opened to allow a couple to step on. Spotting the German shepherd, they paused before boarding the elevator.

"Maybe he let the battery die," Ed suggested.

"David *never* lets the battery die," Mac said. "He plugs it in every night before he goes to bed. It's part of his routine to make sure it's always fully charged. The only way it would go straight to voice mail is if he removed the battery, which would mean he's in trouble."

The elevator doors opened, and the couple rushed off.

Concerned for David's and Dallas's safety, Ed and Mac hesitated before stepping out into the lobby.

Holding onto Gnarly's leash with one hand, Mac was checking the screen of his phone with the other when it vibrated in his hand. He didn't recognize the number. Hoping it was David, he brought the phone to his ear and thumbed the button to answer it. "Hello?"

"Mac, don't say my name out loud," David said quickly. "I don't have a lot of time. They may be tracing your calls."

"Sure thing, son. What do you need this time?" Mac replied with a forced upbeat tone while looking straight into Ed's eyes. He could see that his lawyer had received the message.

Ed took Gnarly's leash from Mac to free up his other hand.

"I killed two cops," David fought the rising anxiety in his tone. "They were going to kill Dallas and me, and I shot them with my own gun—self-defense. Ballistics is going to instantly connect their deaths to me. Dallas and I are going off the grid."

"So what do you want me to do about it?" Mac asked in the standard tone of an annoyed parent for the benefit of anyone nearby who might have been listening.

"You need to find out who's behind this," David said. "Mac, these cops were dirty, and they were after Dallas. They knew who I was—that I was law enforcement. The only ones I gave that information to was Hopkins and his team. The order for the hit had to have come from someone involved in Yvonne's murder investigation—someone inside the police department."

"Got it," Mac said.

"Gotta go."

"Be safe."

Click!

Mac's chest felt tight from holding his breath when he brought the phone down from his ear and slipped it into its case on his belt.

"What happened?" Ed asked in a low voice.

Mac answered him in a whisper. "David shot two cops."

Ed's jaw dropped open. He sucked in a deep breath. "My God." His eyes grew wide. "Every cop in the city'll be after him."

"As soon as they run a ballistics test on the bullets," Mac whispered. "David shot them with his own gun in self-defense. It's in the system. They were dirty, Ed."

"Cruisers are equipped with cameras, Mac," Ed said. "If it was self-defense and the cameras caught it—"

"Most likely, they disabled the cameras before picking them up," Mac said. "Like they'd want their paid hit caught on tape? They have to belong to that gang—the Dirty Six—that Gibbons was telling us about."

"With Tate killed last night and two more taken out today, they're down to three now."

"Plus their leader," Mac said.

"Well, Mac, you know as well as I do that if David is going to get through this alive, we need to get this case wrapped up—and wrapped up quickly. Every cop in this city will be looking for an excuse to kill him before he can say 'I want my lawyer.'"

"That's why I want you to get down to that police station to talk to Gibbons again," Mac said. "Find out what they know about this, and tell her that her leader is someone connected to the Yvonne Harding murder case. David said those cops knew he was law enforcement. He wasn't in his uniform, and no one at ZNC knew that."

"That means Hopkins or a member of his team passed that information onto the cops dispatched to take out Dallas and David," Ed said. "That should narrow things down for Gibbons. Are you going out to find David?"

"No." Mac took the leash back from Ed. "Like you said, this case needs to get wrapped up before David finds himself on the wrong end of a firefight." He pressed a button on his cell phone. "While you and I are working this case on this end, reinforcements in Spencer will be working on Audra's Romeo-and-Juliet murders."

"Might as well," Ed said with sarcasm. "They're not doing anything."

Chapter Seventeen

"You've got to be kidding me," David said when he saw that Dallas had led him out of an alley and onto Fifth Avenue. They were directly across the street from Saks. "We're running from the police, and you want to walk right into one of the biggest and most expensive department stores in the city?"

With a wicked grin, she turned to him. "Think about it, sugar. Anyone in their right mind would be hidin' in out-of-the-way places and shoppin' in dive stores because they wouldn't have much cash or would be usin' stolen credit cards. The police are gonna think like you're thinkin'. What criminal—"

"I'm not a criminal."

"The police don't know that right now," she said. "They're gonna think we're strapped for cash with no credit cards and no way to get help. They aren't gonna expect us to walk into a major department store in broad daylight and spend thousands—"

"I wasn't planning on spending thousands of dollars," David said. "But I get your point." He gestured to her bag. "That phony ID and those credit cards—they aren't stolen, are they?"

"No," she said. "They go to a bona fide account I set up to use in an emergency, and I think this qualifies. Don't worry. I'm not committin' fraud. I'll pay off the credit cards as soon as the bill comes in." She tugged on his hand. "Come along, puddin'. We'll be fine."

Once again, David realized he'd been holding her hand for the several blocks of side streets and alleyways they'd traveled down to get back in the area of Central Park. Her hand felt like it belonged in his. Abruptly, his thoughts turned to Chelsea. A wave of guilt washed over him when he realized he hadn't thought of her since before the shooting.

What's she going to think about me when she hears about this? How can I explain it?

After a quick jog across the street, Dallas led David through the front doors.

Surrounded by marble and glass, he was tempted to back out of the store. He felt that everyone who looked at him would be able to see that he couldn't even afford to pass through their doors.

"Don't be scared, darlin'. I've got your back." Looping her arm through his, she led him to the escalators. "We need to change out of these clothes. Our lives depend on it."

"I'm sorry, Mr. Blakeley is on a conference call," the administrative assistant said before jumping to her feet and running after Mac, who hadn't slowed down on his path from Preston Blakeley's outer office into what he assumed was the network CEO's office. Instead, Mac walked into a conference in which practically every chair around the long table was filled with men and women in suits.

The larger-than-life face of Senator Patrick Brennan filled an enormous wide-screen monitor at the end of the room.

"Now about the upcoming debates," the senator said. "Let's hold off on scheduling them until we find out what shows have the highest expected ratings during the sweeps." He uttered a deep-throated chuckle. "Then have your man contact my inside contact at the party's headquarters to schedule the debates opposite those shows." His chuckle turned into laughter that was joined by the laughter of his off-screen entourage. "It would be cruel to give the people too much to think about this election cycle."

Smelling a platter filled with cookies in the middle of the conference table, Gnarly took a running leap and landed onto the tabletop, which sent the high-level executives flying in all directions. He galloped to the platter and went to work on the sweets.

"Call security!" a woman who had been sitting behind Blakeley yelled to the assistant, who had already run back to her desk to make the call.

"Who's that?" The middle-aged politician's eyes narrowed. "What's going on there, Blakeley?" He craned his neck to get a closer look through the satellite hookup at the happenings in the chief executive's conference room.

When one brave executive tried to cut off the intruder with a punch to the jaw, Mac smoothly ducked the blow, grabbed the flying fist, and twisted the man's arm behind his back before shoving him facedown onto the tabletop. While he was holding him down, Mac turned to Preston Blakeley. "I want a word with you *now.* Someone ordered Ali Hudson and my brother dead, and I want to know who did it."

"Blakeley," the senator said while making a cutting motion with his hand across his throat to someone off camera. "We'll continue this meeting after you get your house in order."

The monitor went black.

Security guards, their weapons drawn, charged into the conference room. "Let him go, Faraday!" the chief of security ordered.

Moving slowly, Mac released the vice president and held up his hands. His gaze remained locked on Preston Blakeley.

"Everything is okay here," Preston said. "We're good."

There was a collective gasp around the room.

"We'll reschedule this meeting for another day," Preston said. "Leave Faraday." Then, taking note of Gnarly, who had finished the cookies and sat down in the center of the table, he added, "And his little dog, too. We have a few things to discuss."

The assistant who had ordered them to call security tapped a button on the table to disconnect the satellite feed before gathering her belongings and following her colleagues out. Once everyone was gone, she closed the doors to leave Mac and the CEO alone.

After Mac had ushered Gnarly off the table, Preston Blakeley gestured for Mac to take a seat, which he declined. "I don't have a lot of time. Every cop in this city is looking for Hudson and my brother."

"Let me get this straight," Preston Blakeley said, turning around in his seat to face Mac. "You seem to think, for some reason, that I put out a hit on Ali Hudson, Yvonne Harding's assistant. My first question is, why would I care enough to want her dead? If I don't like someone, all I have to do is fire him or her—which is what I did in Hudson's case. It's totally legal. Killing her is not only immoral and unethical but also highly illegal—and it would potentially destroy everything I've built."

Mac chuckled. "You're a very wealthy and powerful man. It's been my experience that not all wealthy and powerful people view murder in the same way you claim to. They consider it a more permanent way of eliminating potential problems."

"It's more than a claim," Preston said. "I'm a realist."

"You said you fired Hudson. Why?"

"Because she was Yvonne's assistant. She worked for *Yvonne*—even though *we* paid her. When Yvonne died, we had no need for Ms. Hudson. So I fired her." He pointed a finger at Mac to make a point and said, "Now, Ryan Ritter tried to get me to transfer her so she could work for him, but I told him to discuss that with her." He offered a grin. "I don't know a lot about Ali Hudson, but from what I've seen, she's a smart enough cookie to prefer unemployment to working for Ritter."

"Why do you say that?" Mac asked. "From what I know about Ritter, he's one of the most successful journalists ZNC has. Wouldn't that be a promotion?"

Preston grinned. "I understand you have a daughter, Mr. Faraday."

"Yes."

"I have two. As one father to another, I wouldn't want either of my daughters to work for Ryan Ritter. Don't get me wrong—he's extremely smart. He's a tremendous journalist and has a huge following. Never says anything unless he has the facts to back it up. He's respected by millions. He's good to his employees, who all love him."

"I feel a 'but' coming," Mac said.

"He's also a world-class womanizer," Preston said. "He's fifty years old and unmarried for a reason. He's had his eye on Ali Hudson ever since her first day at ZNC." He uttered a low laugh. "That young lady is tough, though. She's handled herself very well with him. But just because she's a scrappy fighter doesn't mean she should be put on the front lines to have her heart played with."

"Then you didn't fire her because you wanted to get rid of her?" Mac asked. "It was for purely professional reasons?"

Preston shrugged both of his shoulders. "Why would I want her dead? I didn't know enough about the girl to want her dead."

Yanking out the chair that Preston had offered him, Mac sat down. "Were you aware that Ali Hudson was assisting Yvonne Harding in investigating Audra Walker's murder?"

"She was Yvonne's assistant," Preston said. "I'd expect her to help Yvonne with her stories. But I ordered Yvonne to stay clear of the Walker case."

"Why? Were you afraid of what she'd find out?" Mac asked bluntly.

The formerly congenial expression on Preston Blakeley's face evaporated.

"Audra Walker's assistant told me that you tried to cancel her interview with Yvonne Harding," Mac continued. "She even told me that Audra predicted you'd try to have it cancelled because she had discovered that you were a heavy backer of Senator Brennan—who I just now saw leading a meeting. Walker's book implicated his father in the murder of his sex-symbol mistress, Jolene Fitzgerald, who was about to go public with their love affair."

"Audra Walker's book came out at a very inconvenient time," Blakeley said.

"Right when Senator Brennan was making a bid for the presidential run. Now he's planning to take another stab at it. What do you stand to lose if he's implicated in Audra Walker's murder?"

"Brennan lost his bid for president because on top of Walker's book accusing his father of arranging Jolene Fitzgerald's murder, the police made him a person of interest in Walker's disappearance," Blakeley said. "So if you're thinking of accusing me of killing Walker to save my candidate, you're wrong."

"Wouldn't be the first time that a motive for a murder backfired," Mac said. "Walker's assistant also told me that after five minutes alone behind closed doors with her, the interview was back on. What happened in that meeting?"

Preston Blakeley rose from his chair. "I don't have to answer your questions."

Standing up, Mac grabbed Blakeley's arm when he tried to pass him. "You think Audra Walker did her homework? Want to see how well I can do mine? Whatever she dug up, I can dig up too, and I can use it to my advantage, which I will do if my brother ends up dead—especially if I find out you were behind it."

"I am not behind any of this."

"If you're telling the truth, then whatever Walker had on you, I'll keep to myself," Mac said. "I'm not looking to destroy anyone's reputation or life. I only want to find out who killed Audra Walker and Yvonne Harding—"

"Rubenstein killed Harding," Preston said. "The police already said so."

"That's bull!" Mac said.

"He was killed trying to escape."

"Because he realized he'd been set up," Mac said. "Someone had cleared him through security and let him in the building, and he told them that Yvonne was interviewing him for *Crime Watch.*"

"There was no interview," Blakeley said.

"You're right there," Mac said. "Someone cleared Rubenstein, allowing him up to the studio. He didn't have the means to get into the building and up to the studio without someone clearing him through building security."

"Had to be someone on the inside," Preston said.

Mac agreed with a nod of his head. "I believe Yvonne Harding was killed because she was investigating Audra Walker's murder, and the killer thought she was getting too close. Now he's tying up loose ends by going after Ali because he fears she knows too much." He stepped up to Preston Blakeley. "So tell me where you were the night Audra Walker disappeared."

"You think I'm behind this?" Preston Blakeley said with a laugh.

"Two years ago, Audra Walker came back to this building late at night and was murdered," Mac said. "Something happened while she was here that got her killed. According to witnesses, you and Audra Walker got into an argument—"

"That was *business*," Preston said. "Just because we disagreed *politically*—"

"I've investigated more than one murder that was committed in the name of doing business," Mac said in a cold voice. "Where were you that night?"

"I don't know for sure. It was so long ago, and the police didn't consider me a suspect, so … home, maybe."

"How about when Yvonne Harding was shot?"

"That one's easy," Preston said with relief in his tone. "I was up here—in this very office—with my executive assistant on a conference call with the West Coast. There were six people in California who saw me, plus my assistant. We didn't know there had been a shooting until my secretary ran in to tell us." He grinned. "I can prove it. The conference call was recorded, like we do for every one of these meetings. The recording shows my secretary running in to tell me that Yvonne Harding had been shot."

"How convenient for you," Mac said.

"Any other questions?" Preston asked him with narrowed eyes.

"Only one. What did Audra Walker have on you?"

There was a long silence, and Preston Blakeley regarded Mac. "Off the record?"

"All I want is for Ali Hudson and my brother to be safe."

Preston Blakeley lowered himself into a chair at the table. His shoulders slumped. "I don't know how she managed to do it. I was so careful."

"What?"

"Several years ago," Preston said before stopping to pour himself a glass of water from the pitcher on the table. Mac saw that his hands were shaking as he took a long drink. "About a dozen years ago, I was on a business trip out to the West Coast, and I met a woman—"

Mac tried not to scoff. "Audra Walker found out about your mistress?"

"More than that," Preston said in a low tone.

"How is it more than that?"

"I married her," Preston hissed. "We have two children together."

Mac felt his jaw drop open.

"She thinks my name is Blake Prescott," Preston continued. "I make regular trips out to the West Coast, and"—he stopped to drain the glass of water—"she thinks I'm an insurance salesman."

"You have two families?" Mac asked with a gasp. "Why?"

"I don't know!" His eyes wide, Preston Blakeley started to blubber. "It just happened!"

"Were you drunk in Vegas?"

"How did you know?"

To save time, David took a wad of cash from Dallas and went to the men's clothing department to purchase new clothes while she went to the ladies' department. They had arranged to meet in one hour at Café SFA—that is, Café Saks Fifth Avenue.

David had never spent so much money on clothes in such a short amount of time. The lean male clerk dropped a tidbit about aspiring to be a fashion designer and then wasted no time in dressing David up like he was a male fashion doll. David tuned him out when he started admiring his slender hips and tight buttocks.

While the look the clerk had assembled was not in keeping with David's usual tossed-together style, it served his purpose of changing his appearance from a casually dressed visitor from rural Maryland to an upscale big-city slicker. Within an hour, David was clad in a brown suede jacket, a soft brown sweater, and slacks. The look was finished off with matching boots and a wide color-blocked scarf that the clerk had insisted upon. When David stepped out of the dressing room, the clerk was waiting with a brown felt fedora that he'd gotten from the hat department to add "one last touch."

"I just *love* a man in a hat," he told David with a wink.

In that instant, David spotted the security camera high above them in the ceiling.

"They say hats are making a comeback." Taking the fedora, David turned his back to the camera and placed the hat on his head, careful to wear it forward with the wide rim down over his forehead to conceal his eyes from the camera.

"Oh, that's just perfect," the clerk gushed.

Minutes later, David was sitting at a corner bistro table trying to erase the memory of Officer Sauer's face and of how the silver badge he'd been wearing on his chest had shone in the sun.

Why did you make me have to kill you? You had to have taken the same oath I did to protect and to serve, Sauer. Why? What did they offer you that was so great that you turned on your brothers in blue?

David search his mind for terrorists he had killed while on missions in the Middle East or as a police officer—for every time he had pulled his gun and been forced to fire. He had never felt so much guilt over shooting anyone as he did for killing those two men with police badges pinned to their chests.

"Hey, To-*nee!*"

Startled by the loud Jersey accent, David almost knocked over his coffee. He looked across the café into the store and saw a striking brunette with long, silky straight hair making her way toward him. She was wearing a multicolored leather poncho, and her long legs were encased in chocolate leather pants. Underneath the pants, she was wearing high-heeled ankle boots. Between the straight hair and the bold make-up, David vacillated between thinking she was indeed Dallas Walker and thinking she was maybe a high-fashion runway model who had just completed a massive shopping spree and had mistaken him for someone else.

They had agreed that she would refer to him as Tony and he would call her Angelina while they were on the run and in public.

Directly behind her, two uniformed police officers were walking in the direction of the café. With an appreciative grin, one of them took in the sexy gait of the beauty in front of them.

David rose from his seat while Dallas, who was grinning broadly at her makeover, made her way through the tables without knocking anything over with her armload of shopping bags. "Sorry to keep you waitin', sugar, but you would not—"

Throwing his arms around her, David cut her off by covering her mouth with his.

She resisted him until he whispered into her ear and pressed his body against hers. "Police behind you. They're looking for a man and a woman, not a couple," he said. Once again, he locked his mouth over hers while fighting to conceal his face with the hat.

Dropping her shopping bags, she wrapped her arms around his neck.

The scent of her hair reminded him of the fresh, clean scent of Deep Creek Lake first thing in the morning. The taste of her mouth on his made his heart race. Forgetting about the two police officers nearby, his mind filled only with thoughts of her and of the feel of her body in his arms.

He wanted to be closer to her—and to never let her go.

"Can I help you?" David heard a server ask a customer at a nearby table.

"I'll have what he's having," an elderly man chuckled.

"I never," an elderly woman said in response to his laugh.

"I know," the old man shot back.

Jolted back into the present, David released her. Shaking the fog from his head, he swallowed and looked around. There were no police officers nearby—at least not any that he could see. A couple of tables away, an old man shot him a thumbs-up while his wife, who was sitting across from him, looked disgusted by their public display of affection.

"I think we're safe now," David murmured while adjusting the hat back on his head.

"Are you sure?" Dallas replied in a dreamy tone.

David eased her into a chair. Taking his seat next to her, he paused when he noticed a dazed expression on her face. "Are you okay?"

She sighed. "Never better."

"We haven't eaten since breakfast," he said. "You should eat something."

"Food is the last thing I want right now."

He cocked his head at her wicked grin. "We need to move on. I hate being out in public like this. Get ahold of yourself while I take a look at what's in that envelope you took from ZNC." He patted the space on the tabletop between them. "Where is it?"

"Why don't you search me to find it?" she suggested with a playful tone.

Unamused, David rummaged through the collection of shopping bags containing their old clothes until he found her shoulder bag. After finding the envelope, he slapped it on the tabletop and read the front. In black marker, it was addressed to Yvonne in care of *Crime Watch* at ZNC. The return address read simply "Roberts."

"Who's Roberts?" David asked before remembering a conversation he and Mac had had with Yvonne the day before. "Oh yeah—he was the former chief detective investigating your mother's disappearance."

"Caleb Roberts," Dallas said with a nod of her head. "He retired last year. That was when Hopkins took over the lead in the case." She paused before adding, "He was murdered yesterday."

"Yesterday?"

"Yeah, that's right. On the same day that my mother's body was found. He was shot in the head hours after agreein' to let me see his notebook. It was made to look like a suicide, but I'm not buyin' it."

"Yvonne was killed the same day. Can't be a coincidence." David squeezed the padded envelope. It contained something that was rectangular in shape. He ripped the envelope open, thrust his hand inside it, and pulled out its contents, which consisted of a small black notebook and a thick manila folder.

Dallas snatched the notebook from his hand. It had a note clipped to the front cover.

"He must have had a bad feeling that he wasn't going to live long enough for the meeting, so he decided to drop this in the mail to you—I mean Yvonne." He opened the folder, which contained copies of police reports and witness statements. "What does the note say?"

"'Don't trust anyone,'" she said.

"We already know that," David said.

"It also says to ask Officer Milt Sauer 'bout his honeymoon to Australia—and 'bout who asked him to mail the postcard." Dallas looked up to lock her gaze with David's.

"One of the police officers I shot was wearing a nameplate that read Sauer," David said in a hushed tone.

"Damn!" she hissed.

Clasping her hand, he shot her a confident smile. "Don't worry. I've been in tougher spots than this."

She flashed him a toothy grin. "They say not to mess with Texas for a reason, sweetheart." She gestured at the folder under his hands. "What's that?"

"Roberts' bootleg copy of his case file on your mother's disappearance. I guess he wanted you—I mean Yvonne—to have it."

"What's in it?" She reached for it only to have David move it out of her reach and tuck it back into the envelope.

"Not right now. We need to keep moving." He took one of the burner phones she'd given him out of his pocket. "I need to call Mac to tell him about Roberts and his note and to find out if he's gotten any info for us."

"We're only a couple of blocks from the Four Seasons."

"That's the last place we want to go," David said in a low voice. "That's where I'm registered. They'll expect me to go back there. We have to go someplace else."

He became aware of her gazing at him with her cognac-brown eyes, which were then framed with thick, long lashes and bold colors. The touch of blue on her eyelids made her brown eyes more striking. Her expression was different from how she had looked at him before. Lust had been replaced with something softer—deeper.

David swallowed down the wave of emotion rising up inside him. "Any ideas?"

"Some," she said. "You look great in that hat, by the way."

"You look great too," he said while writing down some notes on the back of a napkin. "That poncho suits you."

"Thanks," she said. "I knew you were a great kisser. I just knew it."

A slow grin came to his lips as he handed the phone to her. "You're not so bad yourself," he said with a wink. "You do a pretty good Jersey accent. Can you do Australian outback?"

Effortlessly, she switched to an Australian accent. "What'd you want me t'say, mate?"

David slid the note in front of her. "You need to say this to Mac. It's in code."

Keeping her voice low, she said, "We're usin' a burner phone, so they won't know if we call—"

"As soon as ballistics matches the bullets I put in those policemen to my gun, they'll get a warrant to trace Mac's phone calls. We believe Hopkins or someone on his team is in on this."

Nodding her head, she said, "And if he's listenin' in on Mac's calls, he'll know we're on to him."

"Exactly," David said as he wrote out Mac's phone number across the top of the napkin. "I'll be timing you. You can't talk for more than thirty seconds."

Reading through the script David had written out, she frowned. "You want me to say a lot in less than thirty seconds."

"Any longer and they'll be able to narrow down our location." David was collecting their bags. "Just in case we need to be ready to move as soon as you hang up."

Sucking in a deep breath, she pressed in the phone number David had written out and listened to the phone ring on the other end. Mac answered on the third ring.

"Good-eye, mate," she said. "Just wanted to let you know that I got that note Harold Fitzwater mailed to me."

"I'm sorry, you have the wrong number."

"Don't you lie to me again, you little traitor," she said. "I know he's covering for you. Bob told me everything. What'd you give him to be your fall guy today?"

Finished, she disconnected the call.

Checking the time on the phone, David grinned. "Seven seconds to spare." After pocketing the phone, he handed her an armload of bags and stood up. "Now we need to move."

"Do you really think Mac got anything from that?" she asked, hurrying after him.

"Harold Fitzwater was a lieutenant Mac used to work with in homicide in Washington," David told her in a low voice while they hurried to the main exit. "He took a bribe to allow a murderer Mac had arrested to escape on a private jet to Europe. The cockney accent and your reference to the note tell him that you're referring to the postcard your mother allegedly sent from Australia. The fall guy tells him that one of the cops I shot had something to do with that postcard, and 'Bob' telling you everything tells him that we got this information from Sergeant Roberts."

Keeping his head low so the rim of his hat covered his face, David led her out onto the street.

Chapter Eighteen

Shivering against the bitterly cold autumn wind, Ed Willingham warmed himself with the hot apple cider he'd purchased from a street vendor while waiting for Lieutenant Abby Gibbons to casually bump into him in Central Park during her afternoon run.

"We need to stop meeting like this," she said while pausing to stretch her legs on an arm of the bench. She searched the surrounding area for any sign of someone she knew who might see her talking to the lawyer.

"A couple of hours ago, two New York City cops were found dead along the East River," Ed said with a casual tone. "Were they two of your Dirty Six?"

Standing up straight, she placed her hands on her hips. "Yes."

"The shooting was self-defense," Ed said. "The gun used to shoot them is in the national database."

"Care to tell me which client did the shooting?" she asked.

"Not until you tell me who sent your dirty cops to kill my client."

She uttered a deep sigh. "As far as the good cops doing their jobs know, some thug from out on the street took out two of their brothers in blue while they were on a lunch break. Your client will be safer if he turns himself in."

"So that the surviving three of the Dirty Six can finish the job?" Ed asked in an undignified manner. "Or better yet, maybe the one behind the hit order will decide that if he wants something done right, he should do it himself. I don't think so." He stood up. "I'm here as a courtesy to let you and your police department know that those cops were killed in self-defense. My client is not a cop killer. Now if you don't want his innocent blood on your police commissioner's hands, your department needs to step up your game and identify who's been calling the shots in this muscle-for-hire enterprise that's been operating within your department. A little bird told me that Sergeant Caleb Roberts, the detective who originally had the lead in Audra Walker's disappearance, was murdered yesterday."

With a shake of her head, she said, "That was ruled a suicide."

"Oh," Ed laughed. "The lead detective in Audra Walker's case commits suicide the same day her body turns up, disproving Lieutenant Wayne Hopkins' claim that she took off?"

"Because of the postcard, Wayne had every reason to believe that that was a voluntary disappearance."

"Oh," Ed said. "That's right. I forgot all about the postcard mailed from Australia to an acquaintance of Audra Walker. Tell me, Officer Milt Sauer—"

"One of the cops shot down by the East River," she said.

"My contacts in the State Department tell me he was traveling in Australia."

Abby's eyebrows furrowed. "For his honeymoon. I thought at the time that it was a rather expensive and lavish wedding and honeymoon for his salary. I was told it was a wedding present from a relative."

"Or a killer," Ed said. "And how long did it take Lieutenant Hopkins to close Audra Walker's case when that postcard arrived here in the States?"

"Wayne had the handwriting on the postcard authenticated," Gibbons argued.

"So did the Walker family. They went public saying that their expert claimed the handwriting was not Audra Walker's, and her body sealed in that wall at the News Corps building proves Hopkins' expert was wrong—or lying." The lawyer moved in close to her. "How about if you and I go talk to this expert and ask him which it was?"

"Our forensics experts aren't perfect," she said. "They're humans, and while the science is perfect, humans are flawed."

"Oh, only your cops are dirty," Ed shot back at her. "If Lieutenant Hopkins wasn't involved in Walker's disappearance, or at least in the cover-up, why didn't he get a second opinion from another expert when the Walkers said the handwriting on that card was a forgery?"

Lieutenant Abby Gibbons backed away from Ed. She was sputtering when she said, "Wayne is not dirty."

"If he's not, someone on his team certainly is," Ed said. "My client, David O'Callaghan, is the chief of police in Spencer, Maryland. According to him, those two dirty cops knew that when they took him and Ali Hudson out to the river to murder them. The only way they could have found that out was from Lieutenant Hopkins, who he told while giving his statement after the Harding murder—or a member of his team."

Her face grew pale. "Anyone running a background check on O'Callaghan could have found that out. Journalists have sources—"

"True," Ed said. "But do they have access to dirty cops?" When he stepped toward her, she backed away. "You told

Faraday and me this morning that these goons seem to be one step ahead of you. Have you ever thought to ask yourself why that is? Isn't it obvious? It's because of someone in the department who has access to you and your office."

She swallowed.

"Lieutenant Hopkins was Roberts' partner," Ed said. "He's hungry for fame. Every suspect in Walker's and Harding's murders has the power to give that to him … and he has access to the Dirty Six, who can help the killer cover his or her tracks." A grin came to Ed's lips. "But the Dirty Six have underestimated my clients. Now they're down to three. If they're not careful, they may end up down to zero by the time this is over."

Abby Gibbons was then hugging herself. "I'll call the handwriting expert to ask him what happened with his analysis of the postcard."

"And Hopkins?"

"I'll talk to Wayne."

"When you do, give him this warning: anything happens to David O'Callaghan, and there's no place here on God's green Earth that he'll be able to hide from Mac Faraday."

In the elevator descending to the ground floor of the News Corps Building, Mac was so deep in thought—his mind was reeling with possibilities, many of them bad, of how the whole situation with David was going to play out—that he barely noticed when the doors opened.

Gnarly stood up from where he was lying across Mac's feet and barked.

"Hey, Faraday, wake up," he heard Ryan Ritter call out to him before laughing good naturedly.

Mac broke out of his stare and saw that Ritter was holding the elevator doors open for him. Gathering up the dog leash, he led Gnarly out onto the ground floor.

"Are you looking for Ali and your brother?" Ryan said. "I saw them this morning. Congratulations on hiring Ali Hudson, by the way. You got yourself one rare find there. She's as smart as a whip and easy on the eyes, too."

The reference to his hiring Dallas startled Mac and made him stop, turn around, and face Ryan. His mind working quickly, he concluded that there had to have been a good reason for someone to tell the noted journalist that he'd hired Yvonne's assistant. "Thank you." He forced a grin across his face. "I know a sharp employee when I see one."

Ryan allowed the elevator to move on without him. "What exactly are you going to have Ali do in Deep Creek Lake?"

Recalling Preston Blakeley's warning about Ryan Ritter's womanizing and his pursuit of Yvonne's assistant, Mac realized the source of the journalist's misinformation. "Whatever it is assistants do—assist me."

"In what?" Ryan Ritter fell into step with Mac as he crossed the lobby. "I thought you were retired."

Appearing displeased about the hanger-on they had picked up, Gnarly paused to look over his shoulder back at Ryan and uttered a low growl from deep in his throat.

Thinking fast, Mac replied, "I hired her to assist my wife, Archie. She's an editor. One of the best in the business. Worked closely with my mother for ten years. Now that we're married, we want to travel more, but Archie is in such demand that she needs an assistant." He then added in a whisper, "But don't tell anyone. It's a surprise."

The more Mac talked, the more sense it made. He found himself wondering if Dallas would like to work for Archie, who was putting in full-time hours as a freelance editor.

Remembering Dallas Walker's background, he chuckled to himself.

"Well, I don't know how much you've offered her, but I don't intend to give up trying to get her to come back to New York to work for me." Ryan Ritter reached down to pet Gnarly, but the German shepherd jerked his head out of Ryan's reach and stepped back to brace himself against Mac's legs.

"Usually dogs like me," Ryan said.

"Gnarly's picky."

Instead of going on his way, Ryan Ritter continued to walk with Mac, who was making his way through the throng of visitors moving to and fro on the main floor of the high-rise building. "Can I help you? Audra Walker was a friend."

Mac stopped. "I thought you hardly knew her." He turned to peer at the journalist.

"We only met that one day she came here for her interview with Yvonne Harding, and we really hit it off." A smile came to Ryan's lips. "I had hoped we would grow closer. Who knows where we'd be now if things had turned out differently."

Recalling that Letty, Audra's assistant, had said that Ryan had been quite attentive to Audra, Mac regarded him for a long moment. Finally, the journalist said, "I feel like you have a question for me, Faraday."

"I'm just curious," Mac said. "I keep hearing about what a prestigious news journalist you are. One of ZNC's top stars. How long has your show been on?"

"This new season makes thirteen years." With a sense of pride, Ryan smoothed his tie.

"You've had dinner at the White House," Mac noted. "Interviewed every president, some prime ministers, and movie stars. Audra Walker won Pulitzers and every other award in journalism, but you never had her on your show. Why not?"

"That's something you'd need to ask her publicist about," Ryan said. "It wasn't because I didn't want her. I did. As a matter of fact, on the night she was interviewed by Yvonne, I was here before taping because I wanted to ask her personally to be on my show. We set it up for the next week." He chuckled. "Why would I have been avoiding someone I'd never met?"

"I didn't suggest you were avoiding her."

"Fact is, I wanted her. Audra Walker on my show would have been a guaranteed draw for big audiences." Ryan flashed Mac a wide grin. "You and I think alike, Faraday. We're both suspicious."

"That we are," Mac said. "Do you remember where you went after Yvonne's interview with Walker?"

"Are you suggesting I need an alibi?"

Mac laughed along with him, and then he said, "Can you tell me where you were?"

"As a matter of fact, I can," Ryan said slowly. "Under regular circumstances, I wouldn't be able to remember where I was without having Betty check my calendar." He grinned. "However, as luck would have it, I know exactly where I was that night."

"Where was that?" Mac asked.

"With Yvonne Harding." Ryan's grin turned into a full-fledged leer when he saw shock cross Mac's face. "Sorry. Kind of awkward, isn't it? I mean, with you being best friends with the guy who turned out to be Yvonne's husband. If she had told me she was married—"

"You're telling me that you were with Yvonne Harding all night," Mac said.

"All night," Ryan said.

"I didn't get the impression—"

"Yvonne and I are grown adults. You might say we were friends with benefits. The intimate nature of our relationship has been off and on since she came to ZNC. I remember that particular night because when Audra Walker disappeared, the police wanted to know Yvonne's alibi because of the text Audra received that seemed to have come from her. So—"

Mac nodded his head. "And you were her alibi, which is why you know where you were."

"Jason Van Derk was my guest on the show that night," Ryan said. "Knowing what a fan I am of fine cigars and liquors, he had given me a bottle of very fine fifty-year-old scotch. It was much too good to drink alone, so I took it over to Yvonne's place after the show. We broke it open and … one thing led to another. We were together all night."

"I get your point," Mac said. "How about when Yvonne was shot?"

"That's easy," Ryan said. "I was in makeup getting ready for my show."

"That should be easy enough to check."

"Check away," Ryan said. "This is the first time I've ever been a suspect in a murder." He grinned. "Pretty cool. Any other suspects in Audra Walker's murder—besides me, I mean?"

"Do you know why Yvonne Harding, not *Crime Watch's* star, Pam Wiehl, interviewed her?" Mac asked.

"Because Pam was jealous of Audra," Ryan replied. "They both had the same publisher. Audra sold more books, got bigger deals, and won awards. She got the royal treatment when she came to ZNC." That wide grin crossed his face again. "Plus, I think Jim Wiehl had a bit of a crush on her."

"I was told that Jim is devoted to his wife," Mac said.

"I'm sure he is," Ryan said. "But Audra Walker was a looker, and Jim was fawning all over her." With a shake of his head, he added, "Pam did not like that one bit."

"Do you think Pam was jealous enough of Audra Walker to want to dispose of the competition?" Mac asked.

Ryan chuckled. "Well after Audra's disappearance, Pam Wiehl did get a couple of journalism awards that would have gone to Audra otherwise. One was the woman of the year award from the Women in Journalism Association."

"Interesting," Mac murmured.

"I should say so," Ryan said. "And now that Yvonne Harding is out of the way, Pam is a shoo-in for that award this year." He chuckled. "That's the way to stay on top. Kill the competition." Seeing someone across the main floor's reception area, Ryan raised up his hand like he was hailing a cab and called out a name. Capturing the other man's attention, Ryan quickly shook Mac's hand before trotting off to join his colleague. The two men left the building together.

Inside the security office, Mac and Gnarly stepped up to the counter. Without hesitation, Gnarly jumped up to place his front paws in the counter, causing the guard behind the counter to jump back.

"He doesn't like to be kept in the dark," Mac explained before easing Gnarly's front paws down to the floor. "I'd like to talk to someone about Carl Rubenstein."

The guard at the counter turned his attention to his boss, a huge man in the uniform of the chief of security. "Hank?"

"We've already said everything we need to say to the police investigating Yvonne Harding's murder, Mr. Faraday," Hank said in a low voice while hitching up his pants and puffing out his chest.

"I know," Mac said. "My question has to do with your security procedures."

"If you have questions about our procedures, you'll have to have your lawyer call our lawyer," Hank said. "We do everything by the book. We knew Carl Rubenstein had been making threats against Harding and ZNC, but we received a security form clearing him to go upstairs for an interview with Harding."

"Didn't that strike you as strange?" Mac asked.

"Not really," Hank said. "The news bureaus in this building are always setting up interviews with their biggest enemies. Sometimes they even fake fights and feuds in order to get viewers taking sides, and then they have these interviews and all-out brawls on air. That gets lots of viewers to tune in."

"So you thought nothing of it when a security form came in clearing Rubenstein to go on up for an interview with Yvonne Harding, even though he'd threatened her hours earlier."

"Nothing at all." Hank shook his head. "He must have hacked into the system."

"Is that easy to do?"

"We aren't exactly the NSA here."

"Tell me how your security system works."

"It's all internal," Hank said. "The intranet. All someone had to do was log into the building's intranet using any desktop here in the building; go to security; fill out the visitors form with the name of the visitor, his arrival time, his destination, and the name of his contact; and hit the send button."

"Kind of like when David and I came here yesterday," Mac recalled.

"Exactly," Hank said. "Only instead of going to the security kiosk in the lobby, everything is already done before you come through the door. You walk up to the reception desk, and your badge is all ready for you to pick up. Then you walk through the metal detector and, assuming you aren't packing, you're on your way."

"If the visitors security form was completed online using the building's intranet, your system would say who sent the form based on whose user account the form was sent from."

"Which means that whoever filled out the form needed a user ID and password in order to get into the building's secure network in the first place," the other security clerk said. "The name on the request form is Ali Hudson."

"But she couldn't have used her desktop, because Harding's office and outer office were sealed off yesterday while the police removed Audra Walker's body," Mac pointed out.

"You're right," Hank said. "Plus, the police determined that Ali Hudson was out of the building at the time the request was sent in because her security badge shows that she swiped it going out seventeen minutes before the request was submitted online to our office."

"So we know the visitor's request came from someone else using another desktop," Mac said.

"Could be any one of hundreds of computers." Hank slowly shook his head. "Most of the employees in this building log in when they arrive in the morning and log out when they leave."

"Personally, I don't think Rubenstein was set up," the clerk said. "I think he got someone to hack into our system and to get him a pass into the building so he could kill Harding. He used that plastic gun because he knew that our metal detector wouldn't pick it up. I still haven't figured out how he got the bullets in, though."

"Maybe he used wooden ones," Hank said. "That's what the terrorists are using overseas. If he used wooden bullets, our security system wouldn't have detected them."

"The killer used real bullets," Mac said. "They found a metal shell casing at the crime scene and in the stairwell where Rubenstein was killed."

"If he killed Yvonne Harding, then who shot him?" Hank asked.

"His accomplice," the clerk said. "The inside man I told you about who set up the visitor's pass for him and gave him the bullets for the gun."

"Do you have any way of knowing the IP address of where that form was sent from?" Mac asked. "Suppose someone here in the building who didn't have a log-in to the intranet were to walk up to any of these desktops. Since everyone just logs in at the beginning of the day and stays logged in until they leave, couldn't that someone just fill out the visitors form at any desktop while someone was at lunch, submit it, and then simply walk away?"

Hank's mouth hung open while he processed Mac's question. The younger security clerk got it right away.

"We could just check the IP address to figure out what desktop the request came from." The younger man was already on his computer bringing up the form.

"Then we identify who had access to that desktop," Mac said.

The young security clerk was excited. "Don't worry, Mr. Faraday. We're going to nail this creep!"

Chapter Nineteen

Seriously? I'm running from the police, and I'm going to hide out in the Plaza?

David sucked in one deep breath after another while sitting on the bench across the street from what was considered one of the grandest, if not *the* grandest, hotels in New York City.

It was Dallas' idea.

The police would naturally be searching every hellhole in the city looking for them and would expect them to be hiding as far off the grid as possible. They would never think to look for them in the lap of high society.

David had to admit that Dallas had a point.

Armed with her phony identification and platinum cards, Dallas strolled in with her shopping bags to book a room while David waited across the street. The plan called for her to check in alone. Using yet another alternate cell phone, not the same one she had used to call Mac, she would text David the room number—and nothing more. He would wait seven minutes before crossing the street to enter the hotel and would go directly up to her room.

Once they were both secure in the hotel room, they would stay there until Mac and Ed had managed to clear them.

Across the street, Dallas used a thick Jersey-shore accent to register for a deluxe room and to effortlessly spin a tale about how her trip was an illicit getaway with her lover, "a guy Daddy would *kill* if he knew I was hookin' up with 'im." She slipped the clerk a large tip—an incentive to keep their tryst secret in case Daddy "sent some of his goons."

After getting two key cards, she trotted over to the elevator that would take her up to the ninth floor.

She found it difficult not to notice the elegant, tall woman with long, dark hair clad in a brilliant red-sequined backless dress in front of the elevators. Black jewels dripped from her ears and around her throat. She wore a red hat with netting that fell down across her eyes.

Dallas' first impression was that she must have been a famous model or a movie star.

While waiting for the elevator that would take her up to the room, Dallas noticed the woman in red glance in her direction once—and then twice. The third time, her glance rested on Dallas longer—she was studying her.

Curiosity gave way to nervousness. Dallas hadn't had access to the news. *Are pictures of David and me all over the city?*

The elevator doors opened.

Dallas tried to appear casual as she ran onto the car. With a few graceful steps, the woman in red was standing next to her. Wishing she were already there, Dallas punched the button for the ninth floor. She yearned to be behind closed doors with David holding her in his arms, telling her they would both be okay.

It'll all be over soon.

"Sixteen, please," the woman in red said.

Dallas' hand trembled when she thumbed the button.

The doors closed. The elevator ascended.

"Dallas?"

Dallas jumped and turned to the woman who was eying her from behind the veil.

Her dark eyes were kind. "I thought it was you," she said. "I saw on the news that your mother's body was found. Are you here to find her killer?"

Dallas' mind raced. Somewhere in her mind, the woman's voice and eyes seemed familiar, but she couldn't remember where she knew her from. She had something to do with her mother. But the woman didn't look familiar to her.

That voice. Where have I heard it before?

The woman abruptly held out a business card to her. "Dallas, if you need anything—ever—call me. I owe your mother a big debt. Now that she's gone, I'll pay it back through you. That's what she'd want."

The elevator doors opened, and Dallas practically leaped off the car and ran down the hall. She arrived at the hotel room's door and rushed to open it and slip inside before anyone else could recognize her. Collapsing onto the bed, she waited for her heartbeat to slow down and then realized she was still clutching the business card the woman had handed her. All that was printed on it was a phone number—there was no name, address, or any other information.

"This is getting very old, very fast," Mac told Gnarly while peeling off yet another pair of evidence gloves and tossing into the trash bin after examining the German shepherd's excrement. "You ate those rings two days ago. How much longer can you hold on to them? You better not have left them in the park when you went running with David."

Gnarly gazed up at Mac, a curious expression on his face.

With a sigh filled with disgust, Mac led Gnarly back out onto the street, where he heard his name being called out among the street noises. "Mr. Faraday!"

He made a complete turnaround before he spotted a middle-aged woman dressed in a worn khaki jacket trotting down the steps of the News Corp Building's main entrance. Huffing from shortness of breath, she said, "I recognized you from the news." She stuck out her hand. "I'm Polly Langley."

Hesitant, Mac shook her hand. "This is Gnarly." Sitting between the two of them, Gnarly sniffed at her jeans before cocking his head at her.

"He must smell my cats," she said. "I have two calicoes."

Anxious to return to his investigation, Mac asked, "How can I help you, Ms. Langley?"

"They won't let me inside the building," she said. "I talked to the police this morning, and they won't tell me anything except that Carl wasn't scheduled for an interview with Yvonne Harding last night—"

"What connection—"

With a gasp, Polly clasped her chest with both hands. "I'm so sorry, I should have explained it to you. Carl was my fiancé."

"I thought he was married," Mac said before shrugging. "Well, I guess since his wife, Ruth Rubenstein, was murdered, technically, he wasn't married."

"Carl left Ruth more than a year ago, when he fell in love with me. We were living together and wanted to get married, but Ruth refused to divorce him. And since New York is a community-property state, if he divorced her, he would have had to pay her alimony—half of his work salary. It wouldn't have left us enough to live on."

"Are you sure you want to be telling me this, Ms. Langley?" Mac asked. "This all sounds like a very good motive for him to kill his wife."

Polly vigorously shook her head. "Carl had an airtight alibi. The police know that already. We had friends over for dinner, and we all watched the ball game. There were six of us there the whole evening. Our friends didn't leave until after midnight."

Mac was confused. "Then why do you need my help?"

"Carl didn't make up this interview with Yvonne Harding," Polly said. "It's all over the news that he came here last night to kill her for getting Ruth murdered—"

"When actually, Yvonne did him a favor," Mac said. "With Ruth dead, he was free to marry you and to keep his paycheck."

"You sound just like everyone else, Mr. Faraday," Polly said. "The truth is, Carl was a kind and gentle man. Truly. I get migraines, and when I do, Carl takes such tender care of me. He brings me herbal tea. He keeps the lights dim so that my head won't hurt so bad. Why, the other night, I got one of my headaches during the game and had to lie down. Carl entertained all of the guests, and he came in at every commercial to check on me."

"And then after the murder of the wife he hated, he rushed out to file a lawsuit to profit from her death."

"You make him sound like a selfish opportunist," Polly said, sniffing at him. "Don't tell me that you wouldn't have done the same thing. Put yourself in his shoes. You're working every day and barely getting by, and you're married to a bitterly jealous old hag who's happiest when she's making those around her—even total strangers like that writer she drove to suicide—miserable. If an opportunity to grab a brass ring and to start over presented itself, you wouldn't grab it?"

"Sometimes," Mac answered slowly, "when you find yourself in a position like Carl found himself in, you have to ask yourself how much your happiness is worth. I don't know the particulars of Carl's finances, but I suspect that, considering Ruth was officially branded a troll, he would have been way ahead if he'd cut his losses and removed himself totally from her."

With bitter anger in her tone, Polly said, "Easy for you to say—you're a multimillionaire."

"I wasn't always a multimillionaire," Mac said. "Before my inheritance, I did have to ask myself that very question. It was hard, but I cut my losses and walked away from a very bad situation to start over. Sometimes you have to take the less traveled path to find happiness and peace of mind."

He could see by the deep frown on her face that his advice was not what she wanted to hear.

"Think about this, Ms. Langley," he said. "If Carl had walked completely away from Ruth back when he moved in with you—if he had turned his back on the opportunity to play the role of the mourning husband—then he wouldn't have opened the door for whoever framed him. And he would be alive right now, and the media wouldn't be portraying him as a killer."

Dallas was more nervous than a cat in a room full of rocking chairs.

David had been very specific about their plan. He'd even made her repeat it to him. As soon as she got up to their room, she was to close all of the blinds. Then she would text him the room number. The number only. Not "room" or "rm." Nothing more than the number. Out on the street, once he received the text, David would wait seven minutes—not five or ten—before crossing the street and going up to their room.

The deluxe room was decorated in elegant European furnishings that included a balcony overlooking the city. After tossing her shopping bags onto the king-sized bed and closing the curtains, Dallas sent the text to David and waited.

It was eerily quiet.

Outside, she could hear the traffic. After five months of living in the city, she had managed to tune it out. Now she could hear not only the buzz of vehicles rushing to navigate the heavily congested streets but also the ticking of the clock on the nightstand. Like an ominous symbol of their time running out, the ticking became louder with each passing minute.

Eleven minutes had passed since Dallas had texted him the number, 939.

Dallas was pacing long before the seven minutes had passed. She would've felt better if they had given her a room facing the same street David was waiting on so she could see him out the window. As it was, she had no idea if the police had spotted him or not.

No, they're looking for a blond-haired man in jeans, sports coat, and a blue sweater—not an expensive leather jacket and a fedora. But then I've straightened my hair, put on a ton of make-up, and changed my clothes completely, and that woman in the elevator still recognized me. Who was she, anyway?

Dallas picked up the card she'd placed next to her handbag. *Is she a friend or a foe? Seemed friendly enough.* She tucked the card into her wallet.

What time is it now? Fourteen minutes had passed since she'd texted David the number.

Hearing a sound in the hallway, she hurried to the door and peered out through the peephole. The room across the hall was receiving room service.

David, where are you? Grabbing the burner phone, she pressed in the message, "Where R U?" Recalling David's warning to only use the phone when absolutely necessary, she paused with her thumb over the "send" button.

No. She deleted the text and resumed pacing from one end of the room to the other, stopping during each pass to peer out the window and down to the street for any sign of the police moving in.

To her calculation, he should have been knocking on her door five minutes ago. *A lot can happen in five minutes. How long did it take David to take out both of those cops trying to kill them? It was a matter of seconds.*

Hearing a movement outside the door, she ran to look out the peephole. The server was wheeling the cart away.

With a curse, Dallas backed away from the door. *David, if you're dead, I'm going to kill you.* She threw herself onto the king-sized bed. As soon as her body made contact with the mattress, she heard a rap on the door. A shriek escaped her lips before she ran to it and grabbed the lever. She was about to throw it open when she remembered to be cautious. She peered through the peephole and saw David's fedora.

"Who is it?" she asked in a seductive tone.

"Tony."

Throwing open the door, she reached out, grabbed him by the front of his jacket, and yanked him inside. Before David could object, she threw her arms around him and smothered his face with kisses, forcing him to ease her inside and close the door behind him while she clung to him.

"You had me worried sick!" she said between kisses. "What took you so long? You said seven minutes. It's been over fifteen."

David tossed his hat onto the bed. "I got lost."

Dallas released him. Her mouth dropped open. "Lost? I left you *across the street*. How could you get *lost?*"

Hurrying back to the door, David opened it slightly to hang the do-not-disturb sign on the handle. "As luck would have it, I came in at the same time that a big group was checking in. There was a huge crowd around the elevators. Not wanting to take a chance, I took the stairs." He plopped down onto the bed. "When I came out of the stairwell and onto the ninth floor, I was completely turned around. I've been wondering the hallways for the last five minutes, looking for the room. Then just as I found the right corridor, there was a server coming down the hall. I had to duck back into the stairwell to wait for him to leave."

Climbing into his lap, she straddled him and shook him by the shoulders. "Well you had me worried sick. The least you could have done was call me to tell me that you weren't dead. That would have been the polite thing to do."

Dropping back onto his elbows, David grabbed her arms to make her stop shaking him. He looked up into her light-brown eyes. A grin crept to his lips. "I'm sorry. Next time I'll call to tell you I'm not dead."

Their eyes locked in a long gaze.

Fearing what would happen next, David eased her off him and moved over to the love seat. After shrugging out of his jacket and draping it across the arm of the small sofa, he slipped off the new boots, which had begun to hurt his feet.

He considered switching back to his regular shoes. The last thing he needed if he suddenly had to run was a pair of boots that weren't broken in. He was staring at one of the boots in his hands when he became aware that Dallas was sitting on the bed directly across from him.

"I'm famished." She stretched across the width of the bed to turn on the desk lamp. "Are you hungry, love?"

David did not miss the pet name that she had called him. He had grown accustomed to her terms of endearment. "Sweetie." "Sweetheart." "Dear." "Darlin'." "Honey." Even "puddin'." But "love." That was different.

"I'm not hungry," he said. "You go ahead and order whatever you want from room service. We've taken too many chances being out in public. We should stay put in this room until Mac and Ed make some progress."

A slow grin came to her lips. "Oh, neither of us is goin' anywhere."

"Why does that sound like a threat?" David asked, but she already had the phone's receiver to her ear.

"Are you sure you don't want a New York strip?" Dallas asked with her finger poised over the room-service button on the phone.

"Salad with grilled chicken is fine," he said while digging through her bag for the case file she'd smuggled out of the News Corp Building. "I don't want anything heavy in case we need to get moving fast." Upon finding the folder, he opened it on the seat next to him.

Using her Jersey-girl accent, Dallas put in her orders. When she ordered a bottle of wine, David cast a side glance in her direction.

As soon as she hung up, she slid down to the foot of the bed, where she perched with her chin in her hands. With a sigh, she gazed at him. Seeing a hint of annoyance, she asked, "What?"

"You shouldn't have ordered the wine," he said.

"Why not? I thought you drank."

"I do, but we need to be one hundred percent," he said. "If things go real bad real fast, like they did this morning, we need to have our wits about us. Alcohol, big steaks, and rich desserts will slow us—and our reaction times—down. Understand?"

"Understood," she said so seriously that David wondered if she were mocking him.

"Sorry," he muttered. "I hate to be a wet blanket, but one of us has to be the adult if we're going to get through this alive."

"You only want to keep us both safe." She reached over to brush her fingertips across his thigh. "I get that."

Grasping her hand and taking it off of his leg, he studied her long, elegant fingers. Unlike most women he knew, she kept her fingernails short and unpolished. "I think you're resourceful enough to take care of yourself."

She slipped off the bed. "I realized somethin' while waitin' for you."

Saying nothing, David stared down at her bare feet.

She lifted the suede poncho up, slipped it over her head, and allowed it to hit the floor next to her. David slowly moved his eyes up her body and saw that underneath the poncho, she was wearing a burnt-orange turtleneck sweater that hugged every sensuous curve of her luscious body.

"You haven't once talked 'bout Chelsea," she said. "No attempts to call her. No mention of her. Have you even thought about her today?"

"This was a mistake," David muttered. She moved toward him until she was standing before him. She rested her hands on his shoulders. Her firm stomach was at his eye level. Placing his hands on her hips, he kissed her stomach—once, twice, and again and again, pressing his lips and face longer and harder against her body each time.

Uttering a low moan, she kneaded his shoulders and back.

"You feel so good," he breathed.

She dropped to her knees in front of him.

Caressing her face in both hands, he locked eyes with her as he ran his fingers through her long, straight, silky hair, allowing them to travel down to the very ends of it until he was brushing his fingertips up her soft arms to her shoulders and then up her neck. After tilting her head back, he covered her mouth with his, kissing her fully, tasting her as deeply as he could, and trying to commit the essence of her to his memory.

"David," she whispered when he pulled away. "I don't know what's going to happen later, considering what happened today, with the police, and with whoever sent those dirty cops after us. But I want you to know … no matter what happens … that I love you. I've loved you ever since I laid eyes on you." Gazing up at him with moist eyes, she smiled tenderly.

Struck by the sudden, unexpected declaration from who had to be the most beautiful woman he had ever met—the woman who was kneeling before him and declaring her love for him—David let out a deep breath. "It is so easy to fall in love with you."

She lifted her face to his. Closing her eyes, she waited for him to take her in his arms, pick her up, and carry her over to the bed to make passionate love to her.

Instead, he said, "But I can't."

Feeling him lift his hands from where he was caressing her, sensing him pull away and stand up to put distance between them, she opened her eyes and turned to where he had retreated.

"I'm so very sorry," he said. "I'm not going to say I don't have feelings for you. I do. I'll even admit they're growing stronger the longer we're together … but I'm *engaged.*" He raised his voice. "I'm getting married on Saturday."

"Do you think I *want* to break you and your fiancée up?" Dallas rose to her feet.

"Oh, so you don't want to break us up? You just want a roll in the hay—all casual, with no strings attached?"

Dallas placed her hands on her hips. "I'm not that type of woman."

"If you're not, why did you just now—"

"You can't pick your family or who you fall in love with," she said. "Do you think I wanted to fall in love with a guy who's getting married to another woman in a few days? If I had my pick, I'd fall in love with a guy who wasn't already picked, but that's not the cards we've been dealt."

"Well, before we play this hand, I strongly suggest we reshuffle the deck," David said. "I've already been there and done that. Chelsea and I had a really good thing going back a long time ago, and I let my hormones take over and ended up hurting her bad—really bad. When I remember the look she had on her face when she found out"—he shook his head—"I never want to hurt someone that badly ever again." He sucked in a deep breath. "I've spent the last few years making it up to her and winning her trust again. Now I've made a commitment to her, and I'm not going to go back on my word again."

Refusing to reveal how deeply his rejection was cutting her—and it was cutting her like a knife—Dallas stared at him with wide eyes.

The knock on the door signaled the end of their conversation. "Room service."

David took the gun out from the back of his waistband. "I'm going to wait in the bathroom for them to leave and make sure all is clear. After they're gone, I'm going to take a shower. You go ahead and eat."

He opened the door and stepped into the bathroom.

"Sugar," she said to stop him.

He paused at the door.

"What you said just now was very eloquent," she said. "Tender, even—like how badly you hurt Chelsea; how you spent years makin' it up to her, makin' a commitment, and givin' her your word. But there was somethin' very important that you left out—that you didn't say."

Slowly, David turned to her. "What was that?"

"That you love her."

Chapter Twenty

Mac had concluded that unless a show was being recorded, the usual noise level inside a studio was blaringly loud. After checking to make sure the recording indicator light in the outside corridor on the thirty-sixth floor was off, he pressed through the studio door to find casually dressed crew members and well-dressed on-camera journalists rushing about like entertainers in a three-ring circus.

Mac made his way into the control room and found Jim Wiehl standing behind his wife, who was seated at the control panel. The director and his assistant were filling two other chairs. Each one of them had a furrowed forehead and knitted eyebrows. Mac was wondering what they were concentrating on until he heard David's voice coming from a speaker.

"I'm not wired like that, Yvonne. What happened to you?"

It took a full moment for Mac to realize what he was hearing.

David's voice continued, "You think that you can trap me, lock me up in this concrete cage called a city, and hand me a bunch of toys, and I'll be happy? You know me better than that."

"You recorded the murder." There was accusation in Mac's tone.

All four of them jumped and whirled around. The director ordered the assistant director to turn off the recording.

Jim Wiehl stepped forward as if to block Mac from moving any farther into the room. "Faraday, what are you doing here?"

Refusing to be held back, Mac dodged the executive producer and went up to the control panel. "Looking for Yvonne's killer," he said. "Where did you get that recording? Have you turned it over to the police?"

"We only now found out about it," Pam said. "In all the excitement last night, the sound technician didn't realize what he had. He just told us, and we've been listening to it to see if there's anything on it."

"What about the shot?" Mac asked. "The science of forensics has advanced to the point that scientists can identify a weapon based on the sound of a shot."

"We've listened to it three times and can't hear any gunshot," Jim said.

The assistant director said, "But I think if we can isolate the various noises in the background, we can pick it up."

"Don't do anything to the recording," Pam said in a firm tone. "If we tamper with it in any way, when they catch Yvonne's murderer, the recording will be tossed out of court as evidence."

Mac was surprised by the journalist's order. Based on what he'd been hearing about her, he'd expected her to use the recording for her own professional gain.

"I thought they found the murder weapon in the stairwell," the director said.

"Even so, this recording is evidence," Mac said.

"Pam's right," Jim said. "We'll make a copy for ourselves and give the untouched original to the police." He then ordered the director to contact the police department.

"Can you make a copy for me, too?" Mac asked.

"Sure," the assistant director said. "I can send it directly to your cell phone if you want."

While the director and his assistant went to work, Jim turned back to Mac to ask him about the purpose of his visit. "We only have ninety minutes before we start recording tonight's show."

"We're doing a special tribute to Yvonne," Pam said.

"That's very nice," Mac said. "But I'm also short on time."

"You mean your brother," Pam said. "David O'Callaghan. We have sources with the police department. Somehow, they've connected him to the murder of two police officers. Hopkins is suggesting that this makes them wonder if he had something to do with Yvonne's murder. Maybe murder for hire. He paid Rubenstein to kill Yvonne so he could inherit her money."

"Your security office said that the visitor's request for Carl Rubenstein was submitted while Yvonne was at lunch with David. So there was no way he could have sent in the form—even if he had managed to get access to the building's intranet."

"How about Ali Hudson," Jim pointed out. "Our sources say she's on the run with O'Callaghan."

"She had nothing to do with Yvonne's murder," Pam said, shaking her head. "Ali left for lunch the same time Yvonne did. We all rode down in the elevator together. Yvonne, O'Callaghan, Lieutenant Hopkins, me, and Ali Hudson. Rubenstein was out front with reporters, causing a scene. O'Callaghan was breaking it up when Hopkins and I were going to lunch. I saw Ali cross the street."

Silently, Mac recalled meeting Ali as she was coming out of the building not long after that, when she claimed she'd forgotten her bag and had had to return to her office to retrieve it.

"The police proved Rubenstein killed Yvonne," Jim told his wife. "They found the gloves he was wearing when he shot her."

"But then who shot Rubenstein?" Pam turned to look at Mac. "Everyone saw you go into the stairwell after him."

"Rubenstein was shot from down below him in the stairwell," Mac said. "It could have been an accident. The gun went off when the real shooter tossed it down the stairwell to get rid of it."

"What makes you think Rubenstein didn't kill Yvonne?" Jim asked him.

"Rubenstein told security that Yvonne was going to interview him for *Crime Watch,*" Mac explained. "He could have been lying about the interview, but someone on the inside had to have sent the visitor's notice to security. He didn't have the means to do that."

"Why would anyone in ZNC want to kill Yvonne?" Jim asked.

"Doesn't it seem ironic to you that Yvonne died on the same day Walker's body was found, and Yvonne was the last one to interview her before she disappeared?" Mac asked them.

"I don't like the direction this questioning is going in," Jim said.

"And I don't like that some dirty cops tried to kill my brother and that now he's running for his life," Mac said. "Deal with it."

"We never even knew Yvonne was married," Pam said. "We hadn't even met your brother before yesterday. What makes you—"

"But you had met Audra Walker," Mac said. "I believe whoever killed Audra shot Yvonne and is now after Ali Hudson because she was Yvonne's research assistant. My brother just happened to be there when they tried to kill her."

"Someone is trying to kill Ali?" Pam gasped while taking Jim's hand. "Oh, that dear girl. She's the same age as our Katie."

Jim swallowed. "How can we help?"

"The truth would be a big help," Mac said. "Sources tell me that you didn't get along with Audra Walker, Ms. Wiehl."

To Mac's surprise, Pam clasped her hand over her mouth. Her eyes instantly filled with tears.

Jim grasped her shoulder. "We should talk someplace else. Someplace quiet." With his arm around his wife, the executive producer escorted Mac and Gnarly out of the control room. They then made a sharp left turn to travel down a small inner hallway and through another door that opened into a room that resembled a beauty salon. The spacious room, which included two dressing rooms, a bathroom, and a rear door leading to the opposite end of the corridor, had vanity stations and a staff of cosmetologists and hairdressers.

"This is where all the real magic happens," Pam said. "The makeup department."

Four cosmetologists were busy helping guests and on-air personalities with their hair and makeup in four of the eight chairs. Ian Griffith and the other host for *Crime Watch* were applying their own makeup in the two other chairs.

"When you've been in the business long enough," Pam explained, "you learn how to make yourself up on your own. I can now apply my whole face in under ten minutes."

"But not her eyelashes," Ian Griffith said with a laugh. "Like last night."

"Ian was in here cracking all of us up after my eyelash decided to take on a life of its own during my interview with Lieutenant Hopkins," Pam said. "He followed me back here and had all of us in stitches as he made one joke after another. Who would have thought there were so many jokes one could make about eyelashes?"

"So this is where you were when Yvonne was killed?" Mac asked.

The smile fell from Pam's face. "We didn't know until Ryan Ritter came running in and told us that someone had shot her."

At Jim Wiehl's suggestion, everyone decided to take a short dinner break in order to clear the room and to allow Mac to repeat his question about Audra Walker.

"Why was Yvonne Harding interviewing a Pulitzer Prize–winning author on *Crime Watch*? Why weren't you, the main attraction, doing it?" Mac asked. "Sources have told me that you were so jealous of Audra that you couldn't see straight."

Taking a seat in one of the makeup chairs, Pam said, "Yes, I was jealous of Audra Walker. Very jealous. Everything was so easy for her. She came from a tiny town in Texas—much like the one I came from in Montana—and married an older man with more money than God."

"Unlike me," Jim interjected.

"I've since learned that there are things much more valuable than money and fame." She kissed him on the cheek, causing a soft look filled with love to cross the producer's face. "Audra Walker had everything I wanted when I left Montana," Pam said. "She could drink any man under the table and be as bright as the sunshine the next day. She was skinny. Beautiful. Had two perfect, bright kids. Best book deals from the biggest publishers with the biggest advances, and awards coming out of her ears—yes, I hated her." She choked.

"Audra Walker was also the best friend that anyone could have asked for," Jim said.

Pam grasped her husband's hand. "The type of woman who would lay her life down for you without giving it a second thought." With a trembling hand, she wiped a tear from her eye.

Seeing more tears coming, Jim reached for a box of tissues, which he handed to her. "Three years ago, our youngest daughter, Katie, was offered a job as an assistant to a wealthy businessman in Egypt."

Mac noticed Pam clutching her husband's hands with both of hers. She appeared to age no less than ten years before his eyes.

Jim continued. "She was so excited. The job offered the chance to travel all over Europe first class, all expenses paid for." He sighed. "It was too good to be true."

"Katie went missing less than two days after she got to Egypt," Pam said with a catch in her voice. "Our last communication with her was a desperate phone call from her cell. She said that it had all been a lie, and then we heard her screaming—right before we got cut off."

"We called the embassy, the State Department—"

"Who said they could do nothing." The angry tone in her voice was evident.

With a nod of his head, Jim said, "We hired private investigators. They found that there was an actual white-slavery scam there. They would lure young Western women to Eastern Europe with the promise of glamorous jobs in order to abduct them and force them into becoming sex slaves for wealthy businessmen and leaders in the Middle East."

"Wasn't that the subject of your book that came out the same time as Audra's book?" Mac asked.

"That was how I learned about the problem," Pam said. "Because of what happened to Katie. When she got to Egypt, she was abducted by this ring. When they found out she was a virgin, they auctioned her off like an animal."

"The highest bidder was one of the leaders of ISIS," Jim said. "He intended to make her one of his concubines. Because she was white and a virgin, Katie was quite a status symbol for this animal to own."

"Obviously, you managed to bring her home," Mac said.

"Thanks to Audra Walker," Pam said with a sob.

Jim explained. "When our private investigator told us that a group with ties to ISIS had our daughter, we went to the State Department."

"Who did nothing," Pam said. "Due to their political connections with some of the parties involved in this practice that was accepted in the third world region where they had taken Katie, our State Department didn't want to risk ruining any delicate negotiations taking place at the time."

Mac plunged forward. "But Audra Walker did help bring Katie home."

"It just so happened that at the same time, Audra Walker was being interviewed by one of our affiliates in Italy," Jim said. "I was desperate. Since her husband, Buddy, was so wealthy, and he had so many business connections all over the world, I called Audra and explained what was happening. I asked her—begged her—to help us. Maybe, I thought, the Walkers could pay the terrorists enough money to get her back for us." He sighed heavily. "Audra said to leave everything to her. Fewer than seventy-two hours later, we were hugging our daughter at JFK. Audra personally escorted her home on a private jet after rescuing her from a private compound in Saudi Arabia. Katie told us that Audra saved not only her but also over a dozen other young American women, some of whom were teenage girls, from this camp. Apparently, arrangements were being made to send them off to serve as concubines to terrorist-leaders all over the Middle East. Audra and a group of soldiers who must have been mercenaries brought all of those young women home."

"Without paying any ransom?" Mac asked.

"Katie told us that Audra's group blew up the terrorist compound, an act that Israel ended up getting the blame for—or the credit for, depending on who you asked," Pam said.

"Audra was like"—Jim shrugged—"as casual about bringing our daughter and the rest of those girls home as she would've been if she'd taken them all on a shopping trip."

"She did that, too," Pam said. "I think the whole group cleaned out Harrods before coming back to the States—all on Audra's dime."

Mac started to speak. "But—"

"It made me so ashamed of how jealous I had been of her," Pam said. "As cold as I had been to her, she still—she took such a risk to save *my* daughter. And she refused to—well, she *insisted* that we never tell anyone what she did. Even in my book, I never mentioned Audra Walker and what she did, because she was adamant that I never tell anyone about her involvement."

"I offered to pay her," Jim said. "But she refused. Said it was just one parent helping out another. Her late husband, Buddy Walker, was the same way. You have no idea how much the Walkers gave to charity without anyone knowing—how much they kept secret."

Mac was stunned. When he found his voice, he asked, "How was she able to assemble such a team and break into a terrorist—"

"Audra Walker had a talent for moving effortlessly from high society to the gutter while always fitting in," Jim said.

"That's why she was such a good journalist," Pam said. "She had connections in every walk of life all over the world. Everyone trusted her—because she could be trusted."

"Like when she spent more than a week in jail for refusing to give up her source," Mac said.

"I know a lot of journalists who would offer big talk about doing that," Pam said, "but when it came down to it ..."

"I still don't know how many favors Audra called in to save Katie," Jim said. "The fact is, she did it when no one else would."

Mac glanced over at Pam, who was tearfully staring down at her feet. "I still don't understand why Yvonne Harding interviewed Audra instead of you, Pam?"

"Because ..." Pam started to say. "I couldn't trust myself. If I got in front of a camera with her, I would have broken down and told the whole world what type of woman Audra Walker really was and she told me flat out that she did not want that to happen. We decided together that Yvonne Harding would do the interview."

Mac felt guilty asking his next question, but he needed to know. "Where were both of you on the night Audra Walker disappeared?"

Jim answered without hesitation. "The police asked us about that night, so I remember. We both left the city together as soon as taping was over. We were driving upstate to our weekend place." He added, "I guess you want to know where I was when Yvonne was shot."

"That would help," Mac said.

"I was in the control booth," he said. "My director, assistant producer, and sound technician were with me."

Pam volunteered her alibi next. "I was here in makeup getting my eyelash repaired. We were right in the midst of getting it on when all the excitement broke out. Ian Griffith and a couple of guests and all of the makeup artists were in here when it happened."

With a sad expression, she looked down at Gnarly, who was resting his head on her lap. "You must think I'm awful. Yvonne was murdered, and there I was, fussing about my bald eye."

"Funny what people notice or focus on when things like that happen," Mac noted.

Leaving the couple in the makeup department, Mac picked up Gnarly's leash and led the German shepherd out the rear door, which looped around the corner at the end of the corridor, past the entrance to the stairwell, and back to the elevators.

Once they were out on the street, Mac decided to pass on taking a cab back to the hotel and to instead enjoy the brisk autumn weather. Hopefully, after going over everything that Letty, Audra's assistant, had sent him about the Texan Romeo and Juliet, he could uncover what Audra had seen or heard at ZNC that night—and what had given her the breakthrough on the case she'd been working on her whole adult life.

Mac was a full block away from the News Corps Building when his cell phone vibrated in its case. After digging it out, Mac read the caller ID. It was Ed.

"What did you find out from Gibbons?" Mac asked him.

"She was going to talk to the expert who confirmed that the handwriting on the postcard had come from Walker," Ed reported. "But unfortunately, she can't do that. The handwriting expert is dead."

"Don't tell me," Mac replied while quickening his step. "Sometime yesterday … after Audra Walker's body was discovered."

"Someone pushed him in front of a subway car on his way home last night," Ed said. "Our killer doesn't like loose ends. Gibbons said she's going to talk to Lieutenant Wayne Hopkins this evening."

"Get me her home address," Mac said. "I want to be there when this conversation takes place."

"Maybe it's not Hopkins," Ed said. "Could be someone on his team."

"In either case, I want a face to face with this guy," Mac said. "The longer David's on the run, the more trigger-happy these cops are going to be when they catch him."

Chapter Twenty-One

"Mac, I've got a cab," Ed called to him from where the doorman had hailed a taxicab for them in front of the Four Seasons. "Are you and Gnarly ready to go?"

"Just about." Mac was urging Gnarly to make use of the fire hydrant before getting into the cab when his cell phone buzzed on his hip. Hoping that it would be good news from David, he grabbed the phone to check the ID. It was Doc Washington, the medical examiner in Garrett County, Maryland.

"Hey, Doc," Mac answered the call. "I'm assuming you're calling about some autopsy reports I asked Bogie to pass on to you."

"The very ones," she replied in her low, cultured voice. "You are aware that I'm at a disadvantage because these reports are over thirty years old and because I have no access to any of the physical evidence."

Mac handed the leash off to Ed, who ushered Gnarly into the backseat of the cab. "I'm just hoping you might see something that raises a red flag."

The driver apprehensively eyed the very large German shepherd as if he feared Gnarly would eat him.

"There was one," she replied. "According to Bogie and the police report, the kids killed in the car that went over the cliff were seventeen or eighteen years old, right? They were healthy, young Caucasians, one male and one female."

"Right," Mac said. "Seniors in high school. This incident happened the night of the senior prom. Anything in the report jump out at you?"

"Like that neither of them died in the fire?" she asked. "According to the autopsy report, neither of them had inhaled fire or smoke into their lungs. The girl died from a broken neck. All of the other injuries consistent with a car crash came well over an hour after she was dead."

"She was dead before she was put in the car?" Mac ignored Ed, who was gesturing for him to climb into the back of the cab.

"But wait, there's more."

"Tell me," Mac said, urging her on.

"The boy was not a boy," Doc said. "According to skeletal structure and dental X-rays, I'd put the female at late teens to early twenties, but the male was significantly older. I'd put him in his early to midtwenties. Now I could be wrong. However, this was supposed to be a high school boy from a rural Southern town, right?"

"Supposedly," Mac said.

"So what was he doing with bits of healed-over shrapnel in his legs?"

"Shrapnel?" Mac repeated.

"Shrapnel," she said. "Healed over. It's all over his legs—like he was in the vicinity of a bomb blast."

"Like a soldier who'd seen action," Mac said.

"Thirty years ago," she said. "That was before the conflict in the Middle East."

"It wasn't a suicide pact," Mac said. "It was a homicide. Let me talk to Bogie."

"Mac, I'm at home," Doc said.

"I'm not asking what room you're in," Mac said. "Just hand the phone to Bogie. I need him to do something for me."

"Mac," Ed whispered to him, "the meter is running."

"This will only take a minute," Mac told Ed while Bogie picked up the line.

"Figures you'd catch me with my pants down," Bogie's gravelly voice said through the speaker.

"That is not a visual that I'm looking for right now," Mac replied.

"I can guess what you want," Bogie said. "Doc already told me. Call Texas, and ask if any young couples including a soldier who had seen action were reported missing at about the time of Romeo and Juliet's suicide pact. Are you thinking Audra Walker ran into Romeo and Juliet in New York?"

"But so much time had passed," Mac said. "The only way to prove it would be to prove that the boy and girl buried in Texas aren't who everyone thought they were."

Bogie agreed. "But there's no way a small-town deputy chief in Maryland is going to get the Texas authorities to exhume those bodies. If I call them, they'll tell me where to go."

"Then don't ask them," Mac said. "Call them, and ask if they have any missing couples from around that time period. Make it sound like you've found them up in Deep Creek Lake."

After grumbling that it was worth a shot, Bogie asked how David was doing.

"He's okay," Mac noticed that his voice went up an octave.

"You're lying," Bogie said. "What's wrong?"

"I can't go into it right now," Mac said. "He'll be fine. Ed and I are on top of everything. How's Chelsea?"

"Fine."

Mac noticed that Bogie's voice had gone up an octave. "What's happening with Dr. Love?"

"Do you mean Dr. Seth Blanchard?" Bogie asked. "He's a good stand-up guy."

"Sounds to me like you're rooting for him," Mac said.

"I only want what's best for David and Chelsea," Bogie said. "Wouldn't it be better for them to discover that they aren't *the one* for each other before the wedding instead of after?"

"So he's putting moves on Chelsea?" Mac asked. "I thought this was all in Archie's imagination."

"Let me put it this way," Bogie said. "The hospital gift shop had to close to restock their flowers."

"That's not fair," Mac spat out. "David isn't there to defend himself."

"All's fair in love and war, Mac."

As soon as Mac hung up, Ed urged him into the cab, and the driver, relieved to finally get a move on, hurried as best he could in New York's evening traffic. The sooner he got them to their destination, the sooner he could get Gnarly out of his backseat.

"Gibbons is going to be mad," Ed told Mac several minutes later while handing a wad of bills to the cabdriver, who had delivered them to the apartment where Abby Gibbons lived.

"Especially if she's in on it," Mac told his lawyer as he led Gnarly out onto the sidewalk.

In the front seat, the driver sighed as if he were relieved he had gotten to their destination without being eaten.

"We don't know who the dirty cops are or who's running things. For all we know, she's feeding us a line, and she and Hopkins are running this whole operation together," Mac said.

Ed closed the rear door of the cab and tapped the hood to signal that the cabdriver could leave. "If that were the case, she would have never told us that those cops were dirty."

"She'd look guiltier if she told us they were clean, and we found out they weren't," Mac said. "Better for her to pretend to be on our side and keep us close so that she knows what we know."

"Do you think Gibbons is in on it or not?"

Before Mac could answer, a loud crash followed by a high-pitched scream filled the air. More shrieks joined in before the noise came to a shattering halt as the body of Lieutenant Abigail Gibbons landed on top of the cab that had delivered Mac and Ed to her apartment.

Mac was the first to find his voice. "If she was, she's not anymore."

In the shower, David stood with his face up to receive the full force of the spray. His eyes closed, he was alone with his thoughts of every woman who had raced in and out of his life, every relationship, and every mistake he'd made that had hurt those he loved.

There was his mother, who, lost in her dementia, could not differentiate between him and his father, who had loved her but had also been in love with another woman, the famously brilliant Robin Spencer—Mac's mother.

David was in high school before he saw that the roots of his parents' marital issues had to do with his father being in love with a woman he couldn't have—all because he was too honorable to disrespect his wife by leaving her. In spite of the rumors that claimed otherwise, he never cheated on David's mother. David knew that for a fact, because he had told him to his face when David had confronted him with the rumors.

"Do you love Mom?" David had asked him in the blunt, direct manner of a teenage boy.

"I would never hurt your mother, son," Patrick O'Callaghan had said. That was on the day the principal called him to pick up David after he'd broken a boy's nose for teasing him about his father's alleged affair with the murder-mystery writer who lived at the end of Spencer Point. He found his son in the nurse's office with an ice pack on his black eye.

"But you are cheating on her?"

"No, I'm not," Patrick said. "Robin and I are friends. We may even be best friends. I haven't had sex with her since she moved back here to Spencer."

It was not until much later that David realized the significance of the words "since she moved back to Spencer." He had had sexual relations with her years before, when Mac Faraday had been conceived.

"So you aren't having sex with her," David said. "But you're in love with her."

Dressed sharply in his police-chief uniform—black slacks and white shirt—Patrick O'Callaghan stood up straight and stared at his son.

His silence spoke volumes.

"It's true," David said in a soft voice. "And she's in love with you. It's an affair of the heart."

After another long silence, Patrick said, "You are a very smart young man."

"Are you in love with Mom?"

"I took a vow when I married your mother," he answered. "I gave her my word that I would stay with you and her through sickness and in health, for richer or poorer, till death—"

"And that's the only reason you stay with her, when the woman you love lives only a couple of miles away—because of a stupid vow you took," David said, tossing the ice pack aside.

"A man, or a woman, for that matter, is only as good as his or her word," Patrick said. "That's why I don't give my word lightly. Marriage is a commitment, and a real man doesn't walk away from a commitment—otherwise, his words would have no value, and if his words have no value, then he's not worth anything."

David stood up out of the chair. "What if he made a mistake when he gave his word?"

Patrick stood up to him. "This is not your concern, Son."

"It's my life, and that makes it my business," David said. "I love Chelsea. If something happened and for some reason I thought she was gone, and I married someone else, and then Chelsea, the love of my life, came back, I'd leave the other woman like *that*." He snapped his fingers.

Patrick laughed at his son's anger. "Oh, you young people know so much about life."

"Think about it, Dad," David said. "Mom's crazy—"

"Don't talk about your mother like that," Patrick said.

"It's true, Dad." David raised his voice. "She's nuts. Has it ever occurred to you that maybe loving you and knowing that you're in love with someone else—and knowing that the only thing keeping you home is your stupid word—has maybe contributed to her insanity? Think about it. If you had left her years ago, maybe she would have gotten over you by now—"

"Or killed herself," Patrick said in a somber voice.

"But you'd be with the woman you truly love," David said. "I'm never going to let anyone or anything come between me and the woman I truly love."

The sound of the door closing made David jump out of his thoughts. He almost banged into the shower door reaching for his weapon, which he had placed on top of the folded towel on the bathroom counter.

Through the steam, he could make out Dallas standing in the middle of the bathroom.

"Are you okay?" she asked. "You've been in here for so long, and your supper's getting cold."

David wiped the water from his face. The sound of her sultry voice excited him.

"I'm sorry if I upset you," she said. "I mean, comin' on to you and tryin' to talk ya outta marryin' Chelsea. It was low of me. Like I said, I'm not that type of woman. It's just … I felt this immediate connection, and … I do love you, David."

There was silence, and David felt like he had to reply. All he could think of to say in response to her second declaration of love was "I know."

He heard the bathroom door open a second time. "Well, honey, don't stay in there too long, or you're gonna wrinkle up like a prune—and I don't think Chelsea wants to spend her weddin' night with a prune."

He heard the bathroom door close.

Cocking his head, he waited, half expecting—or was it half hoping?—that she would open the shower door and step in with him.

Opening the shower door, he peered out and saw that she was gone. Disappointment clutched at him.

I'm marrying Chelsea, but I want Dallas. I want to be with Dallas, but I would never want to hurt Chelsea.

"There was somethin' very important that you left out—that you didn't say," Dallas had told him.

"What was that?" David had asked her.

"That you love her."

Among all the reasons I listed for not making love to Dallas and for marrying Chelsea, why didn't I say that I loved her?

"Do you love Mom?" David recalled asking his father that day in the nurse's office.

"I would never hurt your mother."

Why did I never notice that before? He didn't answer my question. Why not? Because Patrick O'Callaghan was a man of honor and integrity. He would have never lied. He couldn't say that he loved Mom because he didn't.

And me? I'm marrying Chelsea—why?

"I never want to hurt someone that badly ever again. I've spent the last few years making it up to her and winning her trust again. Now I've made a commitment to her, and I'm not going to go back on my word again," he had said.

Turning off the water, David stared at the wall, allowing the water to drip down from his scalp, over his shoulders, and down his body.

Is that what this has all been about? Trying to make amends for hurting Chelsea all those years ago? If that's it, how long can a marriage based on guilt last? What will happen if I meet my Robin Spencer later on? I could end up hurting Chelsea worse than I already have.

Opening the shower door, he stepped out and looked over at the spot where Dallas had been standing minutes ago, when she'd told him a second time that she loved him.

What if I already have?

Wrapping himself in a soft plush white bathrobe that came with the Plaza's suite, David went into the bedroom and found Dallas stretched out on her stomach across the bed with her mother's case file spread out in front of her. She was twisting and rotating her bare feet, which were at the head of the bed.

Looking up from the folder, a grin of satisfaction crossed her lips while she took in the sight of him clad only in the white bathrobe. "You're lookin' good," she said. "Refreshed,

I mean," she added. She tossed her head in the direction of his salad with grilled chicken on the table. "Your chicken is cold."

"I'm not hungry." He sat down on the bed next to where she was lying.

Slowly, she raised her light-brown eyes from where he was sitting up to where the front of the robe had loosened, revealing his bare chest, and then up to his blue eyes, which were peering down at her. "You haven't eaten all day."

"Maybe later," he replied. "Would you like to take a shower?"

Looking him up and down, a slow smile came to her lips. "Maybe later." She shifted over to give him room on the bed. "I'm reading the police report for Mom's disappearance." She slid the report in his direction. "I think you should see this."

Tightening the belt on the bathrobe, David stretched out on the bed next to Dallas and picked up the report she had set out for him. The top sheet of the report gave the details of Audra Walker's disappearance.

Journalist Audra Walker had spent the day at ZNC studios being interviewed by their on-air journalists. The last one was with Yvonne Harding, who was interviewing her for a segment of *Crime Watch*. Afterwards, Audra returned to her suite at the Four Seasons. Witnesses, including her assistant, Letty Bolger, who was with her the whole day, saw her return and go to her suite. Letty had the second bedroom in the suite. Audra Walker stayed up to work on her next project. Letty went to bed. The next morning, Letty found that Audra's bed had never been slept in and that she was missing.

Cell phone records indicated that shortly after eleven o'clock, Audra had received a text from Yvonne Harding saying that she had information on her next project and that she should meet her in front of the News Corps Building.

Yvonne Harding claimed she hadn't sent the text to Audra Walker. Not only that, but she also hadn't had Audra Walker's cell phone number. The text had been sent from a disposable—a burner phone.

"Nothing here that we didn't already know." David was aware that Dallas had moved in closer while he had been reading. Trying not to notice the sweet vanilla scent of her perfume, he flipped to the second page of the report.

It was a witness statement from Yvonne Harding. The details of her interview with Audra Walker read the same as those in the assistant's statement. Of course, Sergeant Roberts wanted to know Yvonne's alibi for after Audra Walker had left the studio. After all, the text luring Audra back to ZNC had allegedly come from her.

Yvonne claimed that she left the studio shortly after eight o'clock and went home to her condo in midtown Manhattan, which was within walking distance of the studio. However, she took a cab. Sergeant Roberts had tracked down the driver, who confirmed he'd driven the famous news journalist home that night.

Yvonne was home alone in her condo until approximately ten thirty, at which point Ryan Ritter stopped by sporting a fifty-year-old bottle of scotch he'd received as a gift from the guest on his show that night.

Aware of Dallas watching him, David skimmed the details, which, in a nutshell, said that Yvonne had an airtight alibi for not sending the text to Audra Walker or killing her. She had spent the whole night with Ryan Ritter.

Dallas' low, throaty voice broke through his thoughts. "Yvonne's alibi for Mom's disappearance is Ryan Ritter. Did you know they were sleeping together?"

"Didn't you say earlier that you suspected they had had a fling?" Laying down the report, David saw that she was so close to him that he could see that the outer rims of her brown eyes were green. He felt the heat of her shoulder pressed against his.

"It was just a suspicion. I guess this proves I was right, huh?" She rested her hand on his wrist. "Are you jealous? I mean, she didn't know you two were married, and—"

"Not really." He dared to turn his head and found her head close to his. "Surprised. I knew Yvonne wasn't celibate after we ended it, but I wasn't expecting her to be sleeping with Ryan Ritter."

One of her feet dropped down from where she'd been waving it up at the head of the bed, and it landed between his bare legs and feet. "You certainly weren't." Her mouth was close to his. "Celibate, I mean."

"Stay on point," he told her, aware of her foot rubbing up and down the inside of his calf. "Yvonne said in her statement that Ritter brought over a bottle of fifty-year-old scotch. Knowing Yvonne the way I did, that doesn't make sense. She didn't drink scotch—or at least when she did, she passed out. Yvonne and hard liquor did not mix well. After one drink, she'd be drunk. I mean, not-able-to-drive drunk. She wouldn't have shared a bottle of scotch with Ryan Ritter."

"The statement doesn't say how much she had to drink," Dallas said. "It only says Ryan brought over a bottle, and they shared it. From what she said in the statement, maybe she poured a drink but didn't drink it, and then they spent the night together." She brought her lips close to his. "You should be happy. She has an alibi. She didn't kill my mother."

"Something doesn't seem right about that statement," he said. "My gut tells me it's not right."

"Are you sure that feeling in your gut isn't jealousy over Ryan Ritter?" Dallas rolled over onto her side. "How many years had it been since you two were together? For all you know, she built up a tolerance for the hard stuff." She reached over to slip her hand inside the robe.

"Maybe," David murmured with a deep sigh. "That has been known to happen … just … Yvonne said in her statement that she didn't text your mother. Someone else using her name sent it from a burner phone."

"Or so she says," Dallas replied.

"Said." Struck by guilt, David pulled away from her and sat up. "She's dead—murdered—or have you forgotten?"

She pressed up against his back and wrapped her arms around him. "You're the one saying Yvonne's whole statement doesn't make sense simply because she didn't drink scotch. She didn't give the police a blow-by-blow, but it does say Ritter was the one who brought it over because the guest on his show gave it to him. What's the biggie?"

Leaning back against her, David said, "I don't know."

Holding him close, she said, "But we will know, and we'll find out together, because like it or not, I'm in this with you for the long haul."

He allowed her to slip the robe off his shoulders.

She brought her lips to his. "Whether you like it or not, no matter what happens, even if you do marry Chelsea a couple of days from now, I'll always be with you. Even if I can't have you, I'm always goin' to have your back—because, darlin', I'm in love with you."

He took her into his arms. "I have a feeling I'm falling in love with you, too."

Chapter Twenty-Two

"What do you mean, you don't have access to the crime scene?" the Manhattan police captain said to the chief detective, the half dozen homicide detectives, and the group of uniformed officers. They were all waiting outside the apartment building where Abigail Gibbons, an investigator with internal affairs, had fallen to her death from her tenth-floor apartment.

"Feds trump New York City metro." Lieutenant Andrew Van Patton, a middle-aged career detective in an ill-fitting, crumpled suit, tossed his head in the direction of the fleet of federal vehicles and the crime-scene investigators with "FBI" written in block letters across the backs of their jackets.

"Who called them in?" the captain asked.

"The governor."

The captain's eyes grew wide. "Who called the governor, and why did he call in the feds?"

"I think one of the guys Gibbons almost landed on top of made the call before any of us got here. Obviously, they're friends."

"Where's this *friend* of the governor?" the captain asked.

"Upstairs," Van Patton said, jerking his chin in the direction of the high-rise. "*They* allowed *him* in."

With a growl, the captain ordered the lieutenant to accompany him inside, but two federal agents blocked their entrance. The captain was only further annoyed when he was made to wait while one of the officers called upstairs to the investigating officer, who told the captain he had to wait while the special agent in charge came down to meet him.

"Are you serious?" the captain yelled. "This is *my* city." He ripped his cell phone out of his pocket. "I'm calling the commissioner."

"If you wait, you can talk to him in a couple of minutes, sir," the agent told him.

The captain stopped with his mouth hanging open.

"He's coming down with Special Agent Sid Delaney," the officer said. "He's anxious to talk to you."

The captain turned to the lieutenant, whose face had grown pale. "What … did … your … people … do?"

With her long, slender legs and arms, Dallas reminded David of a colt curled up asleep on the bed. Her thick, dark mane was splayed out across what had been his pillow.

"I love you, David!" Chelsea's had said tearfully. "You said you loved me! How could you break my heart like that?"

He was remembering the night of the Valentine's Day dance. It was senior year. Her confrontation had hit him like an ambush and had been just as painful. She confronted him with his own betrayal when he returned with his buddies to the gym where the dance was being held. He had left her alone for fewer than five minutes.

A lot can happen in five minutes.

David didn't need a blow-by-blow. The smirk on Katrina's face said it all. Seducing the always-loyal David O'Callaghan wouldn't really prove the power of her seduction skills if she kept it a secret.

Trying to avoid both women, David turned away and ended up face to face with Seth Blanchard, Chelsea's friend. The slightly chubby science geek always seemed to be around, even though he'd been delegated to the outskirts of their crowd. A highly respected surgeon, his mother was chief of staff at the hospital in Oakland. His family's wealth and social position should have made Seth a natural member of the in crowd around Deep Creek Lake. However, his mother's reluctance to indulge her son and her insistence on teaching him a healthy work ethic by making him earn his toys kept him out of the fast crowd.

Seth Blanchard was Chelsea's friend. David didn't need to be a detective to figure out that he wanted more. The expression on Seth's face confirmed his suspicion. With narrowed eyes, Seth looked at David as if he'd just kicked his beloved puppy in the ribs.

"Do you love her?" Chelsea tearfully asked David the next morning after he'd finally convinced her mother to allow him to see her.

"No," he said instantly

It was the truth. Never for a second had he ever thought he loved Katrina. His betrayal had been caused by a purely physical desire to be with the sexy girl with a reputation for knowing exactly how to fulfill adolescent fantasies.

From across the room, David looked over to the bed, where Dallas was sleeping. The light from the street outside spilled in through the break in the curtains, casting her in a golden glow.

This betrayal was completely different. His desire to be with Dallas was nothing like his desire to be with Katrina had been. His experiences with women and love and life had molded him into a man completely different from the one he'd been when Katrina had seduced him.

Even so, although this time was different, it was still a betrayal of someone he loved all the same. David closed his eyes. *What am I going to do?*

He heard multiple car doors slam shut. His eyes sprung open. On the street down below, three men were meeting with another man who had just walked out of the Plaza's main entrance. Even from his perch several floors above them, David recognized the thick padding under the three men's jackets as ballistics vests and weapons.

The other guy must have been the chief of hotel security.

David sprung from the window to shake Dallas awake. "Get dressed. We need to get moving. Now!"

To his surprise, she was instantly awake and grabbing her clothes. "What's going on?"

"Cops incoming," David said. "Three of them. I saw them meeting with a suit—looks like he could be hotel security."

Seeing that he was already fully dressed, she asked, "Have you slept at all?"

He shrugged into his jacket and grabbed his hat. "There'll be plenty of time to sleep when we get home."

She threw the poncho on over her head. David was surprised by how quickly she had managed to find and put on her clothes. In his experience, only active-military types were able to move that quickly after being awakened from a sound sleep.

"Maybe it has nothing to do with us."

"We can't take that chance." David handed her the spare gun he'd taken from one of the police officers he'd shot. "Tuck this into your waistband. Don't leave anything behind—especially the case file."

She was already tucking it into the secret compartment in her bag and slinging the bag over her shoulder. After grabbing the gun from him, she stood up and reached behind her back to tuck it into her waistband. To her surprise, she saw that while she'd been asleep, David had combined their belongings into only two shopping bags. They'd had six shopping bags when they'd checked in. "Where are the other bags?"

"I shredded them up, took them down three floors, and buried them in a trash can," he said. "But I kept the receipts. They're in your secret hiding place in your bag. Don't want anyone to find them and trace them to your credit cards."

"You really have been busy." She took in a deep breath. "I'm ready."

After grabbing her by the shoulders, David kissed her fully on the lips. "I love you, Dallas."

"I know." A broad grin crossed her face. "Don't worry. I've got your back." She showed him the gun she had hidden under the poncho.

"Hold on to the back of my jacket, and don't let go. It's going to be hard in those high heels, but you need to keep up."

"You'd be surprised how fast I can run in high heels." She snatched the bag out of his hand, rolled it up as tightly as she could, and shoved it into her shoulder bag. It stuck out a bit, but even so, it freed David's hand.

He put the fedora on his head and was careful to lower the rim to conceal the top half of his face. "Do exactly as I say," he told her while leading her to the door. He held his weapon out of sight behind his back. "We're going to take the rear stairwell and try to go out through the service entrance."

He opened the door a crack. After making sure the hallway was clear in both directions, he gestured for her to follow him. Together, they scurried down the corridor, away from the main elevators. They had made it almost to the end of the corridor, where the hallway broke into a T, when they heard the elevators open down at the other end. Stepping up the pace, David yanked her around the corner, and they ran for the stairwell. At the door, David halted and gestured with his finger to his lips, indicating that she should be quiet, while he eased the door open. No need to slam it so that guests in nearby rooms would hear it.

Once in the stairwell, they ran down the stairs, one flight after another. David would often take two steps at a time.

"How do you think they tracked us down?" she asked in a loud whisper.

"I must have missed a security camera while wandering around and looking for the room," David said. "I thought the hat covered my face, but a camera must have caught me."

Remembering the woman in the elevator, Dallas let out a loud gasp. "Or maybe that lady—"

Her gasp was abrupt enough to make David stop and turn around. "What lady?"

Dallas was breathing hard. "There was a woman in the elevator. She recognized me."

"What woman? What elevator?" David's heart raced with panic. "When we first got here? That was hours ago, Dallas! They probably have the hotel surrounded by a whole SWAT team complete with snipers! Why didn't you tell me?" When she reached for him, he pushed her away.

"She called me Dallas," she said. "The news says they're looking for Ali Hudson. They don't know that I'm Dallas."

"But this woman does," David said. "If she saw your face on the news and figured out that the police think you're Ali Hudson, she could have called them to tell them that you're really Dallas Walker and that you're staying here at the Plaza."

Slowly, Dallas shook her head. "I don't think so," she said through tears. "She was a friend of Mom's."

"Friends turn friends in to the cops all the time," David hissed. "The police are offering rewards for information leading to our capture. I can't believe you didn't tell me. I thought you were smarter than that."

Upstairs, they heard a door open. Grabbing her roughly by the arm, David charged down the stairs, dragging her behind him. He was so angry that he didn't care anymore about being gentle with her. He only wanted to get out of the hotel and as far away from New York as he could possibly get. At that point, he would have considered it a miracle if they were able to make it to the street.

Upon reaching the street level, David stopped. Exhausted, Dallas was clinging to his arm. Holding his finger to his lips for her to be quiet, he cracked open the door and looked out both ways. The alley was dimly lit, with only one streetlight casting the whole alley in shadows. A trash bin blocked David's view of the back of the alley. The opposite direction, which would lead them toward Central Park, was clear.

"Stay behind me," David whispered before leading her out of the stairwell.

They had only made it a few steps before the whole alley exploded into bright spotlights.

"Hold it right there, O'Callaghan!"

Two men silhouetted by the stoplights stepped toward them, aiming rifles at them.

Instantly, David's hands went up. Spreading his fingers wide, he took his finger off the trigger.

Holding up her hands, Dallas stepped forward to stand next to him. Her body shook with sobs. "This is all my fault."

"It's okay, baby," David said. "You made a mistake. We all do." Moving slowly, he dropped his gun down to the ground in front of him.

"Hands behind your head!" said the voice that David then recognized.

As he lowered his hands down to clasp his fingers behind his head, David saw Lieutenant Wayne Hopkins sauntering up the alley from behind a black unmarked cruiser. He had his service weapon aimed directly at him. "You know the drill, O'Callaghan. Get down on your knees."

Wordlessly, David lowered himself down onto his knees and crossed his ankles.

"Get his backup weapon," one of the officers who was still cast in silhouette said to someone behind David and Dallas.

While David had been watching Hopkins, Dallas had been following the same instructions they had given to him.

David felt someone pat down his lower legs until he located his ankle holster and took the small semiautomatic, which he handed to Lieutenant Hopkins. He then moved on to search Dallas. Instantly, he found the gun she'd tucked into the waistband of her pants and the ankle holster she'd taken from the downed officer.

"You know your mistake, O'Callaghan," the police lieutenant said while pocketing David's gun.

Keeping his eyes down on the ground in front of him, David said nothing.

"Being a hero," Hopkins said. "We had no interest in you or Faraday. It would have been so easy to set you and Faraday up to take the fall for your wife's murder, but no. I planted the gloves to let Rubenstein take the fall—you and Faraday were free to go. If you had just left well enough alone and let my guys pick up Hudson here to tie up a few loose ends, you would have been home in Maryland by now."

David glanced over at Dallas, who was looking back at him with tears in her eyes.

Hudson. He called her Hudson. If the woman in the elevator had turned us in, Hopkins would have known she was Dallas

Walker. This wasn't Dallas' fault. Wordlessly, he tried to tell her with his eyes that he was sorry.

"But no, you had to be the hero and kill two of my men—"

"Two dirty cops," David said.

"They were just doing their job," one of the men said before hitting David across the face with the butt of his rifle.

Instantly, David fell to the ground. He felt warm blood ooze from the blow to the side of his head.

"No!" Dallas screamed. "Don't hurt him! He was only trying to help me!"

"Hey, you caught them," someone said from the rear exit that David and Dallas had run out of.

David fought to push back the darkness threatening to overcome him. *Need to stay alert. Have to help Dallas. They're going to kill her.*

"Yeah, thanks to you, Orville," Lieutenant Hopkins said. "We wouldn't have if you hadn't seen O'Callaghan on your security tape and called me."

"Just doing my job, Hopkins," Orville said with a chuckle. "You know what they say: Beat cops don't retire. They're on patrol until they die." He paused. "I expected more officers here for a cop killer. You only got three—"

"This is a special case," Hopkins said quickly.

Suspicion seeped into Orville's tone when he asked, "Where are the uniforms?"

Lieutenant Wayne Hopkins answered his question with three shots.

The hotel security officer dropped dead.

Fighting to stay conscious, David watched the blood flow from the three gunshots that Lieutenant Hopkins had put into the security officer, who had then fallen only a couple of feet away from him.

Behind him, he heard Dallas scream hysterically. He had thought she was a woman who could hold her own, but all of this must have been way more than she was emotionally prepared to handle.

One of the officers rolled David over onto his stomach. Pinning him down with a knee pressed against his shoulder blade, the officer bound David's hands behind his back with flex-cuffs.

Hopkins shook his head at him and made a *tsk, tsk* noise with his tongue. "How tragic. Looks like you added a retired cop to your list of victims before you disappeared off the face of this earth, Chief O'Callaghan."

Through clinched teeth, David cursed the detective, only to be cut off by a sharp pain in the base of his neck. The sting from the injection shot through his body.

"What did you do to him?" Dallas demanded in a high-pitched voice as everything around David went black.

Chapter Twenty-Three

"David is going to be fine, Mac," Ed Willingham said, breaking the silence within the confines of the elevator racing up to their suite at the Four Seasons.

Adding his two cents, Gnarly rubbed his head against Mac's thigh. Mac responded by stroking the dog's head.

Their time spent at the police department swarming with federal agents leading the investigation of Lieutenant Abigail Gibbons' murder had proven to be productive. Based on evidence proving that both of the police officers David had killed were indeed suspected of taking bribes and carrying out murder for hire, among other crimes, David O'Callaghan was no longer wanted for murder. Both he and Ali Hudson were wanted as material witnesses.

Mac and Ed Willingham had chosen to keep Dallas' true identity a secret until they were sure she was safe.

Unfortunately, three of the suspected Dirty Six—and Lieutenant Wayne Hopkins—were still out there, and all were off duty. Mac had no doubt that they were looking for David O'Callaghan and Dallas Walker. When they found them, they would kill them. Two fewer loose ends to deal with.

"David was special ops in the marines, Mac," Ed said. "He's not your average street cop. He knows how to take care of himself."

Mac swallowed. "I know, Ed." He shot him a grin. "You don't have to comfort me. David will be fine. He's gone up against terrorists and killers and hired guns—he's always come out fine."

The elevator doors opened.

With Gnarly leading the way, they stepped off the elevator and headed down the corridor to the suite at the end of the hall.

"You know, I knew your mother for—I hate to say how many years. When I found out about you—when she found you and made you her beneficiary—she explained that she'd had to give you up for adoption, but she refused to tell me who your father was."

Mac paused at the door leading into their suite. "She didn't want to embarrass David's mother."

"I know," Ed said. "But she did tell me that you had a brother—a half brother." He chuckled. "I should have put two and two together then. I didn't know that she and Pat went all the way back to high school together." He sighed. "What I'm trying to say, Mac, is that more than anything else, your mother wanted you and David to be friends—brothers—like you are now."

With a chuckle, Mac pushed open the door and held it open for his lawyer. Gnarly ran in ahead and jumped up to sniff the gift basket Archie had sent to see if there were any goodies left for him.

Mac asked, "On that day you chased me for three blocks to tell me that I had inherited a fortune, did you ever dream that you'd end up here in New York City, trying to save my brother from dirty cops?"

"Someday you and I will sit down and have a long talk about some of the things your birth mother got me into," Ed shot back with a grin. After opening his valise, he removed a thick file and tossed it onto the desk.

Mac checked his cell phone for messages but didn't find any from David or Dallas. After the federal agents had voided the warrant for David's arrest on suspicion of murder, Mac had tried to contact them at the same phone number Dallas had called from to give him the message about the forged postcard. Mac's call had gone straight to voice mail. Most likely, he assumed, they had removed the phone's battery so the police couldn't trace the phone if they suspected the call was from David or Dallas.

Uttering a heavy sigh, Mac opened the minibar and took out a bottle of beer for him and scotch for Ed. Within minutes, the lawyer was completely absorbed in his work on the case and was preparing various defenses. He wanted to be several steps ahead of the district attorney regardless of what he decided to do—which would depend on how things worked out once they brought David in from the cold.

Mac was more concerned with the condition David would be in when they did bring him in. Standing at the window and gazing out across Central Park and the city, Mac wondered where David was and whether he was safe. A chill moved down Mac's spine when the night air blew against the thick window of the high-rise hotel.

Hope he's warm enough.

Glancing down at the phone in his hand, Mac tried to will David to call him. Knowing David, he probably wasn't asleep—wherever he was.

"Have you talked to Chelsea since all this happened?" Ed asked from the desk without looking up from his paper work.

Her name reminded Mac that the last time he'd spoken to Archie, she'd said Chelsea was spending the night at the hospital for observation after having a seizure at the nursing home. There would be plenty of opportunities for Dr. Seth Blanchard—or Dr. Love, as Archie called him—to make his move.

"No," Mac said. "Archie was afraid to upset her with the news after her seizure."

"And David doesn't know she had a seizure and is in the hospital."

Mac shook his head. Gazing down at the phone in his hand, he went over to the door leading into his bedroom. "I'm going to get an update from Archie and try to get some sleep."

"Sounds like a plan," Ed said with a wave of his hand.

Leaping over the coffee table that was blocking his way, Gnarly galloped into the bedroom and jumped up onto the bed. Too distracted to notice, Mac sat on the edge of the bed and thumbed the speed-dial number for Archie's cell. He was surprised when she answered on the second ring.

"Good evening, my love."

It was close to two o'clock in the morning, and he'd expected her to be asleep after a day of taking care of wedding duties while Chelsea was in the hospital. He'd been planning to leave a sexy, even naughty, message on Archie's voice mail for her to receive when she woke up the next morning.

He would have preferred that. Awake, she was able to ask questions to which he had no answers. "Where's David and why is the FBI looking for him?"

After providing Archie with a full rundown of the last two days, Mac concluded with, "But I'm not worried, hon, David can take care of himself." He told himself that if he said it enough, he might start to feel it.

"It sounds like these dirty cops are working for someone else," Archie said. "Do you know who?"

"That's why I'm calling you, dear."

"Really? You need me?" Her voice brightened.

"I'm going to e-mail some scanned photographs to you from a file that Audra Walker put together for a book she was working on. Most of them are candid shots from when she went to high school. I want you to use your facial-recognition program and compare the people in these shots to pictures of my list of suspects to see if you find anything."

"What are you thinking?" she asked.

"The night she disappeared, Audra Walker left ZNC studios totally motivated to return to this book about the Texan Romeo and Juliet," Mac said. "Something someone said or did gave her a breakthrough on the case."

"Anyone at ZNC from Texas?" Archie asked.

"No," Mac said. "And no one there even claims to have known anything about the case. Audra's former assistant has contacted the local law enforcement for the case file, but all physical evidence was destroyed. The case had been closed as a double suicide."

"Then what angle was she planning to take with the story?"

"Suppose it was murder?" Mac asked. "Audra was a witness to Romeo and Juliet's car going over the cliff. It was on fire *before* it went over."

"If it was going to catch fire, it would have after going over," she said.

"Exactly," Mac said.

"If Romeo and Juliet faked their deaths, how'd they send that car over the cliff without them being in it?"

With a shrug of his shoulders, Mac said, "One of them could have placed a rock on the gas pedal before or after setting fire to the car and rolled out right before it went over the cliff. Everyone would have been so focused on the car that they wouldn't have seen them slipping away into the night."

"And since it was a cliff," Archie said, "no one would have thought anything when they found the rock used to hold down the gas pedal inside the car. Very clever."

"I'm sending you pictures of all our suspects here. Maybe one or two of them came from that small town in Texas, and Audra recognized them."

"So they had to kill Audra Walker to keep their secret," Archie said. "E-mail the file over, and I'll get right to work on that."

"I would have thought you'd be tired after taking care of wedding stuff all day," Mac said.

"I need something to take my mind off this wedding," she said. "Seriously, dear, this is one strange wedding."

"Stranger than ours?" Mac asked.

"It's right up there," she said. "Chelsea never should have gone to see David's mother. According to Bogie, Violet really upset her, which Bogie swears is what led to her seizure. Then Dr. Seth ended up being an old friend of Chelsea's. Too good of an old friend, if you ask me."

"So he sent her some flowers to cheer her up?"

"Remember when you and I were in the hospital at the beginning of the year? You'd been shot. You almost died."

"Yes," Mac said, "I remember. I was there. What about it?"

"Do you remember how hard it was to find a doctor?" she asked. "There were nurses and aids everywhere. But if you needed or wanted a doctor, you couldn't find one anywhere. And when you did find one, he wouldn't have any answers for you because you weren't his patient."

"So—"

"Not so with Chelsea," Archie said. "No, no, no! Dr. Seth Blanchard is on her case, and from what I've seen, he's not giving it up any time soon. He was there when I got to the emergency room. He was there when they checked her in. He was there when they took her in for the MRI. He was there to make sure she liked her dinner"—she let out a squawk—"and when she mentioned she didn't like the mac and cheese, he took it and left and came back a half hour later with baby back ribs and fries!"

"Where did he get the baby back ribs?"

"He went to some little joint that the two of them used to go to in high school! So then I had to listen to them spinning tales about how much fun they used to have back in the good ol' days!" Her voice went up an octave. "Mac, I think this doctor has some stalker tendencies. What if Chelsea ends up not being at the hospital tomorrow morning? What if this Seth decides to kidnap her because he wants her for himself?"

"And you're thinking this because he got her baby back ribs when she complained about the mac and cheese?"

"When I was in the hospital and complained about their lousy mac and cheese, no one went out to get me ribs!"

"Darling, I would have if I hadn't been in the next bed over with a bullet in me."

"Like I said, this is the weirdest wedding I've ever been in … And I thought ours took the cake."

"Leave him alone!"

Dallas' voice sounded like it was traveling to David from the end of a long tunnel. Hard fingers pressed on the muscles on his upper arms before he was lifted up from where he was lying on cold concrete and dragged facedown across the floor. When he was dropped, he felt the smooth texture of sheet plastic on his face.

"Wake up!" The toe of a boot connected with his ribs. With a groan, he rolled over onto his side and tried to make sense of his surroundings. Between the drug he'd been given and the fact that his hands were bound with a zip cord behind his back, movement was difficult.

"Stop it!" Dallas yelled before he heard the sound of a slap.

Although he couldn't see her, he sensed that someone had knocked her to the floor.

"Don't touch her," he wanted to scream, but his mouth wasn't working yet. The drug they had injected into his neck still had a strong hold over him.

Lieutenant Wayne Hopkins' voice echoed all around him until he was able to place him a few feet away. Lifting his head, David saw that the detective, who was clad in a long black wool coat and slacks, was standing at the edge of the clear plastic spread across the concrete floor. He was speaking into a cell phone.

"Yeah," the detective said. "We got both of them." He paused to listen to the caller's question. "No, no witnesses or trail. The boys were able to track O'Callaghan down off the grid. As far as anyone will know, he and the girl escaped." A grin came to his lips. "No way Faraday and that mutt of his would be able to find them here. They're all looking for them in the city—not Long Island."

His vision clearing, David looked around and saw that they were on the freezing concrete floor of a building still under construction. Only the floor and outer walls had been constructed. Some, but not all, of the interior walls were complete. Nearby, David saw a stack of drywall and rolls of insulation. Three men dressed in overalls and work gloves surrounded him.

Lieutenant Wayne Hopkins finished his phone call. "It'll be done by the opening bell on Wall Street." With a smile, Hopkins disconnected the call and slipped his phone into the pocket of his coat. "Kill them both."

"Anything specific?" the largest of the three men said as he glared down at David.

"Just seal both of their bodies in the walls, and get it done this morning," Hopkins said. "The construction workers will be back at work tomorrow, and the drywall needs to be dry so they won't suspect anything."

The three officers grinned at each other.

Squatting down close to David, Hopkins shook his head with mock sadness. "Sorry I can't stick around, O'Callaghan, but I have a meeting at the department first thing this morning. The captain is personally supervising the whole department's search for you and Ms. Hudson."

David responded by spitting in his face.

The three officers moonlighting as paid assassins chuckled at the fury that crossed Lieutenant Hopkins' face. The two men locked glares while Hopkins fished a handkerchief out of his pocket and mopped his face.

"As I was saying," Hopkins said while tucking the handkerchief into his pants pocket. "I wish I could make you a little bit more comfortable, but I'm afraid that's out of my hands. You see, Sauer and Logan were good friends, and the boys here are really pissed that you killed them the way you did. I'm sure, being a cop, you understand."

Finally, the feeling returned to David's tongue. "Go to hell, Hopkins."

"You'll get there first, O'Callaghan." Hopkins rose to his feet. Seeing a gun in one of the men's hands, he said, "Use silencers on those guns. We don't want any reports of gunshots."

While Lieutenant Hopkins crossed the floor to take a construction elevator down to the street, the three men chuckled among themselves. Each one of them took a silencer out of his pocket and screwed it onto his weapon.

"You should have just let Sauer and Logan kill you, Chief," the shortest of the three said before delivering a kick to David's ribs. "Because they were going to kill you fast." He kicked him again. "By the time we're through, you're going to be begging us to kill you."

David flexed his stomach muscles in preparation for another blow—but the next one came from behind him when a different officer kicked him in the kidneys. The pain shot up and down his back. David rolled over. He bit his tongue to suppress the cry of pain.

No way will I let them see me suffer or hear me beg. The longer they take with me, the more chances there'll be for Dallas to escape. Please let Mac find her somehow—someway.

"Your turn, Joe," the first officer said to the largest of the three.

Cringing through the pain, David saw Joe grinning down at him. He had his gun, fit with a silencer, pointed at one of his knees.

David glared up at him.

A wicked laugh escaped from Joe's lips.

David braced for the shot. He was so focused on the impending brutal pain in his knee that he didn't notice the abrupt rush of movement behind Joe. It was as if he'd lost time between the dirty cop cackling and him suddenly screaming out in gut-wrenching pain.

A split second later, David felt hot blood spray over him. Blood was gushing out of Joe's throat, where Dallas had plunged the blade of a box cutter.

In their thirst to avenge the death of their friends, the trained officers had completely forgotten to keep an eye on the hysterical and seemingly helpless woman they had bound with a zip cord in the corner. Because they had dismissed her, none of them noticed when she managed to pick up a discarded box cutter blade and cut through the rip cord binding her hands—at least not until she landed on Joe's back. Wrapping her legs around his waist, she forced his head back with her hand under his nose and plunged the point of the razor blade into his jugular. His blood shot out of the wound like water from a hose that had suddenly been turned on. Without stopping, she dragged the razor straight across the assailant's throat.

David regained his composure quickly enough to drop down and roll across the cement floor in the hope of avoiding any stray bullets that Joe might fire off in the losing fight for his life.

Like a mountain lion taking down its prey, Dallas clung to his back while slicing away with the blade, even while Joe clawed, kicked, and thrashed in a vain attempt to buck her off. With blood spewing from his severed jugular vein, he finally collapsed. Joe's agonizing screams were almost drowned out by the sound of semiautomatic gunfire.

"Dallas! No!" Hearing the gunshots, David tried to sit up. He expected to find that Dallas had died—that she'd been finished off by the two remaining officers.

Instead, David discovered all three assassins sprawled out before him. The armor-piercing bullets from the semiautomatic weapon had cut through the ballistics vests they were wearing like they were made of paper. The shortest one was twitching and uttering noises that David recognized as death rattles.

"David!"

He almost jumped up to his knees when he saw Dallas push Joe aside and crawl out from under him. She was covered in blood but seemingly all right.

Behind him, he heard the clatter of a single pair of boots making its way toward them.

"Are you okay?" She ran over to him with a bloody razor blade in her hand. "Thank God the police finally got here."

As their savior drew near, David said, "I don't think she's with the police."

Dallas looked up from where she had cut David loose and saw the tall, stunning woman she had met in the elevator making her way toward them. In contrast to the elegant red dress she had been wearing the evening before, she was clad in black from her boots to her leather gloves, her form-fitting pants, and her leather jacket. She was carrying an AP-9 semiautomatic machine gun in her arms.

Seeing the weapon, Dallas wrapped her arms around David. "Don't hurt him!"

"I have no intention of hurting your friend."

A gravely wounded officer moaned.

Hearing him, the woman in black went over to where he was jerking in pain. Aiming her gun down at him, she pulled the trigger to finish him off. Once she was satisfied that the three assassins were dead, she went back to where David was holding Dallas in his arms.

"The police are now on their way." She held out the machine gun to David. "I'd appreciate it if you take credit for this, Chief."

"But—"

"You're special forces in the marines," she said with a grin. "I'm sure you can think of some way to make it believable. The police will be anxious to believe anything you say if it puts this whole scandal of dirty cops working as paid assassins behind them."

Hearing sirens far in the distance, she hurried in the direction from which she had come.

"Who are you?" Dallas blurted out to stop her.

"I told you, my dear," she replied. "A friend of your mother's. She and I are now even." Turning back to David, she tossed what looked like a stone into his lap. "Now you owe me one, Chief O'Callaghan," she said with a wink before running across the floor, jumping over a low wall, and using the scaffolding to scale down the building without the incoming police seeing her.

"What's that?" Dallas grabbed the stone from his lap to see what she had thrown at him.

Seeing the shiny black jewel, David frowned. "It's a black diamond. One of the world's most infamous paid assassins just saved our lives … and now I owe her."

Chapter Twenty-Four

Lieutenant Wayne Hopkins checked the time on the bank clock while he waited for the traffic light to change and to allow him through the intersection. It was ten minutes before nine o'clock.

In almost half a block, he would pull into the parking garage. He'd take three floors up to the homicide squad. He'd pour himself a mug of coffee and walk into the briefing room to regretfully tell the chief that there was still no news from any of the officers on patrol about the whereabouts of David O'Callaghan or Ali Hudson. Somehow, they must have escaped the city.

Yes, it was turning into a perfect day. With these last two potential witnesses gone, all the loose ends in the Audra Walker murder case were tied up. In a matter of months, the detective would cash in on favors owed to him. In approximately a year, Lieutenant Wayne Hopkins would accept a generous offer from ZNC for his own program and retire from the police department to become a celebrity.

After climbing out of his black SUV, Hopkins paused to admire his reflection in the rearview mirror. He was displeased to see that his hairline was receding higher than he would've liked. *Maybe I'll need some hair plugs.*

Usually when it was approaching nine o'clock, the parking garage would be filled with plain-clothes detectives reporting for duty. To his surprise, the garage was strangely quiet. Even so, Hopkins had a feeling that he was not alone. As he approached the elevators, a noise from the shadows caught his attention.

He stopped and listened.

Grrrrrr.

He turned to look over at four parking spaces. In one there was a luxury sedan, in another, a sports car, and in the remaining two, SUVs.

Everything was still.

He listened again.

He heard only the sounds of the city outside.

You need more sleep, Hopkins.

With a shake of his head, he went over to the elevator and pressed the "call" button.

Out of the corner of his eye, he saw something move in the shadows. Turning his head, he searched for the source of the movement. *Could a burglar be looking to steal my SUV … from the police parking garage? Maybe a felon seeking revenge for an arrest?*

Listening and watching, Hopkins waited with his hand on his service weapon.

When the elevator doors swung open, the sudden movement made him grab for his weapon, causing the woman on the elevator to utter a shriek. Apologizing, Hopkins hurried on while she trotted off.

By the time he reached the homicide squad, Lieutenant Wayne Hopkins had shaken off his paranoia. He sauntered into the squad room with his lies in order.

"Where've you been, Hopkins?" His young partner, Detective Winslow, stood up from the desk across from Hopkins' cubicle.

"There was a car broken down on the way in, and traffic was backed up, so I decided to stop for breakfast." Hopkins checked the time on his cell phone. "Still got time to pour my coffee before the morning briefing, though."

"Briefing was cancelled," Detective Winslow said. "Chief has been tied up all morning with the captain, commissioner, and feds. Scuttlebutt says it's about Gibbons' murder."

Lieutenant Wayne Hopkins' eyes grew wide. His mouth dropped open. "Seriously? Lieutenant Gibbons was murdered?"

"Where've you been?" Winslow asked. "It happened last night. FBI swooped in before any of the locals could get there, and they're taking the lead." He lowered his voice to a whisper. "Everyone says she got too close to that gang of dirty cops she's been investigating, and they whacked her."

"Why didn't anyone call me?" Lieutenant Hopkins shook his head. "I can't believe the commissioner allowed the feds—"

Detective Winslow was suddenly out of his seat and scurrying away. When Lieutenant Wayne Hopkins turned around, he was face to face with his chief, Lieutenant Andrew Van Patton.

"Hopkins! My office!"

The chief spun on his heels and marched off to his office in the corner of the squad room. A blanket of silence fell over the squad. Hopkins could feel the eyes of his colleagues on him while he made his way to their chief's office.

As soon as he crossed the threshold, Hopkins saw Mac Faraday leaning against the wall across from him. With one ankle crossed over the other and his arms folded across his chest, Mac was casual—yet the glare in his eyes was something completely different. As he looked the detective up and down, Mac seemed capable of penetrating through Hopkins' lies and uncovering his secrets.

You have nothing on me, Faraday.

Van Patton slammed his office door. "Where've you been, Hopkins?" he asked in a firm tone.

"Checking around the different precincts to see if anyone's gotten any leads on O'Callaghan," Hopkins said. "Every confidential informant has been put on notice." He smirked over Van Patton's shoulder at Mac. "He killed Sauer and Logan twenty-two hours ago. I'm thinking he's fled the country—possibly with the help of a friend with resources."

Instead of answering him, Mac unfolded his arms and stood up to his full height.

"It has come to our attention that both Sauer and Logan were being investigated by Lieutenant Gibbons of internal affairs for belonging to a gang of dirty cops who were not only taking bribes but also moonlighting as muscle for hire and even performing paid hits," Van Patton said.

"Both Sauer and Logan were on break when they were killed," Mac said, closing in on the detective. "*My* information tells me that they used that break to attempt a hit on O'Callaghan and Hudson—which forced O'Callaghan to kill them in self-defense."

"*Your* information?" Hopkins repeated. "Would your informant be David O'Callaghan, by any chance?" He turned to his chief. "You do realize that if Faraday has been in communication with O'Callaghan and hasn't told the police, he can be charged for obstruction of justice and harboring a fugitive." He turned to Mac. "We could arrest you."

"Actually, it's you who should be arrested." Seeing that a bloody corner of Hopkins' handkerchief was hanging out of his pocket, Mac snatched it and held it up for Van Patton to see. "That is, if the blood I see on this handkerchief turns out to belong to O'Callaghan."

Lieutenant Wayne Hopkins' mouth dropped open. With a loud laugh, he snatched the handkerchief from Mac's hand and shoved it back into his pocket. "If you have an accusation to make, just say it, Faraday. There's a warrant out for David O'Callaghan's arrest for killing two New York City police officers."

"Actually, he isn't a suspect anymore," Lieutenant Van Patton said. "He and Hudson are material witnesses. The feds uncovered evidence in Gibbons' apartment supporting Faraday's claim that O'Callaghan killed them in self-defense."

Mac smirked while Hopkins's confident demeanor fell.

"Which leads to our next question, Hopkins. Did you have a personal relationship with Abigail Gibbons?" Lieutenant Van Patton asked.

"Yes," Hopkins replied without hesitation. "We were having a sexual relationship. We were both the same rank and adults. We cared about each other."

"Would she share her status on her investigation into the Dirty Six with you?" Mac asked.

"No," Hopkins said. "We never discussed our cases with each other. We would just get together for a roll in the hay, nothing more."

"Did you see her last night?" Van Patton asked.

"No," Hopkins sputtered. "I hadn't seen Gibbons in a couple of weeks. Our relationship was completely casual—nothing heavy. We had a no-strings-attached, friends-with-benefits situation—nothing else. I certainly had no reason to toss her out a window. Now am I under arrest? Suspended? Do I need a lawyer?"

Van Patton turned to Mac, who shrugged his shoulders in a sign of resignation.

"The federal agents taking the lead in the Gibbons investigation are going to want to talk to you," Van Patton said. "They'll be here at ten o'clock. Plan to meet with them in interrogation."

"Am I free to go get a Starbucks?" Hopkins asked.

"You can even get a scone if you want." Mac stepped aside, allowing him to pass him in his hurry to escape the office.

Mac waited for Hopkins to trot out of the squad room before turning to Van Patton, who had left his office to gesture for a team of detectives to follow their colleague. "Did you notice that Hopkins acted surprised to learn that Abigail Gibbons was dead—and yet, without our saying anything, he knew she'd been thrown out a window?"

With a shake of his head, Van Patton grumbled. "You do know he's going to run?"

"Of course he's going to run," Mac said. "Especially after he gets a load of the little present I left in his SUV. But, believe me, he's not going anywhere."

His cell phone to his ear, Wayne Hopkins practically bolted off the elevator in his haste to get to his SUV and away from the precinct as quickly as possible. The feds were going to be there at ten o'clock. That meant he had less than an hour to get as far from New York as possible—or to get the biggest, baddest defense lawyer in the city. Even if he managed to escape arrest for murder, the suspicion alone would cast a cloud over his image. His fledgling television career could be irreparably damaged before it even started.

He had to shift his priorities to self-preservation.

Reaching voice mail, he said, "It's all shot to hell. Faraday's brought in the feds, and they're after me. If you don't want to go down with me, we need to make some adjustment for payment. Call me back ASAP."

Approaching the SUV, Hopkins hit the button on his key chain to unlock the door. After shoving the cell phone into his pocket, he yanked on the door handle and found the door was locked. With a growl, he hit the button on the key chain to unlock the doors again and climbed into the front seat.

"Damn it!" His frustration overflowing, he banged on the steering wheel with his fists. *So close! I was on the brink!* Only the month before, he had spent a whole weekend with a shapely brunette who had recognized him from an appearance on *Crime Watch*. Enamored with his celebrity, she had given herself to him freely—and had asked him question after question about being on television and about what Ryan Ritter, Yvonne Harding, and Pam Wiehl were really like.

He'd been inside the world of stardom. Using his resources on the police force, he had managed to maneuver himself closer to the center, and he had been on the brink of breaking into it.

"Damn! Damn! Damn!" He continued to pound the steering wheel. Glaring straight ahead, Hopkins huffed and puffed with fury.

"*Grrrr!*"

Stopping, he listened. Again, the low noise came from behind him.

"*Grrrrrrrr!*"

He turned around to peer into the backseat. Listening, he heard nothing. After jamming the key into the ignition, he started the engine.

Abby Gibbons' voice blasted from the speakers, filling the interior of the SUV. "You're nothing more than a common street thug with a badge!"

His deranged tone almost made his own voice unrecognizable. "I'm an exceptional *opportunist*—not only *seeing* but also *using* the opportunities that life has granted me. That's the difference between common street cops like Roberts who retire to dreary little apartments and the stars."

"Is stardom worth it? Sending those goons, Sauer and Logan, to kill David O'Callaghan—"

"No, Abby! You have it wrong! I sent them to kill Hudson—"

Hopkins pounded the console to turn off the player.

Silence filled the SUV—but only for a moment.

"*Grrrrrrrrrrrrr!*"

Hopkins whirled around to look into the backseat again.

Again, he saw nothing.

After throwing open the door, he climbed out of the car. He took his gun out of his holster and slowly made his way around the SUV, checking underneath it. Abruptly, he sensed movement nearby. Rising up, he looked into the rear compartment of the SUV. Nothing.

You're paranoid, Hopkins. With a sigh, he holstered his gun. *Sooner you get out of the city, the better.*

He hurried around the SUV to throw open the driver's door and climbed in.

Absorbed in his thoughts of how best to make his escape, it wasn't until he had fastened his seat belt and reached for the gearshift in the center console that he noticed the long, furry tail that was spilling out of the passenger seat.

Once again, he heard the low growl—only then it was next to him.

Raising his eyes from the gearshift, Wayne Hopkins looked directly into the eyes of Gnarly, whose head was equal in size to that of the detective.

"So it's *you,*" Hopkins said while slowly reaching for his weapon. "Faraday thinks he can use you to intimidate me. Well first I'm going to shoot you, and then I'm going to skin you and cut off your head and ship you to his mansion on Deep Creek Lake."

He yanked his service weapon from its holster at the same time that Gnarly lunged across the front compartment. His rear leg kicked the SUV into gear. During the fight that ensued, Hopkins' foot hit the gas, and the SUV plunged forward, rear-ending the sports sedan in front of it.

When Mac and the detectives from the homicide squad spilled into the parking garage, they heard the roar of the SUV pushing the small car out of its parking space. Mixed in with the noise were multiple gunshots and the sounds of vehicles being smashed by the out-of-control SUV.

Rounding the corner, Mac saw the SUV rocking and jostling where it had come to a stop after pushing the small red sports car into the rear of the car across the aisle from it. Blood was smeared across the inside windows.

"Gnarly! Stand down!" Mac yelled over the roar of the SUV.

The door on the driver's side flew open, and Wayne Hopkins, covered in blood, spilled out onto the concrete floor. His service weapon tumbled out and landed next to him.

Also covered with blood, Gnarly was standing on the driver's seat, glaring down at the dirty cops' ringleader.

"Now I know what you meant about Hopkins not going anywhere."

Cursing, Wayne Hopkins picked himself up, only to find that every detective he worked with on the squad was aiming his service weapon at him. "Hey, guys, what's going on? Can't you see what happened? Faraday is trying to frame me! He killed Gibbons and sicced his vicious dog on me." Clutching his left hand, which had a bullet hole through the palm, he gestured to Gnarly, who was still growling at him. "He attacked me. See?" He held up his blood-covered hand and arm.

"Put a bullet right through my hand when I tried to protect myself."

"You're a liar, Hopkins," Lieutenant Van Patton said in a low voice.

"We expect that from dirty politicians," Detective Winslow said, "not one of our own brothers."

"You killed Lieutenant Gibbons because she figured out what you were up to," Lieutenant Van Patton said.

Hopkins tried to object. "Now wait a minute—"

"We heard the recording!" Detective Winslow shouted.

"They all heard the recording she made with her cell phone," Lieutenant Van Patton said. "They heard her lay it all out for you. Then they heard you admit to tipping off the dirty cops she had collected evidence against and organizing them so they could put their law-enforcement skills, combined with their lack of ethics, to use in a way that would benefit all of you. They heard her confront you about sending your personal hit squad out to kill Ali Hudson and Chief O'Callaghan—right before you killed her."

"You're a dirty cop," Detective Winslow spat out. "Dirty cops don't just hurt those they've sworn to protect—they ruin the reputation of every *good* cop on the force. It's scum like you who get us spat on—or even worst, ambushed."

Hopkins' eyes grew wide when he saw the whole squad of detectives and uniformed officers, his colleagues, advancing on him. "Chief! Faraday! Stop them!"

"Don't talk to me," Mac said. "They're the ones with the guns."

"You just don't get it, do you, Hopkins?" Lieutenant Van Patton said. "The media and public never notice or appreciate stories about the good cops. Last week, when Officer Koberstein ended up in the hospital after shoving a pregnant black woman out of the way of a runaway car and getting hit, only one news station picked up the story. He'll be in the hospital for two weeks with a broken hip and two broken legs. He'll be in physical therapy for months. He sacrificed his life to save this woman and her unborn child because he's a *good* cop—but no one cares."

"But you, Hopkins," Detective Winslow said. "When the members of the media find out about you, you can bet every news station all over the country will cover it, and we'll *all* be crucified—for what?"

"None of us hardworking good cops will ever be able to get rid of *your* stench," Lieutenant Van Patton said.

"Now, guys," Hopkins said, "I can explain."

"You explained it very well in the recording Gibbons made—right before you threw her out a window," Mac said.

"You're not going to turn me in. You can't. You know what they'll do to me in prison."

"They don't have your back anymore, Hopkins," Mac said, "because you didn't have theirs."

"Assume the position, Hopkins," Lieutenant Van Patton said as he and Detective Winslow moved to take the lieutenant into custody.

Hopkins moved so fast that no one saw he had his gun in his hand until he brought it to his temple and pulled the trigger.

"Mac!" Ed Willingham said as he trotted out from the elevator and into the throng of officers and detectives. Upon seeing Gnarly and Hopkins, who was dead from a self-inflicted gunshot to his head, he stopped short and turned his head away. "I see Gnarly has been busy. I wanted to tell you that they found David and Dallas."

"Tell me they're okay." Mac held his breath and waited for Ed's response, which was a nod of his head.

"They're at the hospital in Long Island. I've got a car waiting to take us now."

Chapter Twenty-Five

In Long Island, Mac strapped a service-dog vest onto Gnarly in order to allow him entrance into the hospital before following Ed into the emergency room entrance. While Ed went in search of a reception clerk who could help them, Mac zeroed in on two uniformed police officers who, he correctly assumed, had accompanied David and Dallas to the emergency room. By the time Ed returned, Mac had left Gnarly with the officers and had found Dallas Walker, who was staring straight ahead and sitting on a chair next to an empty gurney.

"Dallas."

Startled out of her stare, she jumped to her feet and rushed into Mac's arms. "I'm so glad to see you." He felt her stifle a sob working its way to the surface.

"It's okay." Mac hugged her tighter. "I'm just glad neither of you are hurt." Seeing the empty gurney, he said, "David is okay. Right?"

Pulling away from the hug, she sniffled. "They took him for an X-ray. One of the hit men whacked him on the head with a rifle butt. They think he may have a concussion. He definitely has a couple of broken ribs and a bruised kidney."

Mac noticed that both of her hands and wrists were heavily bandaged. "And you?"

"Just some cuts." With a shrug, she tucked her hands under the multicolored leather poncho. "They'll heal. They took us to a high-rise that was under construction. I saw a razor blade on the floor. So I provoked one of those goons into slappin' me so I would have an excuse to hit the floor. When they turned all their attention to David—"

"Who they considered a threat," Mac said.

She nodded her head. "The last thing they expected was for me to go on the offense."

"While you were cutting the one's throat, David disarmed one of the other two and killed both of them. The officers who brought you here told me." Letting out a breath, Mac shook his head. "I'm really impressed. Everyone is. You two seem to make a good team."

Her cheeks turned pink. "I think so."

"Looks like you have company!" a nurse announced when she wheeled David around the curtain into the examination room.

To Mac's surprise, Dallas rushed forward to kiss David on the lips. When she pulled away, he caught her by the back of the neck and kissed her again.

This is not good. Mac thought. *Not good at all.*

"I see you found us," David said while Dallas and the nurse helped him out of the wheel chair and back up onto the gurney. He had a nasty bruise on his left cheek and his forehead.

"Yeah," Mac said. "It's been a rough twenty-four hours. But not as rough as it's been for Wayne Hopkins."

"I hope you nailed the bastard," David said through gritted teeth.

"He offed himself," Mac said.

"Even better."

"But he didn't kill Mom," Dallas said. "He was the detective on the case."

"Second to Sergeant Roberts." Mac noticed that she had moved in close to David on the gurney so that she was half sitting on it. Her hand was resting on his thigh. "He didn't kill Yvonne Harding either. According to the checkout log for building security, he signed out more than five minutes before Yvonne was shot."

"He was covering for the killer." Remembering that he'd heard Hopkins talking on a cell phone at the construction site, David sat up. "Do they have Hopkins' cell phone?"

"I'm sure it's either in his SUV or on him," Mac said. "Why?"

"Because if they do, they have a line to who is behind this. Hopkins reported to someone that he had picked Dallas and me up. Whoever he was talking to on his cell phone gave him the order to kill us."

"Hopkins wouldn't have been stupid enough to do his dirty business on his own phone," Dallas said. "And how much do you wanna bet that whoever was givin' the orders was usin' a burner phone?"

"Yeah, but if the boss man or woman doesn't know that Hopkins failed to tie up his loose ends and that he's dead, he or she could be feeling a false sense of security," Mac said.

"And could make a mistake," David said with a grin.

"Do you know who it is yet?" Dallas asked Mac. "Do you know who killed Mom and why?"

"I think I do," Mac said. "The problem will be proving it."

"That's never stopped us before," David said.

"No, it hasn't." Mac gestured toward the bruises on David's face. "That's going to wreak havoc on your wedding pictures." He noticed a silence in the examination room while David and Dallas exchanged anxious glances.

Dallas extracted a cell phone from her bag and scurried toward the door. "I need to call my brother to let him know what's goin' on."

Once she was gone, Mac and David exchanged long looks.

Finally, David took in a deep sigh. The pain in his broken ribs made him grimace. When he was able to talk, he said, "Mac—"

"You don't have to explain to me," Mac replied more harshly than he'd wanted to. He sounded like a parent chastising a child.

"Have you talked to Chelsea?" David asked. "Told her what's been going on?"

"No," Mac said. "One, I had no idea about this." He pointed in the direction that Dallas had disappeared in. "Two"—he sighed—"she's in the hospital."

David sat up as best he could with his injuries. "What happened to her?"

"She had a seizure yesterday," Mac said. "Archie says the emergency room doctor told her it was the stress of the wedding and trying to get stuff together for law school."

With a groan, David covered his face with both hands. "Mac," he whispered, "what am I going to do?"

"The smell of that soup is driving me crazy." Bogie had to restrain himself from digging into the bag for the takeout container of fresh crab soup and hot bread from the Spencer Inn that Archie had ordered and picked up for Chelsea's lunch.

Archie slapped Bogie's wrist when he tried to sneak a fresh roll from the bag she was taking out of his squad car to carry into the hospital. "That's for Chelsea. Poor girl. She was telling me this morning that the bacon they served for breakfast was like petrified tree bark, and the fruit salad was tasteless. She's probably starving to death, and you know how hospitals are. They won't release her until after lunch—at which time we'll go straight to the inn for a relaxing massage and a wonderful girls' night out with the bridesmaids."

"I smell Carmine's pizza." Sniffing, Bogie stopped in the hallway leading to Chelsea's room. "Pepperoni. Italian sausage. Mushrooms. Double cheese. Thin crust." At a trot, the deputy chief hurried down the corridor with Archie behind him.

Chelsea's laughter drifted into the hallway.

Turning the corner to enter their room, Archie stopped when she saw Dr. Seth Blanchard sitting across from Chelsea on her bed. They were eating pizza together. On the floor between them, Molly was taking turns doing tricks for both of them in exchange for goodies.

"Hey, you're just in time," Chelsea said, waving for them to enter the room. "Seth brought me pizza for lunch. There's enough to share."

"Molly loves Italian sausage." Seth grinned at Chelsea. "Just like her mother."

"When I was in the hospital for my broken ankle, all I got was mushy spaghetti and tough meatballs," Archie said in an accusatory tone.

"You weren't my favorite patient." Seth winked at Chelsea.

The blush that came to Chelsea's cheeks made Archie's blood boil. Seeing Bogie reaching for the pizza, she slapped his wrist.

"I brought you crab soup from the inn." Archie held up the bag to show the container to Chelsea. "Along with fresh bread." Then for Seth's benefit, she added, "And as soon as your doctor decides to release you, we'll go to the spa and meet the bridesmaids for a nice relaxing afternoon of pampering."

"Sounds like a lot of fun." While her words said that Chelsea believed it would be an enjoyable afternoon, her emotions failed to say the same.

"Mac and David have been working hard on the case," Archie said. "They should be back tomorrow. Bogie and I have been keeping up with the event coordinator at the inn. Everything is still on schedule for *your wedding the day after tomorrow*. So you can relax."

"Sounds like everything is coming together." Seth stood up from the bed.

In a defensive move, Archie stepped up to the bed when she saw Seth pat Chelsea's hand. "All we need is for you to release her and *let her go.*"

"I think Seth is still waiting for the results from the MRI he ordered yesterday," Chelsea said.

"But you're feeling fine, aren't you?" Bogie asked around a mouthful of pizza. "Doc said that as long as you were feeling okay and took it easy—"

"What has David said?" Chelsea asked Bogie and Archie.

"David's been tied up in this murder case," Archie said. "Believe me, he would call you if he could."

"But he's been tied up solving the murder of his first wife," Chelsea said.

"He went to New York to divorce Yvonne because he wanted to be with you." Archie was uncomfortably aware that Seth was lingering at the foot of the bed. After she fired off a glare in his direction, he announced that he would go sign Chelsea's release and that she would be free to leave.

"You're going to leave your number for me to call you, aren't you, Seth?" Chelsea called after him. "In case I need to get in touch with you."

With a soft grin, the doctor left the room.

Archie glared at the vacant doorway for a long moment before turning her attention to Chelsea, who was picking bits of pepperoni from her pizza and feeding them to Molly. "You do know that you're getting married the day after tomorrow—or did that seizure you had make you forget about that?"

"Seth is my doctor," Chelsea said, "and a good friend. If it wasn't for him, I never would have made it through chemistry."

"From what I can see, he's still trying to help you with chemistry," Archie said without humor.

"The Blanchards are a nice family." Bogie pointed to the last slice of pizza. "Can I have that?"

"Unless Archie wants it."

Feeling as though eating any of the pizza would be akin to betraying David, Archie folded her arms across her chest and gave her head a firm shake. Ignoring her glare, Bogie dove in.

"You're not able to forgive David, are you?" Archie asked her.

"Of course I can forgive him," Chelsea said. "He explained over and over again how this happened. It was a mistake. He was drunk. Back in high school, he was immature, and his hormones overpowered his senses. Now he knows better. Four years ago, he didn't."

"As long as you keep him sober and out of Vegas, you two should be fine," Bogie said.

"You're not helping," Archie told him.

Chelsea waved her hands. "What's done is done. Now Yvonne is dead, and David is free to keep his word and to fulfill his obligation to marry me."

"How romantic," Archie said with heavy sarcasm.

"Archie, why don't you go make sure Seth is signing the release forms." Bogie tossed his gray head in the direction of the door. "I'll stay here to make sure Chelsea doesn't decide to pull a runaway-bride act on us."

Her arms still folded across her chest, Archie went in search of Dr. Seth Blanchard, who she found at the nurse's desk completing some forms. "You are aware that Chelsea is marrying David O'Callaghan the day after tomorrow?"

A chuckle rose from deep in Seth's throat while he handed the clipboard over to a nurse. "You've told me that several times, Archie. You've been trying to make that so clear that I'm almost expecting an invitation from you to drill it into my head."

"Okay." Archie moved in close to him. "Then I'll make this even clearer to you. Back off. As her doctor, you have to see that she's under a lot of stress—"

"Which I believe could have directly contributed to her seizure," Seth said.

"And your making romantic overtures days before she's supposed to marry another man, one who isn't available to defend himself, isn't stressful? You're planting doubts in her mind when she's emotionally vulnerable. That's cruel, not to mention unfair."

"All's fair in love and war," Seth said with a laugh.

Archie moved in like she was going to punch him. Before she could, he turned serious.

"I haven't seen Chelsea since I went away to med school ten years ago," he said. "The stress that caused her seizure—which is nothing to laugh at, by the way—was there before I came back in the picture. Maybe that stress is caused by underlying doubts about marrying David, and maybe it's not. Only Chelsea knows that. But I do know one thing, not only as her doctor but also as her friend: she needs a friend right now to help her identify the source of that stress."

"Did you ever think it was caused by planning a big wedding and getting ready to go to law school?"

"At first," Seth said. "And maybe it's wishful thinking on my part, but in talking to Chelsea, I'm picking up on some underlying hostility toward the man she's planning to marry and spend the rest of her life with."

Archie scoffed. "He made a mistake."

"He married another woman without knowing it."

"Accidents happen."

With a roll of his eyes, Seth turned away.

Archie grabbed him by the arm. "I think you're taking advantage of this whole situation to move in on Chelsea and to break up their engagement while David isn't even here to defend himself."

He grinned. "You're very perceptive, Archie Monday. I've wanted to be more than a friend to Chelsea since high school chemistry, and I've never tried to hide that. I've never been smooth enough to play those types of games. If all this had happened another way—if I had run into Chelsea shopping and had seen that she was happy and thrilled about marrying David—I'd be the gentleman and stay away because I love Chelsea and only want the best for her. I want her to be happy. But that isn't what happened. She was brought into my emergency room by an ambulance after having a seizure. Her blood pressure was elevated. She's exhausted and confused and, frankly, unhappy." He leaned in toward her. "Brides aren't supposed to be unhappy."

Seeing anger seeping into the mild-mannered doctor's demeanor, Archie backed up a step.

"That woman in there is my patient and someone who I care for very much. If I have to save her life and her emotional well-being by keeping her from walking down that aisle and marrying David O'Callaghan, then I'll do everything in my power to keep it from happening."

As soon as Archie was gone, Bogie tossed the crust from his slice of pizza to Molly and sat down on the bed next to Chelsea. With a paternal attitude, he draped his arm across her shoulders. "No matter how mad you may be at David right now, Chelsea, I think deep down you know that he loves you very much and that you love him. You also know that he is not a cheater. What he did in high school was completely due to his immaturity, and what happened in Vegas was because you were gone and out of the picture."

"I know." With a sigh, Chelsea leaned her head on Bogie's shoulder. "If I ask you a question, Bogie, will you tell me the truth? No sugarcoating."

"Sure, kiddo."

"Why did David's dad marry Violet?" When Bogie didn't answer, she raised her head and looked over at him.

"Well ..."

"You were Patrick O'Callaghan's best friend going all the way back," she said. "You knew all of them."

"I met Pat after Robin's folks had sent her off to school out of state," Bogie explained.

"But you knew him when he and Violet got married," she said. "You're David's godfather. You were there when David was born. If Pat was in love with Robin Spencer, why did he marry Violet?"

Bogie cleared his throat. "Pat loved Robin Spencer with all his heart. But her folks ended it between them. They sent her away. Even though he loved her, he resigned himself to the fact that he was never going to see her again. He thought he had moved on when he married Violet—"

"Did he love Violet?"

"Yes," Bogie said firmly. "He never would have married her if he hadn't."

"But Mac's mother was *the one.*"

With a heavy sigh, Bogie nodded his head. "By the time Robin came back to Spencer, it was too late. Pat had married Violet and was too honorable to leave her."

"And Violet saw that," Chelsea said in a soft voice. "Even though she had him, she knew his heart belonged someplace else, and the pain ate away at her until she went mad with jealousy and resentment."

"Pretty much," Bogie said.

A weak smile came to her lips. "I guess you might say theirs was an honor marriage—a marriage entered into not because of love but because of Patrick's sense of duty and desire to keep his word." She sighed. "How sad for Violet. The only thing that kept the man she loved with her was his sense of honor."

"Sometimes a strong sense of honor can become a curse," Bogie said. "Pat was pretty much caught in a trap."

"Why would you want to trap someone you love?" Chelsea asked.

"Happens all the time," Bogie said. "In my time, I've known more than one woman who got pregnant on purpose to trap a man into marrying her. I think Violet got pregnant with David on purpose because she knew Patrick would never leave her for Robin if they had a child together."

"It would have been better for everyone if she had just let Pat go, even if he was determined to do the honorable thing and to keep his vows. If she had done that, everyone could have moved on. She might have even managed to keep her sanity."

"That's very true, Chelsea."

"Am I David's Robin or his Violet?"

"You were his first love."

"That wasn't my question, Bogie," she said. "Most people don't marry their first love. Am I David's Robin Spencer—the love of his life, the woman who's going to be on his mind when he takes his last breath—or am I the woman he's re-signed to marry in order to make up for breaking my heart back all those years ago?"

"Only you two can answer that."

Chapter Twenty-Six

"You need to do it now," Mac told Gnarly, who looked at the fire hydrant like he really wasn't feeling it. "Because once we go in there"—he pointed to the News Corp Building across the street—"I'm not dropping my interrogation just because you feel the need for a pit stop. You're going to have to cross your legs and hold it."

As if to demonstrate his opinion of Mac's threat, Gnarly stood up, turned his back on the fire hydrant, sat back down, and thrust his snout up in the air. If he'd had arms, he would have crossed them.

Mac was in the middle of a curse when his cell phone vibrated on his hip. The caller ID read "Bogie." "Think about it," he said to Gnarly while connecting the call and bringing the phone to his ear. "Tell me you have something for me, Bogie."

"Clint Brown and Kimberly Castillo from Marfa, Texas," Bogie said with a sigh.

"Texas' Romeo and Juliet," Mac said.

Bogie continued. "I had a nice long talk with Presidio County's sheriff, who had taken the lead when those two kids died in that car that went over the cliff. Now we both know that DNA wasn't available—"

"They trusted the kids at the scene who said Clint and Kimberly were in the car," Mac said.

"Exactly," Bogie said. "Clint had never been to a dentist, so there were no dental records for him. Kimberly's family believed her friends' ID. However, after I brought up Audra's statement that the car was on fire *before* it went over the cliff and mentioned how she disappeared after publicly saying that she was looking into this case, the sheriff became very open minded. His mind opened even more when I pointed out the shrapnel in what were supposedly Clint's legs. He said there was a young man in the next county over who the military police had been looking for because he'd gone AWOL. That was around the time when Clint and Kimberly supposedly died, but this AWOL soldier was twenty-three years old."

"Early to midtwenties, which is what Doc said was noted in the autopsy," Mac said.

"Plus, this guy was on medical leave after suffering leg wounds from an accidental explosion during a training exercise. Military *does* have his dental records."

"Yes!" Mac pumped his fist in the air.

"Sheriff is going to call the army and ask if they'd like to send over the dental records so we can compare them with the autopsy records for the body identified as Clint's. The sheriff is also going to take a closer look at the woman's body because this missing soldier had a girlfriend who disappeared at the same time. Her name was Carmen Gomez. She was a bartender who worked at his favorite hangout. It was a very popular cowboy bar, and she had a special way with the clientele. According to the sheriff, she was a sexy raven-haired Mexican."

"Mexican?" Mac asked. "The autopsy report didn't show any characteristics in the woman's skeletal features that are commonly associated with people of Mexican origin."

"Yes, but she went missing at the same time that this soldier went AWOL—after she worked a closing shift at the bar. They both disappeared with all of the money in the bar's cash register and safe. The theory at the time was that they stole the money and ran off to Mexico."

"Hmmmm," Mac mused. "You're giving me a lot of ideas, Bogie."

"That's what I'm here for."

"How are the wedding plans coming?" Mac asked. "Everything on schedule?"

"You tell me," Bogie said. "The groom's with you."

"We'll be home tomorrow in time for the rehearsal dinner." Hoping he wasn't telling a lie, Mac felt his stomach turn. Hearing only silence from the other end of the line, Mac wondered if Bogie, a longtime police officer who had a talent for spotting lies, heard the doubt in his voice. "Are you still there, Bogie?"

"Yeah." Bogie's voice had gone up an octave.

"Is Chelsea okay?" Mac asked. "She's not having second thoughts, is she?"

"We'll see you and David tomorrow."

Click!

"Is it me, or was that weird?" Tucking his cell phone back into its case, Mac tugged on Gnarly's leash, and they trotted across the street to the News Corp Building. After making his way through the security checkpoint, Mac saw Hank, the chief of the building's security, waving to him from his office's doorway.

"We checked on that visitor's form sent to security for Rubenstein," he told Mac in a low voice, glancing around as if he expected the killer to cut him off while he was divulging his findings.

"And?"

"The IP address that the form was sent from belongs to Pam Wiehl's desktop," Hank said. "It was sent from her intranet account, too."

"But the contact name on the form was Ali Hudson," Mac said.

"She's your killer," Hank said with certainty. "I've heard about how jealous Pam Wiehl was of Yvonne. You know how these women get when they get older, and pretty young girls start stealing their spotlight?"

"Yes," Mac said, "I know. Thank you for your help, Hank. That information is very useful."

"We've got places," Mac said into his cell phone while waiting outside the studio door.

Gnarly's ears peiked up, indicating that a visitor was nearby.

"The ball is now in play." Mac pressed the button to disconnect the call as Ian rounded the corner.

His ears falling back on his head, Gnarly wagged his tail.

"Well, hello, big guy. How are you?" Ian Griffith knelt to pet the German shepherd on the top of his head as he admired his impressively large build.

"Everything set?" Mac asked.

"We'll be ready to shoot in one, two—"

The elevator doors opened at the other end of the hall, and loud laughter floated down the corridor in their direction. Bent over with laughter, Pam and Jim Wiehl, and Ryan Ritter stepped off the elevator and made their way toward Mac, who was waiting by the doors.

Gnarly uttered a low growl.

Ryan was too focused on Mac to notice. "Faraday, I insist on being invited to your meeting."

"You insist?" Mac asked. "I didn't ask you, because I know how busy you are, and I thought I'd do you a favor. Since you've been cleared as a suspect, I saw no reason to inconvenience you." With a grin, he shrugged his shoulders. "Usually, witnesses run from these type of things."

"Keep in mind that you're dealing with journalists with this case," Jim told Mac.

"I'm a witness," Ryan said. "I was in the control room with you and O'Callaghan minutes before Yvonne was murdered."

"That's right," Mac said. "And then you went to makeup, which was on the opposite side of the studio from the scene of the crime. You were nowhere near the murder when it happened."

Laughing, Pam tapped Ian on the arm. "Which reminds me—I was just telling Jim about that stunt you pulled with my false eyelashes in makeup." She burst into loud laughter.

Ian joined in.

"What happened?" Mac asked.

Wiping his smile from his face, Ian said, "Considering that Yvonne was shot and killed while it happened, it seems tasteless for us to be laughing about it."

"I know," Pam said with a nervous laugh. "But it had everyone in stitches." She turned to Mac. "Ian is such a clown. Sophie, one of the makeup women, took off my other eyelash after the one had come off during filming the other night. Well Ian took both eyelashes, glued them onto his eyebrows, and started walking around, pretending to be a drag queen."

To demonstrate, Ian placed one hand on his hip and, batting his eyelashes, sashayed up and down the corridor while Pam roared with laughter. "He's just awful!"

"Totally outrageous. You'd never believe it." Ryan chuckled. "How ironic that while we were all doubled over with laughter, one of our good friends was having her young life tragically cut short."

After sighing wistfully, Ryan made his request once more. "If you don't mind, Mac, I really would like to be included in your meeting. As a journalist, I've been trained to be observant, and since I was there, I believe I could very well help. As you know, Yvonne Harding and I were quite close. I do want to help catch her killer."

With a wave of his hand, Mac gestured for them all to enter the studio. "The more the merrier."

Once inside the studio, Mac allowed Gnarly off his leash. On duty, Gnarly ignored the snack table Mac had set up for the group of witnesses and suspects he had called together and instead took a position between his master and the suspects. While waiting, many of them helped themselves to the goodies.

Ed Willingham, Lieutenant Andrew Van Patton, and four detectives from the lieutenant's squad had positioned themselves among the guests.

Taking his time, Mac made note of the suspects eying him, the lawyer, and the detectives.

There was Preston Blakeley, ZNC's CEO, who had a political agenda and a business relationship with Senator Brennan. Audra Walker's best-selling book threatened Senator Brennan's political career, which, in turn, would have hurt ZNC, who supported the senator. Blakeley had even tried to nix Audra Walker's interview and would have succeeded if she hadn't blackmailed him into letting it happen. Carl Rubenstein's potential lawsuit over Yvonne's outing his wife as a troll had stood to cost ZNC millions of dollars.

Pam Wiehl had considered both Audra Walker and Yvonne Harding to be her professional competition, as had Ian Griffin. She claimed that she had been personal friends with Audra Walker and that she and her husband owed her, but how far did that gratitude go? Far enough to make her set aside her ambition?

The others were all potential witnesses in Audra Walker's murder—and most of them had also been present during Yvonne's murder.

Mac waited for each one of them to start shuffling around and stealing nervous peeks in his direction before he checked the time on his cell phone. While they waited, he pressed a phone number. They heard his call over a speaker.

"You have reached the cell phone of David O'Callaghan. I'm sorry I'm not available to take your call right now. Please leave a message, and I'll get back in touch with you as soon as possible."

With a look of disappointment, Mac disconnected the call without leaving a message.

"When was the last time you heard from him?" Ed asked Mac.

"A while ago," Mac replied. "I guess David O'Callaghan and Ali Hudson aren't going to join us."

"And Lieutenant Wayne Hopkins, the detective assigned to this case, went home sick," Lieutenant Van Patton said. "Do you want to reschedule this?"

"No, I don't," Mac said. "Are you up to speed with Hopkins' investigation?"

The head of the homicide squad folded his arms across his chest. "Hopkins kept me in the loop."

Mac turned around to face his suspects. "I guess we'll get started."

"Excuse me for asking," Ian interrupted, "but wouldn't you consider it suspicious that you're having this meeting to prove that neither Carl Rubenstein nor you and your brother had anything to do with Yvonne's murder, but O'Callaghan isn't here?"

"Maybe." Mac gestured at the door leading into the control room, which Ed Willingham had opened. "Let's begin in here."

Seeing that the room wasn't big enough for everyone, Mac said, "I'd like everyone to go where they were during the taping of the segment recorded *before* Yvonne's murder. Lieutenant Van Patton, you'll stand in for Hopkins." Pointing at the news desk on the stage, he ordered Pam and the police lieutenant up onto the stage. "I want crew members to go where they were and to pretend to do what they were doing during the taping."

Sophie, the chief makeup artist, waved her hand. "Do you want us to go into the makeup room? We'll be over behind closed doors, so we won't be able to see what's going on."

"But you do have a monitor with a live feed of what's being recorded on the stage," Jim Wiehl reminded them.

Sophie pouted, as did the other three women in charge of makeup. They were disappointed that they would be left out.

"Don't worry," Mac assured them. "You're not going to miss anything. The last place Yvonne Harding was before she came out onto the stage to prepare for her segment was in makeup, right?"

Their faces brightened. "Yes, she was," Sophie said. "She was giving pointers to her guest."

"I was in makeup, too," Ian Griffin said.

"Yes, he was," another one of the artists said. "He was annoying Yvonne with troll jokes."

Escorted by one of the detectives, an attractive young man, the four women scurried off to the makeup department, which was located on the opposite side of the control room.

Ed Willingham was already in the control room with Gnarly sitting in front of him. "Where do you want me, Mac?"

"You're standing in for David," Mac said before calling for Ryan Ritter, Jim Wiehl, and Preston Blakeley to join them in the control room. "It doesn't matter where you stand. We're talking about the events leading up to Yvonne Harding's murder."

One of Van Patton's detectives followed them into the control room and took a position next to the closed door.

After pulling up a chair from the control panel, Ryan Ritter straddled its back and glanced at the room's occupants. "Okay, Faraday, you got all of us here. Shoot."

"First of all, as a career homicide detective," Mac began, "I've learned not to believe in coincidences. For that reason, I find it more than interesting that Yvonne Harding, the last journalist to interview Audra Walker here at ZNC, was killed on the *same* day that Audra's body was uncovered in her office."

"You believe Audra Walker's and Yvonne Harding's murders are connected," Jim Wiehl said.

"I *know* they're connected," Mac said.

"But how?" Ryan asked. "Audra Walker tackled deep, complex murder cases. Yvonne Harding was a television personality." He chuckled. "Not to slam Yvonne in any way. She had a ton of talent, but professionally, she wasn't in Walker's league."

"Ryan's right," Preston said. "They didn't travel in the same social circles. Their only connection was when Yvonne interviewed Audra."

"But Yvonne Harding was investigating Audra Walker's disappearance," Mac said before turning to Jim. "I saw for myself how upset Pam was when she discovered that Ali Hudson was making inquiries into Audra's disappearance. She was so upset that she went to get you, Jim."

"Because the Walker disappearance was Pam's story," Jim said. "Journalists are very territorial. The Walker case was a big story, and Pam is our headline host. Therefore, it was hers. By investigating Audra's disappearance behind Pam's back, Yvonne was infringing on another journalist's story. That's a big no-no in this business, and frankly, I was surprised because Yvonne knew better."

"I'm sure she did." Folding his arms across his chest, Mac asked, "How much headway had Pam been making in *her* investigation?"

Jim shot a glare in Preston Blakeley's direction. "Care to answer that, Blakeley?"

"I don't know what you're talking about," the CEO said.

Jim turned to Mac. "You want the truth?"

"That's why we're here."

Jim tossed his head in the direction of his boss. "Blakeley and Senator Brennan are tight. After Audra Walker disappeared, as soon as the case started to chill, Blakeley made it known not just to *Crime Watch* but to every show and journalist under ZNC that the Walker disappearance needed to be put on the back burner."

"I didn't say any such thing!" Blakeley yelled.

"A fourth grader could read between the lines, Blakeley!"

"If you aren't protecting Senator Brennan, why is every other network in the building devoting twice the airtime we are to the story of Walker's body being found in *ZNC's* walls?" Ryan asked.

"That's not true," Blakeley said.

"My staff has the data to prove it," Ryan said, smirking at Mac. "It's a necessary evil in the news business nowadays. Every news network is owned by corporations, and corporations make political friends and enemies. At the end of the day, the only thing you can count on when it comes to news is that they toed their party's line."

"In other words," Mac said, "if you really want the truth about what's happening, don't trust the news media to give it to you."

Ryan chuckled. "Those are my words."

"In case you've all forgotten, Senator Brennan was on his way to his party's nomination for president before Audra Walker's disappearance, at which point his poll rankings dropped like a rock. If anything, Walker's disappearance killed his political career," Blakeley said.

"His rankings were dropping like a rock *before* Audra's disappearance *because* of her book about his lecherous and possibly homicidal daddy," Ryan said. "Sounds like motivation for him to kill her. It's called 'revenge.'"

"Why would Brennan have killed Walker when he knew he'd be the number-one suspect?" Blakeley asked.

"Brennan was too smart to kill Walker," Mac said. "People like him have it done for them."

"Point is," Blakeley said, "neither Brennan nor ZNC benefited from Walker's disappearance or murder in any way."

"True," Mac said.

With a smug grin, the CEO folded his arms and plopped down into an empty chair.

Mac turned to the director, who was sitting at the control panel with his assistant, each in the same chair he had occupied two nights before. "Can you play that video I requested?"

After a nod of approval from Jim Wiehl, the director hit the "play" button, and the recording filled the monitor in the control room as well as the monitors out in the studio. It was the recording of the final minutes of Yvonne Harding's interview with Audra Walker.

At the end of Audra Walker's last interview, which had been filmed two years earlier, Yvonne Harding asked, "What's next for Audra Walker?"

"Oh, I'm now gonna finish that one project that's been doggin' me for my whole career," Audra said with a wide grin.

"What project is that?" Yvonne asked.

"The true story behind Romeo and Juliet."

Mac turned to Preston Blakeley. "The other night, when Pam Wiehl opened her segment with this clip, you became upset—"

"I wasn't *upset*," Blakeley said.

"You weren't happy," Mac said, correcting himself. "You asked Wiehl why he'd chosen this particular clip."

"Because it was boring," the network executive said. "It was an hour-long interview. Audra Walker was an exciting and passionate journalist with decades of fascinating work under her belt. She had a million stories, some of which involved movie stars and infamous crime figures. This here"—he gestured at the recording—"was the dullest part of the whole interview. Not only that, but Walker disappeared hours later, and the damned book she was talking about was never written. No one knew what she was talking about—she didn't name names. It isn't like she went missing hours after announcing that she was going to reveal to the world the location of Jimmy Hoffa's body. It was some stale crap about Romeo and Juliet."

"Exactly," Mac turned to Jim. "Blakeley is right. Why did you choose this clip?"

"It was the only stuff that our lawyers and board would allow us to use," Jim replied. "The bulk of Audra Walker's interview with Yvonne had to do with Jolene Fitzgerald's death and her affair with Senator Brennan's father. Everyone on the board was either tight with Brennan or afraid of repercussions from the Brennan political machine. This tape was all we had left."

"As a lawyer, I can see how that would happen," Willingham said.

They all turned their attention back to the recording.

"Romeo and Juliet?" Yvonne asked in the interview. "Is Audra Walker moving into romantic tragedies?"

"Actually, it's not so much a romantic tragedy as it is the perfect murder," Audra said in a teasing tone. With a tilt of her head, she arched that eyebrow.

"Freeze it there," Mac said to the director, whose assistant hit a button on the panel to freeze the image of Audra Walker.

"Not so much a romantic tragedy as it is the perfect murder," Mac murmured at Audra Walker's image. "That's what her next project was going to be. She was returning to a project she'd been working on for years—one she'd never gained any traction on until she showed up here at ZNC. Then suddenly, all the wheels clicked in her mind." Making a rolling motion with his index fingers on either side of his head, he said, "It all came together that night."

"Do you know that for a fact?" Preston Blakeley asked.

"Walker's book tour was taking her all over the country," Ryan said. "She had interviews with every network in this building. There's no telling when, where, or from whom she got the break on her story. For all we know, she was inspired by someone at MSNBC." He chuckled. "As a matter of fact, I'd bet on it. Have you seen some of their news anchors? Pretty suspicious, if you ask me."

"If so, why did she mention the project in this interview for ZNC?" Mac asked.

Silence dropped over the men in the control room as they each regarded the others with suspicion.

The cloud of suspicion broke apart when Mac clapped his hands together. "While you're thinking about that, let's discuss the chain of events on the night of Yvonne's murder."

He turned around and looked out the window to where Pam Wiehl and Lieutenant Van Patton were engrossed in a conversation on the stage. "During her interview with Lieutenant Hopkins, Pam's false eyelash came loose. She was able to finish the interview, and then she went off to makeup." He turned to the director. "Tell everyone that the recording is through and that they should do exactly what they did the other night *after* Pam finished interviewing Hopkins."

Out in the studio, noise erupted. Everyone on the crew was talking at once. Equipment was moved and lights were adjusted for the next segment, which was Yvonne Harding's interview with the psychologist about Internet trolls.

"Security confirms that Hopkins signed out downstairs and left the building minutes after finishing his interview," Mac told Lieutenant Van Patton and the suspects who had followed him out to the news desk on the set. "Yvonne came out of makeup and met up with David here at the set where they talked—"

"Argued," Ryan corrected him with a smile.

"I was in a conference call up in my office," Preston Blakeley said.

"Yes, you were, Mr. Blakeley." Mac ushered Ed Willingham to the steps leading up to the stage. "We did confirm that alibi."

Relief washed over the executive's face.

"I don't need you anymore, Mr. Blakeley, but I think you might want to stick around." Mac took the CEO by the arm and moved him over to stand in front of the lawyer. "You can play Yvonne."

Unsure of where this was leading, Preston Blakeley blubbered.

Mac turned around and found Ryan Ritter standing in front of him. "What do you want me to do?" he asked.

"You went to makeup to get ready for your show, didn't you?" Mac asked.

Ryan looked worried. "Yeah, but you want me to go to the makeup department and put on my makeup just like I did the other night? Do you want Pam to take off her eyelashes and Ian to put them on and dance with them, too? That's all a little obsessive, don't you think?"

Mac looked over at Lieutenant Van Patton, who nodded his head.

"If that's what happened." Taking Ryan Ritter by the arm, Mac led him around the control room and through the door into the makeup department. Lieutenant Van Patton followed behind them.

"I don't see how Ian's dancing around with Pam's eyelashes on his forehead is going to solve Yvonne's murder," Ryan said.

"You'd be surprised by how these tiny details can help police catch killers." Mac threw open the door to the makeup room and ushered Ryan inside, where Pam, Ian, guests from the shows from the night of the murder, and the four makeup artists were chatting away. The detective watching over them was in a makeup chair getting what appeared to be a haircut.

"Okay!" Mac said in a loud voice. "Everyone listen up. We are reenacting Yvonne's murder. I want everyone where they were and doing what they were doing in the minutes leading up to Yvonne's murder. Now, where was everyone?"

"I was over here doing my makeup." Ryan went over to a chair away from everyone.

"Do I really have to take off my eyelashes?" Pam asked Mac. "They're such a pain to put on."

"Just pretend to take them off," Mac said.

Sophie picked up a container holding a pair of eyelashes. "We'll role-play with these."

Ian snatched the eyelashes from her hand and opened the case. Raising his voice to an ultrasoprano register, he sang an operetta while he applied a heavy layer of makeup glue to a lash and pinned it to his eyebrow.

While the makeup artists and guests giggled, Pam Wiehl and Ryan Ritter laughed loudly.

Ian Griffin had just glued the other lash on and had begun strutting around when Sophie turned to Mac and said, "I don't remember Ian playing with Pam's eyelashes the other night."

"Yeah," one of the other artists said. "He made a bunch of jokes, but he didn't put them on and dance around like that. That didn't happen at all."

"What are you doing, Ian?" the fourth woman asked. "He said to do what we did the other night."

While confusion crossed the artists' and guests' faces, Ryan Ritter's eyes narrowed to a glare directed at Ian and Pam.

Mac returned Ryan's glare. "No, Ian didn't dance with Pam's eyelashes on the night of the murder."

"You set me up, bitch," Ryan hissed at Pam.

"Because I asked her to," Mac said. "You stated that your alibi was that you were in here when Yvonne was murdered, but you weren't."

"I was," Ryan said. "I was sitting here in this chair putting on my makeup."

"You put it on earlier," Mac said. "I noticed that you were already wearing mascara in the control room while we were watching Pam's segment with Hopkins. You knew you wouldn't have time to put it on before killing Yvonne, so you must have applied it in your office when no one was around."

"I was here in the makeup department," Ryan said before gesturing to his colleagues and friends gathered in the room. "Tell him! You all saw me in this room, sitting in this chair, putting on my makeup for my show!"

"I'm sure you came in here," Mac said. "But as soon as everyone got busy with getting ready for the next segment, you quietly slipped out. If you had been here the whole time, you would have known that Ian didn't put on Pam's eyelashes."

"You would have said something in the elevator earlier when I told Jim about it," Pam said.

"When you were setting me up," Ryan said with a sneer.

"More like testing you," Pam said.

"If you had been here when Yvonne was shot, you would have known that Ian never put Pam's eyelashes on, and you would have said something about it when she told her husband he had. But instead you joined in—even went so far as to join her in recounting the story to me minutes later. Since you didn't know the event never happened, that proves you weren't here."

Ian peeled both lashes off his forehead. "I saw you leave not long after I came in. I don't know the exact time, but you weren't here long—maybe a couple of minutes, tops."

"You were the one who told us that Yvonne had been shot," Pam said.

"I remember that," Sophie said to Mac. "He did come in from the studio—but I didn't notice what time he left."

Lieutenant Van Patton turned to Ryan. "How would you have known Yvonne got shot out there"—he jerked his thumb over his shoulder—"if you were in here?" He pointed to the floor.

"Easy!" Ryan ripped his cell phone from its holder on his belt. "I got a call and went out into the studio to take it because it was too noisy to hear in here. I went out there and heard everyone screaming about someone shooting Yvonne. That was when I came in here to tell everyone."

"How did you know Yvonne got shot?" Mac asked him.

"Duh," Ryan scoffed. "Because everyone out in the studio was screaming about it." He got up from his seat and stepped up to Mac. "Fact is, Faraday, you're reaching to make this case into something it's not. Rubenstein shot Yvonne to avenge his wife's murder. Everyone knows that. Trying to make me out to be the killer"—he laughed—"is completely ludicrous. You yourself said in the control room that Yvonne's murder is connected to Audra Walker's murder. Well tell Van Patton there to check his case file for Walker's disappearance, because it's all right there. I didn't even know Audra Walker. I had only met her that day, here in the studio. Why would I have wanted to kill her? I didn't have a motive, and I was with Yvonne Harding when Audra Walker disappeared." He ticked off his defense on his fingers. "Airtight alibi and no motive. Too bad, Faraday. You've struck out this time."

"Too bad Yvonne Harding isn't around to confirm that alibi," Mac said.

"She confirmed it in her official statement to the police when they wanted to know where *she* was when Audra Walker disappeared."

"She gave that statement because someone using her name had texted Audra Walker," Mac said. "Of course, Yvonne could have lured Audra Walker back here using her own name with a burner phone that she then disposed of. So Hopkins and Sergeant Roberts asked her about her whereabouts. Luckily, she was cleared of suspicion when she used *you* for her alibi."

"Exactly," Ryan said.

"Which made her *your* alibi."

"Not that I thought I would need one."

With a shake of his head, Mac said, "There's a problem with that alibi, though."

"What?"

"Fifty-year-old scotch," Mac said. "Yvonne rarely drank hard liquor, because when she did, it took only one drink to make her drunk—it was almost like a roofie for her. Two drinks would knock her out. If Yvonne was drinking scotch with you that night, then she wouldn't have been a very reliable alibi. All you had to do was give her two drinks, and she would have passed out—giving you plenty of time to lure Audra Walker here, kill her, seal her body behind a sheet of drywall, get back to Yvonne's place, and clean up. Then you woke up next to her, with her being none the wiser."

"I don't have to take this!" Ryan shoved Mac out of the way and stormed out of the makeup department and into the studio.

"You shot Yvonne Harding, and we can prove it," Mac said while following him.

Everyone spilled out of the makeup department to follow them into the studio.

"Oh, David," Yvonne's breathy voice said over the speakers. Her words were followed by a loud *thud*.

As if encountering the ghost of Yvonne Harding, everyone froze in place.

Mac grinned at Ryan's wide eyes. "You did go to makeup, like you said, Ritter," he said over Gnarly's barking in the background on the recording. "While you were back there, the sound people started doing a sound check on Yvonne's mic. They didn't pick up everything, but they did pick up enough to prove that you shot Yvonne."

They heard a clang in the distance.

"That's the slam of the studio door when Carl Rubenstein ran out," Mac explained. "When he got up here to the studio, discovered that no one was expecting him, and saw Yvonne collapse, he put everything together. He discovered he was being set up and ran."

The clang was followed by a crash, Gnarly's barking, and Mac's yelling, "Gnarly, no!"

"Yvonne, stop it!" David's voice was loud and anxious. "Stand up!"

"Why did David tell her to stand up? At that point, he didn't realize she was hurt," Mac said over the screaming of a crew member on the audio. "That scream is a crew member seeing the blood."

"Obviously," Lieutenant Van Patton said, "O'Callaghan didn't know she'd been shot. I didn't hear the shot." He turned to his detectives. "Did you hear the shot?" They all shook their heads.

"David," Yvonne gasped.

"The killer used a silencer," Mac said. "Between that and the racket here in the studio, no one heard the shot—not even David. As a matter of fact, on my way out the door to pursue Rubenstein, Jim Wiehl stopped me. Assuming Yvonne had fainted, he asked me if she was pregnant."

"Somebody call nine-one-one! Yvonne, darling, stay with me. You're going to be okay," David said.

"No, I'm not. Hold me, David."

Tears were forming in the listeners' eyes.

"I'm here, darling," David said. "Don't try to talk."

"You're right, David, I'm not the same woman."

"Ambulance is on its way, baby. You got to hold on. What happened, baby?"

"Why would he be asking her what happened if he knew that she'd been shot?" Mac asked Ryan.

Yvonne's voice was weak. "Baby … that's what you used to call me."

Abruptly, Pam Wiehl's voice sounded over the speakers. "What happened? We heard someone shot Yvonne?"

"I came running over as soon as *you* told me that someone had shot her," Pam said to Ryan in an accusatory tone. "Why would you know that if David O'Callaghan, who was holding her, didn't know—unless *you* shot her?"

Mac waved his hand to signal for the assistant director in the control booth to stop the audio, which had brought many members of the crew to tears. Most of them were glaring at Ryan Ritter.

Stepping up to Ryan Ritter, Mac locked his gaze with his and asked Jim Wiehl, "How did Lieutenant Wayne Hopkins end up on the list of law-enforcement experts for *Crime Watch*?"

Jim looked over at Pam, whose eyes grew wide when she answered him. "Ryan recommended him. He used him for a segment on his show and said that the camera loved him and that he knew his stuff. So I called him in one day."

"As a matter of fact," Preston Blakeley said, "Ritter has been campaigning for ZNC to give Hopkins his own show."

"Somehow Lieutenant Wayne Hopkins found out you killed Audra Walker," Mac said while taking his cell phone out of his pocket. "Maybe while he was questioning Yvonne Harding, she revealed that she had passed out. I can see you spinning things around—under the guise of helping Yvonne when Hopkins and Roberts questioned her about Walker's disappearance—and coaching her. Hopkins must have caught on." He grinned. "Somehow, Hopkins realized you had used Yvonne to establish an alibi for yourself, so you offered to help make him a star in exchange for cleaning up your mess." He pressed the button on his phone to dial the preprogrammed number.

"If Hopkins said that, then he's lying." Ryan Ritter turned around, taking in the faces of his colleagues and subordinates, all of whom were staring at him, their faces filled with suspicion. "He's conjuring up this whole conspiracy with nothing concrete to go on. Hopkins?" He scoffed. "He said he had a dream of being a television star, and I'm a nice guy, so I put in a good word for him. That's all!"

Ryan Ritter jumped to attention.

Mac studied the screen on his phone.

Ryan's breathing quickened.

"Don't you think you should answer that, Ritter?" Mac asked. "It might be Hopkins." He lowered his voice. "I think his goons ran into some problems on Long Island."

Ryan Ritter followed Mac's line of sight to where David O'Callaghan and Dallas Walker had entered the studio through the back door. Even though they had changed clothes and freshened up, the bruises and welts on their faces were evidence of their ordeal.

"We've got some bad news for you, Ritter," Mac said in a low tone. "Hopkins and his hired guns failed miserably in their job of tying up your loose ends. And there's more bad news." He gestured to where Lieutenant Van Patton was holding up an evidence bag with a bloody cell phone in it. "We got Hopkins' phone and the list of calls he made to the burner in your pocket."

With wide eyes, Ryan stared at the phone in the evidence bag. Slowly, a grin crossed his face. He broke into a laugh. "Burner in my pocket?" He extracted a cell phone from his pants pocket. "Are you talking about this?" He continued to chuckle. "Maybe Hopkins was calling this phone. I wouldn't know. I just found it in the men's restroom less than an hour ago. I was on my way to turn it into lost and found when I ran into Pam and Jim downstairs." He tossed the phone to the police lieutenant. He winked at Mac. "Nice try, Faraday."

"You did have an arrangement with Lieutenant Hopkins," David said. "You were the one giving him orders behind the scenes to tie up your loose ends."

"Like I said, I'm a nice guy. I put in a good word for him with ZNC's producers to use him as a law enforcement expert. I didn't ask or expect anything from him in return."

"I got the impression that it was more than a good word when you suggested I give Hopkins his own show," Preston Blakeley said. "You brought it up again just yesterday."

"Was that before or after he closed the case for Yvonne's murder with Carl Rubenstein named as the shooter?" Mac asked.

"After finding the gloves Rubenstein tossed in the stairwell after he shot Yvonne," Ryan said.

"While there's gunshot residue on the gloves indicating they were worn while firing a gun," Lieutenant Van Patton said, "there's nothing to positively connect them to Carl Rubenstein. Not only that, but forensics found nothing on his clothes or body to prove he had shot a firearm."

"Yet, Hopkins insisted Carl Rubenstein was the shooter," Mac said, "hours after accusing me of shooting Yvonne in the back to free David up to marry someone else this weekend."

"A marriage Hopkins already knew about when he questioned me right after the murder," David said. "No one here in the studio knew Yvonne and I were married except you because you overheard Mac and me talking in the control room about my wanting a divorce."

"I already admitted I told Hopkins about that and you said that as a police chief you understood," Ryan said.

"Actually, it was *you* who told me that as a police chief I should understand," David said. "Thing is, no one here at ZNC knew I was a police chief. The only person I told was Lieutenant Hopkins while giving my statement."

"Which means you had a conversation with Lieutenant Hopkins a second time *after* he questioned both David and I," Mac said. "I suspect that was when he decided to remove us as persons of interest in his investigation and go back to who you originally intended to frame—Carl Rubenstein." He added, "Dead men don't put up as vigorous of a defense as live ones."

"Yes, I had a second conversation with Hopkins after he questioned you," Ryan said. "Big deal. But it was by no means as sordid as you're making it out to be." He pounded his chest. "I'm a journalist. I was pumping the homicide detective investigating the murder of a good friend for information. And yes, he told me that you were a police chief and, because they found gloves with gunshot residue in the same stairwell that Rubenstein tried to escape down, they were focusing on him for the shooter."

"What if I told you that's not what Lieutenant Wayne Hopkins told us?" Mac asked.

"I'd say he's lying."

"Even if he's got recordings of your phone conversations to prove it?" Mac countered.

"Like the one you two had this morning when you gave him the order to kill both of us?" David asked. "You specifically told Hopkins to seal our bodies in the wall of a building under construction like you did with Audra Walker."

His eyes narrowed, Ryan Ritter locked his gaze on David O'Callaghan.

"In spite of all your efforts, you've still got loose ends, Ritter," Mac said.

"Why'd you kill Yvonne?" Pam asked with tears in her eyes. "She was your friend!"

"Because he found out I was investigatin' my mother's disappearance," Dallas announced.

A collective gasp sounded throughout the studio at the revelation that the young woman they had known as Yvonne Harding's assistant was actually Audra Walker's daughter.

Years of fury bubbling to the surface, Dallas charged up to Ryan with David directly behind her—trying to keep her emotions in check. "You were sittin' right there on the corner of my desk with a big bunch of yellow roses, tryin' to sweet-talk me into goin' to lunch with you when Roberts called. You must have seen his name on the caller ID. Was that when you decided to take out Yvonne and me, or was it after Gnarly sniffed out my momma's body just a few feet from my desk—where you buried her and let her rot like garbage!"

"Now I see it." Ryan Ritter laughed. "All these months, you reminded me of someone, but I couldn't put my finger on it. That double-backboned attitude should've told me."

"Careful, Ritter," Mac said. "Your accent's slipping."

Ryan sneered at Dallas while David held her back. "One brick shy of a load—just like your mother."

After jabbing David in his broken ribs, Dallas slugged Ryan across the jaw so hard that she managed to knock him backward and almost off his feet. She would have hit him again if David hadn't thrown his arms around her, lifted her off her feet, and carried her out of punching distance. Holding her close, David spoke softly into her ear.

"Why?" Pam asked again. "I thought Ryan and Audra Walker had only met that night she came here for her interview with Yvonne."

"That's what he wanted everyone to think," Mac said while trying not to chuckle at Ryan Ritter nursing the bloody nose Dallas had given him. "Ryan changed his name and had a lot of cosmetic surgery over the years, but somehow, someway—maybe it was something he said or did—Audra Walker recognized him for who he really is."

"Who's that?" Ian asked.

"Romeo of the book that Audra Walker had been working on for all those years," Mac said.

"Ryan Ritter is Romeo?" Dallas gasped.

Mac explained, "Clint Brown. Supposedly, he died in a suicide pact with his high school sweetheart, Kimberly

Castillo, thirty years ago, the night of their senior prom in Marfa, Texas. Audra Walker was friends with Kimberly. She was there at the lovers' point when the car that her two friends were in caught fire and went over a cliff. Supposedly, both bodies were burned beyond recognition. But something about that suicide bothered Audra for years."

"The car catchin' fire *before* it went over the cliff," Dallas said.

"Then a week later, during the memorial service, Kimberly's father's home was broken in to. Her brother and his girlfriend were murdered, and several thousands of dollars and jewels were stolen out of a safe."

"Too much of a coincidence," David said.

"Over the next thirty years, Audra kept going over the details of the case," Mac said. "Maybe she heard about the young army soldier and his bartender girlfriend who disappeared around that time. After hearing about how the Mexican barmaid had a way with men and recalling what a Romeo Clint was, I could see how Audra started putting things together."

Mac leaned toward Ryan. "How long did you wait before killing Carmen after she helped you pull it off? I'm assuming you were the mastermind of it all."

Mac studied the lifetime of fury working its way to the surface of Ryan Ritter's face. "It was about more than a simple burglary. It was about avenging your father's death. An eye for an eye. Your father died working for Castillo, so you seduced and then killed his only daughter. We can assume that Kimberly, who trusted you, gave you the combination to her father's safe, which had in it thousands of dollars in cash and precious jewels. Kimberly's brother and his girlfriend walked in, so you killed them, too. The heartbreak of losing his children led to Castillo's death six months later."

The corners of his lips turning up in a smirk, Ryan said, "You can't prove any of it."

"I noticed you didn't say that you didn't do it," Ed Willingham said, "but that we can't prove it."

"Which isn't true," Mac said. "DNA was in its infancy then, but it isn't anymore. We now have enough evidence to get your DNA and to compare it to the DNA of your deceased parents, which will prove that you are Clint Brown. The police in Texas are already comparing the dental records for a missing army soldier to the body you'd planted at the bottom of the cliff to make everyone think you were dead. It's only a matter of time before the police in Texas will want to know where you were during the memorial service when Kimberly's brother and his girlfriend were killed and the safe was broken in to." He paused and shrugged. "And that's why you killed Audra Walker—to keep all of that from happening."

Ryan uttered a low chuckle. "Out of everyone here on this earth—if anyone had been perceptive and keen enough to finger me, it would have been Audra Walker. I had planned to not be here on the day of the interview. But I had to see—after all the changes I'd made to my appearance, the voice lessons, the years of extensive training to get rid of my Texas drawl, and the decades spent cultivating my poised New England persona—if *she* would catch on."

Ryan's frown filled his entire face. "She nailed me within minutes. That cock of her head. The look in her eyes. I tried to tell myself that it was just my imagination. I even agreed to have her on my show the next week. And then, as she was leaving, she said she had a special surprise for me." He gritted his teeth. "When she called me Tex, I knew."

Mac picked up where Ryan had left off. "So you took a bottle of scotch over to Yvonne's to get her drunk and to establish an alibi. As soon as Yvonne passed out from the scotch, you lured Audra here, where the ZNC studio offices were being renovated, and got rid of your problem."

"You killed my mother," Dallas hissed at him.

"He's going to jail," David said to soothe her while smoothing her long, dark locks. "We got him now."

Dallas spat in Ryan's direction. "I hope you rot in hell."

"You'll be right there with me," Ryan chuckled while whipping a gun out from under his suit coat.

Screams filled the studio. Crew members ran for cover. Gnarly charged him.

Reaching for his gun, David threw himself in front of Dallas. Before he had a chance to take aim, three shots rang out, each one striking Ryan Ritter in the back.

With a look of surprise, Ryan Ritter dropped to the floor.

Confused, Mac, David, and the police detectives looked around for the source of the shots.

Standing in front of his wife, Jim Wiehl held up his hands; a semiautomatic was dangling from his fingers. "Don't shoot! I give up!"

Ed Willingham went into instant defense-attorney mode. "It was defense of another. Ritter was going to shoot Dallas Walker." He waved his hand at every member of the crew in the studio. "You're all witnesses."

Lieutenant Van Patton took the producer's gun from him. "We all saw what happened, and we'll make sure the district attorney knows." With a sigh of regret, he took out his handcuffs. "We're going to have to take you into custody."

With a sense of resignation, Jim Wiehl turned around and clasped his hands behind his back. "Make sure Dallas gets back to Texas safe and sound," Jim told Mac. "We owe that to Audra."

"I guess this makes you and Audra Walker even," Mac whispered to the producer.

Mac saw David wipe the tears from Dallas's face. Their heads were bowed toward each other, and their foreheads were pressed together.

Tomorrow is David and Chelsea's wedding rehearsal. Their wedding is the day after that. Or is it?

Chapter Twenty-Seven

"That's great, Ed," Mac said into his cell phone while the wine steward opened a second bottle of champagne.

Dallas Walker had insisted on treating Mac and David to dinner, which she called "supper," at the Four Seasons to thank them for their help. Feeling like a fifth wheel, Mac had tried to beg out, claiming that he didn't want to leave Gnarly alone in their suite, but she'd insisted.

Seeing the evening-theater crowd eating before the show and Dallas grasping David's thigh under the table, Mac felt not only like a fifth wheel but also like an underdressed fifth wheel. David didn't look much better with an ugly bruise across his forehead and a welt on his cheek from his encounter with Hopkins' goons.

At least he's alive.

In contrast to David's and Mac's casual appearance, Dallas had purchased a form-fitting, royal-blue, backless cocktail dress in the hotel dress shop that showed off her long legs, which went on forever. She wore her thick, dark hair in loose waves. In a town full of high-fashion models, Dallas seemed to fit right in. Mac noticed more than one head turn when she walked into the dining room. A look of pride filled David's face when she arrived at their table and greeted him with a passionate kiss that he enthusiastically returned.

Mac felt his heart sink. *Poor Chelsea. It's happened again.* But Mac sensed that Dallas was not Katrina or Yvonne. Dallas was different from all of David's other women. During their time on the run, they had formed a deep, intense connection built on a mutual dependence on each other. Mac doubted that David had ever had a relationship like the one he was embarking on with Dallas. She was definitely a handful.

David looked at Dallas with the same deep love that Mac looked at Archie with.

Thinking of Archie, Mac wished that she were sitting next to him at their table, enjoying the champagne with them. He felt an ache in his chest when he thought of her not being in his bed when he finished dinner—or was it supper?—and went up to the room.

After disconnecting his call with Ed Willingham, Mac broke through David and Dallas's heat-filled gaze to deliver another piece of good news. "Jim Wiehl is on his way home. With the dozens of witness statements, including the statements from Lieutenant Van Patton and his detectives, and Preston Blakeley's phone calls to his influential friends, Jim was released without bond. The district attorney is already discussing charging him with justifiable homicide. He won't have to spend a day in jail."

"That's good." David picked up his champagne glass. "A toast to the good guys coming out on top."

After they had all sipped their champagne, Dallas turned to Mac. "What did Wiehl mean when he said he owed my mom?"

Remembering that the Wiehls had said that Audra had insisted no one know about what she'd done to help their daughter, Mac lied. "I think he felt responsible for what happened. He was the executive producer, and he had invited her to be on the show, and—" Feeling himself rambling on, he stopped.

He sensed by the cock of her head that she wasn't buying it. David was having trouble buying it as well.

"Good champagne." Changing the subject, Mac set down his glass and turned his attention to David. "I'm impressed. I knew you were good, but three dirty cops? You were tied up, and you managed to free yourself, disarm one of them of his machine gun, and take them all out."

"Dallas took out one of them." David squeezed her hand, which was clutching his thigh under the table.

"Still," Mac said.

"Someone else was there," David blurted out.

"David," Dallas warned him in a hushed voice. "She said—"

"I have to tell Mac," David said. "He's been after her."

"Who?" Mac asked.

David reached his hand into his pocket. He then placed the black diamond in the center of the table between them.

Mac almost jumped out of his seat when he grabbed it. "*She* was there."

"She was on our side," Dallas whispered across the table at him.

"Good thing," Mac said. "From what I know about the Black Diamond, if she hadn't been, you'd both be dead now."

"She was protecting Dallas," David said.

"Why?" Suddenly suspicious, Mac looked her up and down.

Dallas shrugged her shoulders. "I ran into her in the elevator at the Plaza. She recognized me and knew Mom—how, I honestly don't know. Mom knew a lot of people. Suddenly, she turned up in Long Island. She gunned down those killers. When I asked who she was, she said she owed Mom—kind of like what Jim Wiehl said."

"Then she gave me this diamond"—David took the black jewel from Mac—"and said I now owe her. She called me by name—"

"David told me that she's a very infamous paid assassin," Dallas said. "I don't understand how my mother would've known her."

"You never saw her before?" Mac asked Dallas.

"Her voice seemed kind of familiar, but I have no—"

"Sleeping with the Enemy," Mac said.

"What?" David asked.

"The book that put Audra Walker on the map," Mac said. "She went to jail for ten days because she refused to give up her source."

Dallas was nodding her head. "I was just a little girl then. *Sleeping with the Enemy* was 'bout a superior-court judge in Washington State who'd hired a hit man to kill her husband. Mom's source was the hit man, and the justice department wanted her to name him, but she wouldn't turn him in."

"She never did name her source," Mac said. "Maybe it wasn't a hit *man* but a hit *woman*. That's why the Black Diamond owed your mother—and saved your lives."

"I don't like owing her," David said. "I don't care if she did save my life—she's not getting a free pass in my town."

"Your mother certainly collected an interesting group of characters and sources." Mac took a sip of his champagne.

"What put you on the trail of Ryan Ritter?" Dallas asked Mac. "I never would've suspected him. I saw him every day for the last five months and totally bought his New England roots."

"I have a suspicious personality," Mac said. "First, for someone who wasn't involved in the case at all, he seemed to be around a lot, voicing his opinion and trying to point us in various directions."

"He wanted to know how much we knew," David said.

"And then when he thought he wasn't on our radar, his ego refused to allow him to simply walk away," Mac said. "Ritter was too much of a narcissist to miss an opportunity to flaunt his getting away with murder."

"Okay," Dallas said. "So Ryan's behavior put him on your radar but not on mine. I still don't understand how you managed to connect him to Mom's Romeo-and-Juliet case."

Mac shrugged. "He must have had a motive."

"How 'bout bein' crazy as a bullbat?"

"Now there's no such thing as a bullbat," David said.

"There sure is, sugar," she replied. "Back home I see 'em every night after dark."

"Do you mean male bats?" David held out her glass to the server who had returned to refill their glasses.

"No, they're *birds.* You probably know them as nighthawks." After taking a sip of the champagne, she asked Mac, "What clued you in to Ryan Ritter's connection to Mom's unfinished book 'bout Romeo and Juliet?"

"Your mother," Mac said. "Her assistant told me that this whole project was one that she'd never finished. She would only go back to it between bigger projects. And yet suddenly, out of the blue and for the first time, she publicly said it was her next project. Knowing your mother, my guess is that her making that statement on the air was a signal to the perp that she was on to him." He sat back in his seat. "Her disappearance meant the killer got that message."

Slowly, Dallas recalled her mother's last interview. "Why didn't you think it was the Wiehls? They were 'bout the same age as Mom and from out West. They said Montana, but they could've made all that up like Ritter did."

"Because your mother had known them for years," Mac said. "If she was going to suspect them of being Romeo and Juliet, she would have done so much earlier. No, she had her breakthrough that day, and, as it turned out, Ryan Ritter was the only one who met Audra Walker for the first time. To confirm my suspicions, I sent the pictures from your mother's files—the ones of Clint and Kimberly and all of our other suspects—to Archie so she could run them through a facial-recognition program. Clint had a lot of cosmetic surgery done to change his facial features, but not enough. The program proved I was right. Ryan Ritter and Clint Brown are one and the same."

Dallas let out a breath. "He killed his Juliet and her brother and the brother's girlfriend and—"

"Not to mention the young man from the army whose body he dumped at the bottom of the cliff," Mac interjected, "plus the bartender he enlisted to help him carry out the murders and steal enough money to get out of Texas."

"And he got away with it for so long," Dallas said.

"He would still be getting away with it," David said, "if he hadn't flaunted it. He just had to show off his complete metamorphosis to your mother so he could get off on getting away with all those murders right under her nose. She recognized him right away."

"Which forced Ritter to kill again," Mac said.

Dallas said, "His ego ended up bein' his fatal flaw."

"I can see Ritter getting the plastic gun through security's metal detector," David said, "but what about the bullets? The police found a metal shell casing in the prop-and-set area."

"He stole the bullets from Jim Wiehl," Mac said.

"That's right. Everyone knows Jim Wiehl is always packin'," Dallas said.

"Including Ritter," Mac said. "The murder weapon used the same type of bullets as Jim's gun. Three-eighty caliber. We took a look at the box of ammunition that he keeps in his office and found some were missing. If the bullets in the murder weapon came from Jim's box of ammo, forensics will be able to prove it. As it so happens, Wiehl's office is right next to his wife's. We believe that Ritter stole the bullets when he used Pam's desktop to send the visitor's request for Rubenstein."

"I still can't believe he actually *planned* to slip away out of that crowded make-up department to shoot Yvonne with all those people around and he almost got away with it," Dallas said. "If I was gonna commit murder, I'd want to do it with no one else around."

"He was working on the principle of getting lost in a crowd," David said.

Nodding his head, Mac said, "I once investigated a murder case where a middle-aged woman's husband had left her for his much younger mistress. The wife decided to host one of those lingerie parties. She had a sales rep, some models, and about thirty women at her house—along with several pitchers of margaritas. Once the show started, the wife stole the keys to one of her friend's cars, slipped out the back door, and drove to her husband's mistress's apartment. When she got there, she went in and shot them both while they were in bed, and then she got back in the car, drove home, and went in through the rear door. She was gone less than thirty minutes, and none of the guests missed her. They all thought she was in the kitchen or the bathroom or something."

"How'd you catch her?" Dallas asked.

"She was in such a hurry to get back that she ran a red light, and a traffic cam took the car's picture," Mac said. "The car's owner contested the ticket, saying that she was at the party and that she had witnesses. Forensics blew up the picture of the driver behind the wheel, and it was the wife. The picture—and the date and time stamp on it—put her only two blocks from the scene of the murders when she was supposed to be hosting a party."

Dallas' mouth dropped open. "Which means that havin' a party can be a cover-up for murder," she said in a low voice. "How interestin'."

"But how did Ritter kill Rubenstein?" David asked.

"That was totally by accident," Mac said. "Ritter had no reason to kill him. I think he was planning to toss the gun and gloves into the stairwell to frame Rubenstein—not kill him. With a homicide detective in his pocket, he would have had no problem—Hopkins would've connected the gun to Rubenstein, who had motive to kill Yvonne. As luck would have it, Gnarly slipped out the door after Rubenstein, and I was right behind Gnarly when Jim Wiehl stopped me at the door."

"Cutting off Ritter's escape," David said. "There he was, in the studio, with the murder weapon on him. Not a good situation. He had to do something, and he had to do it fast, before they locked down the studio."

"So he decided to slither out the makeup department's back door," Dallas said.

"But he needed everyone to leave the makeup department," Mac said. "Think about it. If he went running in and then out the back door, people would have noticed it. He needed to get everyone's attention focused on something or someone besides him. How better to clear out a room than to go in and announce that there's been a murder? Unfortunately for him, he announced that Yvonne had been shot before anyone realized at that point that she had been. As soon as everyone cleared out, he went out the back door, ran around to the stairwell, and tossed the gun."

"He literally tossed the gun down the stairwell." David was nodding his head. "It hit a bannister or a step or a wall and discharged, killing Rubenstein."

"My guess is that Ritter was seconds ahead of me," Mac said. "After tossing the gun, he hid behind the door when

I went into the stairwell and waited for me to get down a couple of flights before taking off the gloves and dropping them. That's why I didn't see them. Then he slipped back into the hallway and went around to return to the makeup department through the same door."

"Was it Ryan Ritter or Lieutenant Hopkins who sicced Officer Tate on me?" Dallas asked.

To answer, Mac turned to David. "Do you remember when we were in the control room and I asked where Ali Hudson was? The assistant director told us that she was at a dental appointment. As soon as Hopkins was through with his interview, Ryan Ritter was on his cell phone. According to the phone logs for the burner we took from Ritter, that call was to Hopkins' burner phone. They spoke for three minutes. Two minutes later, Hopkins signed out of the lobby."

"Since you weren't in the studio, Ritter couldn't shoot you at the same time he killed Yvonne," David told Dallas. "You were out of the building and Ritter knew it would be on lockdown. So he called Hopkins to arrange to have one of the Dirty Six get rid of you."

"That's why Ritter kept callin' me all night," Dallas said. "He was miffed when he saw me the next day—told me that he was worried 'bout me. I thought he was tryin' to get in my panties."

"When in reality," David said, "he was trying to find out where you were so that he could send one of the Dirty Six to kill you."

"Probably the same snake who took out Detective Roberts," Dallas said.

With a nod of his head, Mac said, "Van Patton told me that one of Roberts' neighbors recognized Tate from a photo lineup. The police located what they believe was Tate's burner. Hopkins had tossed it in a trash bin between the alley and the News Corp building after killing him."

"Why?" Dallas asked. "Why take out Officer Tate just because he failed to kill me?"

"Tate had been living beyond his means, which had drawn the attention of internal affairs, and he was on suspension," Mac said. "When you got away, Hopkins must have decided that was the last straw. For all Hopkins knew, you could identify Tate, in which case he could blow Hopkins' whole operation if he got arrested. Hopkins must have decided to cut his losses and to kill him. The last call on Tate's burner was to Hopkins."

"Hopkins' burner phone also had calls to Ryan Ritter's burner, as well as phones recovered from the bodies of every one of the Dirty Six," David said.

"Which ties them all together," Dallas said.

"Exactly," Mac said. "Hopkins' burner is proving to be a treasure trove of information. The call log shows calls to well over a dozen burner phones around the time of a number of crimes that Lieutenant Gibbons suspected to have been connected to the Dirty Six. Internal Affairs suspects they were crimes for hire and Hopkins coordinated them."

"So Rubenstein seemed to be nothin' more than a patsy," Dallas said.

"The news was already out about Rubenstein's wife's murder," David said. "Rubenstein was out front with a news crew, making waves. He was ripe for Ritter to frame for murder."

Dallas took a sip of her champagne. "Rubenstein may not have shot Yvonne, but I don't think he was any angel either."

"How are you able to climb stairs in those high heels?" David asked Dallas while she galloped up the third flight of stairs to the one-bedroom apartment they'd managed to find in Brooklyn.

After dinner, Dallas, who wanted to check out a hunch about Ruth Rubenstein's murder, insisted that David and Mac take a cab with her to the apartment of Polly Langley. Once again, Mac tried to beg out, claiming that Gnarly would be lonely. Saying that his expertise as a homicide detective would be essential to her proving her theory, Dallas refused to take no for an answer.

After Dallas knocked on the apartment door, a plump middle-aged woman answered it. Her eyes opened wide upon seeing Dallas in her royal-blue cocktail dress and high heels, carrying an evening bag.

"Is Polly Langley here?" Dallas made no pretense of not trying to see into the small apartment.

"May I ask who wants to know?" the woman asked with suspicion.

"Mac Faraday." Mac shifted over so the woman could see him. "Polly and I talked yesterday about Carl's death. I wanted to let her know that we have some answers about what happened."

The news made the woman step aside and invite the three of them in. "I'm Sandy Williams, and this is my husband, Vic."

In the cozy living room, Vic, a big man with a thin beard, made a halfhearted effort to rise from the recliner and to shake David's hand while Sandy called into the bedroom for Polly. A big cat was lounging across the back of the chair where Vic was watching a horror movie. The volume was up so high that they had to talk loudly in order to be heard.

"We saw on the news that Ryan Ritter was shot and killed," Sandy said breathlessly. "Some unidentified sources are saying that he was involved in Yvonne Harding's murder and maybe in Audra Walker's, too."

"Does that mean Carl was set up?" With hope in her eyes, Polly Langley rushed into the room and stepped up to Mac.

"We believe so," Mac said. "Because of the media attention he got when he threatened to sue Yvonne Harding and ZNC, the killer—"

"Ryan Ritter?" Sandy asked.

While Polly and her guests devoted their attention to discussing the details of the shooting that had resulted in the death of Carl, Dallas eased backward toward the bedroom and peered inside. Her suspicion confirmed, she stepped back into the living room's doorway and shot a smile in David's direction.

"Ryan Ritter seemed like such a good man," Sandy said. "So sophisticated and well educated. He was a distant relative of the Kennedys, you know."

Thinking about Ryan Ritter's fictional background, which included ancestors going back to the Mayflower, Mac and David exchanged glances.

"We can't discuss the details of the case," David said. "But we wanted to let you know that the forensics evidence indicates that Carl was accidentally shot when the killer tossed away the gun."

Tears came to Polly's already red eyes.

"It's so tragic," Dallas said. "Sad enough to bring a tear to a glass eye when you think about it. If someone hadn't killed his wife, Ruth, then Carl would still be alive today."

Polly hiccupped.

"Figures," Sandy said with spite. "Ruth was trouble with a capital *T*. She was nothing more than a jealous shrew—driving that writer to suicide."

"She was a bitch on wheels," Vic grunted while popping open a can of beer.

"I'm a member of that book website, and I saw all those horrible, awful things Ruth and her troll friends said about that writer and her book," Sandy said. "I had no idea it was Ruth until Yvonne Harding revealed it on the news. But

I'd read the comments. When Melissa O'Meara committed suicide, and it hit the news, Ruth's comment was 'Good riddance. If she was so weak, she had no right being a writer.'" Anger seeped into her tone. "She drove that young girl to suicide, but she was so consumed with bitterness and jealousy that they had eaten up every bit of human decency and compassion that she might've once had inside her."

"That's why she was on disability," Vic said. "She'd become such a bitter old hag that she couldn't hold a job—she actually got a doctor to sign off on it. She stayed home in her bathrobe all day collecting disability—which is paid for by us stable, hardworking folks who pay taxes—so she could troll the Internet and make good people's lives miserable."

"Whoever killed her was doing a public service," Sandy said.

"But if she were still alive, then Carl would be, too, because he wouldn't have been set up to go to the studio, where he was killed," Dallas said.

When Polly burst into tears, Sandy rushed to get a tissue for her.

"Have the police made any progress in their investigation into Ruth's murder?" Mac asked.

Unable to speak, Polly shook her head.

"Carl Rubenstein sounds like he was a good man," David said.

"Mac told us 'bout how he used to take really good care of you when you'd get headaches," Dallas said. "You get migraines?"

"Yes," Polly said. "Bad ones."

"Didn't you tell me that you got one the other night?" Mac asked. "You had company for dinner, and you watched the game?"

"Vic and me and the Seinfelds," Sandy recalled. "You made that pork roast with acorn squash, Polly. Delicious. You said you'd give me the recipe."

"Then you got a migraine," David said.

"My aunt Trudy gets migraines," Dallas said. "Sometimes she has to go to the emergency room to get a shot. Did you go to the hospital that night, Polly?"

"No," Polly said. "Usually, I just take some over-the-counter medication and go to bed."

"Is that what you did the other night?"

Sandy turned suspicious. "What's this about?"

Dallas didn't let up. "If you're like Aunt Trudy, you probably had to turn off the light. Aunt Trudy says light only makes the headache worse, so she has to lie down in the dark."

Polly raised her eyes from the floor to look at Dallas and then Mac and then David.

Mac drew her attention back to him. "How long were you alone in the bedroom in the dark that night, Polly?"

"Why are you asking her that?" Sandy stood up from her seat next to her friend.

"Sandy," Dallas said, "the other night, the night Ruth Rubenstein was murdered, did you go into the bedroom to check on Polly?"

Sandy stared at her with wide eyes. "No," she replied in a soft voice. "Carl did." Her mouth dropped open. Pointing to the front door, she added, "We were all right here. She couldn't have gotten out—"

"She used the fire escape." Dallas pointed to the bedroom.

"Sandy, tell them!" Polly said.

"But Carl checked on her during every commercial," Sandy said. "He would have said something if she'd left."

"All that proves is that he was in on it," Dallas said.

"You can't prove—" Sandy said.

"Polly would've had to take the subway or a cab to get to the Rubenstein place," Dallas said. "Am I correct in thinkin' she has a monthly pass for the subway? All the police have to do is check to see if she used it durin' the kill zone."

"Unless she used one of our cards," Vic said. "All of the coats and purses were in the bedroom."

"Then we'll tell the police to check everyone's passes," David said. "If all of you were here together watching the game, then how could one of your passes have been used on the subway—unless Polly used it to go to the Rubenstein apartment to kill Ruth and free up Carl so that he could marry her?"

"It's only two blocks to the subway and three stops to the Rubenstein place," Dallas said. "Polly could've gotten there, killed the troll, and made it back here in a little more than an hour."

"Polly would never kill anyone!" Sandy said. "She wouldn't. Tell them, Polly!"

Polly broke down into loud, hysterical sobs.

Sandy jumped back from the sofa as if her friend had just announced that she had a contagious disease. "Polly, did—"

"It was all my idea." She raised her red and swollen eyes to look up at each of them. "She was an ugly, bitter troll filled with nothing but spite and jealousy. Nothing enraged her more than seeing others happy. The only way we could be free of her was if she died." She sniffed. "It was just like Vic said. When I tightened that cord around her ugly little neck and choked the life out of her, I felt like I was doing the world a public service."

Epilogue

"Do you have any more murders we need to solve?" Mac asked while closing the rear door of the cab that had returned them to the Four Seasons. Dallas was grasping David's arm with both of hers.

Mac had noticed that whenever possible, Dallas had her hand on David somewhere. During dinner, she had rested it on his thigh. In the cab, she had held his hand. It was as if she were afraid of losing him—which Mac concluded was most likely the case.

"We're good for now," she said.

In the lobby, Mac felt that awkward moment he'd been hoping to avoid. He wanted to go upstairs to the suite and call Archie—to have a few minutes of quiet talk alone with her, even if it was only on the phone. But with the way Dallas had attached herself to David, he half expected her to go upstairs with them, which meant less of a chance for privacy.

She's been living in New York for five months. Doesn't she have her own place? Mac didn't even know where she lived. When she needed something, she'd buy it at a nearby shop. *Is she planning to jump on the plane and go back to Spencer with us? Thank God I don't have to explain her to Chelsea. That'll be David's job.*

Thinking it would be rude to ask Dallas about her intentions, Mac preferred to let David take the lead. And he finally took it in the lobby, with a glance and a toss of his head in the direction of the elevator.

"Well," Mac said on cue. "I need to get upstairs to check on Gnarly before he eats all of the furniture." He gave Dallas a kiss on the cheek. "See you later."

"If I have anythin' to say 'bout it." She shot a cryptic glance in David's direction.

Grateful to escape, Mac hurried over to the elevators and was doubly thankful when one opened up immediately to carry him upstairs and away from whatever was about to happen.

"I guess it's time for us to talk," Dallas said with a heavy tone.

David led her by the hand over to the sitting area. Gesturing to the love seat, he said, "Let's sit down."

Even as he took a seat, she stood in front of him. "I don't wanna sit down. When people tell me to sit down, it's to give me bad news."

"Okay." Feeling awkward looking up at her from the love seat, David stood up. He took both of her hands into his. Peering into her light-brown eyes, he swallowed.

Gradually, her face filled with dread. She sat down on the love seat. "You're goin' back to Spencer to marry Chelsea, aren't you?"

With a sigh, David sat back down. "I have no idea what I'm going to do."

"You said you loved me." In spite of her effort to be strong, a sob escaped from her throat.

"I do, Dallas." He kissed her hand. With tenderness, he stroked the top of it from the wrist down to the fingers—

studying it like he wanted to brand it into his memory forever. "I really do love you in a way I've never loved anyone—in a way I never thought I could love. You came crashing into my life and turned everything I thought I wanted to do, everything I thought I felt, and everything I thought I knew right on its side."

"But?"

He dragged his gaze from her hand to her face. "I love Chelsea, too."

Feeling weak, Dallas slumped in her seat. David took her into his arms.

"I don't love her the same way I love you, Dallas," he said. "That, I do know. But I love Chelsea too much to hurt her by going back on my promise to marry her—not after all that I put her through. We could have a happy marriage—"

"Even if you're in love another woman?" Dallas asked.

"I *am* in love with another woman."

Dallas sat up tall. "I'm not gonna be your mistress."

"I wouldn't ask you to be." David caressed her cheek. "You mean too much to me, and I can't allow you to cheapen yourself like that. If I do marry Chelsea, it'll have to be goodbye forever."

Tears spilled from Dallas' eyes. David pressed his forehead against hers.

"I wouldn't be able to trust myself around you," he said in a soft voice. "And there's no way that I would disrespect Chelsea by cheating on her."

"But you *will* be cheatin' on her, my love," Dallas said. "Even if we never see or speak to each other ever again, you'll be cheatin' on her—not with your body, but with this." She pressed her hand flat against his chest.

David wrapped his fingers around her hand.

She lifted his head by the chin to force him to look her in the eyes. "You need to ask yourself, if you truly love

Chelsea and don't wanna hurt her, whether you can marry her on Saturday knowin' that you'll be cheatin' on her from the very instant that you say those vows?"

David reach up to touch her hair. She was so close that he could feel her body heat. Her scent filled his head so that it was difficult for him to think of anything except grabbing her and making love to her right there and then—in the lobby of the Four Seasons. He combed her hair with his fingers.

She looked up at him through her long eyelashes. "Say somethin', my love."

"I would love nothing better than for you to be with me in Deep Creek Lake," he whispered. "I have a nice big house right on the lake. It's not a ranch, but Spencer is a great little town. Yvonne left me enough money that you'd be free to concentrate on your investigative journalist career as a freelancer, and I could take care of you."

She blinked. "You wanna take care of me?" The corners of her lips curled.

He clasped her face in both his hands. "I need you, Dallas. You make me feel whole. Without you, I would feel like a part of me were missing." He kissed her hard on the mouth as if to commit her kiss to his memory so he would never forget her—or maybe so she would never forget him.

Excited to finally have some company, Gnarly stretched out across the sofa and rested his head in Mac's lap. It took several calls before Mac was finally able to reach Archie on her cell phone, and when he did reach her, she was difficult to understand.

She and Chelsea's bridesmaids were out on the town in Oakland, Maryland, for the bride's bachelorette party, and Archie had gone over her limit in champagne. Luckily, neither she nor any of the bridesmaids were driving, because Archie had been proactive enough to lease a limousine to drive the drunken ladies about town without worry.

"I guess you ladies are having lots of fun," Mac said after getting a blow-by-blow description of the male strippers who had provided the main event for the evening. "That should have helped Chelsea forget about her discussion with her future mother-in-law yesterday."

"I wouldn't know," Archie said.

"Why not?"

"Chelsea's not here."

"Huh?"

"She didn't come," Archie said. "She was still too tired after her seizure yesterday and wanted to rest up for the rehearsal and the wedding. But she insisted that we all go without her."

"You're having the bachelorette party without the bride?"

"Well the groomsmen are out having the bachelor party without the best man and the groom," Archie said.

Reminded that the bachelor party was indeed that night, Mac sat up so fast that he knocked Gnarly in the snout, causing the dog to sneeze. "How are they having the party without me? As the best man—"

"Bogie took the police department and the groomsmen out on your credit card."

"Where'd he get my credit card?"

"I gave it to him," she said. "Mac, is it just me, or is this the weirdest wedding ever? It's even weirder than ours. The groom is in New York, trying to divorce a wife he didn't know he had, and the bride is just plain absent. The bridal party is taking bets on whether this wedding is actually going to happen, and, in case it doesn't, on who is going to call it off."

The door to the hotel room opened. After slamming the door behind him, David went into his bedroom—and then he slammed that door as well.

"Who are you betting on?" Mac asked Archie.

"One thousand on the bride," she said. "Why? What's happening there?"

"I'm betting one thousand on the groom."

The chartered flight was scheduled to leave JFK at ten o'clock the next morning. David was already packed when Mac got up. One look told Mac that he hadn't slept a wink the whole night.

"Is Dallas staying on in New York?" Mac asked in the cab on the way to the airport.

"She's going back to Texas today," David said. "She misses her dog."

Mac reminded himself that Dallas had mentioned Storm, her Belgian shepherd.

The cab pulled up to the hangar where their chartered flight was waiting. Brooding in silence, David followed Mac and Gnarly onto the plane. During the whole hour that the jet waited its turn to lift off, David said nothing. Meanwhile the flight attendant served the flight's two passengers drinks, covered up Gnarly with a fleece blanket, and made sure everyone was comfortable.

Unable to take David's silence any longer, Mac finally asked, "What are you going to do?"

"Try to take a nap, but I don't think it's gonna happen."

"I'm talking about with Chelsea."

As if he feared Mac could see the truth in his eyes, David directed his focus to the clouds passing by during the jet's flight toward Maryland.

"Are you in love with Dallas?" Mac asked.

"Yes."

"Then you can't marry Chelsea," Mac said. "You can't take those vows knowing that they're a lie. It's not fair to Chelsea, and it'd be foolish of you to deprive yourself of the happiness you could have with the woman you love all because you don't want to hurt Chelsea by backing out of your wedding."

David's voice was soft when he finally said, "I do love Chelsea."

"So do I," Mac said. "Which is why I'm resigning as your best man."

David jerked in his seat to look at Mac. He expected a grin to cross his face to indicate that he was joking. But Mac was serious.

"If you're in love with another woman, you can't marry Chelsea," Mac said. "You think you can spare her by going through with the wedding? You won't be sparing her. She'll be humiliated when she realizes that you're in love with someone else—and she will find out, not from any of us, but from you. She may not realize it on the day of the wedding or during your honeymoon, but she will figure it out—just like your mother figured out your dad was in love with Robin. Then your worst nightmare will become a reality. You'll be repeating Dad's life—a lifetime of loving someone you can't have because you made the mistake of marrying the wrong person." He paused. "We can only pray that Chelsea won't go mad the same way your mother did."

"That's a low blow," David said.

"Your wedding is going to be in thirty hours." Mac sat forward in his seat. "The time for being subtle has passed. My job as your best man is to stand up in front of that church and witness your vowing to love, honor, and cherish Chelsea with all your heart. I can't do that if I know that it's a lie."

The server arrived with a second round of drinks for both of them.

Numb, David took the drink Mac handed him.

Then, a grin crossed Mac's face. "Besides, you can't get married anyway."

David turned his gaze to Mac. His forehead furrowed.

Mac tossed back his drink. "Gnarly ate your wedding rings."

David's mouth dropped open. With a gasp, he looked over to where Gnarly, who had heard his name, was raising his head. With wide eyes, the German shepherd looked over at the two men.

"What kind of best man are you?" David asked. "You let your dog eat our wedding rings?"

"I think he deposited them in Central Park that morning you took him running." Mac ordered a another drink from the flight attendant.

Sitting up in his seat, David pointed at Mac. "You know, all of this is your fault. I would not be in this position if it weren't for you."

"How do you figure that?"

"I wanted to go to the police station with you," David reminded him. "But no! You insisted that I go with Dallas to ZNC because she needed someone to protect her. If you had let me go to the police station with you and Ed, then I wouldn't have fallen in love with Dallas! So"—he pointed at Mac—"all of this is your fault!"

"And we wouldn't have come to New York, where you met Dallas and fell in love with her, if you hadn't gotten drunk in Vegas and married Yvonne without knowing it! Who gets married without knowing it?"

"What kind of best man feeds the wedding bands to his dog?"

The flight attendant trotted out with another round of drinks for them, which they both tossed back.

Mac was relieved when his cell phone received a call. The caller ID read "Archie." When he brought the phone to his ear, she let loose with a string of shrieks and unintelligible sounds. "Archie, calm down. What's going on?"

"She gone!"

"What?" Mac jumped out of his seat. "Who's gone?"

"The bride! She ran away!"

"Who's gone?" David was standing next to Mac. "What happened? Is it Chelsea?"

Mac swallowed. "Chelsea ran away."

"Are you kidding me?" Breathing heavily, David lowered himself back into his seat. "No!"

"She left David a note," Archie said, "and her engagement ring."

"She left her engagement ring," Mac told David.

"Are you going to feed that to Gnarly, too?"

"She also left a note for you," Mac said.

"Read it to me," David said.

Fearing that the letter would include personal information he would prefer not to hear, Mac suggested they wait until the plane arrived in Deep Creek Lake, but David insisted he needed to know what the note said right then. Putting the call on speaker phone, Mac sat across from David. They both bowed their heads over the phone Mac was holding between them.

Archie's voice was soft when she read it.

My dearest David. I love you so very much. I have loved you for the longest time. Marrying you would be the fulfillment of a fantasy. That's why this is such a difficult letter for me to write. In the last couple of days, I've come to realize that we've been living a fantasy. Do you remember when you asked me to marry you?

You said you wanted to make things right. Now I realize that a big part of our relationship since I came back home has been based on trying to go back to our youth, a time before the real world stepped in—a time before you hurt me by sleeping with Katrina. You've been trying to make it up to me—maybe to earn my forgiveness—while I've been trying to forget about the pain you caused me.

Thing is, David, I have forgiven you. Maybe you haven't forgiven yourself—and that's why you want to make things right by marrying me.

As much as I love you, and as much as marrying you would be my dream come true, I do know that if we go through with the wedding that one day—someday, maybe not today or tomorrow, but someday—your true love will come crashing into your life, at which point you'll be too honorable to leave me to be with her.

On that day, we will be repeating your parents' mistake.

I'm sorry, David, but I don't want to be your Violet. I want to be someone's Robin.

And I want you to be free to be with your Robin, whoever she is, when she comes into your life.

Don't be sad, David, because you don't have to make things right with me. They already are right. That's why I am releasing you from your obligation to marry me.

Finished reading, Archie said, "She then says she's gone to the Poconos with Seth Blanchard and will be back Monday to pick up the rest of her things from your house, David." She let out a sob. "I am so sorry."

After a long silence, Mac asked, "What do you want us to do, David?"

David sucked in a deep breath. "We're going to Texas."

Not sure if he'd understood him, Mac asked, "What?"

David was gesturing for the flight attendant, who rushed to his seat with another round of drinks. Taking his, he said, "Tell the pilot to change course for Dallas, Texas."

Before she could turn around to run to the cockpit, Mac stopped her. "Wait a minute. I'm going to Deep Creek Lake."

"Mac," Archie called out from the phone, "what's happening?"

"David's hijacking the plane," Mac said into the phone. "I'll have to call you back." He disconnected the call and turned his attention back to David. "You can't just change course."

"Yes, I can," David said. "It's a private plane. You yourself said I belong with Dallas. I want to be with Dallas. Chelsea called off the wedding. So now I'm free to be with Dallas." He turned back to the flight attendant. "We're going to Dallas."

"No, we're not," Mac said before turning back to David. "I don't want to go to Texas. I want to go home to my wife, and besides, you have over two hundred wedding guests in Spencer who are expecting a wedding. Chelsea ran off to the Poconos with Dr. Love, and you're taking off for Texas. What about the guests?" He threw up his arms. "Someone has to be there to tell them what's happening!"

"Tell them that Gnarly ate the rings," David said with a grin.

"What do you want me to tell the pilot?" the flight attendant asked.

"We're going to Dallas," David said at the same time that Mac told her they were going to McHenry, Maryland.

Confused, the flight attendant folded her arms.

"You can drop me off in Texas before you go home to Deep Creek Lake," David said. "I took a week off for the honeymoon, so I'll spend it in Texas with Dallas. By the time my vacation time is up, Chelsea will have moved out, and I can bring Dallas back home with me."

Mac chuckled. "You're bringing Dallas Walker back to Deep Creek Lake to live with you?"

"I know it's fast," David said. "But she and I talked about it. With the money Yvonne left me, I can take care of her while she devotes herself to her career as a freelance investigative journalist."

Mac sat up in his seat. "You're going to take care of her?"

David nodded his head.

"And you told her that? That you were going to take care of her?"

David's forehead furrowed. "Yes, I did."

Mac laughed.

"What?"

"You have no idea," Mac said.

"No idea about what?"

Mac waved a hand at the flight attendant. "Tell the pilot to change the flight plan. We are now going to Dallas, Texas. Tell him to make arrangements for us to land at the Walker Ranch—on their private airstrip, if possible."

The flight attendant hurried up to the cockpit.

"Private airstrip?" David murmured.

Throwing his head back, Mac laughed. "Oh, this is going to be so good!"

Spencer Manor - Next Day

"Okay, Bogie," Mac said into the phone, "I understand. Tell Jeff that the therapist's emergency counseling session will be covered under hazard pay at the Inn." He blew Archie a kiss when she set a plate containing his half of the submarine sandwich she had made for lunch and some chips next to his elbow. She responded with a kiss on his forehead before slipping into the dining room chair across from him.

Sitting up tall next to Mac's chair, Gnarly eyed the sandwich.

Mac hung up the phone with a deep sigh.

"You can't say you were surprised," Archie said while eying her to-do list for cancelling the wedding. "All those guests came in from out of town for David and Chelsea's wedding, only to have both the bride and groom bail out on it. It's only right that someone cover their bills at the inn."

"I still think I won the bet," Mac chuckled.

"The bride called it off," Archie said.

"David didn't even make it back to Maryland," Mac said.

"But Chelsea ran away first," Archie said. "Turns out that while her bridesmaids were watching male strippers, she was sneaking out of town with Dr. Love under the dead of night." She added with a naughty grin, "Which means I won."

"Who would have thought?" Mac shook his head. "You should have seen David's face when that plane landed on the Walker Ranch's private airstrip."

Archie laughed. "David honestly had no idea that Dallas' father was Buddy Walker, Texas billionaire?"

"Or that the Walker Ranch consists of five hundred thousand acres across four counties in the state of Texas," Mac chuckled. "He took the news well. He only had to put his head between his knees for about half the flight." He paused, and then a slow grin came to his face when he said, "And then he saw Dallas waiting at the airstrip, sitting on top of one of her prize quarter horses. She brought a second horse for David. They were literally riding off into the sunset when the plane took off to bring me back home."

"Look on the bright side," Archie said while slapping Gnarly's snout back from the sandwich with one hand. "Neither the bride nor groom ended up hurt. They both found their soul mates."

"At least one of them should have stuck around to help cancel all of this stuff." Mac uttered a groan while looking over his to-do list. "Well, David inherited nine million dollars from Yvonne. He can cover the guests' hotel bills." He crossed the item labeled "Hotel Reservations" off his list. "You talked to the caterer?"

"The inn's event coordinator is handling that," she said. "Since the food had already been purchased and it's too late for the entertainment to get another booking, I suggested that the inn go through with the event—only instead of calling it a wedding reception, we'd call it an Oktoberfest and invite all of the hotel's guests. That way, everyone has a good time and nothing goes to waste."

"Very smart." Mac kissed on the nose. "Beautiful and smart."

Grinning, she said, "Pretty clever if I must say so myself."

"How could we have been so stupid as to think those two were ready to get married?" Mac asked. "Even though we were that stupid, it's still not right that you and I have to do all the work."

"This is what we signed up for when we agreed to be the best man and the matron of honor." She tapped his list. "It looks like you only have one more item not checked off. What is it?"

"Cancelling the honeymoon, which was our wedding present to them. Ten days on a private island in Nassau, Bahamas. All paid for. No refund at this point. Money down the drain. Unless …" A wicked grin worked its way across his lips.

She raised her eyes to meet his. "You know, we've been working *very* hard."

"*Extremely* hard."

She laid her hand on his.

"I'd say we've been working so hard that we've earned a relaxing vacation," Mac said.

"You're getting no arguments from me."

"I think we *deserve* ten days on a private island." Moving toward her, his voice was husky when he sad, "Just you, me, the sun, the surf, and the seagulls." He pulled her out of her seat, picked her up, and twirled around with her in his arms.

"Sounds heavenly." With dreamy eyes, she gazed at him. "Would it be *right* for us to take David and Chelsea's honeymoon for ourselves?"

Mac put her down. "We can feel guilty about it during the flight to our island." He checked the details on his list. "The plane leaves McHenry at midnight tonight. By this time tomorrow morning, we'll be making love in the cabana, with no one around except the seagulls."

"I need to pack!"

When she attempted to trot toward the stairs leading up to their bedroom, Mac pulled her back. "It's a private island! All we need are our passports."

"What about swimsuits?"

Mac smiled at her.

Catching on, she grinned back. "I'm game if you are." With that, she threw off her sweater and dropped her pants. With a flourish, she struck a pose before Mac, wearing only her underwear. "I'll let you unwrap the rest."

"I can't think of a better way to kick off a second honeymoon."

With a shriek, she ran up the stairs, with Mac in hot pursuit.

Alone, Gnarly eyed the stairs they had rushed up and the two halves of the submarine sandwich abandoned on the dining room table.

He waited.

It must have been a test.

The only sounds in the house were Mac's and Archie's laughter upstairs—until the bedroom door slammed, signaling that they were too preoccupied to care about the two plates of food on the dining room table.

Those poor sandwiches looked so neglected.

It was just too easy.

Gnarly looked from one sandwich to the other. They were his for the taking.

No guts, no glory!

In a single bound, Gnarly snatched up the first of two lunches.

Moments later, as he stretched out on the deck, looking out across the lake, he licked his chops and thought, *"Yes, life is grand on Deep Creek Lake."*

The End

About the Author

Lauren Carr

Lauren Carr is the international best-selling author of the Mac Faraday and Lovers in Crime Mysteries and the Thorny Rose Mysteries.

A popular speaker, Lauren has appeared at schools, youth groups, and on author panels at conventions. She also passes on what she has learned in her years of writing and publishing by conducting workshops and teaching in community education classes.

She lives with her husband, son, and four dogs (including the real live Gnarly!) on a mountain in Harpers Ferry, WV.

Visit Lauren Carr's website at www.mysterylady.net to learn more about Lauren and her upcoming mysteries.

Check Out
Lauren Carr's Mysteries!

All of Lauren Carr's books are stand alone. However for those readers wanting to start at the beginning, here is the list of Lauren Carr's mysteries. The number next to the book title is the actual order in which the book was released.

Joshua Thornton Mysteries:

Fans of the *Lovers in Crime Mysteries* may wish to read these two books which feature Joshua Thornton years before meeting Detective Cameron Gates. Also in these mysteries, readers will meet Joshua Thornton's five children before they have flown the nest.

1) A Small Case of Murder
2) A Reunion to Die For

Mac Faraday Mysteries

3) It's Murder, My Son
4) Old Loves Die Hard
5) Shades of Murder *(introduces the Lovers in Crime)*
7) Blast from the Past
8) The Murders at Astaire Castle
9) The Lady Who Cried Murder *(The Lovers in Crime make a guest appearance in this Mac Faraday Mystery)*
10) Twelve to Murder
12) A Wedding and a Killing
13) Three Days to Forever
14) Open Season for Murder
16) Cancelled Vows

Lovers in Crime Mysteries

6) Dead on Ice
11) Real Murder
17) Killer in the Band *(May 2016)*

Thorny Rose Mystery

15) Kill and Run (featuring the Lovers in Crime)
18) A Fine Year for Murder (September 2016)

Killer in the Band

A Lovers in Crime Mystery

Summer has arrived! The Thorntons expected it to be a summer of change and change it does, but not in the way Joshua had expected.

Joshua's eldest son, Joshua Thornton Jr. (J.J.) has graduated at the top of his class from law school and is returning home to spend the summer studying for the bar exam. However, to the Thornton's shock and dismay, J.J. decides to move in with Suellen Russell, a lovely widow twice his age.

The May/December romance, bonded by a love for music, between the symphony conductor and young musical prodigy had bloomed many years earlier.

The move brings long buried tensions between the father and son to the surface. When a brutal killer strikes, the father and son must set all differences aside to solve the crime before J.J. ends up in the crosshairs of a murderer.

Coming May 2016!

A Fine Year for Murder

A Thorny Rose Mystery

After ten months of marital bliss, Jessica Faraday and Murphy Thornton are still discovering and adjusting to their life together. Settled in their new home, everything appears to be perfect ... except in the middle of the night when, within the darkest shadows of her subconscious, a deep secret from Jessica's past creeps to the surface to make her strike out at Murphy.

When investigative journalist Dallas Walker tells the couple about her latest case, known as the Pine Bridge Massacre, they realize that Jessica's nightmares may be suppressed memories of a murder she had witnessed long ago.

Determined to uncover the truth and find justice for the murder victims, Jessica and Murphy return to the scene of the crime, a winery owned by distant relatives, with Dallas Walker, a spunky bull-headed Texan. Can this family reunion bring closure for a community touched by tragedy or will this prickly get-together bring an end to the Thorny Rose couple?

Coming September 2016!